MW01697915

PIRATES

Pirate attack. Savage storm. Mob hit. A fight to the death.

T. Seamus Farley and Saul Elbein

Elbein Ink LLC

PIRATES

Published in the United States of America by Elbein Ink LLC.

ISBN: 979-8-9942691-0-7

Elbein Ink, LLC

Contents

Chapter One

Midnight found David Doorman sleepless. He lay on his back in the v-berth of the sailboat *Caesaria*, his eyes skittering over the fiberglass just inches above him in the v-berth. He didn't see the patterns in the gel coat above him. All he saw was the image of his father's purple-faced rage.

He'd seen his father angry before, of course. More and more often, recently. His father seemed never to address him without yelling. But this time, David had to admit that his father's rage was completely reasonable. What David had done this afternoon was so stupid as to be unforgivable. And the damage his fumble-footed screw-up had caused would fall entirely on his father to repair. As if Dad had hours and hours of his free time to repair things that never should have been broken.

David needed to apologize. He knew he should have done it at once, rather than laughing in his father's face. But the heat of Joe Doorman's rage left little hope that an apology would be accepted, much less that David's blunder would ever be forgotten.

David's eyes welled with tears. He shook the tears away. At 14, he was too old to cry. He was old enough, though, to clench his hands into tight fists and swear, fluently and bitterly. When he ran out of curses he made up new combinations.

The very absurdity of his last few constructions calmed him. His eyes stopped their nervous movements. He managed to take a few full breaths. He resolved to apologize to face his father man to man in the morning, whether his father accepted the apology or not.

The resolution calmed him enough to succumb to the exhaustion that a long, difficult day had left him with.

Then he heard the sound. His eyes sprang open. He half sat up, his head cocked to hear more clearly.

A burbling sound penetrated the familiar creaks and clangs of a sailboat at anchor. It was unquestionably the sound of a powerboat motor. Maybe more than one. The deep bass resonated in the tiny cabin. As he concentrated on trying to decipher it, it grew louder. Closer.

Maybe they weren't as powerful as they sounded, or as close. He knew that water transmitted sounds easily over long distances and the hollow cabin of the sailboat might be amplifying them. But even so, the motors sounded big. And close. And getting closer. None of which should be happening. Particularly at night.

Hundreds, perhaps thousands of isolated islands littered the huge lake, each with multiple coves and beaches. There was more than enough room for everyone. That's why, his father had explained the first time they'd "anchored out" on *Caesaria,* you didn't anchor in the same cove as another boat. Unless invited.

David's heartbeat began drowning out the worrisome sound. He rose to his knees as he felt the hair standing up on the back of his neck. This was serious. He had to warn his father. Every crew member had a duty to mention anything that he thought might threaten the safety of the boat and crew.

But then he froze. How did he know whoever this was wasn't invited? If they had been and he sounded the alarm, he'd make a fool of himself once again. Dad hadn't mentioned having visitors, but then, after this afternoon's catastrophe, they had not exchanged any polite words.

It seemed late to have visitors, though. David didn't know how late it was, but it felt like the middle of the night. He should report what he heard. But on the other hand, his father, back there in the open-air cockpit, must hear the sound better than David could. If Dad wasn't alarmed—and David couldn't feel the boat shifting with his father's movement, or hear him warning them off—then David should just stay quiet and stay where he was.

The rumbling of the motors suddenly stopped. David listened intently. Were they gone? Had they finally discovered *Caesaria* anchored in the spot they wanted and gone elsewhere? He started when a distinct bump echoed dully through the cabin. It had to be a hull tapping *Caesaria's*. Then the sailboat rocked and the sound of feet clomped on the deck.

They weren't his father's footsteps. Neither were they footsteps of someone used to being on a boat. But if they were the drivers of whatever those marine engines were that David heard, they had just come off a boat. It didn't make sense that they'd be uncomfortable coming aboard *Caesaria*.

It was all weird. A chill ran up his spine. David's heartbeat threatened to choke off his breathing. He didn't know what made him fearful, but the hair was standing up on the back of his neck.

He peered through the gap in the privacy curtains that screened off the v-berth from the cabin. He could see down the length of the salon—which was empty—and out into the cockpit. The cabin's lights lit the middle section of the cockpit all the way to the stern. David knew his father was out there, in the cockpit, probably lying on one of the settees right outside the wash of light.

A stranger stepped heavily out of the darkness into the middle of the cabin. David could see only part of his body. A tall man, as far as he could tell. Dressed completely in black. Wearing a mask, also black. The man's whole body exuded aggression, like the bullies at school. David felt his chest constrict with fear.

Before David could analyze his conclusions, another man stepped into the light. Also dressed in black, a bandana up around his nose and mouth, shorter and more wiry than the first. This man stared at the first one, his gaze intense. Perhaps uncertain. Perhaps concerned.

The taller man took no notice. He leaned down toward the side of the cockpit, his upper body and face now hidden in the shadows. He must be bending over the settee where Joe Doorman usually napped. Then David heard his voice, a nasty rumble. "Wake up, old man." His voice was low, gruff, sounding like nothing so much as the bad guy in a Western.

The man stepped closer to the settee, cocking one hand over his shoulder. A threat. A clear threat that he was about to punch Dad. Or hit him with whatever he held in his hand.

"Wake up, old man, or I'll fuckin' wake you up."

David almost laughed. It was like something out of a film. Almost comical. It couldn't be real. Not something that would ever happen in David's life. Or on *Caesaria.* What was it, then? A roleplaying game? A costume party? A practical joke?

His voice gravelly with sleep, Joe Doorman finally responded. "What do you want?"

"What do we want?" The man rocked back with laughter, glancing over his shoulder toward his partner, encouraging him to share the joke. His threatening hand still raised, the man peered at his victim. "You know what we want. We want fuckin' loot, man."

David started. Loot? Were they pretending to be pirates? They weren't dressed like any pirates David had ever seen in the movies.

"Sit down and let's talk about it," Doorman suggested. It was the tone his father used when humoring an idiot. A tone he heard often.

"Talk?" The big man took an aggressive step toward Doorman's settee, shaking the hand raised in threat. David suddenly saw what he was holding. A handgun. David caught his breath, but before he could think how to react, the big man swung his fist down in a vicious chopping motion.

David heard a horrifying *thonk*—

***

Joe Doorman had been lying back on one of the cockpit settees, trying to let go of the frustrations of the day. He loved this boat, a place where he could relax and let everything go. He loved the view from where he lay in the cockpit, gazing up into the eternity above him. His eyes traced the polished aluminum mast soaring forty-five feet into the night sky, seemingly holding up a black canopy of brilliant stars. Beneath the protective cover, he imagined the sailboat *Caesaria* floating untroubled on the deep.

Tonight, though, *Caesaria's* crew was far from untroubled. In his mind's eye, Doorman saw lightning flickering on the horizon. His eyes snapped open in alarm. Over him, though, the night was cloudless and the heavens silent. He closed his eyes again and tried to shake off his unease.

Tomorrow there would be storms between him and David. He would have to deal with the aftermath of the latest blowup. Of course, Doorman would apologize for losing his temper, but he had a bad feeling that his temper over the last few weeks—months?—had created damage that couldn't be erased so easily. Every time he addressed David these days he found himself yelling. It was true that David was undisciplined and didn't listen, but Doorman wasn't happy with the way he handled his frustration. After all, David was merely a boy.

Doorman knew he was stressed. Of course he was. With every successful prosecution, with a growing reputation, he'd been rewarded with still more work. Stressed at work, yes. But his family deserved better.

And he would do better. Starting tomorrow morning, as soon as David woke up.

The commitment to address the issue with David should have calmed him. It wasn't the only issue at home, though. There was also Deborah. His wife of fifteen years had been acting strangely. For weeks—for weeks upon weeks stretching so far in the past that Doorman couldn't remember when it started—he had noticed a certain distance between them. Part of it he'd ascribed to his job. He was always preparing for the next big trial and never had the time to be able to stop and figure out what the problem was between them. It was a conversation that would require care and attention, but with unending trial preparation and trials sucking up all his time, there had simply been no opportunity.

And now, next week, another big trial coming up. Doorman had already spent days, nights, and weekends preparing. There would not be time to have the talk this week, not with having to take time off for this week of "quality time" with David. No, not "having to." Doorman knew his growing estrangement from his son threatened to become a permanent breach. At least with Deborah he had built years of goodwill. Enough history and enough credit to put the conversation off until things simmered down. The tension with David required emergency action. So he'd left the remainder of the trial preparation to his staff and taken off.

Could he squeeze a few minutes into his schedule to talk with Deborah after the cruise and before Monday's opening statements? It could be little more than a gesture. He couldn't afford to get distracted with deep emotional issues when he was about to dive into an important trial. The prosecution of a major mafia figure was important to the DA. Important to his own career. Important to the citizens he had sworn to protect. If only Deborah could have just kept it to herself for a few weeks so he could concentrate all of his energies—

No, that wasn't fair. She had been keeping it, whatever it was that was bothering her, to herself. And he'd allowed the job to become all consuming. But that's what life as a trial lawyer demanded. Particularly a trial lawyer in public service. The job did not allow work-life balance.

It suddenly occurred to Joe Doorman that he was excusing himself for having strained relationships with every member of his family. He knew too many trial lawyers who were married to their work and divorced from their wives and children. He'd fallen into that trap. He needed to do something about it.

OK, he'd take a little time Sunday night when he and David came home and before the trial started. Or think about coming home a day early so that he and Deborah could talk. David would lose a little of his father-son time, but he would just have to understand.

The promise to address both of his family problems made him feel a bit better. But it did not relieve him completely. There was still one other threatening cloud on his mental horizon. There was still the little matter of a rumor of a contract on his life put out by the mafia don headlining next week's trial. Rationally, there was no reason to take the threat seriously. He'd been threatened many times before by angry defendants on their way to prison, but everyone knew that nobody ever killed a prosecutor.

Still, Doorman couldn't ignore the threat. But he couldn't do anything about it, either. Not about the rumor. Not about Deborah's discontent. Nothing but get some rest before what promised to be a difficult day tomorrow. So he lay back and tried to float down into the depths of sleep. And he was in fact actually drifting away, sinking into a disturbing dream of strangers on his boat, browbeating him, when a piece of steel slammed into his head with a hollow *thonk* that shot bolts of pain throughout his body and made his head spin and his ears ring.

***

David heard the sound clearly. It sounded like someone had dropped a big, juicy watermelon on the deck. He didn't know what it was, but he could have sworn he'd heard someone's muted cry of pain. Was his father fighting the men who demanded loot?

"Whoa, whoa, whoa," David heard the smaller man cry. He watched through the opening in the privacy curtain as the man grabbed his companion's arm and pulled him away from the settee. The second man's voice sounded shrill as he complained: "Whoa, whoa, whoa, man! We wadn't gonna hurt nobody. We was gonna do it and git. We had a...a understanding. Remember?"

The big man laughed. "I think we got an understanding, the Captain and me. We had a regular meeting of the minds." He elbowed his partner, looking for a laugh.

David watched one of his dad's legs flop into view as his foot dropped down to the cockpit sole. Limp. Motionless. David stuck his fist in his mouth to keep from crying out. Something told him that he needed to stay quiet and unseen.

The tall man turned back toward the invisible settee. "So now that we've reached an understanding, would you care to escort us to the treasure, Captain?"

David suddenly understood that this was no practical joke. This was real. They were criminals. But—pirates? For real? On a lake? On this lake?

It was ridiculous, but it was the only thing that made sense. Pirates were robbers. Pirates invaded boats to rob them of treasure. Pirates dressed all in black. Pirates beat up captains to keep them in line. That was what David was seeing, right here on the family's boat. But he couldn't believe it. Pirates on Lake Lanier?

David saw his father's other leg swing down into the cockpit. He watched as his father rose to his feet and stood unsteadily. The big pirate stepped back to give Doorman room to get to his feet, wavering, then stumble as he came down the short ladder into the cabin.

David sucked in his breath when he saw his father in the light. Blood streamed down his father's face from where he was holding his head. He was grimacing and shaking his head as if to clear it.

The boy's heart clenched in his chest. He'd never seen his father hurt, never mind bloody. He couldn't process it. It couldn't be real. No, it had to be a practical joke. A prank. Wouldn't David blow everything by rushing through the salon and into the cockpit?

A chill ran through him. What if what he was seeing was real? What if they really were pirates and they'd just attacked his father. For real?

But even if they were pirates, even if his father was in danger and needed help, what could David do? He was no match for two adults. Not big, violent men. He couldn't take them on face to face. No, if it was real, his best choice would be to stay hidden and look for an opportunity to help his father. Somehow.

David watched Doorman take a shaky step down the companionway ladder, pushed in front of the pirates. Dad stumbled on the last step into the salon and fell to his knees at the foot of the ladder. He stayed where he fell, holding his head.

"Loot, man," the big pirate snarled. "We want loot. Get on with it."

Doorman had fallen at the foot of the ladder, down on the cabin sole next to the navigation station. Groaning, he pulled himself up onto his knees, holding on to the top of the nav station. It was sturdy chest with drawers, topped by a slanted tabletop table. The top provided room to unroll a chart for navigation and lifted for chart storage. David watched as his father began rifling through the storage under the hinged top, his head barely high enough to see underneath. Fumbling blindly, he seemed to be searching for something.

It made no sense. Dad never put anything in the space under the lifting top. It was a rule: the chart space was reserved for charts. Charts went under the top, valuables went into designated drawers. It was one of his sayings: *Never put anything on top of the charts. When you need a chart, you don't want to have to dig around for it.* Dad knew the rule better than anybody. So why—?

Doorman lowered the top and then began pawing through the drawers. His movements scared David; they were jerky and uncoordinated. His voice was worse. He muttered a stream of unintelligible words as he rummaged. David could barely hear what he was saying, but it sounded like nonsense. His father was always articulate, even when he was spitting mad, but now he was spouting gibberish.

The big man stood on the bottom rung of the ladder, blocked by Doorman's body from coming down into the cabin but watching impatiently. The smaller man stood on the top rung, leaning around the big man to watch.

"Put my wallet someplace," Doorman mumbled loudly. "Must be in here somewhere. Wallet. Watch. Keys." He opened and closed drawers in turn, pawing through them once, and then distractedly all over again.

David bit his lip. Another of his father's sayings that had become a family joke: *If you always put your things in the same place, you always know where they are.* Which, David's mother had pointed out with a laugh, didn't explain why Dad could never find his car keys when he was running late for court. And now his father knelt at the navigation station, searching drawers where the only things ever stored there were flashlights and navigation tools and maybe a winch handle or two. Never his wallet.

Doorman slammed the last drawer closed in apparent frustration. He bent down with a groan to open the bottom cabinet of the nav station. He even stuck his head inside. Now David knew: he must be hurt bad. Even half asleep, his father would know that the only thing in that cabinet was *Caesaria's* bank of batteries.

David turned his attention to the pirates. He examined them closely, trying to memorize everything he could see. You were supposed to pay careful attention to what criminals looked like when you saw them committing a crime. He'd learned that from the crime shows. He noticed that the black suits that the two men wore were wet suits, like the ones divers or personal watercraft drivers wore as protection from the lake's frigid waters. He could see the water dripping from their suits down onto the ladder. He couldn't see their faces, but he might remember their voices. Would it be enough to identify them?

Doorman kept up an odd, disconcerting patter as he searched and then searched again. The pirates could do nothing but stand uncomfortably on the ladder. Was that an accident? Was Dad intentionally keeping them from coming into the cabin? Was Dad protecting him? Relief coursed through him. Method to his madness, as Dad would say. It would mean that his father was not as hurt as he seemed.

The pirates exchanged angry whispers, annoyed with Doorman's lack of progress as Doorman continued fiddling.

Then Doorman's eyes locked on David's. Glared, almost. David watched his father very distinctly compress his lips and give a slight but emphatic shake of the head. A signal. David thought it meant: *Stay out of it!*

Relief washed over David. If he was still capable of giving directions—despite the blood, despite the shaky voice, despite the gibberish—he still had things under control. But if this was all real, if they really were bad guys, David didn't want to "stay out of it." He could help. If his father would let him.

Doorman mumbled a long string of particularly loud nonsense at the two black-clad men. They stared at him, exchanging confused looks. The moment the pirates took their eyes off him, Doorman made eye contact with David again. Camouflaged within the flow of gibberish, he enunciated clearly: "Get off the boat. Out the hatch. Go!"

David didn't understand it at first, distracted by the stream of gibberish. By the time he understood that it might be a direction to him, Doorman had already looked away, shaking his head as if fighting the buzzing in his head, taking up his wild mumbling again and catching the intruders' attention by trying—and failing—to stand.

David wasn't sure what to do. Was it an order? He was supposed to climb out the foredeck hatch right over his head. But the scene paralyzed him. The pirates hulking over his father. His father bleeding all over the place. Apparently unaware that he was talking gibberish.

He needed help and David wanted to help fight off the pirates. Not to run away.

Get real, though. He wasn't brave or a fighter. Junior high had proven that. These were big violent men—bigger than the bullies at school, more violent than the worst of the kids who picked on him. How was he going to stand up to these two gorillas? Worse, it was two against one without him and only maybe two against one and half with him on his father's side. Worse still, the thugs had a gun. They'd swat him aside like a mosquito. He could only "handle" them by avoiding them.

That must be why his father ordered him to go. Dad dealt with criminals every day. He knew how to deal with them. If he wanted David to get out, he must have a plan that needed David to get out of the way.

A thought cheered him. Dad must want David to go for help. David didn't want to leave the boat, or leave his father to fight alone, but he'd already done enough damage today by not following instructions. Now that he'd seen that his father was still in control of himself, David knew he wouldn't be leaving his father helpless and confused. He'd probably better do what he was told.

"Up the hatch" and "now." There could be no misunderstanding of what that meant. David sat back on his haunches to pull on his waterproof shoes—stored in the v-berth in case of emergency, of course—and looked up. The handle to open the plexiglass hatch cover was right overhead. He twisted the handle and pushed the cover up and out of the way, ready climb quietly out.

Chapter Two

The foredeck hatch measured just over a foot square. It opened from the V-berth right onto the foredeck. David only had to stand up in the open hatch and pull himself through. He had done it many times, slipping out without making any noise that might alert his parents to his sneaking out. Getting out would be the easy part.

What then?

The first priority had to be his father. Dad needed help. Even if he wasn't hurt as badly as he pretended he needed help before anything really bad happened. It didn't seem right, though, to just leave him to the mercy of the intruders. Not with him hurt, blood streaming down his face, at the very least, stunned. How could David just go? But Dad had been clear. David had already gotten himself in enough trouble today by not doing what he'd been told to do.

He slid backward on his knees to center himself under the hatch. Pushing the hatch fully open, he boosted himself quietly up and clear of the hatch cover. Never in his wildest dreams had he thought that learning to sneak out the forward hatch might be important.

Out on the deck, David shivered. It was dark. The night was so silent and so black that the stars might all have gone out. A gentle breeze smelling of fish ruffled his hair. He bent to ease the hatch closed. That way, they wouldn't have any idea that someone had escaped. He wished his father could see him thinking ahead, heard his father's voice acknowledge it wryly: *For a change.*

He huddled on the foredeck, shivering from the wind, cold piercing him after the stuffy v-berth. He decided to get to the dinghy tied to the stern and use it to go for help. The shortest path would have been to race along the side deck, through the cockpit, and jump down into the small boat. That wouldn't work, though: the pirates would grab him as he passed. The only other alternative was slipping overboard and swimming quietly back to the dinghy. A look at the black, impenetrable water sobered him.

There must be other choices than leaving the sailboat. After all, what he wanted was to attack the intruders, hurt them at least as badly as they had hurt his father. That would help Dad more and a lot faster than rowing to shore.

But it still came down to the same odds: one kid against two big men.

A surprise attack might even things a bit. It might give his father time to seize the moment while the pirates were surprised by David's sudden appearance. If only he had a weapon! Then he could attack them from behind.

But there were no weapons. His parents had always been dead set against guns aboard. The boat hook might work, but it lived in a cockpit locker; he'd never get through the cockpit to the locker without getting caught. The flare gun? Even worse, in the cabin with the pirates.

There must something to use as a weapon! David couldn't think of anything but his fists. Without a weapon to even the odds, fighting them would be hopeless. It kept coming back to that.

That left only one option. His father's option. David had to go for help. If he could get to the dinghy that was tied off at *Caesaria*'s stern, he'd be able to do what Dad ordered him to do. He'd have to swim for it, though, to stay out of sight. He looked down again at the water and shivered.

His knees shaking, David slowly rose to his knees and grasped the bow railings. He cast one last look aft, hoping for inspiration, any idea at all, that would justify his not going into the water. The lights of the cabin cast pale swaths of light onto the side decks through the portholes and out into the cockpit. He doubted he'd make it to the dinghy unseen except by swimming.

He stared into the darkness over the side. The black water stared back. Bottomless. Impenetrable. For years he'd swum in it and dived in it and never thought twice about it. Just hours before, he'd been bobbing around in it and laughing his head off at capsizing the dinghy and getting dunked underwater. But that was in the daylight. Now, David imagined the cold blackness closing around him. Unseen things lurked below his kicking legs. Huge catfish. Water moccasins. Loch Ness monster type things rumored to hide in the depths. Creatures lurking in the depths, looking hungrily up at the surface, waiting for flashes of meat to plunge into the depths.

David took a deep breath to try to gather his courage. He couldn't dive in: it would make too much noise. He'd have to lower himself, inch by inch. Somehow, that was worse to contemplate. He lay back down on his stomach, stretched out full-length on deck. His teeth chattering in anticipation of the cold water, he grasped the rail with one hand and swung one leg over the side. Then the other. The water closed around his legs like vises as he lowered them into the water. He bit back a sob as he let himself slowly down, feeling the water swallow his calves and then his thighs.

When he got to the end of his reach, the water had hold of everything up to his waist. It was too late to reconsider, but he hung desperately for a moment by his fingers. Nothing could keep them from slipping. He'd committed himself to this—to letting go and dropping silently into the lake—but now that he couldn't back out, he instinctively fought to retain his hold. In seconds he could no longer feel his fingers. His shoulders went numb soon after. Then his hands lost their grip completely.

He plunged into the forbidding water and sank like a stone. The cold blackness closed over his head. David kicked fiercely back to the surface. He wanted to shout out his terror, but knew if he opened his mouth he'd drown. He blew his breath violently as he struggled to the surface. His head shot into the fresh air at the instant he could no longer hold his breath. He treaded water, coughing and gasping.

The intruders were only a few feet away, right on the other side of the thin fiberglass hull. He made himself stop thrashing, treading water as slowly and quietly as he could, sucking in the clammy air without making a sound. He hoped. Sinking down in a slow dog paddle, he made his way toward the stern of *Caesaria*, trying not to think about the freezing water, or the monster catfish, or the creatures from the depths that were swimming up even now to explore the tasty piece of meat that had just dropped into their home. All that mattered now was not making any noise.

The dinghy appeared ahead only as a dark shadow drifting on the darker abyss. Threatening horns poking into the sky startled him. He swallowed water in his surprise, but it brought him to his senses. It was only the pieces of the broken mast, poking their ends up against the night sky. The cause of his disgrace.

Disgrace. The afternoon's disaster that had provoked his father to a temper tantrum. That reminded him of the dinghy's oars. When he capsized the dinghy this afternoon, they must have been flung out of the boat. Had he let them float away? He hoped not with all his heart.

When he had finally dog-paddled to the stern of the sailboat, David stopped swimming and treaded water again. What was his next step? Pulling himself up into the dinghy from the water was possible: Dad had made him practice getting himself back aboard the dinghy from the water before he would let David take the little boat out by himself. He'd done it to his father's satisfaction, so he knew he could do it now. The problem was that it always caused lots of thumping and splashing. He needed a quieter way to get on board.

The sailboat's folding swim ladder was still lowered at the stern of the sailboat from when he'd climbed aboard earlier. That was good luck. He could climb up a couple of rungs of the ladder and step across into the dinghy. Cautiously, he paddled over and tested his weight on the ladder. He didn't know how much noise the sailboat would make when he stood on the ladder, or how much the motion of the boat might give him away when he stepped up. Remembering the fumble-footed footsteps of the pirates, he didn't think they'd notice. Still, he had to be careful. Gingerly, he put one foot on the bottom rung and slowly transferred his weight, trying not to slosh the boat or splash. When no outraged sounds rang out, he pulled himself up. He tried to keep his head out of the wash of light from the cabin and clung, bent over, half in the lake but out of sight except to someone leaning over the transom.

Of course he knew that a painter secured the dinghy to one of the two stern mooring cleats. *Caesaria* used the cleats to tie up to a dock, so there was one on each corner of the stern. Right now, the port side cleat, within arm's length of where David perched, held the painter for the dinghy.

Surprisingly, the cleat on the starboard side, which should have been unused, had two other painters attached. For a moment, it bewildered him. Wait, though. Obviously, the pirates tied their boats there. Sloppily. Pirates maybe, but not sailors.

David leaned over toward starboard, braving the creaking complaint of the swim ladder as his weight shifted. Peering through the dim light, he followed the painters with his eyes. They led to the other edge of the transom, where he saw the barest sliver of a PWC, just visible in the gloom. That explained the engine noises he'd heard. And the wet suits. And the bump against the hull.

Wait a minute. Why not grab one of the PWCs to go for help? They'd be a faster way to get to help than a dinghy with a broken mast. A perfect solution. If the thugs left the keys in the ignition.

The possibility presented gambles upon gambles. Could he chance the possibility that they'd left the keys? That the engines would start? Even if they did, he'd be making a bigger gamble. That the noisy risk of trying to steal a PWC would be better than the quiet risk of taking the dinghy for help. David juggled the possibilities, unable to come to a decision. The cold night air turned even the gentle breeze into torture as it blew on his soaking wet clothes. That put an end to his calculations. He had to move or freeze.

The dinghy. That was easiest. From the ladder, he turned back to trace the line of the dinghy's painter. He could see it tied to the bow cleat of the dinghy, but he couldn't see the sailboat's mooring cleat, over his head on the top edge of the transom. It had to be just toward his left. He reached up to feel for it. He found it. His fingers found the knots, too.

He cursed silently. His father and his rules! *Never do it halfway,* his dad always said. About everything, but particularly about mooring. *You never know when you may need to rely on that knot to hold.* So now that David needed to rely on the knot—rely on it not to hold, but rely on it for a quick, silent release—his probing fingers proved to him that his father's habit had made it virtually impossible to untie the properly tied mooring knot. Not with one hand. Not by touch. David summoned the image of the tight parallel lines that made up the properly tied cleat hitch—Dad always tied the hitch carefully and tightly, of course—but imagining it didn't help. His fingers couldn't decipher the knot. He'd tied them a million times, and untied them a million and one, not ever having to look. But that was from the top looking down. From below, unable to see the rope or his fingers, figuring out the knot was beyond him. Particularly in the cold and the dark with pirates just a few feet away.

David sank back down, his teeth chattering. He didn't have a knife to cut the line. There was no way to sneak into the cockpit to untie the painter without being seen. He might make a quick, loud dash for it, and maybe it was possible to untie the line before the robbers caught him. Or he could climb aboard the dinghy from the swim ladder and use the dinghy as a platform to stand up and untie the line.

That had to be the safest bet. He reached for the dinghy with his one free hand. The little boat sloshed loudly as it moved toward him. Cringing, he froze and listened for a reaction. Nothing. David stretched a leg over the gunwale of the boat to pull it closer. He meant to slide silently in. In the dark, though, he misjudged the distance he'd have to clear and fell into the boat. The thump of his body hitting the bottom of the dinghy thundered in his ears. The pirates must hear it. It would bring them out. He'd be caught. It would all be over.

Sure enough, a voice rang out. Heavy footsteps stomped up the companionway ladder to the cockpit. David quickly slid into the darkest shadow of the broken mast and boom, praying the shadow would hide him. He heard heavy footsteps above him in the cockpit, then hard breathing just over his head, the sound of a frightened animal defending its turf.

"What was that?" It was the big pirate, yelling from the cabin.

"Hell if I know," a shaky voice answered from right over David's head.

"Check on the Sea-Doos!"

David felt *Caesaria* slosh as the little pirate moved to the other side of the cockpit. "They're OK." The sailboat sloshed again, followed by the sound of feet clomping down the companionway ladder once more.

David lay wet and silent, afraid the big pirate would come up to look for himself. The bilgewater in the bottom of the dinghy soaked into him as he cowered, afraid to move. Once again it was the cold that finally made him stir. He got up cautiously and even more cautiously moved to the bow of the small boat, pulling gently on the painter to close the gap with the sailboat. The dinghy glided up toward the stern of *Caesaria*. David fended off with a hand to keep the collision from making noise, then ran the other hand along the painter to where the rope ended with a knot around the stern cleat.

Again he tried to un-cleat the line without raising his head to look. Still, he couldn't decipher the knot. Now, his cold fingers made it even harder.

Suddenly, he imagined what the scene must look like from the cabin. What the criminals would see, spotlighted by the wash of cabin light, would be a pale white hand-sized spider scrambling over to the knot, trying to untie it. He barely stifled a guffaw. If the pirates were scared of noises in the night, what would they think of a disembodied hand attacking the knot?

He finally gave up trying to untie the rope blindly. He'd have to see it. David stuck his head up as far as he dared, far enough to hear the murmur of voices in the cabin. He saw two heads of hair looking away from him. What he didn't see was his father's head. Where was he? Had he fainted? Could he be—?

No. No. No. Dad wasn't hurt badly enough to have died. Focus on the knot!

In a few desperate seconds, he uncleated the line and dropped quietly back into the dinghy. With a gentle push at the sailboat's stern, the dinghy shot away from the sailboat, skating across the lake water as if on ice.

David couldn't take his eyes off the empty expanse that now yawned between the sailboat and the dinghy. It grew ever wider.

He'd planned to row across the lake to the mainland to get help. Now the gravity of the task descended on him like a suffocating blanket. Alone in a small boat in the middle of the night. Without help in the middle of the lake. What if a storm came? What if the crooks chased him? What if the dinghy sank?

His plan to row across the open lake for help drowned under the enormity of the darkness around him. In the pitch-black darkness of the night, the beach in the cove *Caesaria* anchored in seemed more achievable. Better, at least, than a night out on the lake in a small boat alone. He could stay on the beach until morning. When it was light, he could row across the lake. See where he was going, in the daylight. Row a straight course to someplace that looked occupied.

But that might only be better for David. His father—hurt, bleeding, hostage to pirates—needed help now. There was no telling what would happen if David didn't act tonight. And if morning found David on the beach merely yards away from the pirates, they'd see him and capture him. Then his father would never get help.

No, he had to get out of sight of the attackers and he had to get help. There was no choice. He had to row for shore for help now.

The oars, though. Where were the oars? He remembered seeing them leaning against the midships thwart. But wasn't that before he capsized the boat? He groped blindly around the bottom and found nothing.

Might Dad have put them away? Surely, his father must have cleaned up the mess David had made as soon as he'd sent David below in disgrace. Dad would probably have put them where they belonged, in the oarlocks. David's hands searched but still couldn't find them. His blind search became more fevered. Without the oars—particularly with a broken mast, which meant no sail—the dinghy wouldn't be going anywhere.

Frantically, he reached over to feel around in the bow area hidden under the broken spars. He supported himself on the boom, which was lying at an angle, supported by the butt of the broken mast. His fingers brushed something that might have been an oar, if he could only reach far enough to grab it.

As he leaned forward to grasp what he'd felt, his weight was too much for the pile of broken wood. The boom shifted. It fell off the supporting stump of the mast. David fell with the boom, whacking his head on something he couldn't see. He managed to stifle his cry. But the boom slammed loudly onto the gunwale of the dinghy and fell overboard with a splash.

David froze, waiting for a reaction. Nothing happened. After listening for agonizing long moments, David leaned over the side to snag the mast before it drifted away. To let the spar float away into the lake would be terrible, almost as bad as breaking it in the first place. Just as he snagged it, *Caesaria* erupted in panicked shouts.

A figure scrambled out of the cabin, yelling. Two more figures followed, one shadow pushing another up the companionway ladder and out into the cockpit. Voices rang out: loud, muddled. Orders.

Counter-orders. Arguments. Then the sailboat's engine sputtered to life. In a moment it burst into a full-throttled roar. *Caesaria* accelerated away, its stern digging down into a frothy wake produced by the full power of the motor.

David could hardly believe it. It had to be his father at the wheel, gunning the gasoline motor and steering *Caesaria* away. Away from their an anchorage. Away from the island. Away from David. Abandoning him!

The sailboat charged away from where David sat in the dinghy. The PWCs wallowed uncertainly in the boat's wake. David watched, tired, afraid, scared, and all of that meant that it took him longer to understand what was happening than it should have. With the anchor still down and the boat charging ahead, the sailboat would quickly reach the end of its anchor rope and then be yanked back by the anchor. If it continued at full throttle, the rope would pull the bow of the boat back toward the anchor in a big circle. If the crew of the sailboat didn't stop it, the boat would motor around in circles until its fuel tank ran dry.

It happened almost at the moment David foresaw it. The sailboat charged ahead to the end of its anchor rode. The rope stretched to the extent of its length, and stretched until it was wire taught, and then jerked the boat's forward motion to a stop. The engine continued pushing, but with the anchor rode allowed the bow to move only one way: sideways. Its leash jerked by the anchor rode and still under full throttle, *Caesaria* turned and roared back toward David, heeling over as it fought against its restraint.

Voices exploded in the cockpit again. David could hear them over the noise of the roaring motor. A shadow scrambled out of the cockpit and stumbled forward to the bow pulpit. The shadow fell full length on the foredeck, then scrambled up, undoubtedly cursing. It was easy to imagine one of the pirates kneeling on the bow, holding on for dear life to the bow pulpit while trying to saw through the rope with his one free hand. Cutting the anchor rope under tension would be like trying to cut steel wire.

But then, with a sharp *twang!* the anchor rope parted. The engine noise eased. The quiet night reasserted itself. *Caesaria* relaxed down into the water, turning out of its circular course and heading for open water, as though relieved to be set free.

David watched, dumbfounded. He'd expected to leave the boat behind as he went for help. He didn't expect to be left behind himself. Now he felt himself shrink in the enormity of his situation.

Left behind, abandoned in a small broken boat, in the dark of night, on water so empty and so evil that it might have been a graveyard at midnight. The weight of the night's catastrophes overcame him.

David became a little boy again. Helpless. Abandoned. Sobbing in despair.

Chapter Three

Four months before pirates attacked Doorman's boat, two business meetings took place. They happened on the same day of the same year and at the same hour. And unbeknownst to any of the conferees, both meetings addressed how to deal with the same problem.

Prosecutor Joe Doorman's meeting was more like a circus than a pre-trial preparation session. People flowed in and out of his office apparently at random. Trial lawyers, criminal investigators, law enforcement agents, witnesses, and informants all appeared and disappeared at random. They shared only one trait: the urgent need for the lead prosecutor's immediate attention, right now.

The lawyers were doing what trial lawyers did: juggling. While working on Doorman's prosecution of a mob boss, they struggled to find time for the everyday routine of a prosecutor. Doorman himself, even as the lead, juggled running from court to court to take plea bargains, attend hearings, argue motions, then go back to his office to sift through piles of evidence on a half dozen cases and investigations, write motions, and prepare other cases for trial. All while trying to finish his preparation on the next big case.

Doorman held sway in the center ring, where the main show was taking shape piece by piece. In several months, he was set to start the largest mob prosecution in the city's history. If successful, it would cement his growing reputation as a top-notch prosecutor. And assure the re-election of his boss, the District Attorney. Important case. Important consequences. And as always, with every trial, every task demanded the highest priority attention and demanded it right now.

The other meeting was considerably more sedate, the cast more static, and the atmosphere distinctly hostile. The handful of surly men in a restaurant in Milan, Alabama, less than 200 miles from the prosecutor's, were meeting about Joe Doorman. Or, as the leader of the meeting had just announced to his stunned team, the untimely death thereof.

The atmosphere in the restaurant was hot. Hot because July in Alabama is an oven. Hot because of the pizza ovens. Hot because the little hole-in-the-wall didn't have working air-conditioning. Hot because of the smoky, greasy pizza smell that billowed out of the kitchen. And hot because the discussion had turned contentious. Their argument—if not their glowering at other customers—cleared the other customers out of the only Italian restaurant in Milan, Alabama.

If the regular customers had stayed, they would have heard one of the conferees spit: "You gotta be kiddin' me!" The outrage in the speaker's voice shot around the room, echoing around the empty booths and tables, trickling into the traumatized kitchen, and boomeranging back to settle heavily over the four men.

"Kill a prosecutor? It ain't done!"

Two of the attendees froze. Their arms sweated against the vinyl tablecloth as their watery iced tea sweated in its glasses, and now their colleague's words turned their sweat to ice. Even the speaker quailed at the tone of voice that had come out of his mouth. His eyes shot over to the boss to see how badly he'd screwed up. Around the table everyone held their breath and watched the boss carefully.

Number One—as he insisted on being called in public—just sat. Smiling, unbothered. Impervious to the heat. Impervious to his men's arguments. Impervious to the knowledge that he was the only African American who ever ate at Mi Familia. The owners didn't care for the fact that he'd returned to commandeer their restaurant for a second time, and once again commandeered the largest table. Number One didn't much care what the owners thought.

A leader led. Sometimes by going where they were not welcome. Sometimes by listening to his people argue while he kept his silence.

Number One knew how to play this moment of near mutiny because Number One had studied. He devoured everything he could get his hands on about organized crime. He knew, for example, from *The Godfather* and from *The Sopranos* that the Feds were always surveilling organized crime, so he insisted on using only coded names in public. He knew that a successful leader of men had to ride above the storm, so now he listened with every appearance of patience as his men bitched. He knew that only a loser lost his temper at insubordination, so he smiled serenely and steeled himself to ride like the *Titanic* through the icebergs. Implacable. Unstoppable.

He was determined to make a name for himself. Whatever he had to do, he'd do. Right now, Number One only ran a small crew, but he intended to get big. Big-big. Boss-big. Not just to command more of the Milan drug-and-prostitution trade big, either. He was already the master of the little town of Milan. He had bigger goals.

He aspired to Atlanta, first. Then Chicago. Then, no telling how high he might go in the organization. He'd never minded starting small—hell, he'd started small already. What mattered was moving up. First, to get noticed by the big boys in Atlanta. Get talked about in the meetings in Chicago. Make a place for himself on the national scene. Get invited to come up to work with the big boys in Chicago.

Number One knew what he had to do to get there. He had to do something to get noticed by the right people. Something big, really big, something to set the grapevine humming. Something to earn the respect of the Powers That Be in Atlanta and the Bosses in Chicago.

Something just like the perfect opportunity that had fallen into his lap.

Unfortunately, starting small meant working with people without ambition. He cast expressionless eyes over the three men in front of him and stifled a sigh. His associates were professionals, their experience proven by multiple engagements in prisons, jails, lockups, juvenile detention. They were experienced, but not men with vision. They might be too small to see the potential in this huge opportunity.

Meanwhile, Number Three, the first speaker, not having been slapped down, repeated himself as he was prone to do. "Nobody kills prosecutors. It's stupid. We'd call all kinds of crap down on our heads."

Number One smiled at him. The Master of Milan didn't need to argue with underlings.

Number Two smiled faintly and let his eyes wander the main street of Milan just beyond the cracked picture window as though disinterested. "Who's the target?"

Number Three leaned toward Number One and lowered his voice. "I'm just saying this ain't done. You gotta lotta other irons in the fire. Why mess something that ain't our business?"

Usually when Three talked, One listened. After all, Three had been a member of the Gorgonzola Crime Family out in the Bay Area. He'd been a good soldier and taken a term in prison for the family. Three knew the Organized Crime community. If Three didn't think it was a good idea, it wasn't.

On the other hand, being the boss meant acting like the boss. It meant making decisions. It meant rising to the challenge when mutiny threatened. Sometimes it even meant leading your crew into the shit just to prove that you were the boss.

"We're doin' it. You want to make a reputation for yourself, you gotta accept responsibility. You gotta accept opportunity when it comes." One tapped his finger emphatically on the greasy table to underscore his point. "This is it."

"Why don't we just shoot ourselves?" complained Three. "You kill a prosecutor, you're gonna have every cop in every state and federal agency hunting us."

Number One smiled blandly, though a careful observer might have seen the slightest twitch at the corner of his mouth. A leader listened. A leader explained. "We aren't going to kill a prosecutor. We aren't going to do anything. We are going to find someone else to do it." He looked around at the Milan Mob, making eye contact with each of his crew individually. "Now, who do we know that can do it and keep their mouth shut?"

The three exchanged glances. The question was confounding. Between them, they knew dozens of hard cases. Guys from the joint, guys who claimed to be stone-cold killers, guys (and a few gals) who had the tattoos and had the long sheets to prove it. But when it came right down to it, not even the murderers were cold-blooded enough to actually kill a policeman or a prosecutor. They might get mad and off their old man or their old lady or maybe a brother-in-law; they might accidentally take a shot at a cop who was on their tail. But not premeditated, like. To actually plan a hit on a prosecutor? None of the men around the table knew anyone who had been so stupid.

Number Four hesitantly spoke into the silence. "I might know some folks." He spoke slowly, working the idea around like a pinch of snuff between cheek and gum. "A coupl'a hard cases. I think they'd take the contract. They never done time for it, neither, so they'd be off the radar." Never done time for it because they'd never done it before. But they were looking for a new gig. And they were desperate.

Number One squinted. "Who?"

"You don't wanna know nothin' about 'em," Three interrupted quickly. "That way you got, like, deni-, uh, deni-, you know, whatchacallit."

"Deniability," One suggested.

"Denabilly, denabilly, yeah." Number Four bobbed his head rapidly. "You gotta have that." He wanted to divert the conversation away from who his candidates were. He didn't want to admit that they were his mother and her husband. Number One might suspect him of only recommending them because he had worked out a cut for himself. Which would only be fair. Hell, it was what any one of them would do if the situation was reversed. Number One didn't have to know family secrets. If Four worked it right, neither would his mother or her husband.

Three muttered, "It's stupid. It's suicide."

Number One leaned across the table. Discussion was one thing; calling his ideas stupid another. "You don't like the way I'm running things, you can feel free to just run along." He gestured toward the street with his chin. He smiled grimly, then looked each member of his team in the eyes to make sure they all got the message.

Number Three shut up and buried his gaze in the grime on the tabletop. People who pissed off Number One might end up hurt. Three didn't want to end up in prison for a stupid stunt, but he even less wanted to end up dead.

He also didn't have a lot of career options at the moment. Fleetingly, he thought of calling his parole officer and narking out the whole crew. They were turning out to be a dangerously stupid mob. He could turn over the whole deal, get the cops to give him into witness protection. The only problem was, his PO was a prick. As soon as she found out how he'd picked up the information, she'd probably bust him for "consorting" and put him back in the joint, just to be mean.

Like it or not, he was stuck with One, for now. He made a show of hanging his head and knuckling under. Then he buried his burning face in a glass of watery iced tea and hoped One couldn't read his mind.

Number Two, meanwhile, sat silent and nearly motionless. His mind traced a track almost identical to Three's. He was stuck too, in a crowd of idiots. In his case, it was temporary. Once he made his report to the FeeBees, he would certainly get yanked out. The Birmingham Field Office of the FBI had recruited him on his very first night out of prison and convinced him that it would be in his interest to worm his way into One's organization. They'd made no promises of what they could do for him, and plenty of threats about what they'd do to him if he didn't. It wasn't the way law enforcement was supposed to work.

They must want a man inside because they wanted information. And now—now that he had information to trade, information about a hit on a prosecutor—he'd be able to get them to pull him out. Get him the new identity they'd promised. Sort'a promised, anyway. The more details he knew, the more he'd have to trade. So, he had to hang in for a while. Dig a little more, too.

"Who'd you say the new client is?" Two asked.

Number One started to answer.

Four interrupted as a thought occurred to him. "What's the pay?" He'd been imagining the conversation he was going to have with the old people. He'd better figure his cut before he talked to them so he didn't have to do the arithmetic on the spot.

Number One laid it out for them. "Retail price is fifty big. We're gonna take a little fee of twenty, maybe negotiate it to twenty-five. Give the contractors the rest, twenty-five or thirty." He looked around at the faces, each frowning slightly as they figured out their portion of the take. "We don't want to get greedy," One warned.

Two whistled. "That's a lot of money! Who did you say wants him dead?"

Number One ignored the question. He picked up his fedora by the brim and flipped it onto his head as he stood. "That's it then. Let's get to work. Find us a contractor, gentlemen."

Number Four promised, "I'll get it done, boss," and followed his colleagues out onto the street. On the way, he had to hide his smile. This contract would come in handy. The old folks had been having kind'a a tough time. A couple of thousand bucks would tide them over until they could find something stable. A no-risk pyramid scheme or maybe a credit repair scam—some clean, honest white-collar grift that even old people might manage and that the Feds would never prosecute. This hit deal wasn't quite their thing, but mother's new husband saw himself as a tough guy, so he wouldn't be able to resist. And, really, how hard could it be? Point and shoot and disappear.

As for himself—well, he wouldn't mind half a dozen Benjamins in his own pocket, too. Maybe a little more. It would give him a parachute, a chance to get away from One and his little gang of wannabes. Maybe even start his own thing.

As they left the restaurant, Number Four and Number Two marched off in opposite directions. Both were heading for their usual pay phones to take their first steps on the road to a different future.

Chapter Four

Four months after the fateful meeting in the pizza shop, the subject stood shakily at the wheel of his thirty-foot Catalina sailboat. *Caesaria* charged ahead at full throttle into the dark night. The quiet cove with its mysterious noises disappeared behind her, lost in the roaring engine and foaming wake.

The two interlopers stood as close to Doorman as they could get. He felt both of them shivering. The air wasn't all that cold; it must be the adrenaline from their panic of a few minutes ago. Only as the dark cove and its threatening noises disappeared into the night behind them did the pirates start to relax.

From the moment he saw them, Doorman suspected they might be the hired killers supposedly stalking him. The way they hulked over him, masked and mean, the way they viciously screwed the gun barrel into his forehead, the brutal hammer-blow to his head—it all fit. Doorman could guess what would come next. Now that they were safe from whatever monsters they imagined had attacked the sailboat in the cove, they could get on with looting *Caesaria.* And then, once they didn't need him to pilot the boat, they'd dispose of him.

Joe Doorman stood between them, holding on to the wheel with a death grip just to stay upright. His head spun dizzily. A headache pounded behind his eyes. The cut on his head stung. His eyes didn't sync up, so he couldn't focus on the steering pedestal compass right in front of him. Then there was the dizziness. It came and went in waves. Sometimes he had to blink forcefully to return to seeing single images. His hearing was off, too. Sounds waxed and waned.

Thankfully, blood wasn't still dripping into his eyes. He'd wiped gallons of blood off his head onto his pants. His hands were still sticky from it. Dried blood glued his hair to his scalp. If skulls could feel, his skull felt brittle. His brain felt brittle: Doorman had to keep his head steady to keep his brain from shattering like glass.

The one thing he didn't feel was fear for himself. It surprised him, given the imminence of a meeting with mortality. But Doorman's first death threat had come years ago. Terrifying, the first time, but it made him come to grips with the fact that sooner or later someone might come for him. After a dozen or so, he'd gotten used to the idea. It was like a smoker accepting the fact that smoking could kill them. After a while, it was just part of the landscape.

Fear for David, though—that was different. If the killers killed Doorman, they'd have to kill any witnesses. Even if he fought them to a draw—and with odds of two against one, a draw was the best he could hope for—David was likely to be hurt. He needed to make sure David was out of the firing line and then...well, whatever happened happened.

In the panic of a few moments before, while the thugs charged up the ladder to check the startling noises, Doorman had managed to check the V-berth. David was gone. A quick glance when the killers forced him topside proved that the dinghy was also gone. David must have taken it.

Doorman was dizzy, probably concussed, yet the thought of David safe sent a thrill of relief through him. Thank God David had followed instructions for a change. Thank God the killers had found him up here on the boat, not at home. And thank God Deborah was safely at home.

Wandering fuzzily along that path, though, wasn't all that comforting. Sure, David was out of it. But he was also out alone on the lake, in a boat that had been damaged. At least it appeared to be floating in good trim, the last he saw of it yesterday afternoon.

That only left David's seamanship to worry about. Doorman himself had taught David to sail and to row and even to navigate the confusing geography of the lake. The boy had some skills, at least. Sailing skills. Rowing skills. Survival skills, even if elementary. He'd be alone, but he was safer out of reach than he was as a hostage, even somewhere out there on the huge lake. David wasn't helpless, though he acted that way sometimes. He was a reasonably good sailor when he applied himself. He could handle himself on the water, when he focused on what he was doing.

It wouldn't be easy for the boy. The darkness of the night, the loneliness, witnessing the attack on his father: it would all freak him out. But if David simply applied what Doorman had taught him over the years, he'd be safe.

That was, if he applied himself now. And if he'd been paying attention then.

Paying attention: that was David's problem. Take the disaster earlier in the day. The whole scene had been infuriating. After they'd sailed out of their marina and found an empty island cove to anchor in, in the late afternoon, Doorman busied himself putting everything aboard *Caesaria* back in order for spending the night at anchor. Particularly given the way the cruise had started back at the docks, he figured David could use some time to decompress. He suggested David take the dinghy to explore while it was still daylight.

Doorman stood watching as David very carefully stepped from *Caesaria's* side deck onto the dinghy. But onto the little boat. Not into. Not the way he'd been taught.

Doorman watched, unable to stop the boy as he stepped directly onto the top edge of the vertical side of the dinghy. Doorman watched him do it, even knew why his son chose to step on the gunwale just as he'd been instructed never to do. It seemed like a natural move. After all, the dinghy floated several feet below the level of the sailboat's deck. Stepping from the sailboat into the bottom of the dinghy—the right thing to do—meant a long stretch for short legs. On the other hand, the little boat's side rail invited his footstep, looking like it was just the right height to afford a comfortable step down onto the gunwale, and then another comfortable step to the dinghy's bottom.

David had been warned. Many times. "Never step on the gunwale," Doorman told him every time they boy made his way into the dinghy. Weight on the extreme outboard side of the hull could cause the dinghy to capsize. David should have understood that by now.

For whatever reason, David stepped directly onto the gunwale. The dinghy tilted in slow motion under his weight. The side dipped low enough to let the lake water pour in, and then as the dinghy rocked, David lost his balance and fell full length into the boat. His weight alone might not have caused the dinghy to try to turn turtle. But the weight of the water pouring into the boat and the weight of the tall wooden mast flopping toward the side, together caused the boat to roll wildly, and as it rolled, the mast slammed onto the cabin top of the sailboat. Even so, the mast might not have cracked had David not grabbed onto it to save himself from falling. David's weight—concentrated in a few inches on the weakest section of the mast, with a sideways load it was not meant to handle—snapped the hand-crafted spar in two. David and the better part of the mast fell into the water. David disappeared underwater.

Doorman dived into the water to save his son. He didn't think about it, didn't hesitate. He recognized the danger immediately. David could swim, but being in the water with a spar meant being in the water with tangles of wire rigging and lines and possibly a sail, all of which threatened entanglement and drowning. By the time Doorman fished the boy out of the water, he was livid.

David's failure to follow instructions was one thing. Another was the work that was going to be required to rebuild. Doorman's trial schedule barely left him time for sleep and family, never mind boat-building. His schedule wouldn't let Doorman get to it for months and months. Followed by months and months of cutting, shaving, planning, scraping, sanding, finishing, refinishing, re-refinishing and then finally stepping the mast.

A pang of guilt hit him. Doorman could admit to himself that he was inordinately proud of the little boat he'd designed and built with his own two hands. It was his first build, and, like all first boats, he'd overbuilt. His announced intention was to build a tender for *Caesaria*. In truth, he'd built it to learn how to build a small boat, with the hope that David would get interested in the process. More than that, working on a project together would give them a chance to spend time together without the usual friction. None of that had happened. Of all the best-laid plans, almost the only one that had come to fruition was the physical existence of the dinghy itself.

And now, Doorman hoped that if the little boat's hull wasn't damaged by David's blunder, the dinghy might just save his life. And his father's.

If the hull wasn't damaged. Nothing that happened yesterday should have compromised the hull, but there was no way to be certain.

A wooden boat might spring a leak anytime. No matter how careful Doorman had been and how much he'd overbuilt, he had never built a boat before. A new builder never recognized what mistakes he might have unknowingly made. Nor an experienced builder, for that matter.

Even if the dinghy's hull was intact, David might have a tough time getting anywhere in it. His fumble-footed stupidity had rendered it a sailing dinghy that couldn't be sailed. At least the boy could row, if both of the oars survived the capsize. Had they? Doorman could not drag from his memory the slightest clue whether he'd fished two oars out of the water. If David even had only one oar, he could always scull—Doorman had taught him how (or had he?)—and if worst came to worst, he could paddle. David had always been a better paddler than a rower, anyway. Doorman prided himself on not indulging in magical thinking, but now could only hope that at least one oar survived. Then David could go for help. Hopefully in time to prevent—

As he conned *Caesaria*, standing between his captors, Doorman instinctively turned his attention away from hopes and dreams and returned to certainties. Whatever trouble David might have with the dinghy, one thing was certain. His son was off *Caesaria*. Out of the line of fire. Safe from these thugs.

Unless he drowned swimming to the dinghy or after catching an errant wave on his way to get help...

Joe Doorman shook off the thought. David was able to swim. David would swim, and David would row, and David would do anything he could to survive. There was no use thinking about all the bad things that might happen. Worse things were likely to happen on this boat than out there.

What he regretted now was the way he'd addressed David's blunder. In retrospect, it was clearly just an ill-considered step. Why did he lose control and yell at the boy? Why did he let David make him lose control so often? Doorman didn't know himself. It was something he'd have to think about. If the assassins left him enough time in whatever remained of his life to think about it. He feared he'd sent David off into the dark night with bitter condemnations ringing in his ears. It would be terrible if the last thing David ever heard his father say was critical.

He fiercely pushed the thought away. Getting murdered would have to be a problem for another day. Right now, he had to figure out a way to survive. He didn't need to worry about David. David had all the tools to save himself. He had a boat that was safe and sound that would carry him to shore. He had oars, and he could row. Once ashore, he'd undoubtedly seek help.

As for his own survival, Doorman refused to spare a thought for someone coming to his rescue. If his new companions were hired killers, the chances were small that anyone could save him before they acted. Losing an ounce of energy on false hopes would only make him sloppy. He was likely only to have small windows of opportunity to strike out, and he couldn't afford to miss one while he was distracted by daydreams of a passing hero saving him. Better to concentrate on the two assailants. If he survived, he'd want to get as much information as he could into the hands of the police.

Yet the motivations of the men perplexed him. Right now they behaved more like children on a lark than hardened killers. Frightened children at that, pressed close to him as he steered, quaking with fear. He'd known and prosecuted truly hardened criminals: con men, bank officers, real estate developers and even a few murderers. They exuded self-confidence, not fear.

What if the two were not killers at all? What if they were just juvenile delinquents playing at piracy? Doorman dismissed the question. It was wishful thinking. With an organized crime trial starting next week and other death threats against witnesses and now the lead prosecutor, it was likely that the armed men showing up on *Caesaria* in the middle of the night were here to kill him. Even if they seemed so unprofessional.

The way they were acting—and Doorman's intuitive reaction to them—didn't make sense with whom they were supposed to be. If they were killers, he should be terrified. He wasn't. Nor did their conduct make practical sense. If they were going to kill him, why bother looking for loot *first*? They'd have plenty of time afterward for a leisurely search. And why bother covering their faces? They weren't going to leave any witnesses. What was the point of all the drama—"We want loot, man!"—when it would be quicker to simply shoot him, toss the boat unmolested, and disappear?

Of course, hit men didn't have to be smart. Or experienced. They could be killers and incompetent at the same time. Or be both killers and stupid. The storied tenacity, intelligence, and subtlety of the Mob was fiction. Like all criminals, they lived in fear that someone would find out they were all just pedestrian thugs. These two might well be bush-league thugs who didn't know how to execute a hit. He'd still be dead, whether they did the job professionally or not.

The problem, Doorman recognized, was that he was thinking like a lawyer. If they intended to cause him serious bodily injury, he was entitled under the law to defend himself with maximum force. Including killing them before they could harm him. If they only intended to burglarize the boat, he wasn't entitled to unleash that level of violence. Not entitled under the law, certainly. And he was not sure he could justify using deadly force if they were just misguided kids.

Misguided kids. He desperately wanted to believe it. But he didn't have that luxury.

If they were killers—and he had to assume from their battering him with a gun barrel that was what they were—he had to respond with deadly force. They'd set the terms of engagement. Whatever a court might decide later, he had no choice but to assume that it was kill or be killed. And if it turned out that they were just kids acting out—tough luck for them.

At least he didn't have to worry about David and Deborah being safely out of the line of fire.

***

Meanwhile, the two thieves huddling near Doorman for reassurance were beginning to feel silly. The panic-fueled adrenaline rush had faded. Their knees still shivered a bit. Their breaths still hissed shallow and fast, but now they were taking big gulps of air to calm themselves.

The thumping and splashing in the cove behind them had scared the hell out of both of them. More than that, though. Something about that cove on this night spooked them. There was something sinister in the air back there.

At first, they'd thought the noises were a distant boat's wake crashing up on the shore. Then, they thought that one of their PWCs had come untied and the waves were bumping it against *Caesaria*'s hull. But the noise was different from wakes on a sandy shore or the bumping of hulls.

At the first of the sounds, they'd locked eyes, questioning each other about whether the other heard that. When the sounds continued, Blackbeard watched Billy start to lose it. First, his friend grew still and his eyes grew wide. Then he flew totally out of control, dancing around and slapping himself. And to his shame, Blackbeard felt the panic infect him, too.

Their hostage had put the idea in Billy's head. As Doorman had made his way up toward the front of the boat, the part he called the "v-berth," searching for his wallet, that's when the bumping started. The guy called out over his shoulder: "Don't worry. It's just one of those big beavers."

The little man grabbed Blackbeard's shoulders and shook him. "Beavers! Beavers!" Then Billy actually screamed: "Beavers! I hate beavers!"

The big pirate watched, open-mouthed, as Billy began hopping up and down and turning in circles and slapping himself about the head. Blackbeard feared he'd knock himself out. All the time chanting, "Beavers?" Blackbeard watched, astonished. Who hated beavers?

Then the hair stood up on the back of his neck as he remembered the sudden loud splashing. The impenetrable black water. The solitude of the night. The whispered rumors of monsters hiding in the who-knew-how-deep depths of the lake. Suddenly his friend's panic got hold of him, too. Beavers or not, there was something—something evil—out there!

Only when they'd left the cove behind and Blackbeard was able to breathe great gulps of the fresh, sweet air did his thinking return to normal. He blew out his breath in disgust. *Lake* beavers? Who'd ever heard of lake beavers?

Blackbeard looked over at his compatriot. Billy was a piece of work. Why he hung out with the little guy he didn't understand. Their job called for speed: quick in, quick snatch, quick out. Here they'd been on the boat for more than an hour and hadn't even begun doing what they'd come for. They had a whole damn boat and a whole damn prisoner under their control but hadn't scored a damn thing. Worse, Blackbeard didn't know where their captain was taking them.

"Slow down," the big man ordered. He stepped back from the helmsman, displaying the gun subtly like he'd seen them do in the movies, just to show who was in command. "What's your name, old man?"

"Captain Bligh. What's yours?"

The tall pirate laughed. "OK, Captain Bligh it is. You can call me. ..hmm...let's see. Christian?" He grimaced. "No, call me Blackbeard." He pointed at his smaller partner. "That there's Billy the Kid."

"Don't call me kid."

Blackbeard winked at him and turned his attention back to the captain. "Where are we?"

Doorman shrugged. "Hell if I know."

"We're lost?" cried the small pirate.

Blackbeard saw Billy start bouncing on the balls of his feet. He jumped in to foreclose another demonstration. "We're not lost, damn it. We just don't know where we are on the map." Why the hell had he taken Billy along in the first place? These outbursts were getting on his nerves. It was hard enough dealing with police and boat owners and hostages, without having to deal with Billy and his beavers.

He stepped away from Doorman and brandished the gun. "Captain Bligh is going to take care of us. Aren't you, Captain?"

Doorman stole a glance at the gun. It was a rusted old .22. That gave him comfort: a professional killer would hardly use a gun in that condition. Unless of course he wanted something cheap and untraceable. On the other hand, as rusted and beaten up as it was, it might not even fire.

"The Captain knows where we are. Or he'll figure it out," Blackbeard assured Billy. "Ain't that right, captain? Now why don't you just run us around in circles for a little while. We got some business to take care of. Billy, you go below and see what you can find. Don't make too much of a mess."

***

Joe Doorman conned the boat around in an aimless circle, still ruminating on the same question: If they weren't the killers, who were these guys?

They might be organized crime customers he'd put in prison. A little young for that, maybe. They could be fresh out of their first short prison stay. Looking for revenge on the prosecutor who put them there. They didn't look familiar, but prison could change you. Their voices didn't sound familiar either. The names? He'd nailed Billys, Bills, Williams but nobody who he'd thought had the hatred to come back and find him. As for Blackbeard, it was obviously a pseudonym, but probably a takeoff on his real name. Black? Blackie? Beard? Beardsley? It didn't ring any bells.

He shrugged and turned his attention to the lake. Blackbeard's question was a good one. Where the hell were they? The constellation of islands barely visible through the gloom didn't look familiar. The lights on shore didn't jog his memory. As the boat circled, Doorman kept swinging his eyes, looking for landmarks. Peering into the dark hurt his head. The images kept turning into double vision.

Something was bound to jog his memory sooner or later. He'd been sailing this lake for years. It was easy to get momentarily disoriented, with few differentiating features to punctuate the uniform wall of pine trees that covered every inch of every shoreline. Eventually, though, some familiar landmark would always show itself and he'd recognize exactly where he was. If he knew where he was, he would know what his options were.

Options. Few when outnumbered by 2 to 1, even without adding in the gun. The options ranged from fist fighting to shooting off a flare to jumping overboard. Which one depended on where he was and how close he was to anyone who might see a flare or dry land within swimming distance.

For the moment, though, he had to admit that he was lost.

Would David be lost too? Would he be able to get himself out of the middle of the lake, or for that matter, out of the cove where they'd anchored? What if the boy hadn't gotten to shore? Or what if he'd fled to the nearest land—the cove's beach—and then had never gotten off the island? What if he couldn't find the oars or wasn't able to jury-rig the mainsail?

David wouldn't be able to go for help in those cases. Doorman cursed himself for expecting a young boy to save himself, much less bring help to fight the intruders. He'd end up lost, and Doorman would have to go looking for him. Once he fought off the pirates.

But first things first. Where were they now? Through the pain and dizziness, Doorman tried to remember what course they'd taken from the marina to the island. Usually as soon as he left their slip at Lakeland Marina, he'd keep a running plot of their course on the chart. A best practice, even if unnecessary on inland waters. But a best practice he always followed because he wanted David to always follow it. A best practice as a navigator and a best practice for teaching your son. Doorman had failed on all accounts. He hadn't even opened the logbook. It was such a deceptively easy course yesterday afternoon. A short line-of-sight sail to an easily seen overnight anchorage before heading out for their cruise the next morning. There was no need for a dead reckoning plot, unless something unimaginable happened like being hijacked by pirates or assassins and getting smacked in the head with a pistol.

Now, with no plotted course and no dead reckoning plot, all he could do was to try to remember their course leaving Lakeland Marina. With his head thrumming like a banjo string, remembering wasn't easy. Their heading out of the marina toward the night's anchorage had been the usual one: say, 270 degrees toward the west side of the lake. That would put them in the location of one of only a dozen or so small islands off the opposite side of the lake. Then, when the goons had forced him to rush out of the anchorage, the boat meandered on an erratic course. Doorman thought they'd gone east after that dizzying doughnut while pinned down to the anchor. When the anchor rode was cut, they'd headed off on a tangent. But what heading was anybody's guess.

So Doorman guessed.

Call it something like 110 degrees from their original course. So, 110 degrees added to 200 degrees—or was it subtracted from? Doorman's head spun with the attempt to do the calculation. He tried to push through the static to do the numbers, but he couldn't quite bring them into focus. The reciprocal of a compass bearing of 110 was...what? Something like...250 degrees? Maybe 300 degrees? Maybe a little less?

The prosecutor glanced at his captors to make sure they weren't paying attention. Then he eased onto a heading that split the difference: 275 degrees. At this point, a guess might send them in more or less the right direction...or not. In either case, better than wandering aimlessly around the lake. The course itself would prove itself right or wrong in time. If the pirates let him have time.

He glanced around to take stock of his captors. Blackbeard had sunk down onto a settee, staring out at the water with a vacant look.

He looked so much like a forlorn David that Doorman had a fleeting impulse to put his hand on the man's shoulder to comfort him. Just then, the tall man spoke. "Hate this lake. All that useless water. All you pissant boaters with your big, rich boats."

Billy appeared in the companionway and clomped up the ladder. "Voil-uh!" He held both hands up in victory. One hand clutched Doorman's wallet, the other Doorman's cell phone. He tossed the wallet to Blackbeard. As Blackbeard yanked open the wallet and pulled out the bills, Billy fiddled with the phone.

"Lookee here." The big man held up the five $100 bills Doorman had withdrawn from the ATM yesterday afternoon. The bills riffled in the wind as Blackboard flipped the wallet toward the lake. "We got us some loot!"

"Whoa!" screamed Billy, lunging for the wallet as it hit the lifelines, dropped to the side deck and then skidded toward the water. Leaping toward the rail, reaching for the wallet, the boat's sudden motion left Billy teetering between falling overboard and staying dry. Doorman saw his chance. He jerked the wheel quickly to starboard to put the rail down and tip Billy into the water.

Billy lurched and slid headfirst toward the lake. Blackbeard grunted with the effort of reaching across the cockpit to grab Billy's belt and haul him back into the cockpit. He screamed: "What the hell are you doing?"

"Credit cards!"

"We don't want credit cards. Cash! Only cash. You can't trace cash, you dimwit."

"What about his ID?" gasped Billy as Blackbeard dropped him the cockpit.

"Why the hell do I need the man's ID?" Blackbeard smiled a hard smile at Doorman. "He said he's Captain Bligh. Isn't that good enough for you?" Billy scrambled up onto one of the lazarettes to sulk. Blackbeard turned to their captive. "Find us a cove, old man. I don't want to be out here in the open in the daytime."

Doorman looked up at the sky. The sky was still dark, the stars bright, but his watch told him it was only a few hours until first light. Relief swept over him. David would have an easier time in the daylight. Someone might rescue him. Somebody might see *Caesaria*. Help might arrive. Something might happen.

A beep and an electronic voice startled them all. They stared toward the source of the sound and found themselves staring at Billy. He was holding Doorman's cell phone out at arm's length like a venomous thing. An electrified voice sounded tinnily from the speakerphone: "Hello? Hello? Who's there? May I ask who's calling please?"

Blackbeard grabbed the phone from Billy's hand. With flailing thumbs, he managed to hit the power button to turn the thing off. Then he pitched it angrily at Billy, catching his partner full in the face. "What the hell did you do?"

"I was just pushin' buttons," Billy whined through his hands as he massaged the place the phone hit him.

"You're a damn idiot," Blackbeard thundered. "You must've called somebody by accident. Keep the damn thing off. In fact, don't touch anything unless I tell you." He took a pace toward the cabin, then back, the only movement the small cockpit allowed. He aimed a kick at his bowed companion, snarled, "Fuck it!" and stooped to scoop up Doorman's phone from where it had bounced off Billy's face. He reared back and heaved it out into the lake. "Why don't you get your ass downstairs and see if you can stay out of trouble. Maybe try find anything else that's worth anything."

Billy scuttled below.

"What an idiot," Blackbeard muttered. "It wouldn't surprise me if he called the police by accident."

Doorman kept his face carefully blank. Billy might not know what he had done, and Blackbeard might not know, but Doorman did.

Billy must have hit the auto-redial button. The last call Doorman had made was yesterday in the late afternoon, to tell Deborah they were anchored and bedding down for the night. At this early hour of the morning, and with her husband and son out on the water, a hang-up call from Doorman's cell would set off alarm bells in her mind. She'd try to call back when the call dropped. And when she couldn't reach her family, Deborah would call out the dogs. Starting with the phone number he'd posted prominently on the refrigerator door.

All he and David had to do was to survive until help arrived.

Chapter Five

Deborah Doorman drifted, almost asleep. With her son and her husband out of the house, sleep wouldn't come. To make it easier, she'd made the mistake of inviting the dogs up into the bed. The theory was that they would give her enough security to get a good night's sleep. Instead, they crowded her, one against her back, one on top of her legs. That left a narrow sliver of bed for Deborah, not enough to relax. She ended up tossing and turning all night, waking up over and over to try to shove this limp dog or that muttering dog aside.

She was hovering just at the surface of sleep when the phone rang. She answered with a mumbled greeting, aware that it must be the middle of the night. Half asleep, she mumbled: "Hello?"

Nobody responded to her greeting. That woke her fully. "Who's there? Who's calling please?"

A faint sound trickled out of the receiver. She could not distinguish words, but she was certain that she had heard human voices. Then the line went dead.

Deborah put the phone down thoughtfully. She lay back in bed, thinking. The dog that had taken advantage of her momentary absence scrambled to keep from becoming a pillow.

She tried to dismiss the call and concentrate on getting back to sleep. She was losing the struggle. She told herself that it was just the fear of a sleepless night that kept her from drifting off.

Deborah tried lying still with her eyes closed. People said that if you acted like you were going to sleep, you'd probably fall asleep. When that didn't work, she tried reciting affirmations that she was actually falling asleep. Then a yoga exercise of successive relaxation.

Finally, desperate, she tried counting sheep. She visualized a paddock of sheep, jumping in ones and twos over a fence. She kept count as the passed over, until it failed for the same reason it always did. Every time she started to fall asleep, she lost the count. Then she had to start over, driving her more fully awake each time.

At last, she gave up on the sheep, too. She sat up and began to look over at the clock. She stopped herself. If she did not look, she would not have to wrestle with just how little time was left for sleep. There would still be a chance that she might get back to sleep.

If she looked at the clock, though, any chance of sleep would evaporate. If it was before one, she would try to go back to sleep, always conscious of how little time was left to sleep. That was more than enough to keep her awake. Invariably, she would give up in the early hours of the morning. If it was after one, she wouldn't even bother to try. She'd know there was no point in trying to sleep with so little of the night left. Better to make use of the hours than to lie awake staring at the ceiling. "Making use" usually meant cleaning, always hoping it would put her to sleep. But the more she did, the more she would find to do, until inevitably, she would go to work, frazzled.

She told herself not to look at the clock.

Warned herself not to look.

She looked. Two thirty. No sleep tonight. Might as well get up and do some cleaning.

Two thirty, though. Pretty early for someone to call. She picked up the phone and pushed the caller ID code. Joe's cell number came up. Why would Joe call her at 2:30? More importantly, why would he hang up?

She was almost certain she'd heard someone yelling on the other end. Why would Joe be yelling? At this hour of the morning, he couldn't be yelling at David. The child would be asleep, and he slept like the dead. Then who? And why did Joe hang up when she answered?

With fingers shaking in a sudden chill, she punched the autodial number for Joe's phone. An electronic ring sounded in her ear. Once. Twice. Half a dozen times. Then a recorded message: "The cellular customer you have reached is not responding. Please leave a message at the beep." Deborah left a message.

She got up, threw on a robe, and pattered into the kitchen to start a pot of coffee. The dogs followed her. Snuffling and grumpy, they nosed the back door. She let them out. She considered leaving the door open a crack so that they could come back in without scratching. But Joe's insistence on physical security in the last few months had unnerved her. She closed the door. Locked it. Turned back to watch the coffee maker.

The call troubled her. The recording troubled her even more. It meant that he'd turned the phone off or that it had died. Why would he turn his phone off when he was out on the boat? And why would he turn it off after he'd just called her? Besides, would Joe Doorman turn off his phone while he and David were out on the boat? No way. Not Joe. Not ever. He'd be monitoring the weather. Maybe his texts and his email too.

The dogs scratched to come in. She opened the door for them, then relocked the door. She poured herself a cup of coffee and sat down at the table. One hand wrapped around the coffee cup, she rested her head in the other and thought.

There was undoubtedly a good explanation for the phone call. It could be that Joe hit the recall button by accident while trying to call someone else. But who would he be calling at 2:30 in the morning? Or he might have hit the home number by accident. But by now he should be asleep, not handling the phone.

Anyway, what could he possibly be calling about at this hour? Weather? When sailing, weather was always a concern. She reached over to turn on the weather radio. The forecast sounded clear. No storms in the immediate area. There was that strong cold front, stalled up in the Midwest, now starting to move southeast toward Atlanta, but its arrival in Atlanta wasn't predicted for any time soon. It certainly wasn't a concern now. Anyway, Joe would have known about the forecast before he turned in. There would have been no reason to call home because of a weather change some time in the future.

She was probably overreacting. She always worried when she was alone in the house. And when Joe was out of town. The strange call hit her hard because it had called her attention to her unusual anxiety. Yes, that must be it. She was worrying about worrying. It was nothing more than that.

But being honest with herself, she knew there was more to it than that. It highlighted a stubborn anxiety she'd been trying not to think about. For weeks she'd felt an undercurrent of uneasiness between herself and Joe. There was something he was avoiding talking about. Or something that he was hiding.

Could it be a woman? Ridiculous. Of course. She'd never had reason to suspect anything like that. If anything, he seemed less interested in intimacy than usual. Sure, all the old wives' tales said that you could always tell when a husband strayed because they started being cool to the wife.

Cheating, though, wasn't in Joe's nature. No way. She was sure. He was the straightest, most reliable man she'd ever known. More likely, it was some kind of medical thing that worried him. He was getting to the age where that happened. But if it were only that, why wouldn't he tell her? They had no secrets from each other.

Maybe it was something wrong with her? They were older now, not the lithe young things they had been before David. He might think that she'd let herself slide: become too fat, or too saggy, or too gray. But surely he would have found a way to talk to her about it. Their talk was embarrassingly candid. Whatever it was, why would he hide it from her?

All that was crazy, though. It was most likely just this next trial. He was always preoccupied before trial. And this trial was a really big one. Important to the DA's political future, important for Joe's career, important for the DA's office to get this win. Lots to worry about there.

A big case and a dangerous one, too. Mafia types didn't take kindly to being prosecuted and jailed. Or so she'd heard. Was he was worried about his own safety?

Inconceivable. He was fearless.

Worried for his family? Not that he'd admit. Deborah had gently probed Joe about any potential danger. "Mafia wannabes," he'd scoffed. "Big talkers." The news reports were less dismissive. The news said this particular defendant had been the number two man in the Atlanta Family and gone rogue. The talking heads suggested that he tried a coup and got punished by being narked out to the cops by the thugs of the Big Boss, though how they could know that was anybody's guess.

No, it couldn't be any of that. It was most likely just Joe being Joe, always anxious while preparing for trial. This wasn't any different.

Except that Joe had been different. These last few weeks, he'd been more intent than usual on deadbolts and window locks. More insistent on dropping her off at the hospital and even coming back to pick her up before heading back to his office to work for a few more hours after dinner. He had talked again about buying her a gun, only stopping that nonsense when she told him that she'd just toss the thing in the first dumpster she saw. He'd even posted a "hotline" number on the fridge, because (he said) the police now had a patrol assigned to their neighborhood and they'd respond instantly if anything happened.

"What kind of 'anything' are we talking about?"

"There's really nothing," he'd said. But "nothing" was clearly a lie. He wouldn't be doing deadbolts and window locks and escorting her to and from work and buying guns unless "nothing" was something. Her guess was death threats. After more than a decade of living with a prosecutor, she knew there were always death threats. Hot talk by hotheads, he'd say. Boys yelling "I'm gonna kill you!" on the playground. It didn't mean anything.

The additional security precautions suggested he thought otherwise. She'd pressed him a week ago about whether he'd been getting more threats than usual. He'd as much as admitted that he had by avoiding answering her question. "Whenever you take on a big case, the bugs crawl out of the woodwork." He then put his arms around her and pulled her close for what was supposed to be a reassuring hug. He'd done everything but pat her on the head and tell her not to worry her little head about it. She remembered resisting the embrace. His dismissal of her concern irked her. She insisted he answer. "What kind of 'anything' are we talking about, Joe?"

"We should take a few precautions, just because it's smart. The world's gotten crazy. But really, sweetheart, nobody almost ever tags a prosecutor. They go after cops on rare occasions, but never lawyers. We're not worth the ammunition." Sitting sleepless in the kitchen tonight, it occurred to her that police officers probably told their spouses that assassins went after lawyers, not cops.

Joe Doorman was a particularly effective prosecutor. He might well be worth the ammunition to someone facing prison. Like the mafia don who was his next target. That luminary just might be desperate enough and vicious enough not to follow the Mafia Code that supposedly excluded innocents from the line of fire.

All this made her increasingly nervous. Deborah considered digging out the police hotline number. But why bother? Even if Joe had called home because he was in trouble—not likely, she reminded herself—the police were local, while he was forty miles up the road. Forty miles too far for the local police to help him. If he needed help, he would have called someone near the lake.

The whole police hotline thing was useless, too. She'd worked it out for herself. Most of the people Joe prosecuted were financial criminals. Accountants, mortgage brokers, lending officers. They weren't violent.

In any case, Deborah figured that people who really wanted to hurt you could find a million ways to do it. Burn your house down. Bomb your car. Shoot you from across the street. The thought that it was useless to try to protect yourself infuriated Joe, but it gave Deborah comfort. In the hospital, she'd seen a million ways that death could creep up on you. You couldn't worry about everything.

No, actually, you could. You could worry about every little thing. Worry yourself to death. That was the million and first way death could get you.

She had been getting her own death threats, but never told Joe. He had enough to worry about. Her threats related to the clinical studies she was coordinating. Her department was studying what might be the first-ever treatment for a new, deadly form of hepatitis. Hepatitis X had suddenly exploded on the scene. The disease, peculiar to the Deep South, had taken both physicians and health experts by surprise. A diagnosis of the disease—the most virulent of the strains of hepatitis yet discovered—meant death within a year. With Hep A and B and C and D and E receding into the background, the sudden appearance of Hep X had baffled hepatologists across the country. The doctors could only watch as a small but increasing number of patients died without an effective treatment. A small independent pharmaceutical had formulated a potential treatment, and Deborah was running some of the preliminary clinical trials. If they panned out, it offered the first glimmer of hope.

Hope, not cure, if it worked. But the treatment was a long way from approval. These studies were the only avenue for Xers to get the chance of treatment. Anybody she rejected from her hospital's pharmaceutical studies might reasonably see rejection as a death sentence.

The market for the drug would be lucrative, but the pharmaceutical company was wary. Not least because the drug was the intuitive brainstorm of a Birmingham epidemiologist. What odd meanderings of thought had led Dr. Aaron Cohen of the University of Alabama, Birmingham, to think about pig's feet as the vector? A wacky theory, and coming from a doctor from Birmingham, Alabama, of all places. Nothing that gave the company a lot of confidence in its chances to work. So, they kept the human trials small and the inclusion criteria onerous. There wasn't room for many test subjects. Deborah had to reject most of the patients who wanted to participate in the trial. Even then, candidates had to accept the chance they'd get a placebo instead of the drug. Some begged her to cheat on the double-blind procedure and slip them the drug. Some offered her bribes. A few threatened her.

Most of these people were desperate but harmless. By the time they were diagnosed, most were too sick to do anyone any injury. There might be a few nuts out there, people who thought that if they had to die an untimely death, they might as well take the messenger with them. Or survivors who wanted the medical establishment to feel the same pain they felt when they had to helplessly watch their loved ones die.

Deborah had not told Joe about her threats. There had been only half a dozen. Several had come by telephone: whispered, inarticulate. Others were anonymous notes mailed to the department or the drug company.

She smiled through the steam of her coffee. Death threats for Mrs. Doorman. Death threats for Mr. Doorman. The Doorman household was certainly getting its fair share of threats. The thing was, the threatening callers and writers weren't very specific. It wasn't like they'd call up and say, "Mrs. Doorman, this threat is for you," or "Mr. Doorman, this threat is for you." Perhaps Joe was fielding some of her threats and she was fielding some of his. Wouldn't it be funny if there was someone who had first been "unjustly" convicted by Joe and then denied lifesaving treatment by her?

No. Not funny. Not ever, but especially not right now. Not with Joe out of the house. Not with the phone call she'd received. Peering through the steam of her coffee, she frowned at her own anxiety. It was probably baseless. Surely, Joe was safe on the boat. Surely, Joe and David were safer on the boat than at home.

Still, the question lingered: If nothing had happened, why would Joe call her at 2:30 and then hang up?

With a sudden shrill of panic, Deborah went to the kitchen to dig out the police hotline phone number Joe had left for her. With an embarrassingly shaky voice, she told the dispatcher why she'd called. Then she sat down to wait for the police, finished her coffee, reconsidered, and cursed herself for acting like an idiot.

She barely had time to finish her coffee, put on a robe, put away the dogs, and get the living room straightened up when the police cruiser pulled into the driveway. She seated the young police officer at the kitchen table and offered him a cup of coffee. She wished she could offer him a doughnut but decided that he was probably sick of doughnuts by this time of the night. Then she realized that the whole doughnut thing was an outrageous stereotype, and on top of being ashamed of her weakness for calling him, she was ashamed of herself for succumbing to the stereotype.

She saw the officer frowning at her, looking perplexed. She realized that she'd been looking at him blankly while she mused about doughnuts. Deborah tried to pull herself together. "Sorry, Officer. I'm half asleep. What did you ask me?"

"You offered me coffee. I said, 'No thank you. I just came from the Doughnut Hut.'"

Deborah snorted, barely getting control before the coffee spilled out of her nose.

The young officer, who had to be only a few years out of elementary school, blushed. "So you're Mrs. Doorman?"

"Yes." She faltered, seeing herself through his eyes. Just above medium height, short dark hair, a reasonably trim figure—for a woman her age, she conceded—but right now, rumpled and puffy from the sleepless hours in bed. Deborah pushed at her disordered hair, feeling really stupid about summoning this child barely older than her son. Just to say something, she asked, "Do you know Joe?"

"Everybody knows Joe Doorman. He's a star. I mean, I've never had a case with him. I don't do organized crime investigations. If we ever have a case that looks like it's a Mafia case, we hand it off right away to the Organized Crime squad of the PD, and then they work with the DA's Organized Crime Unit. But he taught some classes at the Academy. He was great. Really funny. He must be great at home." He blushed. "I mean, you know, like witty."

"Listen, Officer, I appreciate your taking the time, but really—"

"Oh, you know, that's my job. The sergeant put me on special patrol in this area because Mr. Doorman lives here. We kind of swing by to keep an eye on him. On y'all, I mean. I didn't know if he was married or anything. That's why I was over here so quick when you called. I figured I'd better find out what's going on here." He took out his notebook, looked for a pen, and, blushing again, accepted her offer of a pencil. "Dispatch said something about more threats?"

Deborah should have felt safer with a cop in the house. She didn't know what she'd expected, but whatever it was, it was not a boy with a gun. She had a vision of him standing alone, gun drawn, facing down a rough circle of dark-suited thugs, sucking his thumb and calling for his blankie.

She took a deep breath to keep from giggling, then began telling him what led to her phone call. Finally, she stammered to a stop. "This is really stupid, isn't it? I mean, it's probably nothing. You don't have to tell him, do you?"

"Eventually he'll probably find out. I mean, if it is nothing, I guess he won't be very concerned about you calling. If it is something—" The levity drained out of his expression as his brain realized too late where his mouth was going.

He tried again. "Most of these calls are nothing, you know. Just people getting panicked. But let me do this. He's up at the lake, you said? So, what I'll do is, I'll give Hall County a call and ask them to keep an eye out for Mr. Doorman. I'm sure it will all be fine, but I don't want you to worry."

He stood and headed for the door. With a hand on the doorknob, he turned back. "Hey, I forgot. If you do hear from him, the sergeant wanted me to tell Mr. Doorman that the FBI called and wants him to call." He dug in his pocket and handed her a card. "That's the agent he should call. Special agent in the Birmingham field office." He shook her hand. "I'll pass your concern along. Somebody will follow up in the morning."

Up until now, Deborah had been drowning in embarrassment at having diverted a policeman from his patrol. She'd wanted to rush him out the door. The comment about the FBI, though, stopped her. "You said 'more' threats." She'd learned a little about cross-examination from being married to a trial lawyer and raising an adolescent boy. Like the importance of pretending you knew more than you did. Her voice as carefree as she could manage, she asked: "Have there been any more since...last weekend?"

"Not really. Just the one rumor."

The one rumor. That sent a stiletto of fear into her heart. Joe hadn't said anything about a rumor. A rumor about what? She forced a chuckle. "That rumor. Yes. So ridiculous. Who'd believe it?"

He put on his expression of a hardened lawman telling hard truths. "A man as big as Mr. Doorman is, I'll bet every goombah within two hundred miles of Atlanta wants to kill him." He grinned. "Probably including a few judges and defense attorneys." He guffawed at the cop humor.

"There are always rumors," he allowed breezily. After all, he was a hardened professional, tempered by the street. He'd seen and heard every manner of human perfidy. His year in uniform had seasoned him into a crime-fighting machine, and he was glad to share his street smarts. "Rumors. Threats. All that stuff. You wouldn't believe what we hear. We don't take it very seriously. Anyway, nobody's heard anything about a mob hit on a prosecutor in years."

Mob hit? Her blood turned to ice. She forced a laugh. "Well, won't Joe be proud, now that he's made it to the big leagues. Must've been some rumor."

Boy Wonder leaned forward to confide his secret. "The way I heard it, the DA told Mr. Doorman to get out of town and not to come back until just before trial, because he wanted him around to try this big Mafia case. Doesn't that sound just like a politician?"

"Just like a politician."

"Anyway, we're on it and so's the FBI. We'll look after him, Mrs. Doorman. Don't you worry." He stood and carefully adjusted his cap at a jaunty angle. "Now, don't you hesitate to give us a call if you need anything. Good night."

He took his leave and left Deborah with her worries, a vast span of empty time until sunrise, and a house to clean.

Chapter Six

David Doorman looked out at the spot where *Caesaria* seemed to have disappeared into the night. He shivered. Above him, the huge expanse of dark sky pressed down on him, its weight unrelieved by the uncountable pinpoints of light punctuating the murk. The stars were the only light: he could barely make out the details of the dinghy he was sitting in. The lake appeared to be black, the movement of waves felt but unseen. Below him, the bottomless abyss lurked, biding its time, waiting to suck him and the little boat down into the depths, never to be seen again.

A wave of shivering shook him. What had felt like a soft, gentle breeze on the beach now felt like a torrent of arctic air. A torrent with teeth as it blew on his wet clothing, freezing him.

He felt lost in the biting wind, the inky plane of sky above him and the depths below. On his own, utterly abandoned. And worst: he was truly lost. He didn't know where he was on the lake. Or which way to go to find help.

After a time, he realized his feet felt colder than every other part of his body. For a few numb seconds he stared toward where his feet must be, if he could only see them. He couldn't quite grasp what the feeling meant. His feet felt wet. There was water sloshing around his shoes, though there wasn't supposed to be water inside the boat.

He struggled to come up with a reasonable explanation. Maybe there wasn't actually water in the bottom of the boat; maybe it was an illusion brought on by the cold and darkness. Or maybe there was water inside the boat, but only water he'd splashed into the dinghy when he'd clambered in. Nothing to worry about.

Relieved, he looked around to see if he could orient himself on the island he had just left. At first, he could distinguish nothing in the darkness. But then he saw a shadow in the night. It was only slightly darker than the rest of the black night. The faint rustle of waves on the sand reached him, confirming that the island was there. And it was close. Should he row to the island, instead of trying for the mainland?

David was still pondering minutes later when his feet demanded his attention again. Now it felt like water was filling his shoes. Had it been that way before? He hadn't paid its depth much attention. Without being able to remember just how deep the water felt before, he thought that this seemed different. More water than he would have splashed into the dinghy when he clambered in. Even if he had, he felt certain that it was getting deeper as he pondered. Now almost covering his shoes.

Not unless the boat was leaking.

Wooden boats just naturally leak, his father's voice reassured him.

But not this much! This boat wasn't just leaking. It was—

David cried out and put his hand down to gauge the depth of the water. It was a lot of water. Over his shoes, now. Rising up toward his anklebones. High and rising.

That meant there was a hole in the boat. A big hole. Panic shot through him. If the boat sank, what would he do? He looked over at the dark shadow of the island. Swim for it. That would be his only option if the boat sank.

The idea of swimming in that inky black water yet again terrified him. Who knew what was lurking down there? Catfish big enough to chew a leg off. Nests of snakes. Old broken tree limbs that could impale a leg. Coils of barbed wire that could tangle up his feet and drag him down.

He grabbed an oar and started paddling to get the dinghy moving. At any other time, he would have set the oars in the oarlocks and pulled easily over to the beach. Now, though, all he had was one oar. He didn't think as he thrust it over the side. He was too frantic to complete a real paddle stroke, too frantic to get out of the blackness surrounding him to the solid land. He heard himself whimpering as he dug wildly at the water. The pitiful sounds ringing in his ears made him even more frantic.

Oddly, it was the boat's erratic motion that pierced the panic threatening to overwhelm him. It presented a mystery, a problem to be analyzed and solved, distracting his attention from the fear. He noticed that the bearing of the island kept moving (the *relative bearing*, Dad's voice corrected). It moved to the side of the bow, swinging to nearly behind him. To starboard. Over the bow. Back to port. It could only mean one thing. He was paddling in a rough circle.

David Doorman knew how to row and paddle as well as he knew how to sail, and what he had been doing wasn't the right way. He stopped slapping the water, wrestled his mind away from the terrifying meaning of the water creeping up toward his shins, and thought about how to row with one oar. It must be the same as a canoe. He gently dug the tip of the oar into the water and pulled. The boat moved smoothly, turning away from the side he was paddling on. He tried the same on the other side; now the boat turned the opposite way. One turn canceled out the other. Like a canoe. He knew how to handle this. He tried it, then settled into a steady paddling rhythm. Five strokes on one side. Five strokes on the other. Five again. And another five. Over and over.

The island looked no closer, but its bearing steadied to a narrower arc. The dinghy rewarded him by beginning to move in a coherent course. After a time, the trees loomed higher in the sky. He was closer. He kept at it, his count (five on one side; five on the other) using the rhythm to drive away thoughts about being a kid alone on a huge lake, abandoned by his father, halfway to a deserted island, in a boat sinking underneath him. He paddled and he paddled, losing himself in the mindlessness of the movement.

A grinding sound erupted from under the boat. It startled him. A moment of fear struck him. Rational thought told him that he'd grounded on the beach, but fear swept away the discipline that had allowed him to paddle the ungainly craft to shore abandoned him. He jumped out of the boat, onto the beach, sprinting away from the cursed boat in squishing shoes. He was yards away from the dinghy when he realized that being out of the dinghy meant being even more fully exposed to the wind, with no hull to protect him. If his feet weren't immersed in cold water, the wind hitting his full body made him colder than ever.

He steadied himself with deep breaths and took stock. The sky had already begun to lighten. At least now he knew where east was. It would still be awhile until sunrise. The lake was still empty. He'd hoped to see *Caesaria,* but there was nothing but an unbroken plane of dark water. Empty.

His father had left him behind, alone, marooned on a deserted island. "I love you more than anything in my life" was a lie. One more lie. Just like, "As soon as this trial is over we'll—." Or "Just let me get through this brief and then we can—" And "I'll always have your back." Yeah. Sure. Like now, Dad.

But he had no sooner heard the accusations in his head than shame flooded through him. Dad was every bit as trapped as he was. Worse: he was trapped with two violent pirates. And hurt. And, David realized, helpless. David not only couldn't expect Dad to save him, he needed to save his father.

With a new resolve, David marched back toward the dinghy. He was ready to try again to go for help. The boat didn't welcome him. In the night it looked like nothing so much as a prehistoric sea monster hunkered down on the beach. Staring at it, he found himself reliving his nightmare of the boat almost drowning him. He felt again the water gathering in the bilges, felt but unseen. He could feel it sloshing around his legs, getting steadily deeper. He relived his certainty that the boat it would sink within sight of the beach, close enough to see the looming trees, too far to swim...

The reverie stopped David cold. His stomach knotted. He wrapped his arms around himself to protect against the cold and the fear. He didn't have a boat that worked. Without one, how could he possibly help his father?

A wave of misery hit. He squatted on the sand, trying to get warm. Soon he was overcome: cold, exhaustion, hopelessness piled on him. Tears came, but he could not summon the strength to raise a hand to brush them away. Soon the weight of all the day's disasters piled onto him, each disaster weighing him down until at last their combined mass pressed him to his knees. He folded into forlorn bundle on the sand and soon dissolved into a deep sleep.

***

David Doorman awoke where the backwash of hysteria left him: on his side, curled in a fetal position, in sand that smelled of old fish. He heaved himself up into a sitting position. Then, with great effort, he forced his frozen limbs to unbend and stood. He brushed the sand from his face and clothes, though it stuck like glue.

He felt used up, like a battery that needed charging. The sun peeked over the trees on the eastern shore but radiated no warmth. The lake provided no comfort. There were still no boats to be seen. He was still alone.

Cold and exhaustion made his stomach clench. Hunger too. He'd refused dinner last night on *Caesaria* to show his father how sorry he was for wrecking the dinghy. Now he regretted it.

The association of hunger and the lake got him thinking. He glanced over at the dinghy, wondering if the ice chest had survived. There it sat, just where he'd tucked it into the dinghy yesterday. He couldn't understand why it hadn't floated away when the dinghy capsized. (*When you capsized the dinghy!* Dad's voice corrected.) It didn't matter. It meant that he had food.

He walked to the dinghy with a hard knot in his gut. He was hungry, but it wasn't just hunger he felt. It was determination. For the first time since he'd gone overboard, he could focus on the one task he had to accomplish. Saving Dad. The only question was how.

First, identify your priorities. Dad's voice, always lecturing. *Don't get distracted by things you can't do anything about.* Like Dad being beaten up and held captive by pirates. Like the boat leaking.

Priorities. His first priority was to summon help. It was that simple. Everything else came after that. And to do that, he had to get off this island.

Standing on the sloping beach that smelled of fish and motor oil, he sighed. A great, deep sigh. Perhaps there was the tiniest remainder of a sob in it, but he was done crying. He had to work to do.

Second, his father said, *make a plan. Ask yourself: what facts do you have to work with?*

The first fact was location. He had to know where he was to know where he could go for help. David thought that sailing with his parents, he had learned every island and every stretch of water on the lake. This island didn't look familiar, though. The chart, left behind on the sailboat, would have helped. Before now, he would have sworn it was so familiar that he would be able to remember it. He couldn't, though. Not when he was hungry and cold. Not when he was wrung out from yesterday and last night.

You should have paid more attention to the dead reckoning when I tried to show you. Thanks, Dad. That's helpful. But he could kick himself for not paying more attention to their course yesterday, or the position of this island. Navigation had always been his father's job. David remembered years of looking over his dad's shoulder as he demonstrated how to keep a dead-reckoning plot. How to identify landmarks. How to take a bearing and use back-bearings for triangulating the boat's position. He always stood at his father's shoulder as Dad worked at the chart table, pretending interest in the laborious lawyer-like explanations. Dad, dads-plaining as always. David wished now that he'd paid attention.

OK, too late for wishes. He had to rely on memory. What could he remember? David tried to remember their course in leaving the marina yesterday afternoon but hadn't paid attention. He remembered that they hadn't sailed very far before anchoring, because they'd started out too late in the day to go too far. What direction had they gone, though?

Caesaria's home marina, Lakeland Marina, was on the eastern edge of the lake, so they couldn't have gone east. That left 180 degrees of possible courses they might have sailed, from 180 degrees in the south to 360 degrees north. But which of those 180 degrees of arc had they actually sailed?

OK. Think. They hadn't pulled out the spinnaker to run north before the south wind, and they hadn't beat into the south wind either. So, they hadn't sailed anywhere close to due north or due south. That left less than 180 degrees of possibilities: some course to the west. More or less.

That narrowed the possibilities, but it didn't help. The lake was huge. From the marina, courses anywhere in the 180-degree arc from south-southwest to north-northwest were possible. That encompassed hundreds of miles of shoreline. Which put this island somewhere off the western shore, where there were dozens, hundreds, maybe thousands of islands. David knew there were fewer marinas on this side and fewer towns than around Lakeland. Farms and houses for sure. Maybe campgrounds and parks. But slim pickings when it came to getting help.

He'd been bouyed up on a wave of satisfaction at being able to analyze the elements that made up his problem. But now he felt the reality and crashed. The solution—anywhere in an arc of 180 degrees taking in the whole west side of the lake—wasn't useful. Not on such a large lake.

He would not give up. I will not give up, he snarled at the dinghy. OK, the lake was big, but it wasn't like it was the Southern Ocean or anything. And it was surrounded by Georgia: marinas, towns, parks, people. It wasn't the ends of the earth. Wherever he managed to get to shore, help wasn't going to be too far away.

Make a plan. Right. First step: get off the island and to the shoreline. Second, figure out how to get to shore. Sure. That was easy. All he needed was a boat.

How else could he hope to get off the island? The dinghy was still the best choice to escape. He looked over at it, as if weighing its feelings on the matter. The boat just sat on the sand, glowering at him, maybe even blaming him for wrecking it. He swallowed down a lump in his throat and edged up to it. Last night's terror radiated out of the sad hull. The hackles rose on the back of his neck.

"It's just a boat," he said out loud to fight off the evil. Inches of water puddled in the bottom, but it looked like the water level that had climbed past his ankles must have drained out. If the water had come in when he was sitting in it and drained out while it was beached, that meant, he reasoned (proud of himself for working this out on his own) that there must be a hole below the waterline. Rocking the dinghy back and forth did nothing to help him locate it. Even if he could have found the hole, though, he didn't have anything to fix it with. A leaking dinghy wouldn't be of any use in getting help. So that was the first fact he had to acknowledge. He was stuck without a boat.

Caesaria might come back. The boy looked up toward where he'd last seen the sailboat. No sign of any kind of boat.

He could swim for it. The closest part of the mainland was probably over behind the island. But even "close," could be an awful long way. He could swim from island to island. Except that the water was as cold as ice. Dad had warned him many times to always wear a life jacket in this lake. Something about upwellings from the frigid depths of the lake. David didn't have protective gear. He didn't have a life jacket. Swimming had to be a last resort.

If only it were summer, he could simply wait. Sooner or later, somebody would want to anchor off this beach, and then they'd find him. Either that, or he could flag down the next party barge or bass boat that happened by.

But it wasn't summer, when the lake was wall-to-wall boats. In the cold months, there wasn't much traffic. That's why his father liked to sail in the cold weather. Unfortunately, it meant that it would be a long wait for a boat to just happen by. With his father in danger and David repeating the word "hypothermia" to himself as he shivered, he couldn't just wait.

Couldn't paddle. Couldn't sail. Couldn't swim. Couldn't just wait for a boat to happen by, not in the winter. "Stuck," he said, letting his hands fall to slap against his legs. "I'm stuck."

His father wasn't going to let him get away with that, even if he wasn't around. *First, figure out what tools you have.* It was one of those stupid things his father was always saying, one of the things that drove David crazy. His little sayings always started with "first," like you wouldn't need to get to the second step, or like every step was a first step. It usually wasn't helpful, and it was certainly not helpful now, when there was not a single tool to be found anywhere.

Wait, though. He did have stuff. Shoes. (*Don't overlook the obvious,* Dad reminded him.) He had an ice chest with a few snacks left over from yesterday's aborted adventure. An oar. A pocketknife on a lanyard. A VHF radio awash in the dinghy, though almost certainly ruined. A ball of string that he didn't even remember throwing in the boat. Bug spray. Waterproof matches. And, of course, the dinghy. A ruined dinghy with a splintered mast. A cracked boom with a sodden sail wrapped around it. Not helping him at all. Taunting him. Reminding him that it was David himself who'd ruined the spars.

He had less than the Swiss Family Robinson or Robinson Crusoe had when tossed up on desert islands. He did have his memory, though. He recalled that the first thing castaways did when they found themselves marooned on a desert island was to explore the island. David turned to look up the slope of the beach toward the crown of the island. The bushes looked impenetrable. Crashing through the brush wasn't an attractive option. But it was either that or stand on the beach and shiver.

His legs trembled with weakness as he walked up the slope. Cramps threatened, a gift of the cold wet sand that he'd slept on. A tiny voice suggested that if he could just sit for a minute to let the first rays of sunlight warm him as the sun rose just over the trees on the far shore, it would warm him up. Give him energy to explore. Warmed up, rested, he might even think of some new solution to this problem.

David sat down, arms wrapped around his knees for warmth. Not intending to sleep, just to rest while the sun worked its magic. He concentrated on keeping his eyes open. After the fourth or fifth time he forced them open, he couldn't fight anymore. His eyes closed. The sand pulled him down into its clammy embrace. He sank into a dreamless sleep.

***

The sun woke him. Shining in his eyes from directly overhead. Shoot. He'd slept 'til noon.

He'd slept too long, but he felt better. He stood up and stretched. All the books he had read made it sound like castaways would fall asleep practically unconscious, dropping where they stood, and then wake up and not know where they were. David knew exactly where he was and what his predicament was. After sleeping, at least he felt rested and confident that he'd find a way to get off the island to find help.

Before it got any later, he'd explore the island to see what was here and figure out where he was on the lake. Next, he'd gather all his things together to prepare for the trip. After that, he'd simply paddle to shore and find help. Exactly how he'd accomplish any of that...well, it all depended on what he found when he explored.

He took the ice chest out of the dinghy and set it on the beach. He gathered his things—there were so few!—and put them in the chest. After thinking for a moment, he put the ice chest back in the dinghy, in case there were raccoons or something that could get into it. Then he went to explore.

In the early afternoon sun, the cove looked like something from a dream vacation. The air was cool—David guessed it was about 65 degrees, warm for fall—and a light breeze blew the fragrance of the pines at him. Sun sparkled off the dappled water.

David walked toward the trees. Where the sand ended—the north end of the beach—he had to clamber up a steep slope to get into the woods. Then he had to crawl on his hands and knees through a thicket of bushes. Blackberry bushes pulled at his clothes, and their thorns tore his unprotected skin. Rocks dug into his knees.

Finally, he broke through the bushes and into the forest. The island had looked as if it was completely covered with pines. Now he found himself wandering not in a forest but in a giant cathedral: a green ceiling of pine needles over his head; a thick red carpet of pine straw beneath his feet; the overwhelming incense of humus and pine in his nose. Below the trees' high canopy there were a few scraggly bushes and dozens of fallen tree trunks. The only sound was the wind. The eerie moan from all around him as it passed through the trees made David's stomach clench. He pushed the feeling away and walked on, looking left and right for anything that might be useful.

It was easy enough to walk in this forest. The tall trees had kept the underbrush at bay. David struck out along the perimeter of the woods, marking his progress by constantly checking the lake and the beach off to his right. The island had a slight crown, making it impossible to see both edges of the island at the same time. Still, something told him this bit of land was isolated. Not a little peninsula. Not a part of the mainland. An island.

He couldn't know that, but he knew. There was no logic to the conclusion, just certainty. He could always confirm it: walk directly across the island to the water he could see sparkling on the other side of the crown of land to confirm what he knew. But then he'd miss whatever treasures the lake had tossed ashore. Instead, he kept to his circular path, like castaways were supposed to do.

As he picked his way through the trees, staying parallel to the shore, his gaze shifted back and forth between the forest floor and the water. He didn't know what he was looking for, but it hardly mattered. Anything he stumbled on might be helpful. But there was nothing to see in either direction. On land, only trees, fallen limbs, leaf litter, and bushes. Beyond them, out on the lake, there was absolutely nothing. No boats, no visible marinas, no sign of rescue or help. Just the trees and fallen leaves leading to the crumbling cliffs dropping three or four feet straight down into the lake. And his beach, disappearing into the trees behind him.

After what must have been close to an hour, David saw an expanse of sand and water in front of him through the trees. Thrilled, he scrambled down onto the sand. The sight that greeted him almost made him whoop with joy. A gift from the lake, something he couldn't have hoped to find. Cast up on the beach was a huge piece of Styrofoam. Saved, he exulted and pumped his fists. Now he had a raft!

Big blocks of Styrofoam weren't unusual on the beaches. According to his father, they worked their way out from under the floating docks at the marinas. They were a navigation hazard and an environmental disaster, Dad would complain, watching out for them as they sailed. David looked for them with a different intention. He wanted blocks big enough to make a raft. While his parents sat on the beach and read or talked, David wanted a Styrofoam block for a raft, to escape the boredom while his parents sat on the beach and talked. What they found to talk about for so many hours on end, he couldn't imagine.

David gave the Styrofoam block a nudge with his foot. It was close to two feet thick and three feet on a side. The nudge didn't move it. He bent down and tried to shove Even when he put his back into it, it barely moved.

The boy straightened up. He knew from experience that the bigger the Styrofoam blocks were, the more waterlogged they became, and the more waterlogged, the heavier. No matter how waterlogged, though, the Styrofoam chunks always floated. This one would float if he could get it in the water. To move it back to his beach, he would need a paddle so he could float it back. So, back to the dinghy for his paddle.

He scrambled up the slope toward the forest and started to retrace his steps. Then he stopped. If he went back the way he'd come, he'd see nothing but what he'd seen before. If he continued his circular path around the island, though, he might find something new. He might find an abandoned canoe—it happened—or maybe a pirate's treasure, maybe even something better than a treasure: an oar. He turned around and continued his walk around the island.

He had barely gone a few dozen yards when he saw another beach through the trees. So, there was another beach on the island. He jumped down the slope. And there was his dinghy, with the ice chest nestled inside, alongside the oar.

David turned around and stared back at the way he'd just come, incredulous. The Styrofoam had been sitting a few yards from his beach the whole time. If only he'd gone left to circle the island, rather than right, he'd have found it in minutes.

Oh well. Bad luck that he started off in the wrong direction. Good luck that he wouldn't have to carry things very far to get them to the Styrofoam block.

A glance at the sun made his heart skip a beat. It had been overhead when he started exploring. Now it was decidedly tilting down toward the west. If he didn't get started soon, he'd end up having to choose between getting caught on the lake in the dark or spending another night on the island. The idea of another night cold and alone made him shiver. Now that he had a raft, he shouldn't have to spend another night all alone. The sooner he got started, the quicker he could get back to civilization.

David picked up the ice chest and lugged it back to the Styrofoam. Within a few minutes, he'd made the few trips he needed to get everything useful out of the dinghy to The Raft. Not just a waterlogged, discarded chunk of Styrofoam anymore. The Raft.

He felt a tickle of excitement. Yesterday he'd headed out on the dinghy for a make-believe adventure. Today, he was going to embark—yes, that was the right word, embark—on a true adventure. He'd sail this raft right out of the middle of nowhere to a park or a boat ramp or a marina. There would be amazement on shore when he paddled up in his strange craft and jumped off. He imagined himself standing tall and mature and waving aside the shouted questions and ordering them off to go rescue his father...

David shook off the fantasy and set to work loading The Raft. All his stuff sat nicely on the top side. If the water turned choppy, though, something might fall off. Using the blade of the oar, he hacked a divot in the Styrofoam to secure the ice chest. Then he dug a hole into the foam so that he could secure a tree branch as a short mast. Not that The Raft needed a mast. But a rag at the end of a branch might make someone sailing by take a second look at what might otherwise pass for just another block of Styrofoam.

Then he was ready to go. David stood in the water and worked The Raft back and forth until he'd inched it partway into the water. Then, sweating and straining, he manhandled it out into knee-deep water.

The best thing about this craft was that it could not sink. The worst thing was that it could only barely be steered. At least he'd only have to worry about getting it going in one direction. East, he thought, looking up to judge where the sun was setting and then looking at a point on the shore opposite for a destination to aim at.

David gave The Raft a final back-breaking shove into deeper water. It just barely floated off the bottom. He clambered aboard. Then he used the oar to pole out into water where the oar wouldn't touch bottom. Then he dipped his oar into the water to begin his voyage.

Chapter Seven

In the fresh light of the new morning, Hall County Deputy Sheriff Thurman P. ("Tramp") Martin leaned back in the captain's chair of his patrol boat to watch the live comedy show unfolding in front of him. A grin cracked the weathered contours of his face. His amusement wasn't, strictly speaking, very professional, even if it was the product of professional experience with interagency cooperation. He was idling in his patrol boat just off the courtesy dock of the largest marina on the lake in his professional capacity. The show was just an added perk.

It was a beautiful morning. The county patrol boat rocked with the gentle reassurance of a baby's cradle. Behind him, his twin outboards whispered a reassuring duet of burbles as they idled. The new sun warmed him. Sunbeams danced off the blue-green water. Overhead, a flight of Canadian geese swooped over in final approach to their accustomed gawky landing. This was the kind of glorious morning that justified Tramp's braving lousy weather, unhappy boaters, and the jokes and jibes of the landlubbers in his department.

This morning's special show, though, was truly a treat. A brand-new, shiny speedboat was engaged in crashing repeatedly into the steel understructure of the dock. Presumably the driver was attempting to dock his craft, not scuttle it, but it would be discern that intention from his actions. The guy was repeatedly driving his thin fiberglass against the dock's steel framework. After each attempt failed, the guy backed off and did the same thing again. And again. And again.

Fragile fiberglass versus steel: not a fair contest. Clearly the driver of the boat (he didn't deserve the courtesy of "captain") had little experience docking a powerboat. In fact, from his continued repetition of the same mistakes over and over—not varying his approach and of course not achieving any different results—it was clear that the driver was none too smart. Not that Tramp wouldn't have guessed that from the flashy, attention-grabbing logo splashed along its hull.

The docking situation wasn't even difficult. It was true that there was the slightest little whiff of wind from the lake that tended to push a docking boat toward the dock. It was also true that a bit of backwash from waves reflecting off the shore might tend to push the boat at an obtuse angle away from the dock. Even so, it was hardly a complicated situation. Had the offending boat been driven by almost anybody else, Senior Deputy (Marine Detective) Tramp Martin would have gone alongside and offered some friendly pointers.

But this wasn't just anybody. This was the newest federal intrusion into local law enforcement prerogatives. The screaming logo on the side of the boat proclaimed it the FLEET patrol boat. Tramp had just seen the acronym in an interoffice memo from the sheriff himself. A memo warning of the imminent appearance on the local scene of a Federal Law Enforcement Emergency Task Force. Which meant that at the controls was an FBI agent, sent by The Bureau in Washington, D.C. to save the day for the poor benighted hillbillies enforcing the law in the South. What Tramp was watching was just exactly what he would have expected of yet another half-assed, ill-considered federal intrusion into local prerogatives.

No local law enforcement agency welcomed the FBI's meddling. There just wasn't much local law enforcement could do to resist their interference, however. You couldn't refuse their help without being threatened with having your federal funds cut off. Funds for training would be slashed; access to Federal Law Enforcement Training Center courses would be withheld; a shit storm would blow back along all of the arteries and veins and capillaries of the law enforcement body politic until...well, (to mix metaphors, as Tramp often did in his flights of fancy), until the cows came home.

You couldn't fight them. You couldn't sweet-talk them into treating local cops as equals, because to the FBI it was patently obvious that no one was equal to The Bureau. And you couldn't co-opt them by cooperating with them. Their idea of cooperation was using lesser law enforcement as gofers.

That left passive-aggressive resistance as the only possible resistance. Some of which was damn funny. Like calling FBI agents "FeeBees." A play on The Bureau's initials carrying the added implication that they were both feeble and ridiculous. Then there was a favorite riff on The Bureau's initials that retranslated them as "Famous But Invisible" to celebrate the Bureau's habit of making big promises but then never showing up to help. Another favorite acknowledged the Bureau's habit of taking control of any high-profile case they could, only to let it die a lingering death, uninvestigated: "Famous But Incompetent." But Tramp's personal favorite was being displayed in living color right in front of him, right now. "Effing Big Idiot" pretty much covered it this morning.

A face appeared at the window of the marina store that overlooked the dock, drawn by the noise or the repeated thumps. The young clerk crashed out of the store's door and careened down the gangplank. He skidded to a stop at the spot where the FLEET boat was battering the dock. Grabbing the coil of mooring rope from the dock, he pantomimed throwing it to the driver. The FeeBee, grateful for the help, abruptly shut down his motor and reached out for the line. Not to moor his boat, but to pull himself out of the cockpit. But the FLEET boat hadn't been secured. Halfway out of the cockpit as the FLEET boat slid sideways toward the dock, the FeeBee got one foot on the dock while the other foot still remained in his boat. To Tramp's delight, the inevitable happened.

The sideward pressure of the agent's weight in the boat nudged the FLEET boat a few inches back away from the dock. The movement caught the agent with one foot on the dock and one foot on the moving boat. Slowly, inexorably, the boat and dock drew apart. The FBI agent found himself doing a classic marine split: he could jump neither for the dock nor for the boat. Tramp enjoyed the realization dawning on the FeeBee's face that nothing he could do would keep him from landing in the water. Tramp gloated, awaiting the dumb bastard's imminent immersion.

Tramp's gloat died in a sour look. The kid from the marina jumped in to save the day. He grabbed the front of the FeeBee's FLEET-branded life jacket and manhandled him up on the dock. Damn civilians—always interfering with law enforcement. "Should have let the jerk fall in," Tramp grumbled under his breath.

The clerk lassoed one of the mooring cleats of the escaping boat with a flip of his wrist like an experienced *vaquero*. A damn good throw. When the kid pulled the boat close to the dock, the FeeBee picked up the rope to try to help tie off his boat. First, he tried to tie the line around the speedboat's thin dodger pole, which would bend at the first sideways pressure, which is what mooring dished out. It soon appeared that he didn't know how to tie a half-hitch around a pole and certainly wouldn't know a bowline if it bit him in the ass.

Which was forgivable in someone who clearly wasn't a boater. What wasn't forgivable was The Bureau putting a non-boater in command of a powerful boat on the biggest lake in the Southeast.

The youngster took the line out of the FBI man's hands and, with barely a wasted motion, wrapped it around one of the stern cleats on the patrol boat. Then, with another effortless flip, he cleated a bow mooring line and, making no comment, turned back to the dock house. Without even rolling his eyes. The FBI man stood watching him go, trying both to catch his breath and call questions to the kid's retreating back.

Tramp watched the kid go, impressed. The kid hadn't cursed the idiot once. Hadn't even shaken his head in disgust. If he'd rolled his eyes, he'd done it when his back was turned. His momma done brought him upright.

Tramp pulled into a courtesy slip. With practiced ease, in seconds, he docked, shut down his motors, tied his boat up, and jumped onto the dock.

He held out his hand to introduce himself. "Tramp Martin. Hall County Sheriff's Department."

"Special Agent Brashears Livingston Thomas." The FeeBee offered a Bureau-issued handshake, then added his credentials. "Special Agent in Charge, Federal Law Enforcement Emergency Task Force, Federal Bureau of Investigation." He handed Martin a business card printed on thick cotton stock with a raised gold seal. Hall County provided Tramp thin business cards with a black-and-white logo, printed on flimsy stock with the cheapest black ink by the lowest bidding, county-approved, friend-of-a-county commissioner's copy shop. No raised gold seal for county employees, but at least the ink didn't (usually) rub off on your fingers.

The newcomer's card clarified that he was not only an FBI Special Agent, and not just the "Agent in Charge" of the Southeast task force, but no less than the IIIrd in a long line of Brashears Livingston Thomases. God help us all.

"My friends call me Livingston."

"Well then," Tramp drawled. "You can call me Senior Deputy Marine Detective Thurman P. Martin." He looked over the fed's patrol boat. "Pretty fancy boat you got here."

Thomas stepped next to him to help admire the boat. He didn't quite hook his thumbs in his belt, but Tramp could hear the swagger in his voice. "It's a state-of-the-art cruiser. The latest communications equipment. Single Sideband radio. VHF. All the best navigation equipment. Loran. GPS. Radio direction finder. Radar."

"You sure enough need all that satellite navigation equipment out there on our local ocean. Pretty damn important. Almost as important as a Chapman's."

The FeeBee frowned at the unfamiliar reference, but kept right on talking. "We have the latest maps, too, loaded on the GPS. DIA did a special satellite run to support our operation."

Too bad they hadn't supplied a second-hand copy of Chapman's "Piloting and Seamanship." Or tuition to a Power Squadron course on piloting a powerboat.

The federal agent leaned toward Tramp with a conspiratorial grin. "I might be able to get permission from the Bureau to share the DIA intelligence. In the spirit of federal-local cooperation."

Tramp considered accidentally nudging the condescending asshole into the lake as a comment on his appreciation for "cooperation." In fairness, though, there were times when he would have liked to have had some of the satellite technology. It was pretty easy to get lost on the lake, particularly in bad weather or emergencies. The lake presented challenges even for experienced boaters, and even on the most innocent of days.

It was hard for people to understand how dangerous Lake Lanier was, in part because it was hard to appreciate how big it was. "Immense" barely covered it. It covered nearly 40,000 acres and held 637 billion gallons of water. More than the size, though, it was the irregular shoreline that made navigation tough. More than 500 miles of heavily wooded irregular shoreline surrounded the lake. That didn't include the islands fringing the perimeter all the way around. There were so many islands and so many little coves that unless you knew which landmarks to look for, you could search for a long time before you figured out where you were or where you were trying to get to. Unfortunately, the landmarks were almost exclusively groupings of pine trees that all looked like other groupings of pine trees.

To assist in navigation, the Army Corps of Engineers and Lake Lanier Association had put numbered buoys and navigation lights around the lake. It helped a little, as long as you knew to look for them. And if you could pick out the numbers on the buoys from the background clutter. But no satellite navigation system was going to help a newcomer tell the difference between the different landmarks. Or match the names of geographical features shown on the maps to the locals' names for them. Locals called one cluster of islands the Three Sisters and another the Three Amigos. There was Chattahoochee Bay and False Bay and Fried Pork Chop Bay. Sailors sometimes called one narrow, windswept passage Cape Horn. None of those names appeared on any official map, and certainly not FLEET's Washington-approved, high-tech, satellite-aided, DIA-issue computerized maps. But if you learned Lake Lanier—really learned the territory—in time you knew exactly what each of these beer-induced literary flourishes referred to.

More importantly, even if a new boater wasn't cowed by the size of the lake and the difficulty of navigation without clear landmarks, there were the reefs. The lake was full of rocks that were barely awash. The only way to learn where the obstructions were was to learn to read the water or listen to the local knowledge shared by old-timers. Which the feds had not done. The Bureau never, ever knew local conditions and the Bureau never, ever asked. Why would they ask a local? Everybody in Washington knew the locals were idiots who didn't know Shinola.

Tramp considered for a moment that he probably should show a little Southern hospitality and show the new man the ropes. But he'd had experience with the Bureau. There was no sense in trying to tell a blowhard any damn thing. Particularly not a Federal blowhard who, by definition, was omniscient. And it was more particularly not worthwhile with an interloping, high-tech FeeBee blowhard.

Besides all of which—if that weren't more than enough—Hall County Marine Detective Tramp Martin would be good-goddamned if he was going to cooperate with a Fed trying to horn in on county business. The guy had no rightful jurisdiction here. The best-case scenario for everyone would be for the FLEET boat to tear out its bottom on a reef on its first patrol, before the feds caused any trouble, then to pull out and leave law enforcement to the professionals.

"You've heard about our mission, I'm sure," Thomas was saying with the faintest tone of smugness.

Tramp had. At high volume. The chief had clued him in weeks ago. The way the chief put it, the "God damn Federales" were going to start patrolling Tramp's lake. Seemed that some Bureau hotshot in San Antonio had decided that there were drugs being smuggled across a lake in Texas that spanned the Mexican border. So, the Texas region requisitioned a boat to put a stop to the drug running and of course created a multi-agency task force to justify the expense. Once the Texas region bought a boat, every other region fought to justify one for its own region. Some guy in Atlanta proved that there were hundreds of Personal Watercraft stolen from the lakes in Georgia (for which there was documentation) that got shipped to the Carolinas and Florida (which was a rank guess) to be shipped transnationally in support of international terrorism or drug smuggling or child sex trafficking (which was bullshit). That gave the Bureau "a lame-brained, dumbass excuse"—the chief's words—to put a patrol on the busiest lake in the Southeast. The chief raged that they'd all be a lot better off if every single goddam PWC got stolen from Lanier and shipped to Africa or Mexico. That would prevent half of the lake's yearly accidents from happening. And get rid of the FBI, too.

Tramp had listened patiently as the chief raged. He was a good guy, a good chief, and a good boss, even if sometimes he failed to live up to the Serenity Prayer. This latest federal effort certainly required an exercise of "wise enough to know the difference." Though face-to-face with Special Agent Blah Blah Blah the IIIrd, Tramp reflected that "lame-brained" and "dumbass" pretty wisely characterized the Federal effort.

Meanwhile, the personification of the Federal Effort continued his story. "Headquarters got a report that two PWCs were hijacked off the lake last night."

Tramp frowned. "Headquarters?" The FBI in Washington had picked up a report from North Georgia? Why would offense reports from the City of Gainesville, County of Hall, State of Georgia, come to the notice of the The Bureau all the way up there in DC?

"FLEET Regional Headquarters in Atlanta," Thomas clarified. "I drove up here as soon as the call came in."

"Wait. You live in Atlanta?"

"Right. I live close to HQ—Headquarters, you know—so I can pop in whenever we get a call." The FeeBee gestured toward the cell phone hooked to his belt in a waterproof case. "High tech, satellite-linked, double-encrypted. I'm on call twenty-four seven. For cases just like this one."

Tramp cocked his head to one side like a confused Airedale. "Let me get this straight. You get an emergency call and you just scramble into your boat and zip out to the scene. Right then. Right as it's happening. I mean, after you drive thirty-five, forty miles up the road to get here. Which should only take about what, an hour?"

It was dawning on Thomas that there was a problem with the deputy's attitude. In DC, they'd warned him that the locals might be challenging to work with. Of course, local law enforcement was jealous of the Bureau's greater budget and expertise. And local law enforcement (Thomas's boss predicted) wasn't going to be happy being shown up by the Bureau's greater resources. On the locals' own turf, no less. The bubbas would hate watching modern law enforcement techniques outperform the traditional hillbilly way of handling things.

Thomas knew it must be hard for locals like this Tramp character to watch a stranger come in with greater resources and knowledge and handle an investigation better than they could. Still, he didn't see how any patriotic American citizen could refuse to assist the Bureau in its work. Which was, when you got down to it, nothing less than Protecting America From Our Enemies. But here, right in front of him, was a deputy who clearly hated the Bureau. Nevertheless, they both had a job to do and it was time to get to it. If the local was invited to join the Bureau's efforts, how could he resist? "Let's get started on our investigation," the FeeBee suggested.

"You do that. I've got to go talk to a man about a horse's—"

"Wait a minute," the FBI called out to the deputy's retreating back. "Don't talk to any witnesses without me. First, we need to surveil the scene and gather physical evidence..."

The deputy paused, turned. "You better do the surveilling. I never took French."

The FeeBee grumbled. "That's not very cooperative."

Tramp had already left the man behind on the dock. In the Lazy Holiday Marina office, he threw himself down in a visitor's chair. He'd known Skippy Dale since high school. They saw each other a couple times a week during Tramp's patrol, a few times a month at church, and once or twice a year at Gainesville High's annual homecoming barbecue. Nowadays, Skippy served not only as the dockmaster of the largest marina, but also the de facto mayor of what he liked to call "the lake community." Tramp thought of him as Mayor Roy Stoner to the Chief's Sheriff Andy.

Tramp put his feet up on Skippy's desk and pointed out the window at the dock. "That there is one sorry—"

Skippy good-naturedly swept Tramp's boots off his desk. "Guess you heard about our problem."

"Nope. I only heard you had fresh coffee and doughnuts."

"I got no doughnuts and two stolen PWCs. Two WaveRunners that were down at the service dock. They somehow got gone." Tramp knew the stolen PWCs weren't necessarily WaveRunners. The little boats went by any old name: WaveRunner, Sea-Doo, Jet Ski, the generic Personal Water Craft, and, among the fishermen and sailors they constantly harassed, a lot of other names much less polite.

"Isn't that a little unusual this time of year? PWCs at the dock, I mean."

"Our mechanics are busier this time of year than during the warm weather. Season's over, people bring them in before they put them in their garage for the winter. My guys were doing engine tests and left 'em in the water overnight. I guess they figured nobody in their right mind would ride off on them in the fall."

Tramp snorted. As far as he was concerned, "nobody in their right mind" described every single person who rode the damn things. It seemed like not a single PWC jockey knew the law about boating drunk, or the navigation rules, or radio etiquette. The only thing they were rational about was protecting themselves from the lake's frigid waters. Give them credit for some smarts, at least: they favored fully insulated dry suits in the winter, wet suits in the summer.

Tramp held out a hand for the information on the stolen water vehicles. Skippy handed over a list of the serial numbers and descriptions. Scanning the information, Tramp mused, "I guess your security guys didn't see anything."

Skippy scowled and shook his head. It was a long-standing quarrel between them. The board of directors at Lazy Holiday Marina hired lazy security guards. They carefully guarded the main gate into the facility from their climate-controlled booth, their minimum wage salaries not justifying the effort of policing the grounds on foot. Any thief, no matter how drug-addled, knew to avoid the gate. They'd come in by water or wade along the shore, where there was no security at all.

"They're probably long gone," Tramp said, folding the list into a breast pocket. "But I'll keep my eyes open."

"How many does this make this year?"

Tramp totaled up the thefts in his head. "Coupl'a dozen. Half a dozen at least in the last month."

"Out'a control, man. Almost feels like there's a gang workin' the lake. Don't laugh at me, Deputy. I'm just tellin' ya what my gut says."

"Wouldn't hurt my feelings if they stole every one of the damn things," Tramp snorted. "That'd cut down drunken boating arrests by ninety percent, probably cut accidents down by the same number. And that's an official opinion of the Sherriff's department, by the way." He stood to leave.

The federal agent appeared in the doorway to block his exit. "OK," Thomas enthused, "I'm ready to get started." He squeezed by Tramp, sat officiously in the chair Tramp had just vacated, and flipped open his badge holder for the benefit of the Dockmaster. "Special Agent Thomas, Federal Bureau of Investigation."

"Special Agent *in Charge*, Skippy. Let me introduce Brashears *Livingston* Thomas. The Third."

Thomas's smile faded a little, not quite seeing the joke. "I'm the local law enforcement liaison and the Special Agent in Charge coordinating the Federal Law Enforcement Emergency Task Force. I understand you've had a qualifying event."

Tramp snorted. Thomas's shoulders tightened, but he kept his attention on Skippy.

Skippy had pretty much figured out Tramp Martin's take on the FBI man, and if Tramp didn't like him, Skippy darn sure wasn't going to. "Only emergency I seen is you chewing up my dock with your boat. Now what the hell does the FBI want down here in God's country?"

Thomas was visibly thrilled to be invited to expound on the Federal interest in Lake Lanier. He started with the Commerce Clause of the United States Constitution. Moved on to the principles involved in theft and interstate carriage of valuable goods, to wit: Personal Watercraft. Implications for the Commerce Clause of the United States Constitution. The Bureau's historic role in stopping organized interstate criminal transactions. "We intend," Thomas assured Skippy, "to assist local law enforcement in identifying and infiltrating the organized crime rings perpetrating these crimes." Whether we want their help or not, Tramp added silently. "With aggressive prosecution and asset forfeiture, we intend to put these criminals out of business." Tramp couldn't remember later whether the FBI agent actually pounded his fist on the table during his lecture, but that's the way he would always tell the story.

"'Asset forfeiture?'" Skippy chuckled, his eyebrows raised. "Those boys got nothing to forfeit."

The FeeBee stopped in mid-sentence. "'Those boys'? You mean you've already identified the perpetrators?"

The Dockmaster snorted. "We know them. Yeah."

Tramp jumped in. "We don't *know* anything. Some people have their suspicions." He warned Skippy with a glare. "What we *know* doesn't mean anything if we can't *prove* it."

The FeeBee turned to stare at him, ruminating on questions about the suspects. Tramp figured it was time to go before he had to give both of them a lecture on the difference between knowing and proving. He tapped the papers in his uniform blouse pocket and waved to Skippy. "See you, Skipper. I'll let you know if I find anything."

He was just stepping out the door when he remembered something else. "Skip, listen. I got a call about a sailboat. Thirty-foot Catalina called *Caesaria*. The guy's wife called in to say that she was worried about him. If you see him, tell him to call home, huh?" He waved over his shoulder as he started out of the office.

"Wait a minute," called Skippy. He consulted the dock chart. "*Caesaria*'s one of ours. Doorman, yeah. Nice guy. Wrapped a little tight. I would'a thought he'd be pretty good with a sailboat. But yeah, if I see him..."

Tramp was back in his boat, just nudging it into reverse, when the Special Agent came stomping down the dock. Before Tramp could back away, the Fed knelt on the wooden planks and grabbed onto the frame of Tramp's windshield. Apparently, he was under the impression that his FBI superpowers could overcome a couple of 250 horsepower outboards.

Tramp briefly considered disproving the assumption by gunning it in reverse and dragging the officious bastard into the water. It was not a professional thought and not one worthy of a Hall County law enforcement officer. He hated himself for thinking better of it. Instead, he exercised a little inter-agency consideration and slipped the gear shift into neutral.

"If you have identified suspects," Thomas called over the sound of the motors that Tramp was revving in neutral to express his annoyance. "Why didn't you say so?"

"I didn't want to distract the Bureau with an unscientific guess."

"You know, Deputy, if you would work with...that is to say, if we were to work together, we might be able to solve this incident mor e efficiently."

"I guess if we did, we might."

"If you know who the perpetrators are, why don't we go arrest them?"

"Well now, it's like this. Down in our neck of the woods, we locals don't have the advantage of all y'alls' high-tech intelligence and satellite stuff. Which is good, because we don't want to get all ruffled an' flustered by technology. We prefer to kind'a sit back in our rocking chairs on our front porches and pick our banjos while we're spittin' our chaw on the front lawn, so we can talk amongst ourselves. We gotta rely on the old-fashioned stuff. Like local knowledge. Community relations. Even, you know, old fashioned things like evidence. Which, in this case, we ain't got." He gunned the engine a few times for punctuation.

"If you get me the names, I'll run them on NCIS, print out their sheets—"

"Well, I'll be damned." Tramp slapped his forehead. "Why didn't I think of that? Identify the perps before we charge them! Guess it's lucky we haven't arrested them yet. Thanks. You sure kept me from making a big mistake. Now, listen, I gotta—"

"Are you going to disclose the names of the suspects? The structure of their organization? Links to TCOs?"

Transnational Criminal Organizations. The FBI's latest branding of the product that in Tramp's youth they marketed to Congress as "the mafia." Waves of new brands had taken the place of the old brand: FTOs (foreign terrorist organizations), CEs (criminal enterprises) and OC (organized crime). Most of the campaigns didn't serve up any actual results, beyond providing an evergreen method of generating Congressional funding. But now they were in luck. Now that they'd discovered international criminals stealing PWCs on a rural lake in the hinterlands it proved that TCOs were active in the area. Which required funding. Which the FBI would share with precisely nobody.

Tramp wasn't in a sharing mood either. "Nope. I can't really share mere suspicions. I'd hate to be responsible for prejudicing your scientific inquiry into the case."

He reversed his boat away from the dock where the FeeBee was struggling to his feet, then pushed the gearshift into full forward as he swung the boat into a tight buttonhole turn. As he roared away, the rooster tail of his wake accidentally soaked his colleague.

Oops.

Chapter Eight

Joe Doorman slumped in the cockpit, one hand draped listlessly on the wheel of *Caesaria*. The intense pain in his head had faded. Now it was as though a fragile glass globe surrounded his skull. As long as he didn't make an abrupt move, the glass wouldn't shatter.

Worse was the feeling of being utterly empty. The sleepless night, resisting the pirates, trying to keep them away from David, conning the boat, worrying about where David was and what he was doing, the ferocious ache in his head—they'd all done their bit to drain the last of his reserves. The fierce headache might also be a concussion. And that was the best-case scenario. At worst, it could be a subdural hematoma or a brain bleed. (Thank you, Deborah!)

Whatever the reason, his eyes kept closing of their own accord. He found himself moment by moment waking from a doze. Not what he should be doing, not with killers aboard and his life on the line. Not with David out there somewhere alone.

He should be planning. He should be listening. But he simply couldn't.

Slowly it dawned on him that his guests were engaged in an escalating argument. He fought to focus in on the words through the static in his head. It surprised him to find that he was witnessing something that he'd thought was only fiction: a pirate falling-out. Not about the division of the booty, though. It had begun as Doorman was cooking them breakfast, though he'd been so focused on attacking them he ignored the subject. Now it seemed to be reaching its shrill climax.

Doorman lay back in the mellow sunshine and fresh air and tried to listen. Billy wanted to take the PWCs and their loot and split. Blackbeard wanted to extend their spree by one more day.

These guys still confused him. He'd pretty much decided that they weren't former criminal defendants seeking revenge for their time in prison. Hit men? Logic suggested it. It seemed unlikely to be a coincidence that when there was a contract for his killing out on the street, the two strangers who invaded his boat were *not* the rumored killers. But these guys schemed like small-time burglars.

He should be happy with a bare possibility that they weren't out to kill him. But even a minuscule chance of their being mere delinquents complicated his planning. If they were killers, he could justify confronting them with whatever means were necessary to defend his life. Striking first, brutally and without limitation, would be perfectly acceptable. Even deadly force in his own defense would be legally justified, even if it turned out later they were just a couple of teenagers out on a lark.

If he reasonably believed they were out to kill him. He did. There were two pieces of evidence to support his belief that they were killers. The vicious hit to his head—the serious injury they'd caused—was one. The second was more damning: they'd left him untied and they'd abandoned their masks. That was utterly stupid if they were going to let him live. Reason said they'd allow him free movement and they'd abandon anonymity only if they didn't expect him to be around later to identify them.

As for contrary evidence? They seemed incompetent. They gave off the vibes of kids on a lark. They were frightened of their own shadows, easily manipulated (beavers, for God's sake!), needing an adult's reassurance. It all suggested that they weren't killers, but didn't prove they weren't. Even killers could be incompetent and psychologically fragile.

On balance, Doorman thought a court would find him justified in defending himself with deadly force under these circumstances. But that depended on his being alive to present his case to the police or a court. And that in turn depended on his winning his fight with them. And that in turn depended on evening the odds, meaning finding a weapon to change the balance of power. What weapon, though? With his head so muddled, Doorman could not think of a single one.

The next time they made him cook for them, he could theoretically put poison in their food. If he had any. He could bean one of them with a heavy frying pan upside the head to even up the odds. In fact, he'd prepared himself to do just that this morning, but they'd both stayed carefully out of reach. He'd been within arm's length of a chef's knife, too, but again, they never let him get close enough for him to take the chance of grabbing it and using it. He hadn't found anything outside the galley heavy enough to use as a weapon. There had to be something. It was so easy to get hurt on a sailboat if you weren't trying to, how could there be nothing dangerous to use as a weapon? Even so, nothing came to mind.

There was another option that didn't involve deadly force. Doorman could always slip quietly over the side and swim for it. Especially at night. During the day, they'd see him dive overboard and swim away. What would they do, though? He was pretty sure they wouldn't be able to run him down with *Caesaria*. If the boat were anchored, they probably wouldn't figure out how to raise the anchor on their own or how to start the diesel engine. But they could always take the easy way out: shoot him in the back as he swam away. Assuming that he could even swim with this head spinning and his balance uncertain.

But even if he got to an island without drowning, it wouldn't be hard for them to find him. The islands were small. Footprints in the sand would lead right to him. It wouldn't take long for them to corner him.

The one thing that kept him aboard was David. The boy might well have taken the dinghy and made it to shore. He might be returning with help or returning on his own after summoning the cavalry. If Doorman was gone, having either escaped or been dispatched by the killers, David would return to the sailboat only to have to face the pirates alone.

There was a more likely possibility. David might still be drifting in a disabled dinghy, or stuck on an isolated island, or even lost in the rural jungle that characterized much of the western border of the lake. If the boy needed rescue, who would save him if not Doorman? And to do that, he'd need not only to fight off the pirates, but also to remain master of *Caesaria*.

Doorman wondered if the boy had spent the night on the island where they'd anchored that first night. Had he flagged down a passing boat? Managed to row the dinghy ashore? Tried to get ashore and overturned and...? The thought brought a wave of worry, then nausea. Doorman forced his thoughts away from the possibility of David coming to harm.

No sense in worrying about it, since he didn't have any information about David's condition and couldn't do anything about it even if he did. If he was going to assume anything, he might just as well assume that David was fine. Cold. Alone. Even lost, afloat or ashore. But almost certainly fine.

Almost certainly.

Below, in the cabin, the voices waxed and waned. When louder, the voices broke painfully against the glass sphere surrounding Doorman's head. Doorman almost yelled at them to shut up, but he caught himself. Their fighting was to his advantage. If they couldn't agree on a course of action, they might just abandon their spree altogether. Or be unable to come to an agreement on something as weighty as a murder.

"Listen, you dimwit," Blackbeard raged. "We never had this chance before 'cause we never had a place to stay before. Now we got a base. We go out, hit a boat, then come back and dump the goods, then go out again. We can clean up! Make more money today than we made in a year. And we won't have to steal any more of those Sea-Doos, either."

"I wanna quit. You said we was only going to do this oncet or twicet, then stop for a month so the poh-lice don't catch on."

"Well, I'm sure after all the Sea-Doos we've stole, the police probably know something's goin' on. I agree that we've gotta give this lake up for a month or two. But right now, why not strike while the iron is hot? Why not go out with a bang? Just one more day, Billy. One."

"I jus' don't like it. I jus' don'." Doorman could hear that even though Billy was protesting, he wasn't arguing the point. He was giving in, something Doorman had heard him do repeatedly. Whine. Give in. Rinse and repeat. Not only was he neurotic, he was spineless. Which might explain why he was relegated to the role of sidekick, not equal partner. A useful vulnerability to remember.

Doorman's attention waned. Billy had already apparently acquiesced to Blackbeard's suggestion. Now they were planning the rest of the day's work. Only one part of their plan concerned Doorman: What would they do with him while they were off burglarizing half of North Georgia?

"What're we gonna do with him?" the little pirate demanded.

Doorman's ears perked up. The few moments of silence in answer to the little guy's question chilled him. Finally, Blackbeard allowed, "I guess we'll have to find a way to take care of him."

"I ain't killin' nobody!" shrieked Billy. For once, Doorman felt a soft spot for the whiny little rat.

"Keep your voice down, you idiot. I'm not talking about killing. I'm saying we have to tie him up or maybe knock him out or something while we're out. Then when we come back, we untie him."

"What about when we split for good?"

"I guess we'll tie him back up and call the police once we get away. You know, tell them where he is. Get them to come and untie him."

"What if there's like a hurricane? I ain't gonna be no part of no killing. Not even letting somebody die in a hurricane. You hear?"

"Oh, jeez, Billy, you are such damn idiot. There aren't any hurricanes in Georgia. All we have to do is let Captain Bligh here set the boat up however he wants to, and then he can ride out any typhoons or tidal waves until the police can come get him. That make you feel better?"

Doorman heard the bluster in Blackbeard's voice. The big pirate wasn't all that sure it was safe. Doorman wasn't all that sure that being tied up and left behind was safe either. And he wasn't looking forward to getting hog-tied. The only thing to recommend it was that getting thrown bound and gagged in the cabin was better than getting thrown bound and gagged over the side.

The sudden cessation of the argument made him look up. Blackbeard was climbing up the companionway ladder to the cockpit. He sat opposite Doorman. "Thanks for breakfast," he started, picking his teeth with a fingernail. "You sure packed a lot of food on board. Expecting company?"

Doorman gave a faint smile. It was lucky they hadn't noticed until now that the boat carried extra bedding, extra food, extra clothing, all more than sufficient for one person. He wanted nothing to betray David's existence. Not even with David gone. The last thing he wanted was to give them a reason to wait for the missing person to reappear.

Blackbeard was obviously having a hard time getting started at whatever he'd come to tell Doorman. He sat, silent, fidgeting with whatever was close to hand. Only one thing caught his attention, though.

"What's this?"

"It's called a book."

"*The Truelove*,“ Blackbeard read, ignoring the sarcasm. He peered at the cover: a beautifully rendered square-rigged ship under sail. "Patrick O'Brian, huh? This any good?"

"The best adventure books ever written. One of the finest writers in the English language." Then Doorman cursed himself for not thinking before he spoke. He needed to concentrate on getting information from his attackers rather giving them book reviews. "You read books?" he asked, studying Blackbeard's face.

Blackbeard threw the book back where he'd found it. "Nope. Too busy takin' candy from babies and stealin' their lunch money."

The big pirate leaned back against the cockpit side, still not comfortable saying what he needed to say. "So anyway, the thing is...Well, you probably heard us talking. We want to use your boat for just a little while longer. Do some business up here today, and then we'll be moving along. But we gotta make sure you're not going to get yourself in trouble." He caught a momentary reaction that flashed across Doorman's face. "No, don't get the wrong idea. We aren't going to kill you or anything. We just gotta make sure you stay out of trouble while we're gone."

Billy climbed into the cockpit with a coil of rope in his hand. "You go get ready," the small man said to Blackbeard. "I'll do it." When his partner went down below, Billy told Doorman what they were going to do. "You prob'ly better get the boat set up however you want it." He gestured with the rope. "You ain't going to be able to do nothin' for a while."

Doorman looked around at the cove in which they'd anchored. It was protected from everything but a wind from the east. A wind from that direction was unlikely at this time of year unless they got a cold front. That wasn't a problem, according to the weather report. Of course, the last weather report he'd heard was yesterday's. The weather could change, and in the fall, it could change quickly. Doorman looked at the sky. Tendrils of high, thin clouds had moved in. It was a little unusual for this time of year, but on a normal day of sailing they would not cause alarm. All they would do was suggest he listen to the weather report.

When he'd anchored here, he hadn't anchored with foul weather in mind. All he'd wanted last night—this morning?—was to get an anchor down so he could try to rest before he fell over. Foul weather was always a possibility, though. If he were incapacitated, he wouldn't be able to rig a second anchor later. He'd have to do it now.

Except for dealing with the pirates' paranoia, the procedure was simple enough. He'd set out the second anchor at a 90-degree angle to the first. If the wind shifted in a storm, at least one of the two should hold and their angles would give him nearly 180 degrees of security. He warned Billy that he was going to be starting the engine and then running back and forth between the foredeck and the cockpit. Then he stood and started the engine.

Blackbeard charged up the companionway, bellowing. Expecting what? That now Doorman was hijacking the hijackers? Doorman explained what he was going to do, then handed off the conn to Blackbeard. He reviewed what hand signals he'd use from the bow and then how to work the gear shift and throttle. Then Doorman went up to the anchor locker in the bow. He motioned to Blackbeard to motor forward slowly at a slight angle to the first anchor rode.

Just before the boat got where he wanted to set the additional anchor, he gave Blackbeard the sign to shift to neutral. He lowered the anchor and when he could feel it touch bottom, signaled to Blackbeard to back slowly away, paying out enough rope to allow it to set. It occurred to him that if he intentionally flubbed the set, the anchor might drag and the boat might drift out onto the lake. Any passing boater would see the boat adrift and come to investigate and find him trussed and struggling. A great plan.

Except for all the unpleasant alternate possibilities. *Caesaria* might also hit a reef, capsize and sink. With Doorman tied up and helpless below. Or run up on the beach, cracking the hull, and then fill with water. With Doorman tied up and helpless below. Nope.

When the second anchor was set and holding, he signaled the big pirate to cut the engine. As Doorman came back to the cockpit, he caught the big pirate watching him thoughtfully. Before leaving the wheel, Blackbeard pulled the key out of the ignition and thrust it into his pocket.

Doorman swallowed a reflexive "Good job," just as he mentally shrugged over Blackbeard taking the key out of the ignition. Tied up, the ignition key wasn't going to help him much. If he somehow managed to get free, he still had the sails. Plus, there was a duplicate key in the chart table.

He went below to make sure that the weather radio was on. At least that way he'd get weather alerts. Not that he'd be able to do anything about them, no matter how bad they were. But at least he'd know what was coming.

He was heading back to the cockpit to check on the security of the sails when he remembered the batteries. This morning, while cooking breakfast for his captors, he'd come up with the brilliant plan of running the batteries down to zero. He'd gone through the boat, turning on all the electrical devices to drain the batteries. He wanted the pirates to come back to find themselves stuck on an unfamiliar boat without any power. Doorman already knew they were afraid of the dark. They'd need the batteries not just for light, but to crank the diesel engine. With the batteries dead, they'd be stuck on a lightless, immobile boat. It might cut short their crime spree. They might abandon the boat and Doorman. Hopefully alive.

Now he realized that it was a stupid plan. If he did get himself free, he'd have left himself without resources. He went through the boat to shut down everything he'd turned on. He left on only the anchor light and running lights lit. Not the proper lighting for a sailboat at anchor, but he didn't want some negligent idiot running *Caesaria* down while he lay immobile in the v-berth. Last, he closed and secured the hatches. It would make the cabin stuffy, but it would keep any water outside where it belonged.

He looked around, racking his brain for what else he needed to do. He couldn't think of anything. If he'd missed something, circumstances later would remind him. Probably in a dramatic fashion. Certainly too late to do anything about it.

Climbing back in the cockpit, he found Blackbeard with the nav station's main VHF radio in his lap. Normally the VHF hung on brackets above the chart table. Doorman knew immediately that they intended to deprive him of any opportunity to make a distress call. What surprised him was that the pirates had carefully unplugged it from the power and antenna outlets, rather than ripping it out with brute force. The unexpected delicacy gave Doorman a lift. Hired killers wouldn't worry about tearing a radio out of their victim's boat.

"You stealing my radio?"

"Yeah. I thought I'd take it down to the corner and pawn it." Blackbeard gave a grin. "I figured we'd take it with us to make sure it doesn't bother you while you're resting."

Which made sense—if they only intended to deprive him of its use while they were gone.

There was another explanation, though. If they intended to kill him and leave his disappearance a mystery, they'd need to clean up any traces of violence. Without an obvious clue like a battered radio or dangling wires, the police would just find an empty boat, with no signs of violence and no clue as to where the owner had gone. They'd conclude that the absent sailor was just another of the unfortunate boaters who slipped overboard and drowned while peeing over the side. At least until they heard from David or found a body. The killers would be long gone by then.

"I'm taking this with us," Blackbeard said, interrupting Doorman's thoughts. "I figure the chance of you getting loose is pretty small. But I don't want to tempt you to do something stupid." He pointed toward the v-berth. "Now look, we're going to tie you up and put you in the loft up there."

"V-berth."

"Whatever. I know you won't like it, but that's what we're gonna do. You can lay back and relax. Get some sleep. We'll be back in a couple of hours for lunch and we'll let you loose then. You need to use the bathroom before we tie you up? OK, then, lie down on that sofa thing down there and we'll get you fixed up. Tell me where I can find a clean sock or a towel for a gag."

Clammy sweat broke out on Doorman's forehead. He didn't like the idea of being trussed, but the idea of being gagged set off panic. His palms begin to itch. He felt himself start to hyperventilate. He didn't want to lower himself to pleading, but he was ready to beg or to fight to keep from being gagged. Struggling to keep panic out of his voice, he said, "You don't need to gag me. There's nobody around to hear me yell for help."

Blackbeard studied his face for a moment or two. "You know," the big man said to Billy, "I do believe he's right. We don't need a gag. Billy, go get that roll of duct tape." He smiled at Doorman. "No gag. We'll use tape instead. Can't have you screaming and keeping the neighbors awake. You probably never been duct-taped before, right? Well, let me tell you what you have to do. You got to suck your lips into your mouth and then we'll put on some Vaseline. You got Vaseline? 'Cause if you're not careful and somebody who doesn't know what they're doing rips the duct tape off, it'll take your lips right off. Isn't that right, Billy?"

Billy had personal experience with nearly having his lips ripped off by duct tape? What kind of life had these two been leading? He lay down on the starboard settee in the salon and submitted to getting tied, Vaselined, and taped. There was no point in trying to fight them.

The pirates picked him up—more gently than he would have predicted—and put him in the v-berth. Then they stomped out of the cabin, slammed the hatch boards into place, and motored off. Leaving Doorman alone with his thoughts.

His first thought: Get a few hours' sleep. He needed it. But bonds and duct tape weren't conducive to resting. Neither were worries about David, maybe helpless, certainly alone; or just as bad, ashore, trying to talk some local cop into believing his ridiculous story about pirates and his father held hostage.

A merry-go-round of worries about David assailed him. Spiced with ruminations on the weather. About how he might manage to get free. About whether, if these guys weren't the killers, there really were killers hunting him. And where they were.

None of the thoughts relaxed him. He tried focusing his attention on planning ways to get free and ways he could attack the pirates. The long night caught up with him before he found a solution. His thoughts drifted to recollections of the past. David. Deborah. Days of glorious sailing with a young wife. The last hours before the pirates attacked. And how, a few days ago, he had been the ringmaster of the circus that was the DA's Financial Crime Unit, standing in the middle of the center ring with whip and chair in hand, trying to tame the vicious beasts that prowled around him, growling for attention.

Chapter Nine

Doorman stood at the center of the whirlwind called the Organized Crime Section of the DA's office. It was far from organized. Although the plaque on his door proclaimed him "Chief of Section," he was a courtroom prosecutor more than a manager.

Any trial lawyer would have recognized his office. Stacks of files covered every horizontal surface. They partially hid Doorman, right now standing behind his desk talking on the phone. Files littered the couch, covered the client chairs, filled the space behind the door. Loose papers carpeted every surface that approached the horizontal: the desktop, the top of the computer tower, the windowsills. Even the surfaces that weren't horizontal were covered: walls disappeared behind exhibit boards, photographic blowups, tottering stacks of boxes.

In front of the desk, two young lawyers and a paralegal, waiting for his attention. They, too, were covered up with paper: stacks of files and reams of paper in their arms and hands, awaiting a word with the Chief. Four people—the Organized Crime paraprofessional staff and a messenger from the DA himself—lurked just outside the office door, waiting to catch his attention.

He saw them waiting, knew from the DA's messenger that his boss was summoning him, knew from the waiting staff that there were important matters to decide. He struggled to get off the phone. A reluctant witness was unsure whether she would be safe if she testified and sought reassurance. As he soothed her, he sorted through the papers within reach, throwing this one out, handing that one to one of the lawyers. His second and third lines were ringing, too. Finally, he decided the witness was likely to show up, cut her short and hung up with a sigh, frowned an apology to the waiting multitude, and reached for the button of his second line.

The emissary from the DA recognized her chance. She shouldered a paralegal and an investigator aside, darted by one of the young lawyers, and breathlessly delivered her message. "The DA wants you. He's been trying to call you, but he can't get through." When Joe Doorman didn't respond immediately, she added: "He said right now." She turned and fled to report back to the boss, whom she feared and adored.

Doorman shrugged an apology to the two lawyers waiting to catch his attention. He fixed his loosened tie. "Duty calls. I'll be right back." He snagged his suit jacket from the hook on the back of the door and headed for the stairs, pulling on the jacket as he went. He called back, "You guys answer those other two lines, OK?"

Behind him, one of his associates protested, "We pretty much have this covered," but Doorman was already halfway down the stairs.

Downstairs, outside the DA's corner suite, the boss's secretary smiled over the telephone stuck to her ear, nodded in the direction of the DA's inner office door, and pointed with her chin to a chair. He moved away from her desk but didn't sit. He had too much to do to sit and wait.

While he waited, Doorman bounced restlessly on the balls of his feet. He had so much to do that he'd already decided that his next call would be to Deborah. His wife would be pissed when he told her he was going to have to cancel the short cruise he'd promised David for next week. She'd see it as one more time he'd placed his job over family. David might be disappointed, too. But being a Chief of a section wasn't just a job. There was a responsibility to the city, to the office, to the citizens, to justice...

Anyway, it couldn't be helped. The trial was starting the Monday morning of the week after next. He only had seven days left to discover and fix things that were broken. It wasn't near enough.

The secretary hung up, stood, and tapped softly on the DA's door. She listened for a sign, then ushered Doorman in. Leaving, she pulled the door shut behind her. A bad sign. There were only two reasons the boss ever talked behind closed doors: to read you the riot act or to assign you a high-profile case.

Doorman prayed for the riot act. Anything but another high-profile case right now.

The DA hung up his phone and looked up. "So." He was a big man, tall and dapper. He wasted little time on small talk, unless he was preaching one of his sermons on administering justice and cleaning up the streets. In his unmistakable deep baritone, he stated, "You're leaving on vacation."

"I was hoping to, but—"

"I wasn't asking. I'm saying you're leaving on vacation."

"I would, Boss, but there are all these damn cases piled up in my office." Doorman smiled to take the sting out of his complaint. He'd asked many times about getting more staff and the DA had responded many times that there simply wasn't money in the budget for mob prosecutions when their human resource dollars didn't even cover the staff needed to cover what the voters told him they wanted addressed (violent crime and carjacking and trafficking and drug dealing and senior fraud and...) Doorman had given up detailing the crush of cases too few lawyers were trying to get ready for indictment or trial at any moment in time: everybody in the District Attorney's office was just as slammed.

"You have a pretty good staff. Maybe you should try trusting them with some of the work."

"I have a great staff. The lawyers are really coming around. They're both scheduled to first-chair cases in the next quarter." He paused. "I hope you're not going to rotate them to another unit, now that I've trained them."

The boss smiled. He moved people around the different sections like stones on a Mancala board. There was no telling where Doorman's two associates would end up, or when. At least, the DA wasn't telling now. He intoned: "One of the things a good staff does, is to take delegation—"

"I delegate!"

"I was going to say, 'take delegation and relieve some of the burden off the Chief.'"

"The burden increases faster than the staff." A cheap shot, but he could feel the burden grow heavier with every moment ticking away as he stood here. "You made me responsible for these cases. I'm going to make sure they're done right. And even if I delegated every task on every other case other than the Mafia case, I know you don't want me delegating tasks on that. That's what's on my desk right now. And it goes to trial the week after next."

The DA sat forward, leaning on his elbows on his desk. His eye-to-eye contact was awesome, hypnotic. "Then let's talk about the Mafia case. Jury instructions done?"

"Sure." Doorman tried not to feel insulted at being quizzed. The case was a big one for his unit, but it was a big one for the DA, too. This was an election year and the DA was an elected official. Losing the case would make for terrible press at exactly the wrong time. That made the Mafia case the most important matter for the office this year.

The boss continued quizzing him. Opening? Closing? Pretrial brief? Motions *in limine*? Evidence briefs? Direct and cross outlines? At every point, Doorman assured him that he'd already finished it.

"Then it sounds like you're ready. I thought the plan was you were going to take off and get some rest for a week before the big trial. What exactly requires you to hang around here?"

Doorman hesitated. He couldn't confess the real reason. It just didn't feel right taking a vacation the week before trial. Not when his staff would be working night and day in the weeks before trial on his case, while he was off playing. It would look like he wasn't sharing the burden of the endless hours and 20 hour days. Besides which, problems always cropped up unexpectedly during trial prep. If he wasn't in the office to handle them—

"What, exactly and specifically and in detail is left for you to do?" the DA repeated, not very subtly consulting his watch.

Right now, right on the spot, Doorman couldn't think of a single thing. But his intuition and experience told him there were things to do, damn it. That he couldn't identify exactly what was left undone didn't make him feel better. That was worse than having the To Do list the DA was asking for. At least with that you could address the problems you knew about and check them off one by one. But you couldn't address the unknown problems with a To Do list. Those lay hidden within every case, waiting to blow up at the last minute before trial...

But the DA was waiting, a smile on his face Doorman didn't like. He pulled an unfinished task out of the air. "I need to finish up a digest of all the documents, for one thing."

"Your brilliant and responsible staff can handle that. So hear me on this, Joe. I want you to leave whatever is on your desk and go. There's no sense in being the head of the organized crime group if you're not going to use the resources of the group."

"I can't just *leave* stuff."

The DA pointed an accusing finger at him. "Your problem is that you can't leave stuff *alone*. Now I'm instructing you: Do not come in tomorrow. Do not come in for a week."

"Well, I'm trying..."

"Joe, you're not hearing me. I want you out of here."

The stern tone took him aback. "OK," Doorman conceded with as much grace as he could muster. "I'll finish up today and take off." "Today" was a flexible promise. "Today" ended at midnight. But there was something in the boss's tone that made him curious. "Mind telling me why you're so anxious to get rid of me?"

"The main reason is that you have a major trial in ten days. You look worn out. I think you need the rest. How many cases have you tried this year?"

"I don't know. Six. Seven?"

The DA nodded like Doorman had proven his point. "Right. Six or seven, and this is September. If you were only doing rapes and murders, you could try six or seven a month. You're doing organized crime cases, remember? In case you've forgotten, I'll remind you that they are big, complicated cases that take months to prepare and weeks to try. You can't just keep blasting them out. And this next one..." He shook his head.

"It's under control."

"I don't doubt that. Everything you do is 'under control.' But it's a huge case. That damn judge of yours looks for every opportunity to embarrass this office. This will be our first racketeering trial in front of her. I don't want her embarrassing us in our last big case before the campaign. Now I don't ask much of you, Joe," flashing his Politician's Front Page smile. "Just do me this one favor this one time, pretty please? Take off for a week for R&R before that trial starts."

Doorman raised his hands in surrender. "All right. You're the boss. I've been thrown out of better places than this. But first tell me: what's the other reason?"

"'Other reason? What do you mean?"

"You know, you said 'the main reason' you wanted me out. That means there's another reason, too. What is it?"

The DA took his glasses off and rubbed his face hard. When he finished, he ran his hands through his short hair. Then he stretched. Finally, he put his glasses back on and peered intently at Doorman.

"You know, Doorman, there's not a single other Assistant District Attorney who walks into my office and cross-examines me."

"Senior Assistant. And Unit Chief. And you brought it up."

The boss groaned and rubbed the bridge of his nose with two fingers. After a pause, he muttered, "Death threats."

"Oh, come on. We all get death threats all the time. None of us has been killed yet."

"Maybe not threats like this." The boss turned to gaze out the window. "These death threats come from the FBI." The DA swung his chair back around and stared at him. "The FBI passed along a tip. One of their confidential informants heard that someone is out there gunning for you."

"Hey, Boss. If the CI will testify that one of the defendant's guys is trying to bump me off, let's go to the judge and get his bail revoked. Re-indict to add Obstruction."

"I didn't say it had anything to do with the Mob case. I'm not sure it does. You've pissed off a lot of people in the last couple of years. Not just our friends up the street but some people you've checked in to the county's hospitality center. That's why I want you to disappear for a week. That and the fact that you, my friend, very obviously need a vacation. Take it now. Come back fresh and ready to nail this bastard."

Doorman could use a rest, that was for sure. But not when there was work to do. And there were always more uncompleted tasks left than there was time to do them. But arguing with the boss would be hopeless. Doorman surrendered. "OK. I think this contract hit thing is just big talk, but..."

"Now, what about Deborah?"

"Deborah? She's got to work. It'll just be David and me going up to the boat. Unless you're telling me you think she's in danger..."

The DA waved a hand to sweep away the thought. "No, no. This is probably big talk by little punks. Anyway, I'm assuming you're taking security precautions already."

"Yeah, sure. We've got the dogs. The PD has us on a hot list until this trial is over. They send a car by during every shift. We've got a hotline number that Deborah has memorized. I think we're covered."

"Still wish you'd get a gun."

"Not until the kid's out of the house. Maybe not even then."

"Yeah." The DA leaned far enough back in his chair that he was staring up at the ceiling. Doorman waited, not sure whether his boss was done. Slowly the DA sat up straight, then stood. "So get out of here."

"OK. You're the boss."

"Oh. Is that me? Whenever I talk to you, I get confused about which one of us is."

Later—four hours later—Joe Doorman finally left the office. As he walked out the door, the moon was setting, and the Organized Crime Unit's lawyers were hunkering down below the battlements of paper that covered their desks, relieved to get back to work without constant interruption.

***

Lying on his back, bound, taped, and half asleep, Doorman replayed the meeting over again in his memory. Being the target of a hit was certainly a new twist on the death threat thing. Not enough to keep Doorman from doing his job, but one additional concern on top of a growing collection of concerns.

Litigation and law practice had taught Doorman to focus only on what was important right now. Now he was able to put aside tomorrow's concerns until tomorrow, worry right now only about what needed to be addressed right now. But tied up, he couldn't do anything. Couldn't plan. Couldn't prepare. Could only lie there and await developments.

Wait and worry.

About Deborah, home alone and helpless.

And David, somewhere out on the lake, alone.

And whether—if these guys weren't hit men—where...?

Chapter Ten

Billy and Blackbeard motored away from the sailboat on their PWCs, sweeping into the back channels between the island and the mainland. Billy was grumbling about not heading for home as Blackbeard seethed at Billy's agreeing and then complaining it. All the time, he scanned left and right, looking for profit-making opportunities. After half an hour of finding nothing, they finally found something. In an island cove hidden from the shore, a single houseboat was beached on the sand.

The big pirate throttled back and motioned for Billy to come up beside him. "You know where we are?"

"I donno. Maybe near Two Mile Creek? Marker 17 or 19?"

"We're going to hit that one." Blackbeard nodded toward the houseboat.

"No, no, no. We said we was only going to do it at night."

"We'll both jump on board and surprise 'em. You go in from the right. I'll go over to the left. I'll see you in the salon."

"I ain't going."

"Don't forget your bandanna." Blackbeard pulled his up.

"Not going. Just not going. No, no, no."

Blackbeard waved a sketchy salute, gunned his motor, and roared off.

Billy cursed as his partner sped toward the houseboat. Blackbeard never even looked back. Billy sat on his idling craft, determined not to follow. Blackbeard was always pushing him. Always deeper and deeper into more trouble. He was sick of Blackbeard always just assuming he would follow. Sick of being treated like a sidekick. Like Gromit. Hermione. Robin.

Well, nope. Nuh-uh. Not this time. They talked about how they were going to do boat invasions before they ever got to the lake. They'd agreed on how to do it and be safe and not end up locked up again. The big guy wasn't following their agreement. Billy looked up, formulating his argument to stop Blackbeard now, before—

He saw Blackbeard's boat gliding up to the houseboat.

Billy ground his teeth. He wasn't going to be burglarizing another boat. No way. He was not going back to jail. If Blackbeard was going to be stubborn and stupid, he could be stubborn and stupid all by himself.

It didn't sit right to abandon his oldest friend, though. They'd been friends since grade school. OK, it was stupid for Blackbeard to do it by himself. Anything could happen to one man crashing aboard a boat in the middle of the day. Blackbeard was going to get himself hurt. It took two to be safe. Friends didn't abandon friends.

Just because they were partners in crime, just because they'd been friends for years, just because they'd always had each other's backs, didn't mean Billy would follow him off a cliff. Blackbeard was the guy that the grandparents were talking about when they said, "If your friend jumped off a roof—?"

Damn damn damn. Friends didn't just sit there and let their friends get into trouble. He twisted his wrist to put his boat in motion and rushed to Blackbeard's side. As he got close, Blackbeard glared over his mask and put a finger up against his lips, his eyes critical of Billy's failure to approach silently. Then he waved Billy on to the other side of the houseboat. The little pirate nudged his PWC up against the starboard side of the houseboat, turned it off, and threw one quick wrap of the painter around a rail. When he joined Blackbeard on the rear deck, his partner didn't spare him a thank you. Not even a glance. That was Blackbeard all the way. Taking it for granted that Billy would follow orders.

The two exchanged a glance across the width of the rear deck, then they burst into the salon. It was empty. As was the galley. And the cabins. The owners must be partying on the island.

Blackbeard chortled and jumped to the wheel of the houseboat. Captain Bligh had taught him how to back a boat up, so now he did. As soon as the houseboat's pontoons ground off the beach, the pirate jammed the engines in forward to stop the backward movement and then shut them down when the houseboat was a couple of dozen yards off the beach.

Blackbeard stomped back into the salon, guffawing. He slapped Billy's arm and pointed out one of the windows at the beach. A man and a woman had come out of the bushes, pulling their clothes back on. Old people, had to be in their forties. Now they stood at the edge of the water, screaming obscenities at the guys who'd stolen their boat.

"Ugly," Blackbeard observed, watching the sagging flesh bouncing in outrage.

Billy turned away and wandered into the largest of the large bedrooms. Blackbeard pushed by him to start going through a big closet. Billy went to the built-in dressers and started pulling out drawers and dumping their contents on the floor. He held up a wallet for Blackbeard to see, then stepped over the overturned drawers to start their getaway. He pulled Blackbeard out of the closet on his way. "I got a wallet! Let's get outta here!"

Blackbeard shook him off and picked a book off a dresser. "Hey, look." It was *Master and Commander*, by that Patrick O'Brian dude. "It's the same book Captain Bligh has. Or the same author. Maybe you get a free book if you buy a boat. They all must read this shit." He tossed the book away and pointed to the radio. "Gotta make that call in a minute. I'm going for the undies drawer. Gimme a couple of minutes before you make the distress call."

Billy watched his partner paw through a drawer full of bright-colored lingerie that seemed to excite his interest.

"Ha!" Blackbeard cried. He held up a little zipper bag in triumph. Unzipping it, he pulled out a strand of pearls. "In the pantie drawer," the big pirate chortled. That women hid their goodies in among their goodies always amused him. There must be some reason they all did that. It didn't make sense, but Blackbeard didn't know many women other than his teachers and a few probation officers and lady cops. Maybe he could ask Captain Bligh. He seemed like he was a guy who knew stuff.

Billy started bouncing on the balls of his feet when his partner went to the next drawer. "We're runnin' out of time, man. Let's go! We gotta get out'a here."

"Go. Make the distress call. Be sure to say it's a robbery. What's the marker way down at the south end near the dam?"

"I donno. Could be Marker 1 or 3 on this side. But we're at more like at Marker 17. Or 19."

"Well, duh." Blackbeard pushed Billy toward the radio. "Tell 'em it's Marker 3."

Billy shuffled over to the radio, mumbling under his breath. A piece of tape over the tuning button reminded the owners that Channel 16 was the emergency channel. He turned the dial to 16 and screamed into the mike.

"Mayday, mayday, mayday." He released the mike button, puzzled. "Not 'Mayday.' We ain't sinking. What do I say?" His partner was too busy emptying a purse to listen.

Billy keyed the mike again. "Emergency! Emergency!" That wasn't right, either. He tried again: "Burglars on a houseboat. Near Marker 1. I mean, Marker Number 3. Emergency. Emergency." He released the mike again, puzzled as to what else to say.

Blackbeard strode out of the havoc in the bedroom, holding up a woman's wallet with a grin. He grabbed Billy's arm and pulled him away from the radio. "Time to go." He paused and gestured toward the radio. Billy looked to see what he was pointing at and saw that he was pointing a pistol.

"Whoa! Where'd you get the gun?"

"Move back."

"Where'd' you get it? I threw yours overboard." Billy stuttered to a stop, shocked at his own confession. He stood, his hands opening and closing at his sides. "We said no guns," he said weakly. "I di'n't want to get in trouble. More than we're already in. For hitting that guy. On the sailboat."

"You little weasel," Blackbeard hissed. "Lucky those jerkwads left this one out on the dining room table to replace the one you stole. Someone took care of this baby." He turned and aimed once more at the radio console.

"No shooting!" Billy shouted.

Two shots erased Billy's voice. Blackbeard's was commanding. "Now, let's get going." He escaped out onto the deck as the echoes of the shots reverberated around the cove.

Out on the deck, they found the PWCs floating several yards of open water away. Blackbeard stared. "Well, shit." The backward movement of the boat must have tugged them loose. The only solution was to dive in and swim to them. That made him pause, uncertain. He didn't much like the water. And he hated to get his new gun wet.

Billy brushed by him. "Let's swim for it." He launched himself into the water, then treaded water waiting for his companion. Blackbeard hung back on the deck, tucking the two wallets into the plastic zip lock bag he carried in his wet suit top. Then he gingerly lowered himself into the water.

Billy dog-paddled to his boat. He climbed up, gunned the motor, and sped over to pick up his friend. He delivered Blackbeard to his own craft so the big brave leader wouldn't get his tender little feet wet.

Blackbeard started up his boat, checked that the bag was secure in his wet suit top, jammed the throttle into full power. He threw back his head and howled in triumph as he zoomed toward Billy. Overcome with relief that they were finally leaving, Billy stood up to give Blackbeard a high five. To his horror, he saw his friend turn toward the beach and brandish the gun.

A glance horrified Billy. The old guy was wading into the lake, holding up his drooping pants with one hand and impotently throwing beer bottles with the other. The bottles landed well short of their targets, but the big pirate fired two shots in the air in reply. As the houseboat's owner threw himself on the ground for cover, the pirates turned a couple of noisy doughnuts, whooping with victory. The little pirate realized they'd forgotten to pull their masks up. That they'd given the owner a better chance to remember their faces made him even more nervous.

At least, Blackbeard had finally turned away. He whooped in triumph as he went. He even favored the man on shore with a one-finger salute as he roared out of the cove. Billy followed, celebrating too: that were finally headed for home base.

The two PWCs threaded their way through the islands, heading back toward Doorman's sailboat. Billy searched the indistinguishable islands for home base. Blackbeard searched the beaches and coves for new opportunities. It wasn't long before they stumbled on one.

A spiffy new fishing boat was slowly cruising the overgrown shoreline of an island. A bass boat: two elevated seats way above the water from which casting was easy, though if they were occupied, balance became tenuous. The fisherman fished alone, sitting in one of the high casting seats. He worked a bass bug just off a brushy bank with such concentration that he didn't even look up as the two PWCs zoomed into view.

Blackbeard throttled down to wait for Billy to come up next to him. "Get your mask up." Then he zoomed toward the bass boat, leaving Billy no time to protest. Not to Blackbeard, at any rate. Instead he shouted out his objections to the lonely lake, which wasn't listening any more than Blackbeard was.

Blackbeard blasted into the narrow stretch of water between the overgrown shore and the fishing boat. Just before he would have run into the fisherman's line, he throttled back. The slowing PWC settled as it slowed, pushing its bow wake ahead of it. The hump of water rocked the fishing boat. As it pitched in the bow wake, weight sitting high above the center of gravity in the bass boat found itself wildly rocking side to side as if to unseat its occupant. The fisherman threw his rod down into the boat so he could hold on with both hands, all the while cursing at the son of a bitch who'd upset his boat.

The fisherman regained his balance and turned to look for the culprits just as Billy ran up alongside. The fishing boat pitched wildly again, sending the fisherman face-first into the bottom of his boat. He scrambled to his feet, a long-handled fishing net raised up like a baseball bat, his eyes wild, ready to do battle with the damn sons of bitches who—

Blackbeard held up the pistol for the fisherman to see. Billy cried out to his partner to stop. "No guns!" They'd agreed on this rule before they ever got to the lake. Showing a gun, plus stealing, equaled a felony. Years in jail.

The fisherman immediately abandoned heroism. He dropped the net and held up his hands. "Please, please, please, please!"

"Give me your wallet," Blackbeard growled at the fisherman. "We want your money."

The man patted his pants pockets, then bent down as if to search a storage space in the boat's center console. It was so obviously a ploy that Blackbeard immediately motored close enough to shove the pistol in the fisherman's face. "Pull out a weapon you'll be fish food, Bubba."

Billy wondered where his friend got such stupid lines. But it worked. The fisherman came up with his wallet and handed it over.

"Cell phone," the big pirate ordered, stifling the victim's protest with another wave of the gun. The man handed over the cell phone.

Blackbeard threw it over the boat to where Billy idled on the other side. "Call 911. Tell them there's been a robbery. Same place as the last one. Better, make it at Marker 3 or—wait—maybe 5," he said with a wink. To the fisherman: "You got a radio on that boat?" The man shook his head. "Can you swim? OK, you better start swimming." When the man didn't move, Blackbeard put his foot on the gunwale and rocked the shallow fishing boat. Convinced to abandon ship, he bass fisherman jumped clumsily off the boat, splashing almost to the shore in his zeal to get away.

Blackbeard tore through the wallet. He pulled out several bills, gave a yell of triumph, and held his treasure high. Then he tucked the money away, grabbed the painter of the bass boat and towed it a few dozen yards from the island, before gunning his boat into the channel.

The little pirate followed, grumbling. Blackbeard expected him to follow once more. When they were out of sight of the fisherman, Blackbeard slowed and motioned to Billy to come up next to him. "You make the call? Why the hell not? Well, damn, dude, make the call. We can't let the man spend the night on the island!"

Billy made the report about a boat invasion taking place near Marker 3. Blackbeard snatched the phone from his hands and threw it out into the lake. "You hungry, Billy Boy? Let's go get us a home cooked meal." He rode off in a roar. Billy caught up to him in a minute or so.

Side by side they rode toward the mother ship, conquering heroes riding the sun-dappled water.

Chapter Eleven

Within a few minutes of shoving off from the beach, David rediscovered the problem with trying to paddle a square object without bow, stern or keel. He'd encountered it before, but back when he was escaping from parents, it was one element in an adventure. Now, it mattered that he steer a consistent course. Like the dinghy, but worse, the raft spun to the right when he paddled on the left and vice versa. So he applied the same technique he'd used on the dinghy: a set of strokes on one side, quickly followed by a set of strokes on the other. It didn't work perfectly: the dinghy had a keel, of sorts, that resisted the spinning motion. A square of Styrofoam didn't. Alternating sides didn't produce a straight course, by any means, but at least it more or less moved the clunky raft through the water in more or less in a straight line. He quickly concluded that "more or less" was the best he was likely to achieve.

Working tirelessly, he paused only when pain made him aware of the toll that the Styrofoam had taken on him. Wrestling the dead weight of the thing had strained his back and shoulders and legs as it resisted being launched. Now countless layers of skin had been sandpapered from his knees and shins and his forearms, where they rubbed on the coarse Styrofoam. Leaning way over the side, reaching down two feet to get the blade of the oar in the water, tortured his already suffering back and shoulders. But looking in front of him and behind him, both shorelines now looked equally far away. Progress, finally!

He returned to paddling, buoyed by his success. Still, he couldn't out-paddle looming doubts. The bottomless water still stretched down to black infinity beneath him, just waiting for him to falter. The rank smell of mildewed Styrofoam had begun to make his stomach churn. He worried, too, that his muscles wouldn't hold up to the next half of the journey—if it was even really true that he had actually completed half of the distance. That was the greatest weight on his shoulders: that he was failing at his mission. He worried that hadn't travelled halfway to his destination. It was ridiculously hard to judge distances from eyes 2 1/2 feet above water level. He might have made it only a few hundred yards.

The distant buzz of a powerboat distracted him from pondering the possibility of failure. The sound grew louder as he listened. His spirits lifted. At last! Saved!

The noise grew louder still, suggesting that the boat was speeding toward him. David put the oar down gingerly—even if he would soon not need it, it would be a disaster to lose it—then stretched up as tall as the pitching raft would allow to try to spot the powerboat and get their attention.

He had to get the power boater's attention if he wanted to have a hope of getting rescued. Standing would make it more likely to be seen. Even rising to his knees, though, caused the block of Styrofoam to pitch dangerously. Being seen wasn't worth the danger of being thrown into the lake. He limited his movement to stretching his body as far as it would go with his knees unmoving on the Styrofoam.

At first, he could see nothing, even though the buzzing motor sounded ever louder. Finally, he caught sight of it, bouncing violently over the lake's small waves. It was racing in his direction. Now he just needed the boaters to see him.

He considered trying again to stand. Standing even for a moment would increase the chances of being seen. David adjusted his weight carefully, searching for the best balance. When he looked back at the speedboat, it was much larger and closer. Faster than he thought possible. They'd seen him! Or would pass so close that they couldn't miss him.

Then David's smile of relief died. The speedboat was not just coming in his direction. It was coming right at him. There was no time to wave them off, even if the pilot could see him over the bow. With the boat's speed forcing its bow high in the air, David couldn't see the driver, which meant the driver couldn't see him.

In seconds the speedboat would smash into him. It would be death, not rescue. There was only one choice. David grabbed the oar and started paddling as hard as he possibly could, trying to move the stubborn raft out of danger. He kept an eye on the boat, hoping it would slow, hoping it would turn, hoping it would see him and throttle back.

Whoever was driving the boat didn't slow, didn't turn, didn't see him. It kept on, the bow aimed right at David. A collision was imminent. More than imminent: immediate. Without time to consider his options, David threw himself into the water and dove for the cold, inky depths.

The destruction of The Raft came to David as a soft *thump* a dozen feet above him, barely audible above the threshing of the powerful motors. Only a few feet over his head, the whirling propellers passed so close to him that they deafened him. First the *thump*, then the all-consuming noise, then nothing.

He surfaced gasping for breath just in time to see the boat receding into the distance. It left a final gift: as David gasped for breath, the fast-moving wake slapped him. The wake toppled him back underwater. He surfaced a few seconds later, gagging and spitting. He turned on to his back to catch his breath. He coughed and gagged and sputtered and fought to get his breath back. When he could breathe again, and hear again, he let his feet sink down, treading water, and took stock.

Adrenalin had left him shaky, even if he was relieved to have survived. The Raft wasn't so lucky. The collision had rendered The Raft a few dozen pieces of dirty Styrofoam. Little icebergs of foam bobbing around him were all that was left. He dog-paddled to the nearest one that seemed like it might be big enough to float him. As he tried to climb aboard, the piece flipped over, dunking him head first. He tried a few more times with other pieces and got dunked repeatedly. He gave up.

The oar floated by, and he grabbed it. It didn't provide much flotation, but it was something. Dog paddling in a circle, he spied the ice chest. Amazingly, it hadn't been smashed. Even more miraculously, the top had stayed on. David paddled over and wrapped his arms around it. There was no way he could climb up onto it. His recent experience with the Styrofoam icebergs told him it was too small and floating too high to carry him.

Once he had some relief from dogpaddling, he wondered about the boat. Why hadn't they come back for him? They must have felt the collision. Surely, they'd want to come back to see what they'd hit. But it had not even slowed down, its motor noise receding into the distance.

He treaded water again, this time spasmodically as he tried to keep one hand on the ice chest, the other on the oar. Exactly how he'd swim with all this stuff he didn't know. He briefly considered letting something go. There wasn't enough left of the stuff he'd started out with to give anything up, though. He did his best to secure the other things he'd gathered+. Then he headed for the closest land he could see.

***

David swam and pushed the ice chest. Swam and pushed the ice chest some more. Did it again and again and then over again. Counted kicks until he lost count; counted kicks again; lost count again.

The chest rode high in the water—higher than eye level—blocking his vision forward, making it hard to judge his progress. Every once in a while he stopped to tread water hard, propelling his head another few inches higher above the surface to look around. The land never looked any closer. He'd say something rude that his mother wouldn't approve of, try to rebalance the ice chest, and kick off again for land. Over and over.

The cold water numbed his skin. Sometimes it was just cold; sometimes it was so cold it took his breath away. At first, swimming kept him warm. The longer he swam, though, the more the water chilled him. Stopping to tread water seemed to warm him, but as soon as he stretched out to swim some more, the lake stripped away every ounce of warmth.

It was exciting at first, swimming alone in a lake where he couldn't see either shore. But the repetitiveness started to weigh on him. Stroke after stroke, kick after kick, minute after minute, he repeated the same actions, with no end in sight and no apparent progress.

David had read his father's books about being wrecked at sea. They all said that one thing killed you: giving up. He would not give up. Not ever. No matter how boring the swim became. No matter how dead his limbs felt.

The boy did math problems in his head until his mind was so numb that he couldn't remember what the problem was that he'd posited just seconds before. Then he tried to recite the names of the states in alphabetical order. Next, the state capitals. Countries. Then countries' capitals. Then capitals in reverse alphabetical order.

Meanwhile, he alternated between every form of kick he knew. Flutter kick. Frog kick. Once even the dolphin kick, though he quickly abandoned it when it buried his face in the water.

About the time David came to the realization that he didn't have energy for another kick, he looked up to see trees. The trees didn't quite loom over him, but suddenly they were visible above the ice chest. Somehow he'd managed to swim right to land. He paused to get his bearings, let his legs down to tread water, and screamed when something from the depths grabbed his feet.

With a sheepish grin, David let his feet down cautiously and felt the bottom. It was deep, sucking mud. With renewed strength, he half swam, half slogged toward shore.

David pushed his ice chest onto the shore and staggered up onto dry land. His legs gave out as he shuffled clear of the water. He sat heavily. After a moment, he lay back and stared at the late afternoon sky. The mild sun warmed his face and chest. He'd never understood his parents' attraction to lying in the sun on a beach doing nothing. But right now, it felt great. And he didn't have the strength to do anything else.

After a few minutes, David pulled himself into a sitting position. He didn't have a clue where he was. Or what time it was. The only thing he knew for sure was that daylight was waning and he was going to be stuck on this island for the night. If it were an island.

Where was he? He'd paddled for a long time from the original anchorage. Several hours at least. That would probably mean he'd paddled back east, toward the marina. After the powerboat hit him, he'd swum for what must have been a few more hours. Maybe he'd actually made it to the mainland! The thought gave him a jolt of energy.

He stood on shaky legs with every intention of exploring. But with his feet planted on firm footing for now and the sun warming his shoulders, David discovered a more urgent priority. He was hungry.

He turned and rummaged through the ice chest. Not much was there, and what was there floated half-drowned in the water that had leaked in during his ordeal. He fished out a floating package of peanut butter crackers. Soggy peanut butter crackers. He stuffed one mushy cracker in his mouth and reached for one of the few bottles of bottled water half sunk in the water in the chest. And another package of peanut butter cracker mush. He tucked that one into a pocket.

By the time he'd finished the crackers, he was ready for an adventure. He set off, starting to climb the steep bank off the beach, when he recognized he had chosen to go to the right again. It was bad luck last time. So this time, he turned around and walked down the beach to the left. He passed the ice chest with barely a look, climbed the bank, and headed into the forest.

The trees crowded closer together than they'd looked from the beach. Brambles and thorn bushes and sharp, leafless vines snagged him. In minutes, David's waterlogged skin bled from scratches and gouges.

The terrain looked remarkably familiar. That wasn't a surprise, of course. Every bit of the mainland around the lake looked like this. And for that matter, every island he'd ever explored.

The boy trudged on. He dug the other packet of peanut butter crackers out of his pocket and devoured them. He scrambled over logs and up little hillocks. Only after managing to tear his way out of his millionth thorn bush did David manage to fight his way into a clearing in the middle of the jungle.

It was not that big a clearing. In the center, someone had arranged a circle of darkened stones. A campfire. Yet no one would build a campfire in the middle of the bushes on the mainland. Would they?

Unless he had landed in a park or at the picnic grounds of a marina. That would be good luck. It might even turn out to be the Old Federal Park! His mood lightened at once. That familiar park sat on the same side of the lake as *Caesaria*'s home marina and just a few small coves north of it. It would have been incredibly good luck to have come ashore so close to home. There would be people here, people who would help him.

Landing at the Federal Park, though—that would almost be too much good luck for a day that had seen being marooned, abandoned on the lake, nearly drowned, run over by a speedboat, and choking down soggy peanut butter crackers. Doubting that anything this day would bring him luck, he took a careful look at the circle of blackened rocks. He touched one and found that his fingers came away black with carbon. Campfire for sure. A park for sure.

Maybe he was in luck. There would be people here. Picnickers, campers, and if he was lucky, even a park ranger.

Then he remembered something his father had told him: the law prevented the building of fires at Old Federal Park. David remembered thinking it was ridiculous that you couldn't build a fire in a park. His father explained something about federal environmental rules. At length and in detail, of course. When Dad talked law, David stopped listening.

This had to be an island, then. Disappointment flooded through him. But wait. Maybe he was on the mainland, just not inside the Old Federal Park. Either way, people had used this area, and that meant people would be back sooner or later. The only thing that mattered was that he find people, and that they call the police and the police would go save Dad.

There weren't people around right now. They might be near, though. So, he fought his way through the thicket on the other side of the clearing. He struggled through the brush until it felt like not a single patch of skin remained unscratched and his legs had begun to shake again with fatigue. At about the moment that he was ready to sink down on the next tree trunk, he saw a beach through the trees.

He crashed out of the vines and down onto the beach. Right there, practically at his feet, hulked a forlorn wreck. A wooden craft, abandoned. A wooden dinghy. One with a broken wooden mast. Realization struck hard.

His dinghy. Which meant his island. He was back where he had started from, once again.

Weakness overcame him. His legs folded up beneath him. His arms barely cushioned his fall as he dropped nervelessly on the damp sand. Tears flowed down his cheeks unnoticed. He heard rather than felt sobs that wracked him. Whether he was crying in exhaustion or crying with frustration or laughing at the absurdity of fighting all day to get back to where he'd started from, he would not have been able to say.

When the tears dried, he fell into a daze, staring out at the slowly darkening lake. He told himself that he should get up right now; get to his feet and do something; not lose another moment of the waning afternoon—

And still he sat, staring at nothing.

***

As night fell, David roused himself. Instinct took over. He checked the angle of the sun and saw that daylight was fading. He'd be out here another night. He was already burning cold from the wind tugging on his sopping clothing, not to mention the clammy sand that had worked its way into his pants. He would need shelter for the night. He looked around groggily for anything that might provide it.

All he had was the hull.

David groaned. It always came back to the damn dinghy.

He crawled over to it and struggled to turn the waterlogged hull over. Most of the water had drained out, maybe courtesy of the same leak that had let it in. The thing was still too heavy to lift. Drained by all the exertions of the day and his second fit of crying, he felt hollowed out.

Summoning every ounce of his remaining strength, he wrestled the boat upside down. Once he'd rolled it over, he saw that the curve of the gunwales—so elegant when the boat was upright—formed arches that would let the wind sneak in. He'd freeze at night unless he could block the wind. Maybe he could use the sail? He unwrapped it from around the boom and draped it over the hull like a tent.

In the heavy twilight, David scuttled underneath his shelter and lay in the sand. Shivering. Staring up at the bilges that dripped water on his head. Trying not to wonder where his father might be, or whether he had been badly hurt, not thinking about what he would do tomorrow, or the creepy sounds of animals in the night. And then he slept.

Chapter Twelve

Brashears Livingston Thomas III, Special Agent in Charge, Federal Law Enforcement Emergency Task Force, Southeast Region, roared northeast on the lake in his patrol boat. He'd pushed the throttle right to its upper limit, exhilarated by the power at his fingertips.

The forward thrust of the powerful motors made the stern dig down in the water and the bow rise. It rose so high that it blocked his view immediately ahead. Even if he could have seen over the bow, the hull bouncing every which way on the lumpy water made it hard to actually focus on anything.

That was OK. He didn't need visibility ahead. His special intelligence reports had already informed him that the lake would be empty this time of year. He didn't need to waste the energy on keeping a lookout.

Anyway, he wanted his attention fixed inside the boat. Thomas could feel the jitteriness of the boat, but it didn't occur to him that it was the result of his extreme speed. He wasn't worried, anyway: he'd passed the FLETC high-speed driving course. Obviously, if he could handle a car in emergency maneuvers, he could handle a mere motorboat. Still, the nervous movements of the hull beneath him made him just fractionally anxious. He kept his eyes on the gauges in front of him, trying to decode what they meant.

He was midway down the lake when he heard the police-band radio crackle. No doubt Cheryl calling and it was almost certainly not very important. He ignored it. Headquarters could wait until he got back to the office. And if it was an emergency out on the lake, let the damn locals deal with it. He himself, an FBI Special Agent in Charge, would let them have their little games. He was too *annoyed* with his treatment by the locals to lend them any more help today. Not that he was angry at their obstructionism. The Bureau didn't get angry. It just got things done.

Honestly, though, right now he was growing more annoyed at himself than the locals. He'd left the marina and turned the wrong way on the lake—left rather than right—and wasted half an hour trying to get his bearings. The lake was confusing. The DIA-downloaded maps didn't help. It was the off-the-shelf GPS that finally straightened him out. It directed him to turn around and head for his home port, down south near the city of Buford.

Or was Buford north? Whatever. The GPS would keep him straight.

As he sped on, Agent Thomas's attention returned to the problem presented by local law enforcement. Clearly, Deputy Martin had heard about the ring of interstate thieves. So why was he pretending ignorance? Could he be part of the criminal conspiracy?

A stray glance out at the lake brought Thomas a glimpse of a rock sticking up out of the water. Or a "reef" as the boaters called it, though Thomas knew enough to know there was no coral in fresh water. He turned to the left—"starboard," he corrected himself (or was it "port?")—to avoid it.

The boat skidded. Thomas automatically followed his defensive driving training: he turned into the skid. Oddly, the boat skidded more. The skid turned into something more like an out of control slide over bumpy ice.

Thomas lost his balance and reached for a handhold. He inadvertently grabbed for the throttle lever to keep from falling, slowing the boat. The change of center of gravity and the reduced speed happened to stabilize the boat, though Thomas didn't know that. He didn't know that if he hadn't almost fallen, his boat would have executed a barrel roll. With the calmer and slower ride, Thomas regained his seat and his breath. He gave himself kudos for his quick reaction and throttled back up.

And went back to thinking about Tramp Martin's attitude. Either the deputy knew more about the thieves than he let on, or the man was a bullshit artist. At Quantico they'd heard about locals who hooked their thumbs in their belts and pretended to know everything just to frustrate the Bureau's efforts. Martin seemed to be one of those locals he'd heard old agents complain about: the ones whose most sophisticated knowledge of investigative techniques stopped at finding out where to get the best free cup of coffee.

A loud thump surprised him and caused him to look around. It must be a harder wave than he'd experienced previously. It knocked the boat sideways. Tramp held his breath, waiting for the boat to skid again, but the boat settled back on track. Not bothering to slow, he stood up from the captain's seat at the steering console to look for whatever he might have run over. He saw nothing except, in his wake, scattered pieces of Styrofoam. Nothing unusual there. There were blocks of Styrofoam floating all over the lake. The Bureau's sitrep on the area mentioned that these big pieces of trash presented a constant marine hazard. Apparently, they broke loose from under floating docks all over the place and just floated free. They looked as soft as marshmallows, but the sitrep warned that they could do some serious damage to an outdrive. Thomas didn't know what an outdrive was, so he turned his laser focus back on the instruments in front of him. "Outdrive" was one of the things he would have to look up whenever he got around to it.

But an afterimage stayed with him as he charged down the lake. It seemed almost as if he'd seen someone sitting on top of a block of Styrofoam. That was ridiculous, of course. Someone floating on a block of Styrofoam so far from shore would be in serious need of help. Mental health help. He must have seen something else.

The mirage faded as he returned to the real problem: the locals' know-it-alls. Martin was one. That Skippy character was another. Clearly, Skippy wasn't going to offer the Bureau any help, either. Maybe he was even part of the conspiracy.

Thomas's pulse quickened at the thought. What if it was a conspiracy? A real conspiracy? What if the marina operators were assisting and facilitating the thefts of PWCs? Better yet, what if they were actively involved in the thefts? And what if local law enforcement was getting a kickback to look the other way?

He perked up. Wouldn't that be something: a RICO case on his first posting in the field! Talk about getting noticed: a case under the Racketeering Influenced and Corrupt Organizations Act would earn him plenty of kudos. Particularly if he could parlay it into a civil forfeiture action. Heck, the Bureau might be able to seize the whole marina if Skippy was involved. Might even net some boats, which was probably where the criminals stored their ill-gotten gains, along with the usual drugs and guns. Boy, the guys up at the J. Edgar Hoover Building in DC would take notice of a score like that! It might earn him a promotion.

A squeal from his cell phone dragged his attention back to the present. He throttled back to be able to hear the call. It was FLEET Dispatch.

"Dispatch" meant Cheryl, a Grade 3 secretary. Technically, she was not a dispatcher, only a clerical staffer limited to typing and filing and answering the phone. DC had refused his request that they authorize a real Grade 5 posting, even though no properly organized Task Force Headquarters would dream of functioning without a dispatcher. HQ had made it clear he wasn't going to get one. With the expense of the boat and a headquarters, they'd spent every penny in the budget—meaning "all they intended to spend"—on an outpost in the middle of nowhere. "Nowhere" meaning anyplace other than DC or New York or LA. Thomas didn't need anything more than a GS-3 secretary, "Assuming," the program coordinator quipped, "you can find anybody down there who knows the alphabet." And by the way, if those conditions weren't acceptable, they had a place for him in Midland, Texas. Out there they were having a big problem with thefts of drilling pipe and could use his attention.

Thomas had been in the Army. He'd learned early never to argue with a superior. He'd also learned how to do an end run. He hired Cheryl (who he figured had spent more than one Saturday night reciting the alphabet backwards to law enforcement officers) and made do. Since FLEET needed a dispatcher more than a secretary, Thomas put her in charge of the radios. He called her "Dispatch," and that at least solved the problem for now. Technically, he was guilty of an informal position reclassification that, to be legal, would have required posting the new Grade 4 position. If she worked out, though, he might recommend that they promote her without posting the position. HQ in Washington did it all the time. FLEET Atlanta should be able to do the same.

"Hey, Bubba," Cheryl chirped when Thomas thumbed the call button. She hadn't quite mastered the art of dispatch and treated every radio call like a call with a BFF. She also had the disconcerting habit of pronouncing "hi" as "hey." Everyone down here did it. It wasn't her only verbal quirk. She also called him "Bubba." At least, that's what he thought she said. He couldn't always understand her through that thick hillbilly accent. Sometimes she sounded like Daffy Duck.

"I been trying to get you on the radio for hours. Have you heard what's going on out there? Isn't it just awful!"

That took Thomas aback. "What's going on?"

"Don't you listen to your radio? All those boats being attacked?"

He must not have heard her correctly. "Say again?"

"Bubba, there are boats being attacked all over—"

"State location," he barked.

"At my desk, silly. Where else would I be?"

"The attacks! Where?"

"Down near the dam," she reported, pouty now. "Marker Number 3. And don't forget you were taking me to lunch today. It's past lunchtime."

"I'm on it," he said, then clicked off, wishing he'd clarified that he was "on" the burglaries, not taking her to lunch. He turned on the police-band radio for the first time since he'd been out today. Tomorrow he'd have to remember to turn it on right away. Anyway, it seemed from the chatter that there had been a second boat invasion somewhere around Marker 3.

Where was Marker 3, though? How did he get there? He pulled out the high-tech DIA map and searched.

The precise location of the crime scene turned out to be a little difficult to find. The satellite maps left out some landmarks that a foreign intelligence agency should be denied, but that would be helpful for actually navigating the lake. Buoy numbers, for example. DIA had marked latitude and longitude to the minute and second. Heights of radio towers and hills. Magnetic declination. Just not marker buoys. Nor did the photograph indicate what landmarks could be seen from the water. To the contrary: nothing smaller than an island or a large creek mouth was visible on the map. These landmarks were indistinguishable from water level.

The deputy's jibe about how long it would take him to get to a crime scene now stung more than ever. He lost his usual equanimity, spat "Jeepers!" and threw the map down. There had to be a better map than the satellite map.

Luckily there was a marina to his left—starboard? He headed over. At top speed, he swooped into the previously calm cove containing Lakeland Marina, searching for the dock house. The air smelled like diesel. The water had a rainbow sheen. It was probably from leaking gas. Maybe the EPA should be notified about a chemical spill.

When he found the fuel dock, overlooked by a building with big plate glass windows, he did what he remembered Tramp doing. He managed to dock like a seasoned professional, only ramming the dock once at full speed and maybe twice more, hard enough to upset his footing. Then he gave up on nosing in headfirst and tried backing in. A few more collisions and Thomas counted it a lesson learned: going backward, you had to steer the opposite way.

A boy came running down the dock, pointing at a warning buoy. "Hey, pal! Can't you read? This is a 'no wake' zone."

Thomas bridled at a mere boy calling him "pal." He flipped out his badge. "Special Agent Thomas, FBI. Official business. I need a map of the lake."

"It's still a no-wake zone."

"I still need a map."

The boy turned and shuffled into the dock house with deliberate slowness. He returned even more slowly. He moved as slowly as possible to still be considered moving. In his hand was a colorful folder. Thomas assumed it was what he'd asked for. It didn't look very helpful, though. The pictures he could see on the covers advertised pontoon boats and pickup trucks.

"Twelve ninety-five," the boy stated, holding out his hand for the money while holding the plastic-wrapped map out of the FeeBee's reach.

"I'm on official business." Thomas again held up his badge.

"It's officially twelve ninety-five."

"Do you know who I am?"

"Nope. Not unless you're Mr. Lakeland P. Marina and you own this here business. Price is twelve ninety-five. 'Course, if you were Mr. Marina, it'd still be twelve ninety-five."

Thomas lost complete control. "Jeepers creepers," he cursed. He dug for his badge once more, took out the twenty folded behind the ID, and practically threw it at the boy. "Keep the change," he barked, snatching the map from the kid's hand and ripping into the plastic envelope.

"Don't throw it in the water," the boy warned. "There's a federal law."

Thomas glared at him and spread the map out on top of his center console. The buoys were clearly marked, as were marinas and parks and towns. Scanning the map, he learned that the buoys were marked in sequence up the lake, south to north, from Marker 1 on the west side down south near the dam to Marker 40 something—no, 60—up near the north end. So, Marker 3 sat way at the other end of the lake. Far, far south.

He nudged his motors into reverse and wallowed out of the embrace of the gas dock's finger piers. As he turned the boat toward the lake, he jammed the throttle down. Thomas saw the boy yelling something just as the wake of the patrol boat's turn caught the floating dock and made the boy tap dance to keep his balance. With a wave and a grin, Thomas sped out of the marina.

Now that he knew where it was, Thomas didn't have any trouble finding Marker Number 3. A marker buoy displayed the number, plainly visible against the backdrop of the crowded pines. He ran his patrol boat parallel to the cove behind the marker and toward the beach nearest the marker. He didn't see a distressed boat.

Nothing at Marker 3. Still, there might be a crime scene near Marker 3. It had to be around there somewhere. Thomas sucked on his lips and kept cruising. It took him the better part of half an hour to decide there was no crime scene at Marker 1, or 3, or 5. Of course it could be on the other side of the lake, at 2, 4 or 6. But his response time was dragging on. So he got on the radio to ask anyone monitoring the public channels where the crime scene was located. Someone interrupted him to squawk about trouble up at Marker 9. Thomas found it on the map, back the way he'd come. An incident in progress always took precedence, so he roared back up the lake.

A couple of hours after he received the call from Dispatch, he found the newest crime scene. Standard operating procedure required him to let Dispatch know where he was. To heck with SOP, though. He didn't want to have to listen to Dispatch's commentary on how long it took him to get there, or about how he was standing her up for their lunch date.

He found a buoy proclaiming itself Marker 9. A houseboat bobbed near the beach of the marked island. Thomas deduced that it had to be the crime scene because tied to the stern of the houseboat was the

Hall County patrol boat. There were other boats tied up to the big boat, too: civilian boats.

Thomas slipped his patrol boat next to the houseboat. He intended to do it gently. He played the throttle back and forth, trying to keep the powerful motor from slamming him into the big houseboat. Paying too much attention to the other boat, he misjudged his throttle. As he tried to shift into reverse to stop his forward drift, he accidentally pushed the lever into forward. The FLEET boat slammed into yet another boat. The collision knocked Thomas off his feet and scratched matching gouges along the houseboat's paint and the speedboat's fiberglass.

As he scrambled to slip the boat into neutral, Thomas found himself confronted by a partially naked, full-bellied man standing on the side deck of the houseboat, shouting. "Who the hell are you? Why the hell you smashing up my boat?"

Thomas flipped open his identification and announced his pedigree.

"Oh jeez. First the county and now the Feds. What's next? The goddam Marines?"

Deputy Martin came around the corner of the deckhouse and waved a hearty hello. "Heard you were here."

Thomas stepped out of his boat. He handed one of the speedboat's lines to the incredulous half-naked man. "What do we have here?" he asked Martin.

"I'm sure glad you're here," the deputy said. He came over and put his arm around the younger man's shoulders in a friendly greeting. It astonished Thomas, but the deputy might be ashamed of his earlier lack of professionalism. Or maybe someone back at HQ had talked with Deputy Martin's boss.

Martin was all hospitality now. "Why don't you take control of the scene here. The Bureau probably gives you a lot more classes in controlling crime scenes than I ever got. I'll go run over to the other scene, which I think is at Marker 4. I'll just check it out and see if it's worth your time sifting the evidence down there, too."

Thomas was flattered at finally hearing some deference from one of the locals. "I'll come with you," he offered, hoping not to be taken up on it. He wanted to begin working the fresh scene. It would be his first honest-to-goodness FLEET incident and he wanted to solve it without interference.

"No, no. I got it. It's just a little thing, anyway. This here is probably the more demanding crime scene. It's gonna take someone with special training to begin a full forensic examination of the suspects. Come on to meet everyone." Martin motioned for him to follow and made his way along a narrow walkway toward the bow.

At the bow, a canopy shaded a large party space. It overlooked the beach and the island. Men and women, all sunburned and all loud, filled the deck space.

"This here's Agent Thomas, Federal Bureau of Investigation," Martin announced as he dropped his arm from Thomas' shoulders and made his way through the crowd to the side deck on the far side. He motioned for Thomas to take over and called, "Agent Thomas will answer all your questions." Then he turned the corner and disappeared.

He was not quite running. He was quite definitely grinning. He knew he should be ashamed at pulling such a juvenile trick. The irate boaters would eat the FeeBee up. Just like they'd eat up any figure of authority who offered himself up to listen to grievances.

He figured Thomas deserved it. Not just because he was a prig and an interloper and a Fed. Not more than an hour ago, the Sheriff's Department dispatcher warned him that the chief had just heard complaints from someone at the FBI about the Sheriff's Department's lack of cooperation. Now, the chief wanted to speak with Tramp. Urgently.

Tramp hadn't bothered to call. And wouldn't. Not until he was damn good and ready to hear the chief's whining about the Fed's whining.

He backed out of the cove and headed down the lake for Marker 5. Not that the FeeBee would shake free of the irate citizens any time soon. But if he did, and he tried to follow, let Martin try to find him at Marker 4, way on the other side of the lake.

Back on the houseboat, the federal agent stepped into the limelight. "Special Agent Thomas, FBI," Thomas announced, taking control. "Let's get everyone seated, and I'll interview you one by one. Raise your hand if you're a witness." He took a waterproof pad and pencil out of the special pouch on his FBI waterproof jacket.

The announcement of his identity did nothing to control the scene. If anything, a federal agent made it more chaotic. Argumentative boaters surrounded him, each of them talking at the top of their lungs. He picked out only fragments: advice, invective, and opinion. God damn Feds shouldn't be messing around with their GPS signals. The Fed's luxury tax made buying boats too darned expensive. The FBI wasn't doing anything to stop all this murder and pillage on the lake. If people felt like they could come up here and attack decent people on their houseboats, nobody was safe. Nobody! Wasn't it time that J. Edgar Hoover and his men did something about all the crime in the county? What were they paying taxes for if nobody wasn't doing nothin'?

Thomas held up his hands for quiet. "Did anybody see the crime?"

Nobody had. To all appearances, there hadn't been a crime. At least, not in this quiet cove. They'd all heard about something happening here on their VHF radios and gathered to help. Thomas scanned the crowd and saw a whole lot of drinking and bitching, but not much help.

Nor any knowledge. All they knew were the rumors. Nobody had seen or heard anything remotely like a robbery or a burglary. Nobody knew any facts. Not about anything: not about the robbery reported on the radio. Not the illegal campfire burning on the beach. Not the strong smell of marijuana wafting over the assembly.

The Bureau had trained Thomas to take statements, so take statements he did. He took down the opinion of every citizen who wanted to put their views on the record. He was into his fifteenth (each increasingly short) interview before he gathered that he would have a hard time ever getting any useful intelligence. Or, for that matter, getting away.

"Excuse me. I need to report in." He retreated, tiptoeing carefully around a woman whose bikini displayed disturbingly vast expanses of leathery skin. Thomas pulled out his federal band radio, turned his back, and called his office. "Killer Whale to SeaWorld." Civilians liked to see their public servants displaying their arcane skills. And he wanted to cover his retreat with professional elan.

FLEET Dispatch came back with a giggle. "Oh, Killer Whale, won't you come swim under my ice floe?" She made "ice" sound obscene.

Thomas colored and turned the volume down. "Take down a report, please," he ordered. From the sulky silence as Thomas dictated, the agent knew he'd been a little too harsh. She was a civilian, after all. She just needed to understand that the Bureau spent a lot of time and money projecting an image of unimpeachable rectitude. That image was a critical tool in the Bureau's constant fight against criminality. It was why local law enforcement put their petty grievances aside to help out on Bureau cases.

He softened his voice and gave her a report of where he was and what he was doing. "Put it out on the wire," he commanded when he'd finished. He signed off as she was asking what exactly needed to be put on the wire. Or what "wire" he was talking about.

Tucking the phone away, he looked back to the victims. They were examining him with great interest. He stood tall and proud and proclaimed: "I give you the Bureau's solemn pledge that we'll find the people who did this."

Profound silence followed him as he turned to make his escape. It was almost like these people didn't welcome the Bureau's help. Why they wouldn't perplexed him.

He had barely turned his back before they all started up again with their complaints about the federal government's intrusion into their lives. Thomas decided he'd best go before they really got started. He strode toward the back of the barge to escape the crowd and wait for Martin to reappear. On second thought—a thought encouraged by the half-naked citizens who followed him back—he retreated to his own boat. He pulled out the boat owner's manual and buried himself in the "Introduction to Seamanship" the manufacturer had helpfully included as an appendix. The text was incomprehensible, but it was better than looking like he could spare the time to talk to anyone else.

And heck, as long as he was waiting for the deputy, it was as good a time as any to bury his nose in the manual to find out what an outdrive was. The term was there in the index, but the description in the manual confused him. The drawings did, too. He'd thought the engine for his patrol boat sat below the hump that rose up behind him in the cockpit. Instead, the manual said it was underwater in the outdrive. Or maybe the engine was the outdrive. Thomas wondered just how far underwater whatever that outdrive was and why it was under the water.

Local law enforcement saved him from puzzling it out. Tramp Martin came back around the island and into the cove. He drove right at Thomas's boat and then, with a few nonchalant moves of wheel and throttle, executed a perfect stop. Thomas wondered where the brakes on the deputy's boat were; his boat certainly didn't seem to have any.

The county boat snuggled up against Thomas' boat without a sound—without even a soft bump. The federal agent stood up to grab on to the county boat's windshield. He noticed that Martin had a companion. A big, uniformed walrus of a man.

The walrus jumped aboard the FLEET boat like a mountain goat. "Sergeant Pitts," he bellowed, grabbing Thomas's hand. "Nice'ta meet'cha." Pitts was not only big; he was accomplished at using his bulk to effect. Right now, that effect caused the FLEET patrol boat to heel toward the side where he was standing. The sergeant nudged Thomas out of the way and plopped himself down in the captain's chair behind the wheel at the center console. Thomas' captain's chair!

"Martin thinks we can jump right on their tails if we get crackin'," Pitts roared, putting his hammy hands on the controls.

Martin called over from his boat, ignoring Thomas: "We just got two radio reports. Couple of people marooned when thugs ransacked their boats. Up at the north end."

Pitts bellowed at Thomas, "This Marker 3 bull shit must'a been a decoy to draw us off. Ol' Tramp over there figgers we're an hour or two behind 'em at most." Martin could barely understand the man through his drawl, but he listened closely as walrus-man announced: "We're going to do a little inter-ser-vice co-op-er-ay-tion here, you and me. We are gonna take the east side, and the Ol' Tramper's gonna take the west." He turned the key in the FLEET boat's ignition. As Thomas sputtered inarticulate protests, the sergeant gunned the engine and put the boat in gear, and acceleration threw Thomas deep into the passenger seat. "County's only got the one boat," Pitts roared over the engine. "We 'preciate our federal partners volunteering theirs."

The two patrol boats swept in formation out of the cove. Once clear of the island's grasping arms, each peeled off to their respective assignments. As the FLEET boat accelerated hard into a turn north, Pitts bellowed, "I'll drive," as he jammed the throttle down.

The federal agent, grabbing frantically for handholds, didn't hear.

Chapter Thirteen

The two pirates swept back to *Caesaria*. Their small vessels described curves and curlicues, testaments to their exuberance about a successful mission. Now and then they hollered out rebel yells and zoomed close together to slap each other's hands in high fives. They were not quite unanimous in their reasons to celebrate, however. Blackbeard celebrated the morning's financial success. Billy celebrated the joy of still being free after committing two armed robberies in broad daylight, and better: talking his buddy out of doing any more.

They ran up next to the sailboat in tandem, throttled back, and leaped for the deck. Now practiced pirates, they quickly tied off the PWCs, pulled up the hatch boards that closed off the companionway, and dropped down into the salon.

Blackbeard unzipped his wet suit and dumped the loot on the salon table. Billy grabbed a wallet from the pile and started to thumb through it.

A frenzied thumping echoing through the boat made them both freeze. The sound came from everywhere. Beneath them. From outside. From overhead. It echoed all around them. It was the beaver attack of the previous night all over again.

Their mouths fell open. Their limbs quaked. They stood locked in the poses where the sound had caught them, staring at each other, eyes wide, breath arrested, hearts exploding in terror. The fright they thought they'd put behind them from last night's haunted cove turned out to have only been smoldering. Now it blew up into a full-fledged panic.

Blackbeard felt his skin crawl and his hair stand on end even as he started to sweat and breathe heavily. He watched Billy turn white and his eyes roll wildly in their sockets. It wouldn't be long before he started slapping himself as he danced in place.

Watching his partner sobered the big pirate. He felt rationality return like a cold stream dousing him and looked around to identify the source of the sound. The v-berth. Of course. Where they'd stored their captive. Who was telling them he wanted to be set free.

Blackbeard snatched the wallet out of Billy's hands and slapped him on the head with it. In a friendly way. "Captain Bligh is reminding us he's still tied up. Go get him."

As Billy shambled toward the forward cabin, Blackbeard sat and started methodically emptying the wallets he'd collected. They'd taken in around $1,500. A pretty good take. A pretty damn good take. That plus the jewelry—another $1,000, possibly; and the Jet Skis—call that another $1,000 if they chose to take them too. More than they'd taken in any other month so far. More than they'd taken in several months put together. Having a temporary hideout on the lake turned out to be one of his better ideas, even if Billy didn't seem to appreciate it.

The big pirate fingered the jewelry they'd gotten from the houseboat. He knew nothing about jewelry. Nobody he knew had ever owned any worth talking about. Guys in jail talked about how they hocked it, and that's really all he knew. They said anything that looked flashy was probably junk. Was it good news that this stuff looked pretty old and beat up? Well, he'd get it to a guy in Atlanta and see what he could sell it for. With the $500 they got from Captain Bligh, they already had a couple of months' pocket money. They were on a lucky streak. He hated having to stop.

He looked longingly at the wallets. It sucked that they had to leave the credit cards. Hell, they could run them up pretty good before someone reported them stolen. The cards would give him and Billy a chance to hit the road, get way out of the state, live wild and free while they lined up their next lake.

An illusion. Credit cards left a clear trail, and the trail would lead right to them. He refused to get reeled in by a trail of credit card charges like the kids he'd met in the Juvenile Hall. They were too stupid to understand the problem with using cards was that they left a paper trail right to their doors. By the time Blackbeard met those guys, they had been given a lot of enforced downtime to think about it. Not that any of them were big on thinking.

Billy walked back in, escorting their captive. Blackbeard looked him over. Captain Bligh's cheeks looked reasonably healthy after having duct tape ripped off them. "You OK, dude?"

"I still have my lips. Dude. Thanks for asking. Where'd you learn the Vaseline trick?"

Blackbeard shrugged. "You learn stuff."

What kind of life, Doorman wondered, teaches you a trick like that?

He quickly shook off the sympathy. He couldn't afford sympathy when he might be fighting for his life. He'd been lying in the v-berth thinking about his options, but one fact eclipsed all the rest: two against one was still two to one. He'd need every advantage if he was going to fight them off. Sympathy would just get in the way, make him pull his punches, cause him to hesitate when the time came to act.

What he would have to do to save himself from his kidnappers was going to be ugly. Even if they turned out not to be hit men, just teenagers out on a lark, their lark could easily end in murder. His. Or theirs. What he needed to be doing every moment was to make them doubt each other or their plan.

"Quite a haul," Doorman observed. "What's my cut?"

Billy stared wild-eyed. "Your cut?" He turned to Blackbeard and shrieked: "He wants a cut?" The little guy bounced in his outrage, turning in a circle, slapping himself on the forehead, cursing everyone and everything in an uncontrolled flood. One phrase stood out. "Your cut? Your damn cut?"

"Captain's entitled to a cut," Blackbeard said, mostly to piss Billy off. He was getting a little tired of Billy's demonstrations every time something happened that he didn't like. The big pirate exchanged a glance with Doorman, rolling his eyes. "Don't you know your history, Billy-boy? Pirate captains always got a cut." He tossed the wallet to Billy to distract him and turned to the captain. "'Course, they got hung with the crew if they got caught. You up for that?"

"I don't remember inviting you to sign on as my crew." It didn't hurt to remind them that this was his boat. His jibe about money scored a hit. So what the hell. No reason not to stir the pot a little more.

"I'm entitled to a cut. It's only fair. You're using my boat. You're eating my food. You've made me an accessory to your crimes. Seems like I should be getting compensated." Before that dagger fully sank in, he gave it a little twist. "I'm sure you two split the take fifty-fifty, right?"

Blackbeard saw Billy frown and start to speak up and quickly jumped in to distract him from thinking too much about "fifty-fifty." "Man's got a point, Billy Boy. Maybe we should cut him in."

The little guy truly exploded now. He hated being called Billy Boy, for one thing. And it just pissed him off to no end that he'd taken the risk of burglary and boat invasion and risked a beef for assault, and now this guy wanted a share when he hadn't done shit but lie around the boat all day!

Blackbeard was thinking, not listening. They really could give Captain Bligh a cut. Why not? He mentally juggled reapportioning shares. In exchange for not narking them out, he and Billy could each give up a little of their share for Doorman—say 10% each. Or, better: take it all out of Billy's 40% share.

Better still, cut Billy and his damn antics loose entirely. He and Billy had been running buddies forever, but the little guy was not exactly what you'd call completely on board with the program anymore. They could still be friends, but business was business. Then he could give Billy's entire share to the Captain and not lose a dime of his own money.

And why not replace Billy with Captain Bligh? The old guy seemed like he was pretty cool. No nonsense, no bluster. Maybe he was a teacher or something. He seemed like he knew stuff. Definitely cool under pressure, a big upgrade from Billy. Right now, the captain was standing there chatting with the guys who'd invaded his boat and smacked him upside the head and gagged and hog-tied him. Almost like he was up for anything Blackbeard and Billy wanted to do. Almost like he was up for the adventure.

It'd be cool to do a job with him. Learn some things from an older guy. Find out about sailing, maybe read those sailing books. Seemed unlikely that the guy was serious about being a part of the crew, but he wouldn't be the first guy with a straight job who moonlighted. Like that teacher at the school who wore a Rolex or that teacher who started dealing meth on TV. Nobody could afford a Rolex on just a teacher's salary.

Doorman, meanwhile, reflected on Billy's latest outburst and wondered if the poor guy had Tourette's. He searched his memory for what Tourette's syndrome was and whether it gave him a clue about how to unnerve the guy.

Blackbeard cut into his thoughts. "Captain, why don't you make us some lunch so we can shut this bad boy up."

Doorman squeezed by the two black-suited men into the small galley. He barely suppressed his grin at driving a first wedge between his captors. If they kept arguing, they might get distracted from guarding him. Given an opening, he'd even the odds in a snap. Maybe get one of the chopping knives into Blackbeard. With the big man down, he'd be able to snatch the pistol, and then who'd be in control of the whole situation?

If.

***

After noon, the pirates stowed Doorman in the v-berth again and headed back out. Billy proved less averse to daylight robbery now that he'd opened one of the wallets to find a pile of money. Less averse, but still not exactly enthusiastic. He'd even wormed a promise from Blackbeard that they'd never, ever do this again.

The big pirate found the promise easy to make, considering that he'd already decided they would move on after today. He meant that they'd "never, ever" do this daylight thing on *this* lake and *not for the next month or so*. If Billy thought he meant something different, oh well. Blackbeard wasn't responsible for his partner's misunderstandings.

They rode north to get away from the area where they'd left the morning's victims, motoring along the channels between the islands and the western shore. Blackbeard rode lost in thought. He found the pile of money back on the boat as inspiring as the little guy did. They'd hit houses before, and even some offices and a few schools. Boats had just been kind of out-of-left-field idea. They'd been grabbing PWCs off the lake for a while, but that was really just like stealing a car. Except when you were out on the lake, you were less likely to get caught than when you stole a car. It was just hard to drive a boat away from the lake. It was a nickel and dime thing: boost a PWC, get it on a trailer or in the back of a (stolen) pickup and sell it on the street. The money was nothing to sneeze at, but it was slow going. You could hardly do more than one a night, sometimes two if you got real lucky. But if you only had one trailer and one tow vehicle, grab two and you were done for the night.

These lake burglaries, though: this was a pure gold mine. It was a hell of a lot better than robbing a house. Nobody on the boats ever carried a gun. (The sharp angles of the pistol stashed into the top of his wet suit reminded him that at least one boater had been carrying a gun.) OK, not *nobody.* But not very many people carried guns. And most people out here were pretty relaxed, not to say drunk or stoned, but certainly not considering getting robbed or taking any precautions against it. No burglar alarms, no dogs, no locks. And no police. One burned-out old joker from Hall County who hung out around the marinas to bust people for expired registrations or worn out life jackets. Not exactly the FBI.

They could specialize in lakes. First, clean out Lake Lanier, then cycle through the half dozen lakes in the Atlanta area. Altoona, East Point, Hartwell, and a couple more he wasn't able to think of right off. They'd hit one lake and hit it hard. The next week, they would let that one cool off and move on to the next. They'd be able to do it forever, one lake every week, and never come back to any lake for six weeks or so while working the others.

Hell, they didn't have to stay home in Georgia. Probably shouldn't. They could expand through lakes in Alabama and Florida. They would only have to do the same lake about every two or three months. The local cops wouldn't figure out they had a problem until long after he and Billy had moved on to some other county or some other state.

They'd make lots of money. Almost risk-free. Piles and piles of money. As he and Billy sped through the islands and back channels, the piles of money Blackbeard imagined kept growing.

In the next three hours, the two pirates found two bass boats and a ski boat. The two guys on the bass boats gave up wallets full of money. Both were out fishing solo. Didn't they know anything about safety? Anything could happen out alone on the lake! The only strikeout was the couple entwined on the shiny, leather-upholstered lazarette of the ski boat. Rudely interrupted, they scrounged up only a few bucks between them.

Overall, this boat invasion thing was good money. Easy money. Virtually no chance of getting caught if he and Billy left this afternoon or early tomorrow. Or possibly the day after, if pickings were too good to leave. Even Billy would have to admit that the rich take proved that the new strategy was brilliant. Simply brilliant.

Maybe not "have to admit." Billy's enthusiasm had already faded. He was back to muttering unhappily to himself. What if they hit a boat where someone had a gun? What if the police found them? What if they got caught? Anyway, the well was dry. Ain't no more boats. It was getting dark. And cold. Time to git while the gittin' was good. Blah, blah, blah. Wah, wah, wah.

Blackbeard tuned out the complaining by thinking about their next phase. The next lake, for one. They wouldn't even have to leave town to hit half a dozen lakes. They'd circulate between lakes just outside of town, scattered around the area, and come home and rest before starting over again.

Two more hours of cruising found the sun declining and no more victims. Billy protested, "I wanna go home." Blackbeard hated Billy's whining, hated even more to agree with Billy when he was whining. In truth, though, even Blackbeard was getting tired and a little saddle-sore. Worse, the gun and the plastic bag of loot inside his top were starting to chafe.

Magnanimously, he said, "If what you want is to quit, let's quit." They turned back to retrace their path to home base. In no time they found the Doorman sailboat, floating by itself in its quiet little cove. Blackbeard looked over to see if Billy was happy about calling it a day.

He caught his partner staring at the boat, licking his lips repeatedly, then back to him. Jeez. It never ended. What was he afraid of now? That the cops would be waiting for them? That Captain Bligh managed to get free and was going to ambush them? Blackbeard sped up so he wouldn't have to hear the latest complaint.

Billy headed him off. "It don't look right to me."

The cove looked different for a fact. That happened on this lake, though. Blackbeard had been around the lake his whole life, and there were lots of times that running around the islands in all different directions among the islands and channels would disorient him. Sometimes, if you were cruising through the back channels, the trees blocked your vision of the big landmarks. You'd get all turned around and think you were someplace you weren't.

That was why the scene in front of them didn't look familiar. They'd come up on the mother ship from a different angle and everything looked wrong. It was just like what he read about being a pilot flying in the fog. You just had to refuse to be disoriented. Not second-guess everything. So he waved his arm imperiously to direct Billy to get moving.

The fact was, the disorienting landscape was the very thing that made this lake a great hunting ground. The victims never knew exactly where they were. They didn't know what direction he and Billy had come from or disappeared to. He and Billy would always have such a head start the cops would never catch up with them.

Both Jet Skis coasted toward the sailboat. Both men tied their PWCs to the stern pulpit. Then they climbed up through the walk-through transom and into the cockpit.

"Wait, wait, wait," Billy objected when he got to the cockpit. He turned to stare back at the stern. "Our boat don't have...don't have..." He gestured at the transom but didn't know what to call it or how to explain what felt different.

Blackbeard didn't bother listening to him. If you started answering all of his arguments, there was no stopping him. You had to just push him aside and get on with it. So Blackbeard shouldered his buddy roughly aside and opened the companionway doors.

He'd already swung down into the salon before it occurred to him that *Caesaria* didn't have a swim platform. Didn't have a walk-through transom. Didn't have companionway doors. And once he was down in the salon, he saw a whole lot more that Doorman's boat didn't have.

Bling assaulted him. A luxurious cabin, mirror-polished teak floor, leather upholstery, polished brass light fixtures, first-class stereo...

Blackbeard turned to gape at Billy.

They were on the wrong boat.

Chapter Fourteen

Blackbeard peered around. His jaw dropped. Not because of the supple leather and gleaming hardwood and lustrous brass that surrounded him. Because of their good luck. They'd boarded the wrong boat. That was true. But a big boat and a rich boat, which meant money. From the looks of this sparkling palace afloat, lots and lots of money.

It was also an occupied boat. Muffled noises of human interaction came from somewhere. Blackbeard motioned for Billy to stay quiet. He looked around the salon, inventorying what they could quickly grab and take without having to confront anyone.

His eyes burned, making it hard to focus. The place smelled like a gas station. The fumes made his eyes water and the back of his throat burn.

Even with his eyes burning and watering, he could see the splendor around him. A roomy salon, paneled in dark, highly polished wood. A big cabin forward. Through the open door he could make out full-size closets, built-in shelves, a dedicated valet seat and dresser. All apparently empty.

The sounds of habitation, however, came from behind the ladder they'd come down. There, a half-open door revealed a roomy bathroom in the space behind the ladder and under the cockpit. Passageways on either side of the bathroom led to identical doors. Even with as little experience as he had with sailboats, Blackbeard guessed they opened into bedrooms.

Dull sounds came through both bedroom doors. One cabin with two doors, then? Or two cabins with their occupants engaged in the identical activity?

The big pirate moved silently to the nearest door, waving his partner to the other one. His hand on the door handle, though, Blackbeard hesitated. Nothing said that they had to roust the owners. It would be safer to take what they could find in the salon and be gone before the occupants knew what was happening. But if that was a bedroom behind the door, that was where the good stuff would be.

Blackbeard pantomimed his intention of going in and motioned Billy ahead. He pulled his bandana up over his nose, pulled the gun out of his top, and gingerly turned the doorknob. Taking a deep breath of fume-impregnated air, he burst through the door.

Billy appeared at the same time on the other side of the room. They looked at each other with surprise. Two entrances to the same room? And the size! The aft cabin was huge. Blackbeard couldn't imagine this much room on a boat. *Caesaria* looked like a closet compared to this.

Matching bedside tables sat in the rear corners of the bedroom. Both held expensive lamps and clock radios and the various knick-knacks of living. Along the wall between the dressers, separating the two pirates, a large built-in cabinet held not only clothing but a built-in dresser with a multitude of dresser drawers.

All impressive. But it was the large, round bed that dominated the bedroom and the pirates' attention. The bed was unlike anything that either man had ever seen in real life. Not in any of the houses they'd visited. Never mind on a boat.

The scene playing out on the bed was what really startled them. It was something neither had seen before. At least, not on a boat. And not live and in living flesh. And not from quite this perspective.

The activity didn't stop when they walked in. The man on the bed was so intent on his work he didn't notice the intruders. The girl did, perhaps because she was not a wholehearted participant, or perhaps because, from where she was lying on her back, the pirates stepped directly in her line of vision.

Her reaction—flopping around, wriggling on the bed, uttering little protestations—was hard for the men to interpret. Overcome by the man's efforts? Choking on the gasoline smell? Surprised by the strange men appearing over her customer's back? Trying to draw a breath to scream?

Her writhing did not distract the man any more than her gasping. If anything, the girl's new animation moved him to even greater efforts. It took him a little while to realize that the rhythm of his efforts did not coincide with the girl's vocalizations. He finally slowed down and opened his eyes and then craned his neck back over his shoulder to follow her gaze.

"Oh," he said, freezing abruptly mid-stroke. "Oh, no."

World's stupidest remark, thought Blackbeard, straight from the world's most ridiculous position. Trying not to laugh, he showed the gun, not pointing it at anyone. "Don't get up. We're only after your money."

"Don't kill me." The man disengaged himself. "Please don't kill me. I have a wife and kids. You can take all my money, but please—"

The girl abruptly stopped trying to disengage herself. She reached up to sink her nails into the guy's back like she was trying to pull him down on top of her. She hung on.

Blackbeard looked over to see what Billy made of the scene. Billy was standing opposite him in the other doorway, frozen. Staring at the scene on the bed. What? He'd never seen people—?

For Billy, it wasn't the activity exactly that stunned him. Something about the girl tickled his memory. Her face was familiar, for sure. He couldn't quite place her. He knew her, but who she was and from where...

Blackbeard figured Billy had just never seen a naked girl before. He himself wasn't distracted by the display or the action. He'd seen more than enough female anatomy to satisfy his curiosity a long time ago. Now wasn't the time to compare and contrast the actors or the scene in front of them. Time had started ticking away as soon as they barged through the cockpit into the salon. They needed to get the job done and get out.

He brandished the gun at the naked man. "Give me your money. Or I will blow your hairy ass away."

The man struggled upright, wrestling against the girl's nails. He pulled himself away from her grasp—at the cost of bloody tracks engraved on his skin—and struggled up onto his knees. He tried to pull the sheet away from the girl to cover himself. She fought to keep it. The man gave it his all, pulling at the sheet away with one hand, pushing her off with the other, and that did the trick.

The girl, though, had had enough. Completely exposed, she abandoned modesty completely. She found better uses for her hands. "You pig! What about me?" Her fists punctuated her words.

The battle on the bed didn't interest Blackbeard. He had work to do and these two in front of him were standing in the way. "Get up and give me your damn money," he yelled at the man. "DO IT NOW!"

The shout galvanized the man. He knee-walked to the edge of the bed, staggered to his feet and shuffled to the bedside table, his legs tangling in the sheet. Blackbeard moved back to give him space to dig for his wallet.

The girl made a lunge in the opposite direction. There was another bedside table opposite the one the man pawed through. She scrabbled for weapons, hurling invective all the way. She threw the first thing that came to hand: a cardboard box of tissues. Her aim was true and it beaned her bed partner on the head. In close succession, she followed with a book. A clock. A picture frame. A lamp. A box of condoms. She continued the barrage while screaming invective at the top of her lungs.

Blackbeard and Billy had long since retreated. They ended up backing into their respective doorways like the figures in a cuckoo clock. The man, meanwhile, had dropped to the floor next to the bed, curling into a fetal position to protect himself from the increasingly dangerous projectiles.

The woman paused only when she ran out of ammunition and a clear target. More projectiles beckoned from the side table at the other side of the bed. She barely spared a glance at the man as she lunged for more ammo.

Blackbeard saw his chance to take back control of the situation. He tucked the gun away and rushed forward to grab her. Body-slamming her onto the bed, he wrestled for her hands. The girl now turned her fighting spirit on him, pummeling him like a street fighter. The fact that the fists belonged to a naked girl didn't distract him from hitting back. He wrestled to capture her hands.

Billy had never seen a woman fight this way. Blackbeard and the girl rolled back and forth, grunting and grabbing, snarling and cursing, kicking and spitting. The boat rocked with their movement. After a few moments, Billy started to wonder. Were they fighting? Or were they—

No. It couldn't be true. He'd known Blackbeard all through high school, and then through their time in Juvenile Detention, then on one job and another. Nothing in Billy's experience with the big man would ever suggest that Blackbeard would...well, would do *that.* With a girl.

The wrestling match went on and Billy grew more uncomfortable every second. He bounced on one foot then the other, dithering about whether to get involved. "Hey," he managed to say. Then he tried again, a little louder: "Hey." Then: "Hey now. Hey now."

Billy looked around for help to disentangle the two on the bed. The man still lay curled in a fetal position on the floor. No help there. Billy was on his own.

Billy reached back into the bathroom to grab a bath towel, then stood over the two wrestling on the bed. "Hey now!" Still, neither paid attention. He twisted the towel with a few flicks of the wrist, like he'd done since learning to even the odds with the bullies in their fifth-grade locker room, He'd always been a wizard with a towel. Now his aim was true.

Blackbeard sat up with a howl, cradling his stinging buttocks with his hands. Or perhaps, given the tendency of the end of a flicked towel to curl, he was caring for parts more tender than his rear. In the pause, the girl scuttled away. She retreated to a corner of the bed, eyes as wide as they could be, breathing heavy, focusing first on one man, then on the other, and not sparing a glance for her former...whatever he was.

Blackbeard rounded on Billy. "You hit me." His face purpled with rage or pain or both. His hands shot out to slam Billy against the wall. Hard. Hard enough to knock the little pirate's breath away.

"No girls," Billy gasped. "Them was the rules. We wasn't going to mess with none of the girls."

The righteousness of his partner's objection just made Blackbeard madder. Those were their rules, yeah. But Billy caused this mess! By...by...

Well, Blackbeard didn't know just how, but the intense pain radiating through his abdomen and everything was Billy's fault. He pushed Billy again. Hard. "You hit me, you little shit. Nobody hits me."

Billy slid sideways along the wall to get out of range of the big man's fists. "There wadn't supposed to be no messin' around with no girls, remember? We agreed. No sex, no murders, no guns. Remember? That was our rules, wad'n it?"

Blackbeard tried for a pose of dominance, but with his hands massaging his stinging buttocks, he couldn't quite manage it. Instead, he unleashed a stony stare. Billy didn't even notice, and finally, Blackbeard turned away with disgust. He focused his attention on the boat owner. "Get up." Retrieving the gun from where he'd stuffed it in his wet suit, he snarled, "I want all your damn money, and I want it now."

The man stood slowly, wary of attacks from the front and from the rear. Blackbeard grabbed him by the free arm—the one not holding up the sheet—and dragged him out into the salon.

Released from Blackbeard's attention, Billy finally got a good look at the girl. She'd crouched down against the headboard, watching the big pirate drag the man away. A look of intense hatred lit her face. Suddenly, whether it was the angle or the fact that for a moment her nakedness stopped distracting him, Billy recognized her. And he knew that she'd recognize him, too.

His face colored and his skin turned clammy. She would see him as a burglar. A thug. Not anything he wanted her to see. It was what he was doing, sure, but it wasn't what he was. Not inside.

But even worse than the embarrassment from being revealed to her as a thug was the consequences of her seeing him at all. Now she was a witness who could identify him. Eyewitness-identify him! It was bad. Bad bad. Bad bad bad.

Billy rushed into the salon to tell Blackbeard what trouble they were in. He found Blackbeard and the owner facing off. A vignette of conflict: the big pirate with a pistol in one hand, the other hand palm up, demanding; the victim with one hand up as a shield, the other hand holding up a wallet. The wallet hung in the neutral air between them, neither being given up nor being denied to his attacker.

"Look. I'll give you a hundred bucks. Cash money. Just take the hundred bucks and go. I won't tell anybody you were here. OK?"

"Give me the wallet. Now."

Billy grabbed Blackbeard by the arm and tried to pull him away. The big pirate shook him off, maintaining his vicious eye contact with the man. Billy latched on again, this time holding Blackbeard's arm in a grip that surprised both of them. The little pirate managed to drag his partner toward the bathroom.

Billy kept whispering something that Blackbeard couldn't make out and pulling at him. He bent down to listen to Billy's whisper, still glaring at the prisoner and the wallet through the partially opened bathroom door. "I knew her," Billy hissed. "I knew her. I knew I knew her."

Blackbeard lost eye contact with the owner. He squinted at Billy, trying to understand. "Knew" her? Acquaintance-type knew her? Girlfriend-type knew her? Biblical-type knew her?

No way. Too much to imagine. And even harder to imagine Billy using biblical language to describe it. Which meant that Billy must *know-her* know her. Still, he failed to see how it trumped the task at hand. Which was collecting loot.

Blackbeard shook himself free again. "Big damn deal. You know her. Your own mother isn't going to know *you* when I get done with you! Now get away from me. Before I kill you!"

That word drew the attention of the fat man dressed in the sheet. "No no no," he called through the cracked door, his voice dripping with cooperation and reason. He held out the wallet. "You don't need to do that. Go ahead, take it all. Take the whole wallet. I'll even give you the PIN for my Kroger card. Take all my money. Take all my cards." He laid the wallet down on a table with a gesture of surrender and backed away.

The girl barged into the salon from the bedroom, movement emphasizing the bouncing of her breasts and the oscillating round globes of her rear end. She brushed by the pirates with a cry, making a beeline for the wallet. Unfortunately for him, the owner stood in the way. She crashed into him, reaching around him for the wallet. She snarled as she grabbed. "Give them all 'your' money? That's my money. I earned it. Give it here!"

The owner couldn't find a hand to fend her off. He gave the impression of a man confused by an embarrassment of choices. Escaping from the pirates and keeping the wallet away from the girl and defending himself as she beat on him and not being stripped naked in front of everyone and trying to figure out what part of his body to shield with his hands: he didn't have enough hands. So he stood, perplexed.

The girl wasn't limited by similar considerations. She had nothing to cover herself and nothing to hide behind, so she dedicated both hands and both feet to accomplishing one goal. "Give me what you owe me, pig!" She threw herself on him, her punches and slaps and kicks punctuating her speech. "Pig! Pig! Pig! Give me my money!"

The two pirates peeked out of the bathroom bemused. Blackbeard's annoyance dissolved in the ridiculousness of the scene. Pretty soon, his chuckle exploded into uncontrolled laughter. He grabbed Billy's arm for support as guffaws shook him. He pointed at the flopping man, and then at the flopping girl, and laughed himself utterly beyond control.

Billy didn't see anything funny about it. If it hadn't been for Blackbeard's violent reaction to getting snapped a few minutes ago, Billy might have slapped his partner to snap him out of it. He didn't dare lay hands on his partner again. But they were in trouble. It was no time for the big pirate to lose control. Not on a dangerous daylight robbery. On a lake where they'd left a nearly a dozen other victims, half of them probably already having called the police. The police were undoubtedly right at this moment looking for them. And now a fat naked man and a screaming girl—who knew him!—blocked their escape.

"Shut up, Mary Ann," Billy yelled.

Everyone froze.

"Mary Ann?" choked the big pirate, his hilarity dying.

"William?" said Mary Ann, her head snapping around to locate the familiar voice.

"Who's 'Mary Ann'?" The man pointed. "You mean Chastity?"

The names sobered Blackbeard immediately. He crossed the cabin in a few hurried strides, grabbing the girl by the arm, and dragging her past the fat man to the ladder. He pushed her in front of him up the stairs and into the cockpit and motioned to Billy to get his butt in gear. The big pirate paused long enough to grab the abandoned wallet from the salon table. He paused only to batter the radio into shards with the pistol. He turned to the man still cowering under the table. "I got a bullet for you if you follow us."

As he headed for the stairs, a book on the salon table distracted him. Old-timey sailing ships. Patrick O'Brian. The title something about a cowardly admiral. "Fuckin' epidemic!" he snarled, hurling the book at the owner in rage before joining Billy and the girl in the cockpit.

Blackbeard hustled the girl through the cockpit and down onto the swim platform, then onto his Jet Ski. He thrust the towel at the girl, who'd climbed on the back of the PWC, then straddled the seat in front of her and started the motor. Without waiting for Billy, he gunned the little boat away from the sailboat at top speed.

He checked to make sure that his partner followed. There was no need to check for the girl: her body was glued to his back. Blackbeard looked back toward Billy, silhouetted on his boat against the backdrop of the name painted on the back of the boat. *Käseria*.

Blackbeard's eyes narrowed as he drove away. Weird name. But familiar. And he didn't have time to think about why. Not with a major disaster on his hands.

They buzzed away at top speed, putting as much distance from the scene of the crime sas possible. When they'd ridden far enough away that they couldn't see the sailboat or pick out the island from the background clutter, Blackbeard picked out a small island, then circled around it to make sure it was empty. He knew from the girl's clammy skin and her violent shivering that she was suffering in the cold. Tough.

He ran his boat ashore on the beach and leaped off, not even bothering to help the girl off. When Billy pulled up shortly after, Blackbeard splashed into the water to pull him off his boat, then dragged him out of earshot of the girl.

"'No girls,'" he mocked. "What about 'no names'?"

"I didn't say my name. She did."

The justice of that answer only put Blackbeard off for a moment. "How does she know you?"

"High school." Billy pried himself loose from Blackbeard's hands. "I knew her in school."

"She knows your voice?"

"We used to talk on the phone. A lot."

"Wait a minute. She was your, like, *girlfriend*?"

Billy shrugged, a shy smile tugging at his lips, but that didn't derail Blackbeard's rant. "I don't get it. She was your girlfriend and you didn't recognize her when she was all spread out all over that bed with everything just hanging out everywhere?"

"I never saw her like..." Billy looked away. "You know. That way."

Mary Ann, meanwhile, had stepped off the Jet Ski. She watched the two men argue out of the corner of her eye as she cast around on the sand for something to pin the towel together. The frigid air burned her exposed skin, and the wind whipping under the towel froze everything else. As she searched, she kept an eye on the men. She couldn't quite hear them, but now she watched Blackbeard take a step back, point at her, and grab his head as if what Billy said to him astonished him.

At the other end of the beach, Blackbeard was holding his head and staring wide-eyed at his partner. "Billy the Kid! Billy the Kid with a girl! Who'd'a ever thought—"

Billy flushed a different color than his usual blush of embarrassment. The shame of junior high and high school and the youth home crowded all sense out of him. It lit an anger even he didn't know he possessed. With a cry and flailing fists he rushed the big pirate.

Back on the other end of the beach, Mary Ann watched the attack and heard William yell: "I ain't no faggot, God damn you."

Mary Ann saw the bigger man take the assault without retreating. Then he planted his feet and hauled back with one arm. He shot a fist right into the middle of Billy's face. Mary Ann started forward with a little cry as Billy fell flat. She stopped as he struggled up, rubbing his face.

"I'm sorry," Billy whined through hands covering his stinging face. "I'm sorry. I didn't mean to hit—"

"Don't ever," Blackbeard snarled, "don't ever use that word around me. Not 'faggot.' Not 'fairy.' Not 'queer.'"

Mary Ann watched the bigger man spin on his heel and storm toward her. He glowered as he marched. He was scowling as he approached, his hands clawed his clothes.

Mary Ann swallowed hard. She knew what was coming. She'd been treated rough; she'd been fought over; she'd been assaulted; she'd had to defend herself more than once. The way the big man had overpowered her in the cabin told her he could force her submission any time he wanted. That was the scientific truth: science like biology, like physics. Then there was Mary Ann's truth, a truth that she intended to impress on him like she had on every other man who thought he could take from her whatever he wanted. He might be strong enough to take what he wanted, but she would make him pay.

Blackbeard stormed toward her. She set her feet in a fighting stance. She watched his hands, determined to get in the first punch and to make it count.

Then in a second, he was past her. He didn't pause as he finished pulling off his wet suit top. On his way by her, Blackbeard threw the top at her and stormed by. "Cover that girl stuff up," he snarled over his shoulder." Her eyes followed him as he passed and mounted the Jet Ski. He snarled: "Get on." It was not an invitation

Gunning the motor as Mary Ann climbed behind him, he yelled at Billy: "I'm going back to the sailboat. If you're comin' with me, we'll straighten this out when we get back." Ending in a taunting falsetto: "William."

Chapter Fifteen

Deborah Doorman made it through almost an entire day of work before panic overcame her. The seeds that would flower into full-fledged panic late in the day were planted first thing in the morning, though. She'd made the mistake of telling the unit secretary about the mysterious call.

"He probably dropped the phone overboard." Even though she gave Deborah a pat on the shoulder, the idea was not comforting. Why would Joe be fooling around with his phone in the middle of the night, and what would cause him to drop it overboard?

It got worse. Seeing the look on Deborah's face, one of the staff nurses in the clinic tried to lighten the mood. "Maybe he's busy with the Dallas Cowboys Cheerleaders. He's probably got some naked girl tied to the keel or the jib or whatever you call it."

Deborah laughed. "Joe? Joe is so straight..." She thought better of finishing the thought. "Anyway, he has David with him."

She walked away, half-convinced she had put her concern aside. Worry about Joe and David's safety got the better of her only twice during the day. Both times, she left patients waiting as she ducked into her office to call Joe's cell phone. Both times, a recording declared the number "out of service." Both times she reassured herself that "out of service" could mean a lot of different things.

Considering what some of those things could be didn't reassure her. By five o'clock, Deborah Doorman's outer appearance of calm had worn to a thin veneer indeed. She finally admitted to herself that she was worried. Beside herself with worry, actually. Before she left for home, she dug the police officer's card out of her purse and called. A sergeant said the young officer was off the clock. He didn't know anything about Joe Doorman or a mob trial or any special patrol. But he knew how to get rid of her: he promised to check on it and have someone get back to her. As soon as possible. If not today, by the end of the week.

Deborah drove home, thinking of all the reasons she didn't need to worry.

At home, she dug out the hotline number Joe had left her. Fingers trembling, she punched in the number and promptly got transferred over to an apathetic receptionist. The receptionist made it clear that there was nothing she could do. "If this is an emergency, you have to call 911. But it's not an emergency unless your husband is actually missing." And added a warning: "He's not a missing person for forty-eight hours."

That was too much. "What am I supposed to do, wait two days and then call back?"

"That would be fine. Chief Howard Clark thanks you for allowing the Atlanta Police Department to be of service." Click.

OK, she was not going to get any help there. She'd have to check on her family all by herself.

Stopping only long enough to change out of her skirt and blouse—throwing the work clothes on the otherwise immaculate floor—she stormed out of the house. She sped up the highway to the lake.

***

Deborah got to Lakeland Marina without a plan. Fatigue and worry preoccupied her. She ran down the familiar dock and pulled up short. *Caesaria*'s slip was empty.

She'd known the whole way up to the lake that the boat would be gone, of course. After all, David and Joe had gone to the lake with the intention of taking the boat out. Still, the forlorn slip filled her with unease. In the space where the sailboat should be, there was only black, disturbed water reflected the low gray clouds overhead. Little groups of riffles slapped at the pilings with a hollow, muted clatter. The air felt warm enough, but she smelled a hint of the arctic on the uncertain wind. Along the deserted dock, a loose line here or there clanged against a mast, underscoring the solitude of the lake with winter coming on.

Looking out toward the lake, she saw nothing. Not a single boat broke the stillness. The flat gray expanse of the water scared her. It was what made her resist Joe sailing alone in the wintertime.

Of course, Joe wasn't alone. David being with him comforted her. Surely one of them would call if they ran into trouble. Except, she remembered, she had encouraged David to leave his phone at home while he and Joe spent quality time together. Damn.

The call in the night suggested that something unusual had happened. So did the unanswered calls. And now her entire family was somewhere on the lake, incommunicado.

Or maybe the lack of communication suggested nothing more than that they'd unplugged to interact without electronic distractions.

She made her way off the abandoned docks, back to the car, scrambling for a plan. Since the police weren't going to go look for her husband and son, she was going to have to. That meant she needed a boat. There were rental places in every nook and cranny of the lake. She just had to find one open in the off-season.

It took Deborah an hour to find an open rental place. Red Neck Salvage and Rental, miles south of *Caesaria*'s home marina, sat where a poorly paved county road abruptly dead-ended at the water's edge.

"It's not that I expected to see *Caesaria*," she explained to the proprietor with a self-deprecating shrug. He pushed a waiver of liability form across the counter without making eye contact. "It's just that when I got to Lakeland—that's where we keep her—I realized how empty the lake was. If they're in trouble, there's nobody out there to help them. They might have hit a reef or lost the mast or—"

"Sign there," Rudy "Red" Neck interrupted, thumping a burly finger down. "I don't usually rent out boats this late in the year, but seeing as how you got experience on a sailboat..."

Deborah managed to stifle a laugh. Joe always said that power boaters assumed that sailors were the boating equivalent of Nobel laureates. They probably assumed that if the sailors could figure out what to do with those confusing ropes and sails and stuff, sailors were just smarter. After all, a power boater only had to turn the ignition key.

In truth, Deborah didn't know a thing about motorboats. But she needed to find Joe and David. If this man mistook her experience on sailboats and assumed that meant something about her ability to manage a big houseboat, it wasn't because of anything she'd said. The houseboats lining the rental docks were frighteningly big, but really, how difficult could it be to con them? Heck, they were designed for people who only turned a key.

Red Neck escorted her out of the office and onto the dock. He walked by a few of the sparkling little speedboats, then toward the houseboats. Her mouth went dry at the challenge of trying to drive one of the behemoths towering over her. The smallest were probably thirty feet or more long, with large patios fore and aft and rooftop seating areas on top of their huge deck cabins. The largest looked as big as the Doorman home. They had two-story deckhouses and looked like floating restaurants more than anything that a person would own, much less sail around the lake.

She followed Mr. Neck down the dock, toward where two of the largest boats overshadowed the finger docks. He ambled to a stop and looked up, grumbling to himself. "Don't like this sky."

Deborah glanced up too. She didn't like it either. A high blanket of gray spread horizon to horizon, and below that, feathery fingers of darker gray clouds crept ominously across the sky. The layers looked disturbed, but Deborah couldn't decode them. She asked, "The weather report is all right. Isn't it?"

The man led her on without comment. She considered that he might be uncommunicative or rude or just hard of hearing. On the other side of the next floating mini mansion, he held out his hand to introduce her to a strange little barge. "This here's *Admiral Byng*. My personal work boat. Built her myself. Here's the key. You go on aboard and get her fired up and I'll get the lines."

A small barge floated shyly between two flashy houseboats. A very compact barge. An ugly barge, looking like nothing so much as a wooden shack dropped onto a couple of pontoons. Even its deckhouse looked like a sloppy do-it-yourself job: a garden shed with aluminum windows set into wood shake siding. Nobody in North Georgia would look askance if they came upon it in the woods.

On the water, it looked like something out of a bad novel. Two banged-up pontoons jutted out from under the rusted steel plates of the deck. Behind the shack, stuck precariously on the back, a steel derrick structure loomed. It looked useless and dangerous. Not to mention that it was so rusted that it seemed about to collapse into deckhouse. She wondered if there was actually any healthy metal under all of the rust on the derrick, or for that matter under the decks' burden of rags and discarded fast food bags and unidentifiable scraps of cloth and crushed beer cans.

"*Admiral Byng.*" Deborah tried to keep the anguish out of her voice.

"Yes, ma'am, *Admiral Byng*. He was a great hero, you remember." *Admiral Byng*'s owner didn't care what she knew of marine history. He just wanted to close the deal and be gone. The man shook the key at her. "Here's the key. Start her up and I'll get the lines."

"I thought you had a houseboat for me to rent!"

He glanced at the barge and shrugged. "This late in the season, I don't keep none of the houseboats in service. This is all I got ready to go out. 'Course, she's my own personal boat, but I ain't gonna use her today or t'morra'. You don't want her, that's fine."

"No," Deborah said quickly. "No. I need a boat. I just didn't expect—"

"Well, you know, sometimes you get lucky." Which of them was the beneficiary of good luck was not clear. Red Neck shoved the key into her hand. "She's not very pretty. But I built her with my own two hands. 'Course I built her to work on the docks and she done a little salvage here and there. But she'll go just about anywhere, do just about anything you ask her to, as long as you don't take her through a hurricane. She's just as fine a little craft as you ever seen out there on the water. If you ignore the crane on the back and the welding equipment and all that."

She didn't want *Admiral Byng*, but she needed a boat and this was a boat. Of sorts.

She stepped aboard and walked into the cabin. Or was it a deckhouse? The steering station stood inside the deckhouse at the forward end, just below the window. Trash littered the shack's floor, just as it did the deck. Her breath suddenly coming hot and fast, she kicked the detritus aside and stepped up to the wheel, looking for the ignition and the throttle and the gauges and the light switches and the radio and all the things a boat should have. They all looked strange to her. Almost improvised. Like the wheel. It gave evidence of having been torn out of an old Oldsmobile, right up to the tarnished badge on the hub.

But, oh well. In the end, a boat was a boat. She fitted the key and turned the ignition. The motors started without a hiccup. The man gestured to indicate that he'd released the lines. Deborah shifted the throttle into reverse and backed slowly out of the slip.

It steered heavily, like...well, like a barge. But it steered more or less on the same principle as *Caesaria* under power. She could do this, Deborah assured herself as she backed away from the dock. She crept backward at dead slow, trying not to hit anything with the builder watching.

Once she'd almost cleared the finger piers, Deborah spun the wheel and nudged *Admiral Byng* into forward gear. The motors surged. The barge barely slowed its backward course. The boat's nose turned hesitantly toward the open lake, if a square heap of metal could be considered to have a nose.

Then the motors died. Deborah frantically reached for the key and turned the ignition again. Nothing. She moved the throttles back to neutral and turned the ignition again. Silence.

In the stillness she heard yelling. She saw Red Neck on the end of the dock waving to get her attention. Deborah opened the deckhouse door.

"You gotta kick it in gear sometimes," he yelled over the slowly growing expanse of water between them.

Deborah returned to the controls. She'd had an American Motors Hornet once that she had to "kick" into gear. You had to turn the key in the ignition and press down the gas pedal while you jammed it into Drive, all at the same time. She tried the same thing now. A dozen tries didn't produce any effect. She went back to the open door and gestured helplessly to the owner on the dock.

"You gotta kick it," he repeated.

"I did that."

"No, you di'n't. You gotta go back to the motors and give them a kick." He mimed the motion of booting an engine. "Sometimes the fuel pump gets stuck or som'tin'. I keep reminding myself that I gotta tear them motors down and fix 'em, but I ain't got around to it yet. Go 'head. Get 'er done."

Deborah made her way back along the cluttered working deck of the twenty-five-foot barge. In the process, she snagged her slacks on a ragged cable and punctured her finger on an unraveling seam on the crane superstructure. At the twin outboard motors, she paused.

Kicking wasn't part of her repertoire, particularly when it came to other people's property. Or machinery. Certainly not boats. She couldn't imagine kicking anything on *Caesaria*. Still, she felt a certain satisfaction in the thought of giving this floating piece of crap a kick. She gave the outboard motor a clomp, then looked guiltily over at the owner.

"Naw. Come on, lady. When I say kick, I mean kick them bad boys." He pantomimed it again.

She delivered the instructed correction to the first motor, hurting her foot.

"Now do the other one," the man called. Deborah administered the same medicine to the other of the twin outboards.

"Now go start her up before they forget who's boss!"

Admiral Byng's motors started at the touch of the ignition key. Deborah moved the throttle gingerly into forward. As the barge plodded past the parked boats, she waved to Mr. Neck on the dock.

He didn't see. His face was tilted up to the sky, his lips moving.

***

The *Admiral Byng* moved like a car with flat tires. She didn't respond to anything but the most exaggerated movements of the wheel. She accelerated with the greatest reluctance. The only thing she did quickly was slow down. Deborah started thinking of the recalcitrant boat as "it" rather than "she."

Steering—*conning*, she corrected—Deborah kept a hand on the wheel while she rummaged for the switch to the radio. It clicked on with a burst of static. She tuned to Channel 16, the emergency channel, and turned down the squelch button to reduce the background noise. A hunt underneath piles of papers on the windowsill in front of her produced a chart. A map of the lake, anyway. The map showed roads and parks and marinas, but not a single useful navigation mark. Advertisements for beer, gasoline, and boat ramps, but no depth contours. No buoys. No deep channels or reefs. A tourist map, then. Not a chart.

Still, maybe it would be useful. She propped the map up on the windowsill, pulled a pencil out of the pile of debris. She marked her approximate course and the time at the position of Red Neck's dock. Joe always insisted that whoever was at the wheel kept a rough dead-reckoning plot. She didn't know why, didn't see the point, really, but she wasn't confident enough to break a rule Joe had taught her.

Joe.

She'd had a lot of time to think about Joe and the Dallas Cowboys Cheerleaders. Just a stupid joke. OK. But something about the quip hit home and stuck. It had needled her the whole day, whenever she wasn't concentrating on something else. The persistence of the jibe bothered her more than the quip itself. There had to be some reason why it wouldn't leave. It must have stuck in her brain for a reason.

Of course she knew why and just didn't want to acknowledge what she didn't want to see. She'd never had a reason to doubt her husband's faithfulness before now. Recently, though, he'd been distant. He had spent more time out of the house and until later at night than she could ever remember. Now he always came to bed later than she did. She had the distinct feeling that he was avoiding going to bed with her. These days they seldom snuggled. And recently intimacy seemed to always be preempted by a thousand much more important priorities.

She considered yet again the possibility that the problem might be with her. In recent weeks, in moments of stress, she had found herself examining her reflection, looking for flaws. Like this moment, even while moving slowly out into the lake, she caught herself examining the reflection in the plate-glass windowpane in front of her. She'd didn't like what she saw. She'd gotten old and gained a few pounds over the last decade. Joe had always expressed enthusiasm for older women in general and for her augmented curves in particular. Too much enthusiasm? Too often stated? Was he covering for having grown bored with her? Was he in the midst of a midlife crisis, brought on by spending the day with the hot young women in his office and then coming home to the same old—old!—wife?

She peered through the dirt and through her reflection on the front window. The main body of the lake filled the window in front of her. It struck her suddenly that she didn't have the faintest beginning of a plan. Search for Joe: fine. But that was an aspiration, not a plan. How was she supposed to do that?

She'd start with the first decision, now coming up. Start the search where? Four choices. She had to choose: search to the north or the south, search the east side or west side of the long lake. She sagged under the enormity of the task. It felt particularly draining on top of a sleepless night and a full day. But Joe had to be anchored out there somewhere.

She couldn't concentrate on navigation. Her mind returned to her co-worker's quip. It had struck home because it hit a wound that was already sore. She discovered in that moment that she had already suspected him of cheating. It took an offhand joke to make her see that she knew what she already knew.

Cheating.

That bastard. She should just turn around to go home. Leave him be, wherever he was and whatever he was doing.

But then there was David.

Summoning up her energy, she concentrated on making her first important decision. West seemed the best bet. Joe liked the west side of the lake. She and Joe had anchored all up and down that side, from the undeveloped land around Lanier Bay Marina in the south to the islands around Lazy Holiday Marina in the north.

Deborah turned the barge toward the main body of the lake, intent on heading west. Tried to turn, anyway. It was like paddling one of David's Styrofoam rafts. The two motors were hardly up to the task. They had to punch the blunt bows through the water by main force. It was nothing like the surgical motion of *Caesaria*'s sharp bows cleaving the water in two.

Well, you just have to make do, she remonstrated fiercely. She manhandled the barge out into the lake and set her course for the western side. She throttled up, sitting heavily down on the helmsman's chair, her eyes already scanning the water and shoreline for any sign of her lost family.

Chapter Sixteen

Deborah Doorman found *Caesaria* just after first light and completely by accident. She'd spent the rest of the day and all night after leaving *Admiral Byng's* home circumnavigating the top half of the lake, counterclockwise. She'd looked at every island and looked into every cove she passed to try to find *Caesaria.* Driving this shaking, lumbering barge had tired her, as had staring for hours on end into the growing darkness. Complete exhaustion hit her as the sun rose in the morning.

She must have fallen asleep on her feet some time shortly after the sun rose. She woke to find that she'd lost control of her boat. Left to its own devices, it had drifted off course. She'd opened her eyes to see the tightly grouped islands called the Three Sisters dead ahead. The islands hugged the western edge of the lake, and she was headed right for them. Much too close to the shore. The emergency energized her for a moment, allowing her to wrestle the cumbersome craft back onto a safe course after long, agonizing minutes trying to get it to behave. When she finally got control and turned away from the danger, there, in front of her, riding with proud majesty in a quiet cove, floated *Caesaria*.

She sprang up from her seat at the helm, opened the deckhouse door, and in her irrational relief practically threw herself into the water to swim to her sailboat. It took a minute to calm down. It took another twenty to maneuver the obstreperous barge alongside the sailboat. Then she had to fight to get the barge to stop before it rammed a hole in the sailboat's fiberglass hull. Deborah paused another couple of seconds when she got close, looking at the dirty black tires that rimmed the barge as fenders. Joe would kill her if she left black skid marks on his flawless gel coat. The barge didn't have other fenders. It might be possible to rig something from the trash scattered around her, of course. The filthy rags might not be any easier on *Caesaria's* gel coat than the tires, though.

Oh, to hell with it. She snugged one boat up against the other and tied off one of *Admiral Byng's* mooring ropes to the sailboat's railings. Another misdemeanor in Joe Doorman's book, tying off on a thin aluminum railing. She did it anyway and pulled herself up from the barge's deck up to *Caesaria's.* Her heart fell to see that the sailboat's hatch boards were locked. They could only be locked from the outside.

The dinghy was gone, too. Oh hell, Joe and David must have gone off in the dinghy, fishing or something. She pushed away a niggling thought about all the things "something" could be.

Fine. They were off on a lark. Deborah would wait for them inside. Surprise them. Joe's facial expression would be interesting when he saw her.

Back down over the side, back to the barge's shack of a deckhouse to fetch her sailing pack, then back up into the sailboat's cockpit to dig the sailboat's keys out of her bag. In a second, she had yanked the hatch boards off and climbed down into the cabin.

The air in the cabin smelled surprisingly fresh for being closed up and peopled by two male animals. She smelled a faint hint of perfume in the air, too. Someone must have shampooed their hair or done the dishes or washed out some clothing. Cleaned the boat up, too. It was remarkably tidy for Joe and David occupying it together. The dishes were even washed and drying in the dish drainer. The navigation station was spotlessly clean. There were no dirty clothes in sight anyplace. Everything was neatly stowed. Including a surprise, neatly stowed away on the starboard settee: A girl. Blond. Big busted. Gagged. Trussed up like a pig.

Deborah stepped closer to peer at her, quite unable to comprehend what she was seeing. The girl looked like nothing so much as a Dallas Cowboys Cheerleader. The nurse's snotty comment about Doorman and the cheerleaders shrieked in her memory like electronic feedback. That and the shame of her reply: Joe was "too straight." Until this very moment, Deborah Doorman's consciously held conviction that Joe was "too straight" had been overpowering the intuition that he had been cheating on her.

Here was proof. A Dallas Cowboys Cheerleader in the flesh. Very much in the flesh. The girl was bound and gagged: hands and feet tied and then secured to the overhead grab rail with rope. Duct tape sealed her mouth. A boat blanket covered her generous curves. Barely covered. She lay very obviously naked under the blanket. A plastic tub of Vaseline sat on the table near her.

Vaseline. Deborah didn't know whether to laugh or cry.

The girl suddenly opened her eyes and looked directly into Deborah's. The insolence of her expression made Deborah want to smack her. Instead, she whipped the blanket off the girl. She wore a skin-tight leotard top—no, a wet suit top—with only a towel to clothe her bottom half. The tight top emphasized an impressive figure. The towel would have allowed—oh my God!—easy and repeated access. The Vaseline!

The whole scene disgusted her. The girl boasted exactly the type of body you would expect a middle-aged man to fall for. Large, full breasts; a tiny waist; lean, muscular calves; painted toenails. And more than just well-endowed, she was also fetching: peaches-and-cream complexion, high cheekbones, deep blue eyes. Definitely a type men would lose their minds over.

She also looked like she'd been rode hard and put up wet. Rode so hard that her hair was still drying and a damp smell lingered about her. *Rode hard and put up wet.* Deborah had never felt the import of the phrase so nakedly before.

Deborah felt suddenly sick. The naked slut. The ropes. The lack of bottoms. That tub of Vaseline. No wonder Joe had been too busy to answer the phone.

The bastard.

But why would Joe do this? He had a wife, a child, a marriage of twenty years. A good marriage too, one filled with love and intimacy. Why would he need this whore?

Because his wife didn't look like this anymore? No. It couldn't be that. She'd never looked anything close to this, even in her best days, In recent years, Deborah had found herself standing in front of the mirror many times, staring at the face and figure she didn't recognize anymore, picking out each of the disappointing changes age had brought. Tired eyes. Sagging curves. Networks of wrinkles. Gray-tinged hair.

Deborah realized what she'd refused to let herself recognize over recent years. Each time she'd caught sight of herself in the mirror, she'd quickly suppressed the doubt that Joe could still be attracted to her. When she gathered enough courage to ask, Joe always said that he still found her as beautiful as the day they married. She'd been such an easy mark that when he said those kind words and enfolded her in his arms, she'd melted.

Obviously, he'd been lying. Or maybe he'd been grading her on a curve. (Ha! Large, sensuous curves!) Well, at least now she knew the exact reason that he had been less than attentive. She would never have expected this. She wondered what else he had been hiding from her.

Well. All those secrets Joe had held close to the vest? They weren't her problem anymore. As of now—how stupid she'd been!—he would have free rein to exercise his desires without a wife to get in his way.

But: David, David, David. That Joe had done this—was doing this—she might have to accept. But in front of David? No way. She would never accept that.

A terrible thought struck her. Had Joe planned specifically for *this* when he planned the cruise with David? Did he think this whore put the quality in "quality time"? Could he have decided it was time to inaugurate his son into adulthood with this—?

No. He wouldn't. She was certain.

Almost certain.

She hoped.

David was still a child. His child. Only a pervert would force his child to...to...to...

Deborah sank down on the starboard settee. A few tears trickled down her face. Her marriage was over. Irrevocably broken. It wasn't true, as she'd always believed, that nothing was irretrievable. This was.

All those years, all that hard work. Gone. In a snap of the fingers. There was no way to recover what had been lost.

Had she looked up, she would have seen Mary Ann rolling her very pretty blue eyes at the older woman sitting opposite her, crying. It would not have been a healthy moment for either of them. Fate, or chance, or karma—whatever it was—spared them both.

It took Deborah Doorman a few minutes to come to her senses. She had a series of tasks to accomplish. First, she had to find her son. Then she had to find Doorman. Not to save him. Oh no. She had other plans for him.

But where she might find them out on that big lake, she didn't know. The best course would be to sit down and wait for him to come back. Let him bop down the companionway ladder, with a hard-on for this slutty bitch, and wilt when he found his old lady of a wife waiting. Wouldn't *that* be satisfying.

It would mean having to sit staring at this slut who had broken her marriage. A slut who had the gall now to fall back asleep on the opposite settee with the most adorable sleep sounds. The girl's soft, catlike snores enraged Deborah. How dare she sleep!

Deborah stood up, stomped the one and a half steps to where the girl hung like a side of beef. She ripped the duct tape off the girl's mouth. The removal of the tape made the girl's eyes pop open with surprise and, Deborah hoped, pain. The masking tape came off with remarkable ease.

"You whore!" Deborah spat, overcome with hatred.

"The wife," the girl sighed, licking her impossibly full lips. "Doesn't that just make my day perfect. Can you untie me? I'm getting kind of tired of this position."

***

It took an hour of pointed questioning and incomprehensible replies before Deborah was able to make any sense of the girl's story. Not that she believed it. Still, she could hardly afford not to act on it.

Act she had. She untied the girl and bundled her onto *Admiral Byng*, depositing her on the grimy deck of the deckhouse, and setting off once more to find her family.

Now, back at the wheel of the barge, Deborah looked sideways to where Mary Ann lay on the throbbing deck of the *Admiral Byng*. Back on the sailboat, the girl, freed of her bonds, had quickly pulled on the clothing Deborah threw at her and then immediately fallen fast asleep again. She must have worked hard all night, Deborah thought. She felt a sudden desire to kick the slut when she remembered what that hard work would have entailed and with whom.

Deborah didn't blame her for being a sex worker. Nor for being Joe's...Joe's...well, Joe's whore. If that's what Joe was looking for, it would have been someone else if not this one. No, the girl deserved a thorough thrashing for the fairy-tale story she'd made up about how she came to be lying trussed on the family boat.

You had to be pretty stupid to believe that the girl had been "working" on a "really big sailboat" and then got "kidnapped" by "two men" and brought to *Caesaria*. Kidnapped by Joe? Joe might be a whoremonger, but a kidnapper? No way. And as for "two men," even an ignorant whore couldn't possibly have mistaken David for anything other than a child.

The girl claimed she "didn't know the guy who owned the sailboat." Deborah scoffed. Only when the girl insisted that the guy who owned *Caesaria* had himself been kidnapped and then been taken off on the kidnapers' Jet Skis: then Deborah started considering the possibility that what the girl was saying just might have kernel of truth. Not that she completely believed a single word out of this creature's mouth.

Only one part of the girl's story gave Deborah comfort. "There was no little boy on the boat," Mary Ann insisted. Deborah wanted to believe that no woman with a conscience would stoop to *performing* in front of a child. But would a woman with so little self-respect restrain herself from anything that paid good money?

If she was telling the truth—if David wasn't on the boat during the girl's performance—then where was he? Joe might conceivably have dropped him off at a friend's house on the way to the lake. That way, he could have the girl all to himself. But that meant Doorman and maybe even David would have had to make arrangements before they left for their trip. Even if Deborah could believe it of Joe—and now she could believe anything about him—it was hard to believe it of David. Her little boy, who had never been able to lie to her, would surely have told her that he wasn't *really* going sailing. But of course, David wouldn't necessarily have known. Joe might have lied to him, too. If she believed that Joe hooked up with this creature, it was easy to believe that he might lie to David.

But, but, but...it all diverged so far from her experience with Joe—

"Two other men on the boat," the girl told her. Who could they be? Buddies of Joe's? Partners in sharing this creature?

Impossible to believe.

Almost impossible.

Not impossible, though. She had eyewitness evidence to the contrary staring her in the face. Evidence, in fact, of a whole universe existing that she never would have suspected. A whore. Bondage. Gang bang. Pedophilia. What kind of depraved monster was she married to? You heard stories about middle-aged men going off the deep end. But Joe? But this?

The girl tried to make her believe that the two men who'd kidnapped her were robbing boats on the lake and that Joe was the men's captive. The idea was attractive at first, mostly because it exonerated Joe from at least some of his sins. But in the end, it was ridiculous.

Almost ridiculous.

There was a small chance that it might be true. The possibility that Joe had been taken hostage by criminals (and what of David?) terrified her enough to propel her back onto *Admiral Byng* and back to the current search. This time accompanied by an unexpected passenger. Whether she was saving a trafficked girl or preserving evidence for the coming confrontation with her husband wasn't clear even to Deborah.

Hours later, Deborah had finally gotten her brain in gear. She kept rehashing the girl's story. In the end, the pieces didn't tie together. If thieves had captured Joe, why would they take him with them while they went out to pillage? And why hadn't they taken the girl along? If she was their date, why leave her tied up? Was it some sort of bondage thing? Anyway, who were they?

She kept circling around the same conclusion. The girl must be Joe's plaything and the kidnappers separated her from Joe to keep them from helping each other escape. That made sense, at least. It meant that the girl was lying when she claimed she didn't know Joe.

Good God, was she covering for Joe? The idea struck her to the quick. If the girl was protecting Joe, either he was a damn good client or their relationship was a lot more than just a passing fling. Deborah's eyes welled up once more at the thought. She wiped the tears away and got hold of herself. She still couldn't be certain that she could believe the girl. Maybe the girl simply said anything she thought would get Deborah to untie her.

At least Deborah hadn't fallen for that. While she questioned the girl aboard *Caesaria*, she'd refused to loosen her bonds. She wanted the bitch to suffer, wanted her to lie naked and cold, wanted her to stay hog-tied.

The girl didn't seem to mind being almost naked. She hadn't particularly complained again about being tied or gagged, for that matter.

The only things she complained about were being tired and cold. Which made you wonder how often the girl found herself naked and hogtied—

The thought didn't bear completing.

By the time Deborah pulled the robbers-and-rescue part of the story out of her, the naked girl was shivering. Which made her even more fetching. Deborah understood for the first time why hard nipples and blushing skin were so irresistible to men.

The girl said a lot of other things that didn't make sense. Like Joe being taken away on a Jet Ski. Pirates rescuing her. Then the pirates taking Joe away and leaving her here, hogtied. Something about a "cheese man," left behind on some other sailboat.

Sitting opposite her back in the cabin of *Caesaria*, Deborah had finally had enough of the girl's stories. She snapped. "If pirates *rescued* you, how come you're tied up?" The girl told another version of the same story, which also didn't make much sense: the pirates had rescued her but then bound and gagged her and abandoned her on the sailboat. She must babble whatever garbage came into her head.

If Deborah was going to find Joe and confront him, this girl's existence was at least irrefutable evidence of his infidelity. She would find Joe and then plunk the girl down right next to him. Not even ask him to explain. She wanted to watch him to stammer and stutter as he searched for an excuse. That's why Deborah had dragged her aboard the *Admiral Byng*. But maybe she provide some helpful information, too. Deborah asked her if she knew where the men had gone.

"They went that way." The girl pointed to starboard.

Deborah hustled her into the cabin of the ugly work boat, started up the engines, and bullied the *Admiral Byng* in that direction.

That had been hours ago. Long, weary hours. Unending vistas of indistinguishable trees and gray water and lowering clouds. The search went on and on, hour after hour, as though it would be the same search forever.

But things had changed for *Admiral Byng* and crew. Now only one of *Admiral Byng*'s occupants remained awake. The girl had fallen asleep on the pile of rags in a corner of the deckhouse. The cloud cover had thickened. The freshening wind for the first time sounded a low hum in the rusting metal superstructure. The lake's ripples had grown ever so slightly more defined, and they betrayed the occasional whitecap.

And *Admiral Byng* now sailed in precisely the wrong direction to find Doorman and David. And directly into trouble.

Chapter Seventeen

In the gray light of the early morning, a rusty old jon boat rounded the point of one of the nameless islands on Lake Lanier. The huddled occupants looked for all the world like an older couple out on an early-morning fishing excursion. An eyewitness would have seen only two black-suited figures paddling silently along the shoreline and presume they were sneaking up on the bass that cruised the shallows in the early morning.

In truth, they had shut down the outboard at the first sight of the sailboat that floated in the cove. From the profiles of their wet suits, a witness might be able to guess that one was male, one female, but balaclava hoods would have frustrated any attempt to identify them.

There were no witnesses, though. The two had made sure of that when they cased the island, the cove, and the sailboat. They were moving carefully, working the operational plan they'd put together after careful research, making no mistakes on this first day of the rest of their lives.

They paddled silently to the sailboat's transom to confirm the boat's name. In the gloom, the letters were only barely visible. The woman, paddling from the front, looked back for confirmation. The man in the back gave a thumbs-up sign. This was it. They tied off the jon boat and crept silently up into the cockpit of their target.

In the cockpit, they paused. The man pointed to his partner, gesturing for her to take up her position on one side of the companionway. He unzipped a waterproof pouch velcroed to the chest of his suit. Out came a large handgun. A quiet snap and slight clatter accompanied his chambering a round. He handed the pistol to his partner. She took it greedily and held it to her chest like a lover. The man could imagine the look of pleasure behind her mask. Even as the girl he'd met all those many years ago, she'd loved guns. Had ever since.

The next stop on the operational plan required a carefully orchestrated dance. They'd practiced it numerous times, on several different types of sailboats, until they got thrown out of the boat show. The man put his hands on the companionway doors and got ready to open them. He looked at his partner to make sure she was ready. She nodded. The man began their carefully rehearsed ballet.

Step one: slam open the doors with as much noise as possible.

Step two: push back the companionway slide as quickly as possible.

Step three: move aside to let his partner move by, to drop into the cabin, screaming her lungs out.

Step four: he followed, bellowing.

As he slid down the ladder—his knees were too creaky to jump—he did his level best to scream, too. They'd read on the internet that SWAT teams used screaming the same effect as a flashbang grenade. It made people freeze. Sometimes, according to their research, it made people freeze for the single second it took to shoot them before they could go for their weapons. So the man tried to scream, feeling like a damn fool because men just didn't scream, and his hesitation rendered his scream more of a bellowed squawk. But what could you do when you couldn't beg, borrow, or steal a flash-bang?

Now: step five. The money shot.

They stood in the cabin, back-to-back, screaming and turning a 360 and scanning for signs of their quarry. The woman fanned her free hand in the air to dissipate fumes that choked her. Her partner only acknowledged the smell of gasoline fumes with a wrinkled nose behind his mask.

A single figure shuffled out of the aft cabin to investigate the noise, clad only in his boxers. His sleepy expression and his tousled hair proved that he'd just woken up. He saw the invaders and stopped short.

He stared. His eyes grew wide. His mouth worked soundlessly. His skin drained of color. His bloodshot eyes rolled back in his head as he managed to utter a few syllables of ancient Anglo-Saxon. He crumpled to the floor, unconscious.

The intruders exchanged a stunned glance.

The woman took two steps toward the body, the gun held out stiffly with two hands. Leaning over the prostrate form, the gunner pressed the muzzle viciously into the mouth of their victim. Her partner cringed: it had to hurt. She had always been willing to dish out the hurt. The form on the floor didn't move.

The male intruder quickly turned and searched the boat to be sure there was nobody else present. As he cleared the other rooms, a sudden fierce drumming made him freeze. He looked around to locate the source of the alien sound. It came from everywhere.

Buddy peered out a porthole and saw that it was raining. More than raining: someone had opened the floodgates of the heavens. Water poured out of the sky with such ferocity that the man couldn't see the shore a few yards away.

Damn. The ride back to shore on that stupid little tin boat would be miserable. At least they could use the motor on the way back, because there'd be no one to hear them. The good news was that there was nobody else who was going to be out on the water in this deluge. Shaking his head at the miserable weather, the man completed his search of the sailboat. There were no other occupants.

He returned to the salon to find his partner standing over the body. She'd done the job, then. The operational plan called for "shoot and go" and apparently she'd shot their target. Now it was time to go.

He frowned, though. Had he heard a shot? He didn't remember hearing one. Not the bang. Not that "ooof" from the victim they both found so amusing in the movies, the one that put them into instant gales of laughter.

But there was an inert body at her feet. Evidence that she had indeed offed him. But damn if he remembered hearing anything.

It wasn't the first time that he'd just sort of missed something important. That's what put them both in the joint the last time. He'd missed a stop sign and the patrol car waiting behind it. Unfortunately, the cop didn't miss the bales of product they were hauling up from Savannah. Time to retire when you start missing things.

Wracking his memory, maybe he did sort of remember the sound of a shot. Possibly he could smell the faintest odor of gunpowder. Or maybe he was just smelling gasoline?

The woman still stood over the body, one arm training the pistol down at the corpse. She looked back at her partner, shrugging, her free hand raised in a gesture that asked, "What now?"

What now? She knew as well as he did. The plan called for first securing the kill, then getting the victim's ID, then disappearing. He tapped his face mask: get his ID. The job paid extra if they could confirm the kill. But her eyes above her mask looked puzzled. She repeated the "What now?" gesture.

They weren't supposed to talk once they started the mission. The operational plan demanded complete silence. They'd promised that to each other. An ironclad rule. If nobody ever heard their voices, then one more clue to their identity would always remain a mystery. Not that anybody but them was going to be available to testify.

Pulling down her mask, she mouthed "Buddy! What do I do?"

What the hell, the leader thought. He's dead. He can't hear anything now. Buddy pulled his mask away from his mouth, too. "Get his ID, Lynette."

The rule of silence, broken, now abandoned them both. "He's not dead!"

"Not dead?" Buddy pointed at the body on the floor. "What's that, then?"

"The pig fainted." Lynette nudged the figure with a booted foot. "He said, 'Oh, fuck, not again!' and fell down."

Not again? Well, that didn't make much sense. Buddy shrugged. "Just tag him and let's get out of here." By now the rain had slackened to a hard downpour. If they left now, they'd get wet but not drowned.

Once Buddy's attention focused on the outside, though, he heard a new sound through the rain. There was thunder off in the distance, but there was another sound, too. Some kind of whining sound from overhead. Almost a roaring sound, maybe even a whining shriek. He'd never heard anything like it.

Lynette dragged his attention back to the challenge at their feet. "I can't just shoot him."

"What? Why not? You begged me to let you be the one to shoot him. Remember?"

"He's out cold!"

"So? Shoot him and he'll be out a lot colder."

"No. I can't."

"Oh, sheesh." Buddy stepped over to the body and reached to snatch the gun from her hand.

"No!" Lynette shouldered him away. "This isn't right. You can't shoot someone who's passed out. Wait until he comes around."

"Maybe he'll come around when he hears the gunshot."

"You're not funny."

Buddy eyed her. "I don't remember you ever having qualms about plugging anyone before." She'd once taken out three guys with three shots. His hands had been buried deep in a briefcase, pulling out packets of cash they'd just been given by their buyers. The three Russians had tried to get the drop on them and take both the dope and the money. Lynette didn't stand still for shenanigans. She stopped that play cold. Cold and dead. Three shots, three dead Ruskies. She could be a tough old bitch when someone tried to take what was rightfully hers.

Now, though, Lynette looked away from the would-be corpse. Tears shined in the corners of her eyes.

"Oh, jeez," Buddy muttered under his breath. The last thing he wanted right now was another one of those *you-don't-respect-me* things. Not here on the job. "Fine. We'll wait for him to wake up before you shoot him. Let's at least find his ID while we're waiting."

"The others took it," quavered a weak voice from the floor.

Both assassins looked down in surprise. "Others?" The words came out of Buddy's mouth before he remembered that his face and his voice were both exposed.

"The ones who took Chastity. They took my wallet."

"Took whose chastity?" asked Lynette.

"Plug him," Buddy demanded, suddenly alarmed that she was getting distracted.

Lynette didn't move. Buddy didn't want to wait. He grabbed the gun from Lynette's hand, ready to plug the guy himself.

"Get up," said Lynette to the victim. "Give me your wallet."

"No wallet." The man climbed laboriously to his feet, wheezing. "No money. The others got it."

"Others." Buddy lifted a disbelieving eyebrow, sighting down the barrel at the man's forehead.

"Well, darn it," Lynette looked around for some other means of ID, confused about who the "others" were. "We have to find something to prove who you were."

"Wait a minute wait a minute wait a minute." The owner had by no means been a grammar genius in seventh grade, but he'd mastered past tense. "What are you going to do with me?"

Buddy moved his aim to a spot right between the man's eyes. "See, there are too many of us to play gin and not enough of us to play spades. I guess we'll have to find other entertainment." He glanced at his partner. "Where do you want him?"

"We need the ID, honey."

"Forget the ID. Where do we leave the body?" Buddy looked around for a place.

"Confirmed ID is worth an additional ten," Lynette reminded him.

She was right. They needed the money: they had lawyer bills, not to mention the payments on the RV. Ten K was still ten K. "Let's do him now and then look for the ID later. Worse comes to worse, we can just cut off the tips of his fingers and take them back with us." Buddy got a truly nasty thought. "We could even bring back all eleven 'tips,' if you know what I mean."

Kaufman could barely pay attention with the overwhelming noise from outside and a new unsteadiness of the floor under their feet. But he was clear on one thing: his time to talk his way out of this fresh hell was running out. "You got the wrong guy. I'm not important enough for anybody to want to kill!"

"Someone thinks you are twenty thousand dollars important, Mr. Doorman." He looked into the forward bedroom, then turned to Lynette. "Let's get Doorman up here. Contain the blood splatter."

"Spatter," Lynette corrected. She read crime novels and knew the lingo.

"Doorman? Who's Doorman? My name's Kaufman."

"Right." Buddy prodded the hostage toward the forward cabin with the gun.

The man moved unwillingly but pleaded with new energy. "No, listen. My name's Kaufman! William Robert Kaufman. My friends call me Billy Bob Kaufman! Nice to meet you." He stuck his hand out for a handshake.

Buddy slapped the hand away with the barrel of the gun. "Shut up and get in there."

"I don't deserve to die!"

"Everybody in your profession deserves to die," remarked Lynette from over Buddy's shoulder. She'd recovered from her funk. A helpless man always brought out her mean side.

"Nothing personal," Buddy assured him. "We got a contract. You know? A contract is a contract. You understand that, right, Mr. Doorman?"

"I'm not Doorman! Look, look," he shrieked, looking wildly around the salon for something with his name on it. "Look at the registration! My name's Kaufman!"

"Yeah, yeah. I get it, Mr. Doorman. It's just too bad for you that you're a middle-aged balding white guy just like we've been hired to kill, and you're on the sailboat named *Caesaria*, just where we expected to find you. Everything's right, but you're the wrong guy. Guess you're just unlucky."

"There's an idea." Lynette interrupted, having slowly processed Kaufman's suggestion. "The boat registration could work for ID." She rummaged around the drawers in the cabin.

While Lynette searched, Buddy herded the captive up and onto the bed in the front cabin. The victim curled up in a fetal position, alternately sobbing and gasping and complaining that they had the wrong guy.

"Head or heart, Mr. Doorman?" asked Buddy.

"What?" the man asked.

Buddy repeated: "Head or heart? Head's quicker. Heart's bloodier, but more romantic."

"Romantic? What do you mean romantic?"

"It's *Hedda Gabler*, stupid. You should take more interest in theater." Buddy's first love.

"Wait." Lynette called, staring at a piece of paper she'd found, then stopped to rub her eyes. "My eyes are all blurry. What did you say the name of Doorman's boat is?"

"*Caesaria.*" Buddy pronounced the unfamiliar name slowly. "*See-zar-ee-yah*. This is the right boat. Listen, mister, just make your choice, OK? We're losing time here. Head or heart?" He stepped forward, prodding the man to move a little farther back in the bed.

"Well, we're OK then," Lynette confirmed. "We got the right boat. Name's right here." She held the registration receipt out for Buddy to look at.

"Something's going right for us after all. Let's do it and get out of here."

"Wait, wait, wait," the victim pleaded. He was nearly insensible with fear. "You said you're looking for *See-zar-ee-yah*. This here's *Käseria*, with a 'k.' You get it? Yours is *See-zar-ee-yah* with a 'see,' mine's *Kay-sar-ee-yah* with with a 'kay,' see? It means 'cheese seller.' That's me."

"Cheese seller," repeated Buddy.

"Tomato, pohtato," Lynette said. "Potato, tomahto."

Kaufman banged himself on the chest. "Cheese seller! That's what I do! My name is Billy Bob Kaufman, and I sell cheese! The boat is named for cheese! You can ask anybody about me. Everybody in North Georgia and eastern Alabama and a few counties in South Carolina knows the Cheese Man."

"Come on. Let's do it!" Buddy demanded, trying to interrupt Lynette's laborious reading of the paper in her hand.

"I'm telling you. I'm Kaufman!" He was sobbing. Buddy started to fear that the man would wet himself.

"It's registered to a William Robert Kaufman," Lynette said.

"Yes, yes, yes!" Kaufman moved to get off the bed.

Buddy snarled to hold him back. He turned his head to see that Lynette was beginning to doubt. That was a bad sign. She had never been able to make a quick decision once she started thinking about it.

The delay was beginning to piss Buddy off. The plan was "shoot and go," not a "sit around and talk about it for a while and then go," or "maybe not go." Damn it, Lynette should know better than to deviate from their plan. Buddy looked wildly around for another way to resolve Lynette's uncertainty.

People wrote their names in their books. He reached at random to snatch a book off the table. It was something about sailing. He flipped open the front cover, looking for a name or an inscription.

Inside the front cover, the book's owner had written: *Billy Bob Kaufman*. Buddy cursed, turned around, and grabbed another book off a shelf. This time he opened one called Compton's, the title something like *Troubleshooting Marine Diesels.* Which was ironic, because trouble shooting was exactly what he and Lynette were faced with.

Inside the front cover: Billy Bob Kaufman again. Buddy threw the book at Kaufman. "This whole thing is totally screwed," he complained.

Lynette wasn't any happier. This was supposed to be easy. They'd been annoyed three days ago to find that their target couldn't be taken out while coming out of the courthouse. Then they got lucky momentarily when a helpful secretary let them know that the target was actually out of town. A friendly woman, she commented that she wished she had the resources to take a week off to go sailing at Lake Lanier. She even mentioned the name of his boat. Good luck at last. Or so it seemed at the time.

By now, by the time they had their quarry held at gunpoint, they were already three days into a one-day job. They'd already had to commit three or four felonies just to get to the target. Now it looked like they wouldn't be moving to the next step in their plan—the one they were getting paid for—any time soon.

Lynette let the paper fall to the floor. "What are we supposed to do now?"

"First we kill him."

"I don't really think that's necessary," Billy Bob put in.

"Wait," said Lynette. She stopped to rub her eyes. "Damn. My eyes are still all blurry."

"First we kill him. Then we go hunt down your idiot son and teach him a lesson."

"Now honey. You know he's doing the best he can. You know what it's like when you first come out. He's found a good company and he thinks he's really gonna be going places with them."

Buddy wasn't going to listen to the mama bear defending her cub. Not now. Not on the job. Enough was enough. Back to the plan: shoot and go. Buddy raised the gun. His finger tightened on the trigger.

A tremendous bang startled them all. It made the Cheese King's body fall backward while his face scrunched up in surprise. It also startled the killers. Then the world exploded around them.

A flash of light sizzled in the air around the boat. Before they could even cry out, a second explosion rocked them. Really rocked them, throwing them physically to the flooring of the salon as an intense flash blinded them. A powerful blow from outside threw the boat down on its beam ends. It was as if the freight train they'd heard roaring all around them had just smashed into them. Now it shook the boat angrily.

The victim, not sure if he'd been shot, had rocketed out of the berth just as the first bolt of lightning hit. As he got to his feet, something violently smacked the sailboat onto its side. The three of them ended up tangled in a writhing heap. They landed on what just seconds ago had been the side of the sailboat cabin but was now a floor. They scrambled, pulling themselves upright, fighting against gravity gone haywire and the fire-hose streams of water pouring in through every open port and hatch.

As the water rose quickly around their feet, each reached the same conclusion.

Käseria was sinking. Fast.

Chapter Eighteen

The pirates had shoved off from the mother ship just before dawn. By now, there was not a single happy soul on the two personal water craft that scoured the islands for prey.

Billy wanted to turn back. He kept insisting that they take Mary Ann and go home. "We done enough." "It ain't safe no more." "I ain't goin' nowhere else." On and on. And on. And on.

Even Blackbeard was losing his enthusiasm for the hustle. It had been successful—they should be celebrating a great haul. What spoiled it for him was his pain-in-the-ass partner. All the guy did was whine when he wasn't throwing a fit. Even if you explained it to him, real nice—like "Shut the fuck up!"—he'd go on and on. His unwillingness to get with the program was minute by minute outweighing their shared history.

And then there was the third member of their party, riding behind Billy. Doorman had joined Billy in complaining nonstop. First, he didn't like being bound and gagged. Now he didn't like being dragged along. "I'm not a pirate." "I decline to accompany you." "You will not make me an accessory." Blah blah blah. So much for wanting to join their happy pirate crew.

Blackbeard had convinced him to come along with two arguments. "If I leave you and Mary Ann together, you'll just help each other get untied and probably call the police. If I take you both, you might start thinking about how even the odds are. That means I got to leave only one of you, and I don't want that girl over there around Billy the Kid. She could get hurt. She could get him hurt. So I got no choice. I mean, instead of tyin' you, I could wrap you up in duct tape like a mummy. Either way, we're not taking her with us."

The second argument was more succinct. "I could leave you both here, but then I'd have to, like, knock you both out with a flashlight or something, to keep you out of trouble. I never had much luck knocking people out. I always end up having to keep hitting them to put them out. It's not as easy as it looks on TV. Lots of noise. Blood everyplace. Not fun for anybody."

The second argument won the day. The girl ended up trussed and gagged and left in the sailboat. Doorman ended up in the company of the pirates as they sped around the lake looking for prey. He sat behind Billy, where he could not get at the gun stuffed in Blackbeard's wet suit top.

Not a boat was to be seen. It was strange. You would have thought everybody had abandoned the lake. The uncertain weather probably discouraged anyone with half a brain from leaving the dock. With good reason. The clouds now billowed down toward the lake surface, dark gray fingers punctuated by intermittent puffs of wind that defied direction. The very atmosphere weighed them down.

Blackbeard felt low. A successful hustle, but it had gotten old. After several hours of searching without finding a single boat to pillage, now he was ready to go home. He would have turned back too, if he hadn't had a point to prove. You had to do what you said you were going to do or people didn't respect you. Even if what you said you were going to do was starting to look hopeless.

In truth, he was cold and chafing and starting to fall asleep. Through the long night, he'd sat up watching Doorman in the salon as Billy and Mary Ann secluded themselves in the v-berth. All night, all he wanted was to lie down and rest his eyes.

"Prize?" Doorman had asked while they sat across from each other in the salon. He had clearly meant the girl.

"Friend." Blackbeard rolled his eyes. They both knew whose. If Doorman wondered why Billy's "friend" had to be hog-tied when they left her, he didn't ask. Which was good, because the big pirate didn't care to explain.

The girl was pure trouble. She changed the whole dynamic of their relationship. Blackbeard didn't quite understand it. Billy treated her almost like a sister. Looked out for her. Protected her. Despite their night together in the V-berth, Blackbeard hadn't heard Billy try anything with her. Even though an electric charge sizzled between them that made Blackbeard itchy.

Blackbeard had spent the night worrying about Doorman, too. Something about him had changed. He'd become withdrawn. As if, with Billy preoccupied, Doorman was weighing his options about taking a chance at fighting. The big pirate comforted himself with the conviction that two against one was still pretty good odds for the pirates, even with the damn girl getting in the way.

Now, in the cold morning air—cold even though it was closing in on noon—the big pirate blew on his hands, one at a time as he drove. He was cold. The wet suit chafed at his armpits and thighs. Billy—and the girl, and now Doorman—had all stomped on his last nerve.

He'd hoped for a great last day, but the dark clouds and the increasing wind sucked the fun right out of it. He'd had enough. It was time to call it a day. Get back to the boat, gather up their take, tie up Doorman and maybe the girl too, radio the police to come get them and split. If Billy kicked about leaving the girl, maybe leave him behind with her. Hell, tie them up together if they liked each other's company so damn much.

He zoomed over to Billy to tell him his decision. The little pirate and the Captain didn't have anything to say for a change. They turned their boats in tandem and sped back for *Caesaria*. Just as they turned, the clouds let loose with rain as cold and as hard as hail.

***

Back on *Caesaria*, the three men stood in the salon, dripping rain. What they saw left them all dumbfounded. The settee, where Mary Ann should have been, was empty. The ropes that bound her were neatly coiled in her place.

Doorman broke the silence. "Looks like you been robbed." Anything that threw his captors off their game was a good thing. And if the girl escaped—or had been rescued—then the cavalry would soon be on the way.

But he was also perplexed. The lines used to bind her were not just discarded in haste but flemished carefully into pretty coils. It was the kind of thing an experienced sailor might have done without thinking. The girl wouldn't have. Even David wouldn't have. Only an experienced sailor acting out of habit would do that.

David might have managed to find the boat and climb aboard again. The thought relieved a tension that had settled itself on his brow for days. But it didn't make sense. David certainly would have untied her if he'd found her trussed up. But afterwards, why would he disappear again? And why take the girl with him when he went? And would he pause to carefully coil up the ropes?

The flemished lines called to mind Deborah's delight in producing a perfect, flat coil of rope. But it couldn't have been Deborah. What would she be doing at the lake? How would she have found the boat? Why would she have taken the girl and left? There were scenarios that might lead to a missing girl and flemished ropes, but they were too unlikely to credit. Maybe Deborah had reacted to the hang-up call by calling the police, who barged into the boat and found the girl. Or David had managed to reach shore and get to the police, who found the boat and rescued the girl. It might be possible that a passerby boarded the boat, saved the girl and took her to find help. The tidied cabin argued against any of those possibilities. David or a passerby wouldn't have stopped to straighten up. Any law enforcement officer would have tossed the boat looking for evidence.

There was one other possibility. It made his blood run cold. What if the pirates were not the rumored contract killers after all? What if the rumors were true and the real killers, really hunting him, had found the girl and taken her? Doorman looked again at the neatness that surrounded him. He doubted hired killers would tidy the lines. Downright unlikely that they'd do so in the manner of experienced mariners. Or that they would clean up the cabin after barging in. If they were going to make the girl disappear, why not get rid of the ropes, too?

His thoughts returned to David. If it was David, that would mean that David was safe, able to move around freely, and maybe on his way to find help.

Another question made him flush. If David had found the nearly naked girl tied up where he'd left his father, what would he think?

***

The pirates, meanwhile, resumed their on-again, off-again argument about abandoning their spree. The words that Blackbeard used were not polite. In any case, they were hardly discernible over Billy's exhibition. The guy was in total meltdown: he hopped from one foot to the other, babbling, slapping himself repeatedly and acting crazier than usual.

Blackbeard understood the reaction. He himself was totally pissed at the girl going missing. He'd wanted to keep her away from Billy, but didn't want to lose her. She could be anywhere, doing anything. Like calling the police. Putting a posse together. Whatever.

Not that he had anybody else to blame for her disappearance. He'd tied her up himself because he didn't want to tempt Billy to make it easy for her to get loose. If she'd worked herself loose, it had to be his own fault. Unless maybe Billy had managed to loosen her bonds as they'd left the boat.

"Well," Blackbeard said when Billy's tantrum had blown itself out. "What else could possibly go wrong?"

The answer exploded right over their heads.

Chapter Nineteen

The first thunderclap slapped Deborah Doorman awake. Her eyes snapped open onto an eerie gray-green light coming through the plate glass window. She must've been asleep on her feet. For how long? The light looked like sunset already. Had she been out for hours?

But no, it couldn't be. She'd seen the sunrise only a few hours ago. But that timing hardly seemed possible. It had already been a long, exhausting day. She'd seen the sunrise reflected in the lake water, searched the lake for *Caesaria* for hours, found her husband's little play-toy, and had now searched for hours for the PWCs the little slut claimed to have kidnapped her husband. The bastard. She looked at her watch to confirm that she'd actually done all of this before noon. Most of the day was still to come.

She looked back at the play-toy. All morning the Princess had lain motionless, curled into a little ball against the back wall of the shack. The echoing explosion of the first lightning strike had awakened Her Highness, too. Now she sat rigidly straight, shivering, her eyes wide with fear, her mouth working silently.

A second thunderbolt startled them both. It also awakened an animal spirit in *Admiral Byng*. The barge leapt into a frantic dance that was distinctly unseemly in an old barge. The entire vessel capered.

The wheel twisted in Deborah's hands. The doors to the pilothouse banged open and shut, as though a demon was running in one side door and out the other. Repeatedly.

A demon's wail accompanied the assault of wind and rain, a wail so loud that it drowned out the keening of the girl. She'd scrambled into a bucking corner of the shack and covered herself with the oily scraps piled there. Deborah saw her eyes rolling wildly like a psych patient as her face contorted in a bestial shriek. The storm blotted out whatever sound she made.

Deborah had never heard this volume of sound before, but she recognized it from its weaker cousins. Wind. So much wind that it could only be described in terms of weight, not speed. The weight of the wind pushed the barge around like a leaf in a whirlpool. Tons and tons of wind moaned and screamed in the barge's rusting superstructure and beat the normally placid lake into whitecaps that rocked even the ponderous *Admiral Byng*. The wind slapped *Admiral Byng*'s head around until the barge presented its broad side to the storm's full force. The barge listed dangerously under the force, threatening to turn turtle.

She didn't know what to do. She'd never even conned *Caesaria* in storm conditions. She was proud of herself for having gotten the hang of it so far, but now, whatever expertise she'd gained evaporated. The ugly craft had moment by moment become more and more unmanageable.

There must be something she could do to get control, something Joe would know. With her mind slow and woolly from the night's search, Deborah couldn't come up with a single solution, even a bad one. The gusts of wind shaking the barge's superstructure made it impossible to think.

The wind brutally pummeled the cabin. It shook the walls. It flexed the window in front of her so that the flat pane of thin glass in the makeshift windshield flexed like plastic. It pumped the roof over her head up and down as though preparing to tear it off.

Looking out onto the lake was no less frightening. The sky's lowering black clouds gave off a distinctly yellow cast. Real waves—big four- or five-foot white-capped giants blown by a howling wind down the full expanse of the lake—marched across the lake. Marching down at *Admiral Byng* like an army on the attack.

The waves' endless ranks joined forces with the wind to assault the port-side pontoon. They rocked the barge from side to side. It was hard for Deborah to keep her feet. Somehow, she knew that the barge was about to capsize. She knew she had better find a life jacket before the boat sank. She couldn't without letting go of the steering wheel, and it was the only thing keeping her from getting thrown around the cabin.

A moment of blankness. When Deborah came out of the moment's stupor, she realized she'd been out on her feet. How long had she been out this time? Enough time that the barge had taken on a new motion. When its windward pontoon lifted on a wave, the boat paused before unwillingly crashing back down into the water. Deborah understood—God knew from what insight—that it meant the wind was getting under the boat. The right combination of wind and waves would flip *Admiral Byng* right over.

She took it in dispassionately: a problem to be solved. She needed to do something to keep the barge from flipping. Something, but what? Turn into the wind. The thought came as clearly as if it had been spoken aloud by someone. Someone like Joe. That bastard.

Deborah pushed the throttles of both motors up slowly, afraid that a fast movement might increase the instability already rocking the deck below her. A quarter throttle had no effect. Half throttle had no effect. At three-quarter throttle she could feel the vibration of the laboring motors, but turning the wheel and giving the motors more power had no effect. She jammed both throttles full forward. No effect.

Something from the Power Squadron course tickled her memory. Joe had insisted that they all go to the course together before anyone could take the wheel or touch a throttle. Deborah hadn't expected to learn anything from it, but now she remembered one tidbit. She pulled the lever for the port engine into reverse, leaving the other full forward. For a moment, there was no response.

The boat's yawing steadied. Suddenly it decreased. And just as suddenly, the barge began pitching. The word came to her unbidden from their Power Squadron homework. She'd memorized the unfamiliar words: yawing versus pitching versus rolling. Yawing: moving side to side horizontally. Rolling: oscillating side to side vertically. Pitching: what the barge was doing now, hobby-horsing fore and aft, its bow climbing the waves and then diving into the troughs. Deborah felt sick with alarm at the new motion, until she saw that the bow was coming around. Turning slowly, turning grudgingly, pitching with nausea-inducing abruptness, but by God, turning, turning, turning into the wind.

Slowly: so slowly that Deborah found herself twisting her body in an effort to will the boat's head around. Finally, with the help of a slight lull in the wall of wind, Admiral *Byng* turned. Deborah pushed both throttles full forward against their stops.

It wasn't so much that Deborah's maneuver had worked, she realized, as that the wind had momentarily lulled. She muttered a heartfelt thanks to whichever gods were in charge. The barge surged forward in the blessed calm. The waves did not recede as quickly as the wind, however. They still battered the barge. Relieved of the overpowering burden of the wind, though, the ungainly craft smashed into them joyfully.

Deborah breathed a sigh of relief. She throttled back to stop the jarring and sank down into the chair behind the wheel. The helmsman's seat—a mechanic's shop stool screwed with shelf brackets into the steel deck—still pitched and yawed wildly. She clung to the seat, nursing the hope that the lake would quickly calm as the waves receded. That was the way storms on the lake always blew themselves out.

At that moment, with the pleasant thought barely thought, the wind slammed into *Admiral Byng* again. It no longer blew directly over the bow: it hit from the beam. The abrupt change startled Deborah. The direction was impossible: she'd had the wind coming at her from the side but turned into it. It couldn't still be from her side. Unless—

She did not have time to finish the thought. The barge rocked under a violent assault, rolling and twisting like a thing tortured. Once again, the wind screamed around the pilothouse's sharp corners and tore at the boat's steel structures.

Deborah groaned. Again! But she'd handled it once; she could do it again. She stood tall, starting to execute the same maneuver once more. Heavier now than it had been before, the wind didn't sigh any more, or even whine: it roared, the sound deafening. Deborah noticed the walls around her bowing inward. Panic, long suppressed within her, flickered into flame. Frantically, she worked the throttles and the wheel to turn the barge into the wind again.

The *Admiral Byng* turned even less enthusiastically than before. It turned, at best, a quarter of the way into the teeth of the storm, even with one engine again in full reverse and the other in full forward. The engines ran her crabwise, slowly crawling across the teeth of the storm as it reached its own compromise between Deborah's direction and the storm's muscle. Her sailor's instinct told her that the old junk pile was again right on the verge of broaching. It was all too easy to imagine the barge flipping up and over, cartwheeling across the lake like a blown-up pool toy.

Instead, the force of the storm and the efforts of the motors found a tentative balance. The barge settled into a rhythm, nearly regular, almost predictable, still terrifying. It gave Deborah a moment to catch her breath. The conditions made her heart race and her skin clammy, but having fought two bouts with the wind and survived, she still felt no panic.

Now that the motion became familiar, she had room to think. First: safety. A life jacket. If ever there had been a time to put one on, it was now. She saw a pile of them thrown in a corner, cushioning a pile of grease-stained equipment. They would have to wait until the storm gave her a break to leave the wheel.

Next: the radio. It had made not the slightest noise throughout the long night. Did it work? Did it matter? It wasn't like she needed a weather report. Still, she turned the radio off and on, hoping to prod it to life. Still no sound.

Safe harbor: the next goal. She picked the sodden scrap of map from the floor. Her last penciled position was at 7:30 AM, shortly after what should have been sunrise. Hours ago. Her course at that point had been southerly. In the first squall, she'd turned to starboard, which would be mostly west. After the storm hit, she'd neglected to keep a plot. After all of the noise and motion and confusion, it was hard to puzzle out where they'd been or where they might be now or even what direction they were going.

Deborah shrugged and flung the map away. It hardly mattered where she was. The wind allowed only one direction. The best course she could manage was...well, that way, whatever way the wind was coming from. She guessed it was north, since she remembered someone saying that most storms came from the north.

North, then. Away from safety. As directly as *Admiral Byng* would go, anyway. It would take her directly into the teeth of the storm and leave her equally far from safety in each direction. No nearer to shelter, but at least not any farther away either. If she could just fight her way to someplace near land, there might be a chance to duck into a protected cove.

Admiral Byng bashed her way through the waves. The thunder and lightning had not stopped for a minute, and still kept up a continual warfare only feet above their heads. Minute by minute, the waves seemed bigger. In oceangoing terms, these waves were probably small. Deborah, though, had only sailed lakes—only this lake, actually—and the waves were unlike anything she'd ever seen. Probably bigger too than the barge had been built for. She wrestled her mind away from what that might mean.

Her attention wavered for a moment. The barge immediately veered off the wind. She hurriedly forced it back on course. If the barge turned its side to the wind, she might not be able to get it back. The boat might flip. The image returned: the barge cartwheeling across the lake, spewing junk and passengers as it went.

She could barely keep her eyes open now. Nothing kept her eyes from closing, not even the constant flickering of lightning, the howling wind, the continual drumbeat of thunder, the threat of drowning. She tried to count the hours since she'd last slept but didn't even know what day or what time it was. Hour after hour had passed, every one of those hours filled with no sleep and with growing worry as she searched from island to island and cove after cove, looking for her sailboat and her family. Finding nobody.

Nobody but that worthless girl. Deborah glanced back over her shoulder. That worthless whore, the destroyer of her marriage, was still with her. The girl had curled up again in the corner behind Deborah under the oily pile of rags on the cabin floor. She'd screwed her eyes tightly closed. She might have either died from exposure or passed out.

Deborah suddenly felt ashamed of herself. She'd judged the girl too harshly. The girl looked like nothing so much as an innocent child curled up in bed. Not that she was innocent by any meaning of the word, but she'd done nothing to deserve being dragged into this. The poor thing could probably tell a story of childhood polluted by child abuse, poverty, sexual assault, all leading irrevocably to ending up trussed on a stranger's sailboat naked, the plaything of middle-aged m en.

Hateful, all of them. Joe's sex toy (that bastard). Joe and his friends' sex toy (each of them bastards, whoever they were). The girl, innocent and tragic as her life might be, but still the perfect symbol of Deborah's family's dissolution. Sympathy or no, there was no excuse for what any of them had done.

Deborah's eyes narrowed to steely slits as she considered excuses. The girl wasn't without guilt, however tragic her life. She'd been a willing participant in whatever trysts went on. She deserved no sympathy. She must have been aware of what she was doing to innocent women's marriages when she entertained married men. And she had to know what it would do to expose an impressionable young boy to that kind of conduct. Joe's participation was inexcusable, but what the girl must have showed David was evil. Right now, Deborah would gladly pitch the little bitch overboard. If nothing else, as a sacrifice to Poseidon in trade for bringing her son safely back to her. He was all that was left of her family now.

Her eyelids fluttered with fatigue and her attention wandered and she mused about this day. Today had unexpectedly become the last day of her marriage. It had been crazy to drive all the way out here from Atlanta to try to search by herself. Finding *Caesaria* on this huge lake was never going to be anything more than finding a needle in a haystack. Yet last night—no, the night before last?—she'd motored all night, manhandling *Admiral Byng*, peering into every dark corner. All night on that first night on the lake, she'd gone on alone, searching and worrying and dreading the awful accidents that might have happened to David and Joe. Fire? Sinking? Medical emergency?

But this? She could never have imagined this. This creature, the icon of what had happened to her marriage before she ever even knew anything was happening. And now, on top of that turmoil, the nightmare of fighting this unimaginable maelstrom.

Anger forced her eyes open. That her eyes had once again closed without her realizing it shocked her. She could have killed them both. The wind still buffeted the barge from dead ahead. Thank God she hadn't fallen off her course. The storm brutally reminded her of her duty with a particularly hard gust that rattled the deckhouse and reached a new octave in its whining.

Keeping the barge headed into the wind took all of her strength and what little concentration she had left. Thoughts flashed through her mind and disappeared like the lightning outside the cabin. Like the thought that she was sorry for ever thinking that powerboats must be easy to handle.

She ought to be proud of herself, though. Never having driven a powerboat, she'd done OK. For hours she'd wrestled the wheel, adjusting second by second to the shifting wind and battering waves. Her hands moved constantly on the throttles as if she were an expert. By now she'd even stopped peering out the window in front of her. She didn't have to look to see what she was facing. It didn't matter what was happening outside the window. The only thing that mattered was the fact that she was captive to the storm and the course it forced onto her. So, like an experienced mariner, she stood at her station and steered, playing the throttles and wheel for the best effect.

She dreamed with her eyes open. Once, she dreamed of a dark shape looming to leeward. Another boat? No, an illusion. Deborah knew that when she looked again, it would be gone.

She looked again. It wasn't gone. Looked away. Looked back: it was still there. It must be a boat. A big boat. They were saved!

Or was it too big to be a boat? Maybe it was an island. She stared at it in the weird green light and in the blinding lightning. It stayed there. It was real. It must be an island.

"We're saved!" Deborah called to the girl. When her passenger didn't move, she snapped: "Get up!"

She couldn't see the looming form clearly. It was still too dark, and there was too much rain and spindrift in the air to see very well. If it was an island, it would have a leeward side that would offer some protection from the wind. She didn't even bother to hope for a protected cove. Even a wind shadow would provide relief from the battering. All she would have to do would be to wrestle *Admiral Byng* behind the island.

Deborah used all of her strength and all of her weight to haul the wheel around to point the bow toward the island. It shocked her when the barge turned lithely at her command. Turned on a dime, Deborah thought wonderingly. What did she do right this time that she hadn't done before?

Then suddenly the barge stopped turning. It seemed to stop moving. That was impossible: it was driven by two large outboard motors, deadly waves, the remnant of the wind. As if summoned by her thought, the wind renewed its force, battering *Admiral Byng* once more, shoving the barge up into the air and smashing it back down on the merciless waves. The wheel no longer had the slightest effect. Nor did the engines.

Admiral Byng felt pinned in place, but not immobile by any means. The vessel yawed and pitched and rolled, just as before. The motions felt different though. The rolling felt agonized, with a terrible hesitation at each end of the roll. Each time the starboard pontoon came out of the water, the boat hovered for an interminable second. The boat seemed to be hesitating between the choice of continuing up and over or to settling back into the water. She couldn't decipher the motion. She wished Joe were here to interpret it. That bastard.

She heard a new sound, too. Or perhaps she felt it more than heard it. Each time the port pontoon crashed down, a metallic gong rang out. In the maelstrom, she shouldn't be able to hear a gong. But there it was, resonating through the entire steel structure.

It was not the kind of sound a fiberglass sailboat made. It was not the sound of wind or waves. It was the sound of metal slamming into metal: deck plates hammering pontoons, pontoons hammering whatever other structures held the boat together. But wasn't all this metal welded together? It couldn't be coming apart. Then Deborah recalled her last sight of the disheveled owner and his command to "kick it." Staring dumbly at the sky like a turkey in a thunderstorm. She wondered now if the dumb cluck even knew how to weld.

It took her long moments before she pierced her own stupor to realize what the sound meant. Something in the structure must be badly broken. If the parts separated, if a pontoon came off, if the deck plates separated, if anything separated from anything else, they'd sink like a stone. She and the girl would be pitched into the cauldron. They'd both drown.

At least, Deborah realized, the storm had finally given her a chance to leave the wheel. She pushed herself away from the steering station to scrabble for a life jacket in the pile of life jackets the girl was sleeping on. Sacrificing the girl to Poseidon would have to wait. Shoving the catatonic girl bodily aside, she picked through the pile.

The stack of life jackets, like everything else on *Admiral Byng*, turned out to be a pile of scraps. She clawed through them, throwing pieces this way and that. Finally, she found one that looked whole. Strapless, but whole. She slung it over her neck like a stole. Another proved slightly more intact. She put it around the girl's neck.

Deborah climbed up the pitching deck toward the wheel, fell, scrambled to her feet. A glance out the window told her that the island had receded back into the clouds of rain. Deborah ponderously reasoned it out. It occurred to her that the wind and waves were so strong that they might have bodily lifted up the island—

No. That was ridiculous. *Admiral Byng* must still be mobile. Not pinned, then; stalled by the wind.

Full pressure on both throttles produced only more violent pitching, rolling, and yawing. No change in heading. Reversing one motor only seemed to make the motion worse. The barge might have headed a few degrees more toward the wind, but nothing Deborah tried would get it farther. The wind was pushing *Admiral Byng* around the lake any way it wanted. Nothing Deborah did could stop it. And it didn't matter anymore. She could only do what the storm would let her do, only go in the only direction the wind allowed, until she hit some kind of land.

"Hit is right," Deborah said out loud. She sighed loudly, a sound that if it could have been heard over the screaming storm, might have been a sob. Then she wiped her nose and her eyes with the back of her hand. Until that moment, she hadn't been aware she was crying. Then she began laughing. She didn't know what was funny. A look out the front window sobered her quickly. She saw nothing clearly beyond the bows other than the nearest row of waves smashing into the barge. Beyond that, all was water: water crashing down from the sky, water blown on the wind, angry water surging up from the lake.

Thunder boomed. Huge, reverberating, continuous. Lightning flickered in the boiling clouds, punctuated by occasional crackling strikes that blinded her. When bolts struck around her, they illuminated nothing but killer waves everywhere. The waves and the wind together shoved the barge's high, flat sides leeward at every opportunity.

The storm and Deborah fought for control. The engines strained at all ahead full, but still *Admiral Byng* made no headway. Deborah fought to get the boat under control. Vibrations in the wheel told her that something bad was happening with the steering. With the motors, too: through the throttles, she felt a rattling vibration that might signal that the engines were straining. If they quit under the strain...

Deborah felt herself laughing, the sound lost in the noise around her. If the engines quit, well, she'd just have to go back to the bucking stern and kick the engines. Kick the shit out of them. She giggled, wiped her eyes and her nose.

Deborah and the barge fought the storm while she searched the roiling water frantically for salvation. None could be seen. She might have been in the center of the Southern Ocean, as Joe would say, running for her life. Except, Deborah reminded herself again, here there was land all around her. Not saving land, either: menacing land, fatal land. If *Admiral Byng* crashed into land, Deborah was not sure she could get out of the wreck before it sank, and if she got out, she was not sure she would be able to swim in the churning waves. Never mind dragging the helpless girl with her. Yet land was the only hope.

She found herself chanting. "Give me land," she begged. "Give me land." Then, when the repeated words had become more a habit than a solicitation, a maritime god with a mean sense of humor granted her entreaty.

Violently.

***

Once upon a time there had been a high hill standing sentinel over a pretty valley. Once, before the Army Corps of Engineers dammed the stream running through the valley and rising waters covered the hill. Now the hill remained as nothing more than a narrow spine of rock sticking up from the valley floor almost to the surface of the water. It was just one of many reefs that the lake's boaters knew to avoid. This reef's obstruction warning, a yard-tall white cylinder, had long since blown away. Even if Deborah Doorman had seen the marker buoy through the sheets of rain, she would not have been able to steer *Admiral Byng* to avoid the reef.

Admiral Byng found the reef all by itself. The barge celebrated the occasion with a spine-numbing collision of metal and rock. The port side of the barge ground to a sudden halt on a spine of rock while the starboard side continued on, swinging downwind. The boat's movements described what could only be called a doughnut turn, pirouetting delicately on one broken foot. With a wrenching rasp, the second pontoon ground up onto the rock. The barge's stern settled at first, the waves washing over the engines and the deck and forward into the deckhouse. The deck reared up under the pressure of the waves and wind. The barge screamed as both forces pushed the *Admiral Byng* farther aground.

The disaster wiped Deborah's mind clean. She yelled out to warn the girl. She stuttered, unable to remember the girl's name–unable to think of anything but the barge dying around them.

She shouted, not even able to hear her own voice over the shriek of wind and waves and metal. "Girl! Girl! Get up, girl!" Her passenger opened her eyes, turned her head toward Deborah, but did not move. Deborah could not think what she would have told the girl to do.

The wind seemed to have been waiting for its prey to stumble. Now it grabbed the stricken boat with all its claws and shook it to death. Wind wrenched the hull and tore into the ugly boat's body. Waves pounded at the stranded hull. The water assaulted the battered aluminum hulls and ground them against the reef. The storm wrapped its fingers around every opening and every crack and pried at the deckhouse. Together, they wrenched part of the starboard pontoon free from the deck plates, caused the derrick's supports to snap and crash overboard, and shook the deckhouse free from most of its fastenings.

The shaking threw Deborah onto the deck. She lay on her back, her mouth open in shock as the storm meticulously stripped the poor ugly boat of its features. Over her head, the roof fluttered up into the wind as if readying itself to take flight. A burst of wind took out the front window, breaking it open and whisking the shards away like a puff of smoke. The walls of the cabin house flexed in and out as though they were cardboard also preparing to depart. The deck pounded up and down into Deborah's back. The screech of tortured metal accompanied each dive into the waves' troughs. She saw that every part of the structure would soon be torn away.

Deborah lay where the collision had thrown her. She could not believe what she was seeing. A brief thought about the girl floated through her consciousness and blew away in the roar of the wind. Then the recognition that she'd never get her deposit back now.

She couldn't summon the will to move. Nor the desire to try. It wouldn't matter, anyway. She'd never survive in those waves, and if one of those pieces of flying metal hit her...

It was the waves lapping at her back that got her attention. She rolled onto her knees and groped for the radio. "Mayday, mayday, mayday," she called. She could not hear her own voice over the screaming of wood and metal tortured by the storm. "Mayday, mayday, mayday." She remembered her radio etiquette. "Motor Vessel *Admiral Byng* aground and sinking. Position unknown. Mayday, mayday, mayday." She repeated the call and paused as she'd been taught, to allow a response.

The only response was static. Deborah clawed her way up the grinding deck plates to put her ear to the radio. She turned the volume up as far as it would go. There was nothing but static.

She called and called again, listened and listened again. The barge sank lower and the water rose over the deck. It rose up past her knees, up past her thighs. She called again and again as the wind tore pieces off the *Admiral Byng* and whirled them away into the darkness. Again and again she called and waited and watched as the storm dismembered what had so recently been a utility boat.

She called and called until long after the action was any more than a reflex. Right up to the point that the *Admiral Byng* was no more.

Chapter Twenty

Aboard the bucking, groaning, twisting *Käseria*, Lynette and Buddy clawed their way out of their entanglement with the Cheese Man. The first onslaught of the storm had thrown them all together. Now the killers scrambled frantically around the boat, closing the windows and hatches that were immediately at hand. Yet the water still rose around their legs. They looked wildly for other windows and doors and hatches, filled with terror as the boat lurched and kicked around them. The sounds of the creaking hull and the wailing rigging drilled right into their bones, sending involuntary shudders through their limbs.

Lynette screamed: "We're going to sink! We're all going to die!"

Only Kaufman stayed where he was, prostrate on the floor.

Buddy looked to Kaufman for help. The Cheese Man was sitting motionless on what had been a cabin wall and was now a tossing floor. Buddy kicked him. "Get up here and help, mister."

Kaufman crossed his arms over his chest and closed his eyes. "You're the ones in charge. You guys can figure it out."

Buddy looked at their quarry. This was supposed to be a simple little job, but it was getting messed up beyond belief. And it irked him the way that their victim wouldn't jump to help him and Lynette shut off the torrents of water. It was just inconsiderate. Well, OK, you could understand his point of view, all things considered. Still, c'mon. There were common decencies. "You gonna just sit there and let us all drown?"

"Better than getting shot."

Lynette cried out, staring wildly around her at all the things floating in the churning water rising up past her ankles. She chanted mindlessly under her breath: "Not good not good not good." Buddy was ready to shoot her, too. She always had a stupid comment when you were in trouble. Like yelling "Watch out!" after you'd already fallen. Like pointing out that it was not good that the boat was going to sink. Like repeating, "Not good, not good, not good" when they were on a sinking ship.

Buddy bellowed over the noise. "You're gonna let this boat sink. That right?"

"That's right," Kaufman yelled back. "It'll be a bonus for whoever hired you! Three for the price of one!"

Buddy kicked him a few times out of frustration. What else could you do with someone so irrational? Lynette added a few kicks of her own. Her efforts were ineffectual and probably counterproductive. They didn't want to hurt the only one who could save them. But at least while she was kicking, she stopped repeating the obvious.

Meanwhile, the boat rocked and bucked like a carnival ride from hell. The wind tore at the hull; the waves smashed into the boat with body blows; the water visible just outside the portholes churned unspeakably. The water already inside the boat sloshed ankle-deep, even if you climbed up on the seat backs that had now become the floor. Who-knew-how-much poured in every minute.

Buddy couldn't believe the moron wouldn't help. It was his boat! If it sank, it would drown him, too. What was he trying to do? Be the heroic captain who went down with the ship?

Well, fuck that. And fuck him.

Buddy reached up for the porthole over his head. It was designed to be on the side of the cabin, but now that the side was the floor, the porthole overhead was more like a sunroof. Buddy pulled it open and a cascade of cold water pulsed in, right down on Kaufman's head.

Lynette stared at her partner, aghast. Then she got it. She reached overhead to open another porthole. Another torrent of water poured in.

Kaufman shook himself and looked up. "Better shut that."

Buddy answered him with a stream of one-syllable words, of which the only really polite one was "Nope."

Kaufman pulled himself to his feet and reached up for the porthole. Buddy knocked him back with a vicious slap.

Lynette kicked their hostage a few times more as the Cheese King scrambled to his feet and then wrestled through the killers to get to the porthole. Buddy grabbed him from behind and held him back. Lynette moved in, slapping him as best as she was able in the wildly pitching boat. Buddy let her work off her fury for a few moments. When he figured the guy had probably had enough and that Lynette was calmer for having worked off some energy, he pulled their hostage out of Lynette's reach.

"You gonna save this boat?"

"You're just going to kill me."

Lynette and Buddy exchanged a look. Lynette said slowly, "We...might...not...," all the time staring at Buddy, trying to decipher his intentions.

"'Might not' don't cut it," Kaufman snapped. "If I'm gonna die, so are you. You're going down with this boat. You're going to drown. The fish are going to come eat your eyeballs."

Lynette shuddered. Ever the salesman, always attuned to the "tells" of the buyer, Kaufman caught it and twisted the knife. "They're going to wiggle up inside your girl parts and eat their way up to your heart." Lynette cried out and clutched her abdomen. "They're going to nibble them away. Nibble nibble nibble, little bit by little bit, until you're just a hollow shell. Unless I save this boat. And I'm not saving this boat unless we have a deal."

The horrific vision of the future that he'd planted in Lynette's imagination shocked her into silence. Kaufman turned to Buddy. "You let me live. I let you live. Fair trade."

Buddy hated compromise. It'd been his downfall as a theatrical producer: he refused to compromise with anybody. Not backers, not producers, not directors, not venue owners, not stars, and never a diva like this Kaufman guy. It wasn't a good sign that their target had suddenly developed a backbone. His resistance would make finishing the job just that much more difficult. Why not just blow his sorry ass away right now and swim for it?

A glance out at the lake told him why not. They might be able to swim in rain, but the waves had grown huge now. The wind whipped them into a froth. Between the rain and the waves and the freaking lightning, they'd never make it to shore. As much as Buddy hated giving in, he hated the thought of drowning more. One way or the other, eventually, he'd put down Doorman, or Kaufman, or whoever he was. Right now, Buddy'd have to lie to him to make him cooperate. That had always been his strength as a theatrical producer: little white lies that weren't going to hurt anyone but would make things go smoother. Well, wouldn't hurt him and Lynette, anyway.

"All right." Buddy let go of the hostage.

Kaufman tumbled into the water swirling around the cabin. He scrambled to his feet, eager to exploit a sliver of hope. "I didn't hear any promises."

"I promise." Buddy crossed his heart with his fingers. I promise to kill your sorry ass. I promise to make you suffer. I promise you will live to die another day.

"Give me the gun."

Buddy stared. This wasn't part of the deal. No way in hell.

Wait, though. What was the big deal? Even if the guy had the gun, they still outnumbered him. And Kaufman probably didn't have the *cojones* to use the gun. Most people didn't.

Anyway, right now, Buddy didn't see that he had much choice. Kaufman was the only one who could save them. And Kaufman's price was the gun.

Buddy handed it over. Kaufman stuck the gun in his waistband and motioned Buddy to close the overhead hatch. He directed Lynette forward to the other hatches. Buddy eyed the pistol, thinking he should snatch it back. But no sense in provoking the crazy man until they were safe. If he waited, maybe Cheese Man would shoot his tiny little manhood off by accident.

"Now we gotta get this thing upright." Kaufman pushed past them to pull foul weather gear out of a locker that was more like a basement door. He quickly opened and closed the locker before they could see that he wasn't giving them the extra foul weather gear stored there. The Cheese King wanted them wet and miserable. He started up the twisting companionway stairs. "Let's go save this boat."

Buddy and Lynette shared a look of horror at the idea.

Kaufman opened the hatch doors and loosed yet another torrent of water into the cabin. He pushed the killers through the stream and followed them as they clambered topsides. Kaufman shut the companionway doors behind them and slid behind the killers, noticing that a lull in the wind had allowed *Käseria* to swing part way upright.

The fresh air soothed the back of his throat, even if it was more cold water than air. Kaufman realized his throat was as raw as if it had been burned. The killers' complaints about foul air in the cabin might've been right. Maybe there actually were gas fumes down below. Maybe he'd been breathing polluted air for so long he couldn't smell it anymore.

He turned to business: starting up the motor, getting turned into the wind, raising the anchors. He started up the motor and ordered Buddy to the forward deck. "Get forward and untie the anchor." Kaufman turned to Lynette, pointing vaguely to the boom. "Go up there and get the sail cover off."

Lynette looked at the top of the cabin. It was an easy climb. Except when the boat under her feet was rolling more than 45-degrees and twisting all around as it bounced up and down. All of the rigging streamed with rainwater. As did the deck. There were no dry handholds to be seen.

No way. She shook her head. Not doing it.

Suddenly the boat rolled back level and swung into the wind. Before they could adjust to the new attitude, it rolled on its side, then came back upright yet again. It started drifting backward on the wind, back toward the beach behind them. Buddy crawled and scratched his way back to the cockpit, then fell into the cockpit. His hands were bloody where the anchor line had torn his fingernails away. "It's gone," he panted.

"Get up there and get the sail cover off!" Kaufman repeated to Lynette as he gunned the engine to get the boat moving against the wind.

Lynette looked back at the cabin top, licking her lips nervously. With the anchor gone, the boat was only heeling about 30 degrees. They could do it together. She grabbed at Buddy's wet suit top to get his attention.

She clambered up, followed by Buddy. The gale battered them as they climbed. They clawed at the sail cover, pawed at the clasps, tried to find a zipper or some familiar piece of hardware to remove the sail cover. Their efforts had no effect.

In the cold, Buddy was barely able to use his fingers. Lynette was completely incompetent with anything mechanical at the best of times, even something as simple as the twist clasps that closed the sail covers. They grasped and clawed and scrabbled and tried to hold on to the slippery fiberglass and aluminum while fiddling with the unfamiliar clasps. Nothing they did worked.

They failed so completely that they saved their own lives and Kaufman's. What Billy Bob Kaufman had ordered was the one thing that no sailor would ever do in a storm. That was because the Cheese King, like many owners of luxury sailboats, didn't really know how to sail. He'd never taken classes in how to handle a sailboat. He didn't know the simplest mechanical things, like checking his through-hull fittings for leaks or turning on his ventilating blowers before he started his gasoline engine. He'd never even read a book on sailing unless you counted Patrick O'Brian novels. In sailing, he relied on the same things that had made him a success at selling cheese: persistence, good luck and native charm. And the conviction that since he deserved success.

Billy Bob Kaufman did not know that, had they managed to take the sail cover off, the best thing that could have happened would have been the wind tearing the sail out of Buddy's and Lynette's hands and shredding it into ribbons. The worst thing would be that the wind would fill the sail and knock the boat down, perhaps ending up with it turning turtle and drowning them all. Or drive them out of control onto the beach, destroying the boat. Also drowning them all.

Billy Bob Kaufman didn't know any of this. All he knew was that these killers were idiots incapable of following simple orders. The sail cover was still in place. His screaming at them had had no effect.

Indeed, his crew members had sunk to their haunches at the base of the mast, their fingernails torn to bloody nubs and their muscles frozen with rain and cold and fatigue. They wrapped their arms around the mast and each other and gave themselves up to the brutal assaults of the elements and Billy Bob Kaufman's foul curses.

The wind beat at *Käseria* as it motored out of the cove it had been anchored in. When it left the sheltering arms of the cove, the full force of the storm slammed into them. Waves hammered the hull. Competing forces wrung her like a washrag until every seam, every joint, every surface screamed in pain. *Käseria* was dying and threatening to take everybody aboard with her. But Kaufman didn't know to seek shelter. He didn't know that if he wasn't going to run for shelter, he should try to ride out the storm with his bow turned into the wind, by "heaving to." He'd read the phrase it had always confused him. "Heave" what? And heave it "to" where?

A salesman's luck and native charm favored him for a blessed moment. The wind turned *Käseria* like a weather vane, forcing her nose up into the wind. The serendipitous wind shadow of the next island upwind granted Kaufman the illusion of winning his battle with the forces of the storm.

Proud of his seamanship, Kaufman swung confidently onto a course toward safety. Safety, as far as he was concerned, was his home marina. Port Hideaway Marina, located on the eastern shore, was right over there somewhere. He'd be able to see it, he was sure, once he got beyond the white-capped waves and through the curtains of rain. He just had to turn the boat and speed over.

He turned the boat in what he thought was the right direction, even if it meant downwind. The storm let him go his merry way with the north wind at his back. The wind slackened, Kaufman thought, though in turning away from the wind he'd only reduced its apparent force. A neutral observer might suspect that it was almost as though the storm was sucking him in, letting him believe that he was in control, all the time setting him up for destruction when he tried to turn toward shore.

Kaufman stood at the helm, rain-soaked and wind-whipped. He might be cold and wet, but now that he was back in command, neither the storm nor the killers scared him any longer. He'd saw himself as a modern-day Jack Aubrey at the helm of the sloop *HMS Surprise*. In control, Kaufman thought to himself. Unbowed. Standing firm.

He noticed as they motored with the wind at his back that the wind seemed to have eased. In fact, the wind had completely died away. Kaufman looked around. The sky looked the same: black-gray boils of clouds reaching for his boat. The water looked the same: armies of whitecaps attacking in endless ranks from the north and west. But the wind had calmed; he expected that soon the waves would recede, since the storm had obviously blown itself out. They'd sail easily to the marina. He'd beat the storm! He'd reclaimed the boat! He'd taken the killers' gun! Now he would turn the killers over to the police and be proclaimed a hero!

A fresh blast of wind barreled down on *Käseria* and caught the Cheese King completely by surprise. It almost knocked him from his position at the helm. Then it succeeded in knocking the boat down, its side rail dipping into the lake and the mast almost touching the churning water. Kaufman clung to the wheel as the boat hobby-horsed, slid sideways, and skidded 90 degrees off course. Nothing he did with the rudder or the engine mattered. When the boat gamely struggled to rise again, the wind slapped the vessel down once more.

Once again the storm took control. The wind and waves pushed against the expanse of cabin and hull to overpower the meager efforts of motor and rudder. It smacked the boat down a few more times as if to prove a point.

Kaufman still desperately tried to turn the boat. The storm ignored his puny efforts as easily as it whipped away the whimpering and crying sounds coming from the sodden masses clinging in terror to the mast. After minutes of useless wrestling with the wheel, however, Kaufman felt the boat's motion ease. He didn't know that his efforts had accidentally side-slipped *Käseria* into the wind shadow of yet another small island. By absurd coincidence, it happened to be an island where dark clouds and impenetrable rain hid a castaway taking shelter from the storm.

It was not a big enough island to shelter the big boat. The island was also not a shelter from which Kaufman could make it back to Port Hideaway Marina. But even this island's small wind shadow allowed *Käseria* to regain its feet. Rudder and keel immediately felt the relief and made headway against the wind.

The bow of the boat swung into the relative calm of the wind shadow. It continued swinging north-eastward, almost directly into the wind. The relentless push of the engine soon pushed the boat out of the thin protection afforded by the island and into unprotected water.

One moment *Käseria* was in the wind shadow and upright; the next, it sailed out of the wind shadow and got clobbered by fierce wind and huge waves. The storm took control again. Ice cold shivers ran down Kaufman's back: not just rain finding its way inside his coat, but the beginnings of suspicion that he might not have complete mastery of the situation.

Kaufman had learned persistence, though. The best course of action was to head eastward to the safety of his marina as quickly as possible. He turned the wheel hard over and pushed the throttle down. Yet each time he turned even a few degrees toward the east, the wind whipped the boat out of his control and forced it into a heading of due south. It took every ounce of his strength to get the boat pointed even a few degrees into the teeth of the wind. He'd struggle with the wheel, finally get the bow turned a few degrees, but it kept shying away from confronting the wind. The course never seemed to take.

After a couple of terrifying attempts, Kaufman gave in. He motored ahead in the only direction that gave him any control. North, into the wind. It steadied the boat—if bucking, twisting, skidding and groaning was steady—but full fury of the storm once again battered his exposed skin. The rain and the spray flailed his skin like sandpaper. His sodden foul weather gear whipped around him, chafing everyplace it touched skin. Rain forced its way inside his rain gear and ran down his back in cold streams, joining the intimations of fear.

The boat bucked as though it was a sea creature trying desperately to shed the parasites on its skin. Its normally sedate motion had disappeared in a spate of malevolence Kaufman had never known. The wind and waves threw knockout punch after knockout punch, each with killing force. The parasites held on to their refuge with steely desperation.

Käsaria's engine roared at full speed ahead, dead into the north wind. Surely at least one of the three crew members must have noticed the noise of the engine roaring at full power, while the wind forced them irrevocably backwards. But if any of them noticed, they were too miserable to consider what it portended.

Chapter Twenty-One

Some time during the night, Joe Doorman's voice awakened David out of a dreamless sleep. *Use the tools you have*, the voice suggested. He ignored the advice and went back to sleep.

In midmorning, when David Doorman finally awoke, his father's suggestion popped into his head. He crawled out of the shelter, dusted off the sand and pushed away complaints of stiffness and thirst and hunger and cold. He had a mission now.

Not that the voice had given him useful direction. Dad didn't. He liked to give partial clues rather than complete solutions, because *That way you have to think it through for yourself*. A lot of times, David couldn't figure out what his father was talking about. This time, though, he understood. After all, the main tool he had was the dinghy, and it had only one problem that needed to be fixed. There. That narrowed it down.

With the early morning sun beginning to warm him, David turned and gazed at the little boat. He shivered involuntarily, reliving his panic from yesterday when the dinghy had almost drowned him. This morning, it looked pitiful, like a wounded beast. Worthy of sympathy, not fear.

Sympathy? Sympathy for a bunch of wood stuck together with nails and glue? Wow. He must still be dopey from a night curled up on the sand. He shuffled down to the lake to splash water on his face. The cold water woke him completely.

OK. He had the boat to work with. And the boat had a leak. The only thing he had to do was fix the leak. And to do that, the first step was to find it.

Even after David wrecked the dinghy—yesterday afternoon, or was it the day before?—it hadn't leaked while riding unloaded at *Caesaria*'s stern. The leak appeared only when he climbed aboard to escape from the pirates. That meant that the leak had to be above the waterline, since water didn't leak in when the boat was unloaded. Above the water line, but not too far, because water leaked in only when David's minimal weight climbed aboard. If his thinking was right, that meant that the leak had to be within a narrow zone of the hull extending from the waterline to just a few inches above.

The precision of his reasoning gave him chills. He couldn't wait to tell his father how he'd figured it out. But he had to find the leak first. He got down on his knees and knee-walked around the hull, minutely examining the wood and probing possible weaknesses. There was no obvious hole. There was, however, one place, just above the waterline, where a space between two planks looked bigger than it should.

That must be the place. (*Could be,* his father's voice corrected. *And it might be only one of the places that are leaking.*) His father was big on insisting that one explanation didn't preclude others.

Right. Now all he had to do was plug the leak.

His enthusiasm came to a dead stop. Plug the leak, but without any tools to do it. And without any material for a plug. The realization, the nights without sleep, the cold, his empty belly: all hit him at once. His brilliant solution was no solution. Without materials to repair the hole, brilliant deductions did not get him a nautical inch closer to summoning help.

He dropped to the sand in despair. For a long time, he huddled on the beach, hands around his knees, staring at the boat through ever more violent attacks of shivering and then wrenching sobs. When his crying subsided, he wondered what he'd been crying about. Nothing had changed. He was in exactly the same place he'd been yesterday. David felt himself falling down into a bottomless hole.

Despair. This was despair, he realized. He'd never felt it before. It felt like weakness. It felt like hopelessness. It felt like fear. It felt like a dead end that would never end. A revelation. He'd never personally experienced it before. He didn't like it.

No. He refused to accept it. Despair wasn't going to help. It wouldn't get him off the island or save his father. He couldn't be hopeless. He couldn't be helpless. There had to be a way. He just had to find it.

All he needed was scraps of wood and discarded nails. If he had nails, he could find a rock to use as a hammer. David got to his feet and scoured the beach for nails or wood. But there was nothing.

What about plastic to wedge into the open seam? Nothing.

He could always pound pieces of Styrofoam into the hole. There was none to be found. He sat again, out of ideas.

Despair wasn't going to help. Only fixing the problem would. But how?

Use the tools you have, his father always said. "There are no tools!" David screamed at him. The wind, now freshening with the growing daylight, whipped the words away.

If you can't solve the problem, redefine it. Dad's sage advice, whenever David struggled with a problem. The same advice for geometry, or carpentry, or a chess problem.

Maybe the hole wasn't a hole. Nope. That wasn't going to help.

Maybe tools weren't always tool tools. What kind of tool did he need to plug the hole? Anything that would cut off the flow of water. But without nails, without plastic, without Styrofoam...

But there was his windbreaker.

Stripping off his windbreaker, he climbed into the hull. He went right to the loose area he'd identified from outside the hull and began working. The fix wasn't quick, and it wasn't pretty, but eventually he worked the nylon fabric into the irregularity in the hull. Using a stick, he pushed it as deep as he could, packing it down until the nylon would compress no further. Then he broke the stick and hammered it full length on top of the makeshift patch with a rock. The stick might hold the patch in place.

It looked ugly, but it might work. The possibility that he'd fixed it excited him. Tugging, pushing, dragging the boat, he manhandled it into the water. He was panting by the time it floated in the shallows just off the beach. When he climbed in, the hull sank down beyond the waterline, down toward the load line. David's eyes never left the improvised patch, fearful of what might happen. But there was no obvious leakage. Which either meant he'd located the leak and patched it, or that he was looking at the wrong place. Or, he conceded to his father, he was looking at only one of the places.

There was no way to know but to load the dinghy up and see how the patch worked out in the lake. And as long as he was going to do that, he might as well start for the mainland. He reloaded quickly—choking down one more package of peanut butter cracker mush—and shoved the little boat off the beach.

The boat didn't seem to be sinking as David paddled away from the island. At least not sinking quickly. Water sloshed at his feet as crouched, paddling with all his might over the side. But there wasn't more water in the boat. Not much more water, anyway.

David glanced over his shoulder at the beach perceptibly falling away behind him. The sight exhilarated him. Even after a nearly sleepless night of shivering cold inside his wet clothes, as the activity warmed him, he basked in the glow of having planned and then applied a fix. By himself. Without any adult to tell him what to do. Now he just needed to get to shore.

David turned his attention to addressing the chop that had come up while he was repairing the dinghy. A freshening wind drove it. Sharp little wavelets slapped at the boat as it neared the unprotected main body of the lake. The little boat had always resisted paddling, and now paddling barely counteracted the sideways motion the waves caused.

Paddling wasn't going to get him anywhere. Rowing wasn't possible with a single oar. He sat for a moment, resisting the conclusion that he'd been defeated once more.

His eyes rested sightlessly on the stern. Then they focused on what had been in front of him ever since he'd seen his father build the transom. A notch in the stern. His father had mentioned "sculling." David didn't have a clue what sculling meant, except that apparently you did it with one oar and it had something to do with that notch.

There was nobody around to instruct him. If the notch and the oar had something to do with sculling, he'd put them together and see if he could figure it out. Setting the oar in the notch, David experimented with rowing, paddling, slapping the water. Nothing worked. He was ready to give up and admit defeat. He thrust the oar away from him in disgust. The boat moved forward.

David broke into a grin. He'd never thought of that. It was like a fish's tail, then. He stood up on the rear thwart to get more leverage on the oar. The balance was tricky, but he discovered he could use the oar for balance. He put more energy into pushing and pulling the oar. Not the way he'd been taught to row. But it worked!

Pretty soon, he'd gotten the hang of standing up, working the oar stuck out over the stern, riding the bucking of the boat as he swung the oar from side to side, its blade just under the surface, all the time allowing the oar to counterbalance him. In no time, with less effort than he'd expected, David found he'd sculled way beyond the protection of the cove and into the lake. It was even easier than rowing, in a way. Looking ahead, he couldn't see that the far shore was any nearer, but looking back, the island was definitely further behind. He felt a thrill of victory.

Just as he was thinking about what it would feel like to finally get to the mainland, he noticed that something was happening where his makeshift hull patch was. What had been a trickle of water from under the windbreaker and the stick—something he dismissed as not really significant—had become a stream. Then the stick popped out of place. Water streamed into the boat. He was sinking once more.

The land ahead was no nearer. The island was now far enough away to scare him. If he had to swim it, it was too far. With water pooling in the bottom, visibly deeper every second, David turned the boat around. Failure nibbled at him, along with panic at the increasing water washing around the bottom boards. He concentrated on the race to get back to the beach before the dinghy sank. At least this time he was able to propel the boat efficiently as he raced to beat the leak.

The water was well over his shoes by the time he heard the bow grind up on the sand of the beach. He jumped out and struggled to drag the waterlogged hull a few feet onto the beach. His shoulders ached with the effort of sculling.

Wavelets slapped the transom. It sounded like sarcastic applause, celebrating his latest failure. David realized that the clapping meant that the dinghy was still half afloat, and that the lake could take it if he wasn't careful. Somehow he summoned his last reserves of strength to pull, push, wrestle the boat out of the water.

Then, exhausted, he sat. He could barely lift his arms anymore, much less concentrate on planning what to do next, or even notice that he was falling asleep.

Chapter Twenty-Two

David opened his eyes to a changed world. He was looking up at a threatening sky. When he looked down, he saw rows of whitecaps charging into the cove. The wavelets hit the beach like miniature surf, as if dozens of powerboats were passing by and their wakes were crashing onto the beach.

The cold must have awakened him. The wind—stronger now—streamed off the lake, so cold that it burned his exposed skin. His body felt numb under his wet clothing. Was this hypothermia? Oh, well. There was nothing he could do about it.

The world around him had turned gloomy. It had to be well after noon, which meant the sun should be overhead, but the sky was dark. The clouds overhead must be really thick to shroud the midday sun. That meant that sunset and darkness would come early. His last chance to get off the island today was passing quickly.

He still had the same problems he'd had when he'd fallen asleep, and now a few more. He still had to get off the island with a leaky boat, but now he faced worsening weather, too. His previous repair hadn't worked in calm water. With the wind and waves increasing, the stresses on the hull and the patch would be even greater than before. The patch would be even less likely to hold, no matter how carefully he jammed the windbreaker and a whole cluster of sticks back in place.

Before he let himself feel the despair that threatened to drown him, he reminded himself of what he needed to do. He didn't need a permanent patch to the dinghy's leak. All he needed was a temporary fix, one that would last long enough for the dinghy to get him to land.

Temporary. What did castaways do for temporary repairs? What did the old-time sea captains do? He searched his memory for ideas. Shards of wood. Repurposed nails. Bits of sail cloth—

A word popped into his head. "Fothering." He chased the unfamiliar word through his memory, trying to find the source. Finally, "castaways" and "leak" did it. Fothering was an emergency repair shipwrecked sailors had used in one of his father's sailing books. Who'd done it? Captain Hornblower? Captain Aubrey? It didn't matter. What mattered was that it was a temporary fix for a breached hull.

It might work. All it required was sails and rope. The tools to do it had been right there in front of him—had been right beside him, around him, under him—every moment he'd been rowing the dinghy, just waiting for him to discover them. All he needed was the sail, currently wrapped around the boom, and the sheets from the sail, and some way to make it all into a fother—a thing he had never seen.

He'd only heard the word "fother" and remembered the result. How did it work? And how did you make a—was it a called a "fother"? It was something about wrapping a sail around the outside of a leaking hull. It must work by the pressure of the water outside the boat holding the sail in place. Water pressure must seek out the hole while trying to get into it, pushing the fabric in to plug it. Why they called it fothering David didn't know. How exactly you turned a sail into a kind of hull overshoe—ha! an "overhull!"—he didn't know either.

It occurred to him that at the very least, it would solve the problem of the lake pushing his patch out of place. His patch was applied on the inside, which meant the pressure outside water pressure would push it in. A fother would distribute the force of the water pushing at the patch from the outside over a greater area. If there were other leaks that he hadn't identified, the sail might fix them too. Like a big band-aid around damaged wood.

Excited, David scrambled over to the little boat. First, he pulled his windbreaker out of the gap in the boards. Then he wound it into as tight a diameter as he could. Once again, he pounded it in place from inside the hull with a stout stick and a tree branch.

Dragging the boom away from the hull, he clawed at the sail, unwrapping it from the boom little by little. He untied the sheets and carefully coiled them close at hand. Then, he carefully began wrapping the sail around the hull.

The wind, freshening still, kept whipping the exposed part of the sail out of his hands. He quickly learned to use the blast as a third hand, a helping hand to assist in draping the stiff fabric around the hull. As he worked, he found a way to secure the sail. He used the ropes that served as sheets to secure the sail temporarily while he wrestled the hull right-side up. Before the wind could work the sail out from under his lashings, he threw himself on top of the sail and tightened all the lashings, retying the knots into a kind of cocoon around the hull.

It took hours to rig. In the end, he used not only the sheets from the sail but his shoelaces and the drawstrings from his windbreaker to lash the fabric. Even the ball of string—he still couldn't remember why he'd thought to throw it in the dinghy for his adventure—filled in some gaps.

Done, he shoved the boat into the water to test it. He climbed aboard to weigh the hull down to the load line. As far as he could tell, no water trickled into the bilge. But then, the first patch had seemed successful, too.

He jumped out and gathered his things again. That the Hornblowers and Aubreys of the world had saved themselves this way gave him just enough confidence to load up the dinghy and wrestle it into the water and push off from the island. He didn't want to give himself too much time to think about the likelihood of this fix working. He sculled into the whitecaps that seemed to want to become surf.

If he was lucky, if he pushed himself hard enough, if the patches held, he might be able to get to the mainland before it got dark. If the weather didn't get any worse. If everything worked right, before the little boat sank. If, if, if.

And by golly, it worked. Water dribbled into the hull from someplace under the sail (*some places* his father insisted), but it was only a dribble. The boat wasn't sinking now. At least, not quickly. At least, not so quickly that it would sink the dinghy before he could scull away from the island, across the cove, across the main body of the lake, and to the main shore.

With every sweep of the oar, he gained confidence. This time he'd make it to shore. He was certain.

Until—just after he crossed from the cove into the lake—lightning struck. Real lightning. Deadly lightning. Striking without warning.

The first lightning bolt nearly took his head off. The flash blinded him. The concussion deafened him. An electrical charge tingled in the hair on his arms and pulled at the hair on his head.

The noise of the strike and the echoes reverberated, pounding the hull like a drum. Whether the concussion blasted David off his perch or surprise made him fall, he ended up on the bottom of the boat in the bilge water. More lightning strikes followed one after the other. Thunder boomed out a constant roar. Frantic to get under cover, he scratched at the hull planks he lay on with his fingers, trying to burrow even lower, as far away from the lightning as he could. As he scrabbled, he took one fearful look over his shoulder. Ugly black fingers reached down from the sky to pluck him up. He didn't look again.

Another close lightning strike. Another blinding flash. Another concussion. So close he knew they almost took his head off. More strikes, more thunder, explosions of light and sound, too close together to even begin to count ("one-missis—"). David kept scraping, scraping, scraping at the wood, trying to get even lower, all the while screaming.

After a few minutes, long enough to tear most of his fingernails to bloody tatters, whatever explosive cell had been overhead moved on. All around him, he could see and hear and feel lightning bolts and roars of thunder. At least now they weren't aimed right at his head. He could think.

He had to get off the lake, where he was the highest point for miles. He didn't dare continue toward the far shore. Safety was the island. Right now. But he didn't dare standing on the thwart to scull: he'd be the highest point for miles around, just begging a lightning bolt to find him. He pulled the oar out of the sculling socket and tried to use it to paddle. Paddling with the long oar had been awkward when he could sit up on a thwart, but from his position in the bottom of the boat it was impossible. He edged up to his knees and inched up enough to get the blade of the oar into the water while staying low enough to have a chance to avoid getting blasted.

Cringing at every rumble and every flicker, he paddled desperately, wildly, stupidly. Somehow, he managed to turn the little boat around and paddle it back toward the beach.

That his haphazard paddling moved the dinghy at all felt like a miracle. Or perhaps none of his efforts had any effect at all. It was just as likely that the growing storm dispensed with him as it pleased.

Somehow he got back to the beach without getting struck by lightning.

He got back just before the real wind hit. He had heard it howling for some time, a distant sound, almost like a train rumbling in the distance and to the left and right and in every direction. Only when he felt the first vicious puffs—hammer-blows, not puffs!—did he recognize the sound he'd been hearing.

The bow crunched onto the beach sand. David sprang out and with strength born of panic, yanked the waterlogged hull as far from the pulsing lake as he could. He worked bent nearly double, trying to stay low to duck under the lightning. The full weight of the wind suddenly hit him with an unearthly howl, swatting him down.

He scrambled to the dinghy's bow and wrestled the boat further up the beach, then clear of the waves crashing onto the sand. Once he'd dragged it as far as he could, he let the storm help him push the heavy boat upside down. He crawled under, shaking. It wasn't much shelter. Not against the lightning.

Nor was the hull much good against the wind and rain. The elegant sheer lines turned out to be a liability. The beautifully curved gunwales that his dad had built into the dinghy's sides looked elegant on paper. But upside down, the elegant curves meant that there were openings between the sand and the hull, allowing a torrent of wind to howl through the gap, carrying cold, stinging rain flung horizontally. It was like liquid sandpaper, sandblasting his skin. All the dinghy protected him from was the driving rain from above. It hardly provided protection at all. He was soon soaking wet from the horizontal spray and freezing in the wind.

David hunkered down. He covered up the best he could. His only protection from the howling wind was the ice chest, which had somehow survived another catastrophe. Turned on its side and placed between him and the wind streaming under the overturned dinghy, it blocked some of the wind. The unobstructed wind still howled around it, freezing his head and his feet in torrents of wind that swept low over the beach and blasted sand over every inch of his exposed skin.

Lightning and thunder returned. The storm thundered just over his head. David lay on the wet sand, shivering. Stunned by the storm's power, he could do nothing but cower and hope not to be hit. And regret his pride in the morning's brainstorm. It had been such a brilliant insight! Until it had nearly gotten him killed. Regret and recrimination and helplessness battered him more brutally than any part of the storm.

Nearly helpless against the assaults of wind and rain and blowing sand, he shook with cold and fear. He had only a shirt and pants to protect him from the hurricane. His failure and his helplessness in the face of the assaults of the storm shredded any thought of challenging the storm again.

The storm raged. The tall pine trees on the island bent and swayed like stalks of grass. The unearthly howl almost drowned out the thunder exploding just over his head and the lightning crackling just above the tops of the trees. In the brief milliseconds between deafening thunderclaps, there were other sounds: the moaning of the tortured trees and the terrible hammering of the rain on the wood of the dinghy and the loud hissing of raindrops driven brutally into the sand. All the while, wind beat on the small craft and shook it bodily as though threatening to lift it and snatch it away.

The wind drove the blowing sand and rain into a veil so thick that David could not see the lake any longer. He desperately wanted to close his eyes and sleep. He couldn't. He might not see what was coming to destroy him.

Instead, he lay on his side, his back to the bitter gale. He stared out toward the expanse of water he knew lay to windward. He could not see it through the curtains of water pouring from the low clouds. He could imagine it, though: the wind whipping the lake into a froth and rain pounding down froth in impenetrable curtains.

Gusts rocked his makeshift shelter. David wrapped his arms and legs around a couple of thwarts to hold the hull down. He couldn't be sure his weight would prevent the wind from scooping the hull off the beach and carrying it off. Holding on was the only strategy he had. Nothing more than a paperweight.

So much for what Dad had billed as "quality time."

Chapter Twenty-Three

It had been a disaster from the start, and David knew it was all his fault.

On their first day of their week-long cruise, Joe Doorman had given his son the honor of backing *Caesaria* out of her slip. It wasn't a hard maneuver, even if the slips at their marina were barely wider than the boats. But David had done it before many times, if always with his father standing by his side, ready to jump in to help if needed.

This time he insisted to his dad that he didn't need any help. He'd mastered it. He had memorized the steps. All he needed to do was put the diesel engine in reverse gear and squeeze the throttle forward a touch. That would back the boat clear of the finger docks on either side of the slip. Then he'd push the transmission into forward and put the wheel hard over to turn into the open lane between their dock and the next dock, and head out into the lake. *Caesaria* always turned on a dime. Even with the tight quarters, it should have been easy.

There was one little trick. In shifting from reverse to forward, you had to pause briefly in neutral. If you didn't, his father repeated every time David changed gears, you'd strip the gears. The throttle lever was a little loose, so it was hard to know exactly when the transmission slipped out of gear and into neutral. He knew he would have to work the lever back and forth a bit to feel for neutral. No big deal, except you couldn't take too long finding neutral. Otherwise, *Caesaria* would back into the boats behind. Boats didn't have brakes: you could only stop the backward movement by putting the transmission in forward. So you had to shift gears from reverse to neutral and then neutral into forward, fast enough to stop the rearward movement. Shift too fast, you could strip the gears. And too slow, you'd slam into a boat docked behind.

Yesterday afternoon at the helm backing the boat as he'd done so many times, David kept repeating, "Pause or ruin...pause or ruin...pause or ruin." He shifted into reverse. Immediately he found himself in charge of a sailboat backing toward the million-dollar sailboats in the docks behind. He worked the throttle lever forward and backward minutely, trying to find the place where the transmission slipped into neutral and from which he could push it up toward all ahead.

Caesaria slid backward. The open water between *Caesaria's* stern and the boats behind narrowed alarmingly and got thinner and thinner with every glance. David's attempts to find neutral on the gear shift became more and more frantic the closer he got. If there was a right spot it had to be right here—

He was still trying to find neutral when a hollow *thonk* announced *Caesaria*'s rude meeting with her back neighbor. The powerboaters standing around talking on the dock looked up and stared at them.

Joe Doorman leaped from his position on top of the cabin where he'd been readying the mainsail for setting. He landed heavily in the cockpit, shouldered David aside, and shoved the throttle into forward. He had said not a word to his son as he made the turn and motored out into the lake. He didn't need to. His whole body exuded disapproval.

No, not disapproval. Disgust. Even if David's little mistake did no damage to the spiffy new thirty-six-footer he'd hit. Or to their own boat. He'd failed.

His father relinquished the wheel to him as they cleared the marina's entry buoys. A sign of forgiveness? Maybe. His dad raised the main, then went below to check the battery settings and dog down the portholes and hatches.

Alone at the helm, David glanced up beyond the loosely flapping main toward the top of the mast. The wind indicator was old-school: an arrow on a pivot that was supposed to point into the wind so that you could set the sails. Now, however, it was describing lazy circles in the nearly still air. The sails were drawing, but the wind didn't seem to be willing to take a stand on which way it was going to blow. David kept turning the boat, his eyes fixed on the wind indicator as he tried to discover the direction of the breeze.

Suddenly his father charged up the short ladder from the cabin, incensed. "Can't you keep a steady course?"

Just as David was distracted by the yell, the wind made up its mind. It blew from the wrong side, taking the jib aback. The boat heeled, threatening to jibe. Doorman elbowed David aside and turned *Caesaria* around in an emergency circle that put the boat back under control. With barely a glance at the sails, Doorman brought the boat onto the proper heading to fill the sails, then minutely trimmed the sails with only a few nonchalant tugs, and then stood calmly at the wheel, sailing a boat that was suddenly in perfect harmony with the wind.

The rest of the day his father had not let him touch anything: not the wheel, not a winch, not a line, not a sheet. Joe Doorman had even rushed from the helm to the foredeck to drop the anchor himself as they glided into the cove where he intended to anchor for the night.

He'd said barely a word to David. He didn't need to. David read his father's thoughts as clearly as if they were printed on his deeply furrowed brow. He would have preferred to hear his father scream out the words rather than leave them unsaid.

But the worst part of the day had been still to come.

David, anxious to put distance between himself and his father, loaded the dinghy for a jaunt ashore. He'd collected snacks and bottled water and loaded them into the ice chest. He'd gathered random stuff: a knife, a ball of twine, the handheld radio, a life jacket, binoculars. The things an explorer needed to explore a desert island, or a boy needed to escape his father's wrath. Then he stepped into the little boat.

Stepped in by stepping directly onto the dinghy's gunwale. The entire weight of his body applied to the extreme edge of the dinghy. He knew better than to step there. In a hurry to escape the unpleasant silence on *Caesaria*, though, he did what he knew he must never do.

One foot on *Caesaria,* one on the gunwale of the dinghy. The dinghy tipped toward him under his weight. He lost his balance and had to leap for the dinghy to keep from going in the water. As he fell heavily into the rocking boat, one of his feet kicked up and put a gouge in *Caesaria*'s gel coat. He grabbed for the mast of the small boat to steady himself, but his weight on the extreme edge of the boat overbalanced it and his weight pulled the mast down toward the water. The top of the dinghy's mast slammed onto the sailboat's cabin top. David clung to the mast, holding onto the only thing that would arrest his fall. His grasp concentrated his weight on a few inches in the middle of the mast, the area least braced against lateral strain. The wood announced its outrage with a sharp crack that echoed off the surrounding trees.

David fell between dinghy and sailboat. He sank in ten feet of cold water, upside down, the capsized dinghy bobbing above him among a cloud of flotsam: ice chest, waterproof binoculars, oars, a hand-held VHF radio, and his father. Joe Doorman had not hesitated a moment to jump over the rail to save his son from drowning.

The whole scene, from David's misstep onto the dinghy's gunwales through his somersault ten feet beneath the surface, had been so absurd that even submerged, David couldn't help but laugh. He'd surfaced, spluttering and spitting out lake water, laughing at his own stupidity. He found himself face to face with his father. One look and his laughter died. Dad's face was turning purple with rage. Rage at the misstep, at the broken mast, at the damage to the gel coat, at the gouge in the cabin top of *Caesaria,* and at his son, laughing in his face.

The look on Doorman's face choked off David's laughter. The wooden boat was the product of his father's meticulous handiwork. Doorman was immensely proud of what he'd built. And the pinnacle of his pride was that beautiful, hand-crafted, hand-varnished wooden mast. A mast that David had—apparently in a fit of hilarity—snapped in two like a matchstick, used and then tossed carelessly away.

Together, in silence, they had righted the broken-masted dinghy. Cold, coldly, they followed one another up the swim ladder to the cockpit of the Catalina 30. At that moment, as if his foot touching the deck of *Caesaria* had flipped a switch, Joe Dorman turned into Captain Bligh. A Captain Bligh utterly out of control.

Now, alone in the night, abandoned in the lake, lying shivering in the wet sand beneath the overturned hull, David relived the scene with shame. The older man had stood dripping wet in the cockpit, dressing down his son in a voice filled with barely suppressed violence, delivering the thorough indictment that only a career trial lawyer could manage extemporaneously. David stood before him with his head bowed to hide his burning face and his mind aflame with self-indictment. He knew every charge was true.

He'd deserved every word. Stepping on the dinghy's gunwale had truly been inexcusable. He had known better: Doorman had drilled him on the process of stepping from as close to the center of one boat to the center of another. And there had been no excuse for snapping the handmade wooden mast in two. The only defense David could muster from the depths of his shame was that he hadn't done it on purpose. The words had died on his lips. He could never say to the purple face of the man who'd lovingly crafted it and to whom would fall all of the burden of rebuilding it.

David had known instinctively as his father was dressing him down that the worst part of the disaster was his laughing. His father didn't mention it in his tirade, but it wasn't necessary to mention what they both knew was unforgivable. You didn't wreck a handcrafted work of art and laugh about it. Even if he had been given an opportunity, David knew as he composed an excuse that it would be impossible to explain that he had only been laughing about the ridiculousness of the scene.

Now, stuck alone on an island in a terrible storm, stuck because he'd destroyed the dinghy that would otherwise have saved him—

In English class, they'd covered irony. Here was irony: the kid who'd destroyed the boat having to rely on it for shelter. The boy whose father wouldn't trust him with a sailboat, now apparently his father's only hope of getting saved. The person who'd proved his complete stupidity yesterday now having to use everything he'd ever learned about boats and sailing to try to stay alive and to save his father.

David chewed on this irony as he physically held the broken hull down on the sand against the sucking force of the hurricane raging around him. He stared sightlessly out at the frothing lake, his eyes unfocused and his attention full of yesterday's shameful scene, when a boat suddenly appeared out of the impenetrable sheets of rain.

David sat up as far as the hull let him and stared. Was it real? He stuck his head out of the overturned hull to get a better look. It seemed real enough, though it looked like something out of a cartoon. A weird boat. Wrong, somehow. Not exactly a party barge. Not a houseboat. More like a shack on pontoons. Some sort of metal structure behind the shack. It could have been something out of *Mad Max* or *steampunk*.

It could not be real. But it stayed in his vision, insisting on its own reality. Which meant, David concluded, that whatever it was, it must be here to save him. He always knew that someone would come. Just as he knew that it meant his father had gotten free from the kidnappers and had come back to help him.

Gratitude overwhelmed him. He squeezed out from under the dinghy, stood up to get their attention, and promptly found himself thrown on his face. The wind's blast slapped him down again when he tried to stand again. He tried staying low, scuttling on hands and knees toward the water, screaming at the top of his lungs and waving with one hand while crawling with the other. He'd almost reached the water's edge when the barge wheeled abruptly away.

"No, no, no," he shrieked. "Don't leave me!"

He tried standing again. The wind smacked him down once more. He crawled to the edge of the churning water, ready to wade in and swim after the barge. His hands and knees were already in the water when he saw the rescue boat shudder to a stop, then wheel in a circle.

He didn't have to be told what had happened. David had seen boats go aground before. It had hit a log or a reef hidden under the roiling surface. But nothing in his experience prepared David for what happened next.

The barge began tossing pieces of itself up into the swirling maelstrom. No; it was giving up to the storm what the storm violently stripped off of her. Even from his position on the beach, watching through the curtains of rain and flying debris, David could see that the barge was beating itself to death on the reef. It could not remain afloat long.

It was a terrible thing to watch a boat die. Even one that was only an ugly caricature of a boat.

And what about its crew? There was no sign of anyone on board. There was nothing they could have done for David anyway: they couldn't land the barge on the beach; they couldn't stay still and wait for David to row out to them (as if!). There was nothing David could do for them or they for him. The storm separated them as completely as a mine field.

He scrambled back against the pressure of the wind, heading for the meager safety of his little shelter. Squeezing himself under the dinghy's rocking hull, he watched the odd little barge torn apart.

Bits of the roofing flew off. The derrick on the back deck of the barge canted over and began flapping back and forth as though it was bamboo. The barge's deck quickly bent at an impossible angle from the framework that tied the pontoons together. Bits of the cabin tore off. With each passing minute it looked less like a boat and more like a pile of scrap.

He blinked his eyes to clear the windblown water and sand, just in time to see the deckhouse of the barge dissolve in a cloud of debris. One moment it was there. The next it was just gone. Bits and pieces of the junk that had been in the deckhouse whipped away in an eruption of debris. Now there was nothing left but the two pontoons, the bent metal deck, and two large bags of cloth stuck on the broken deck.

David squinted at the boat. Whatever was stuck on the deck of the barge, it had to be heavy. The wind had torn everything else off of the barge's deck other than those sacks. How could they not fly away?

A head rose out of one of the jumbles of cloth and peered around. Then the other bag stirred. Blond hair streamed out into the jet of wind that blew through the disintegrating structure. David saw a face beneath the blond hair and then a mouth open in a silent cry.

Suddenly, David found himself outside again, trying to stand against wind howling down the beach, calling out to the people clinging to the deck, feeling his words torn soundlessly out of his mouth and whipped away. Those people would drown. Nothing could swim against this wind and these waves, but they'd have to fight both to get to shore. If he didn't do something to help, he would have to watch them die.

But what could he do? The water in the narrow channel between the beach and the wreck wasn't just dotted with whitecaps. The wind whipped around the sides of the island and howled through the trees, curling on itself and tangling with sheets of rain and armies of waves. It was whipping the water of the cove and the lake into a tortured cauldron.

He glanced back at his shelter. Could he use it as a lifeboat? No way. The little boat was barely seaworthy in calm water, never mind in this! The fothering might have worked, but he hadn't put it to the test. And certainly not in the roiling water he'd have to cross. But he had to do something.

Sick to his stomach at what he was going to do, David fought the wind to get back to the dinghy. He pushed it over with the wind's help, then dragged the hull back into the water and tossed in the oar. He pushed it off the beach and then, just as the elements threatened to steal it away from his grasp, jumped in, pushed himself out of the shallows with the oar and held on as the dinghy took off on the wind. For a moment, it looked like he would be blown past the wreck, but he threaded the oar through the sculling notch and managed to steer the small boat onto a collision course.

As the wind blew him closer, he saw that the barge's deck plates had ruptured into jagged teeth. "Don't, don't, don't, don't, don't," David chanted, staring at the jaws of jagged metal waiting to saw into the wooden hull. Don't destroy my hull. Don't flip my boat over. And to himself: Don't do this! Even as he did it.

Despite it all, he kept on. The oar tried to rip itself free of his grasp. He applied all of his weight and all the strength his frozen fingers could muster, straining to keep the little boat heading for the inevitable collision.

***

It might have been the clang of the wooden hull hitting the metal pontoons. It might have been the shudder of the collision. Deborah knew only that an alien sound made her look away from the spectacle around her. She found herself looking right into her rescuer's eyes.

"David," she croaked.

Thank God she'd found him. "Hi, kid," she managed through numbed lips. The wind whipped the words away. She did not have the strength to yell.

David took in his mother with a wide-eyed stare. He felt no surprise at seeing her clinging to the wreckage. He felt only fear. Not just fear of the storm, not just fear for his mother, but fear of the wreck's shards sawing into his wooden hull. However his mother had ended up here, he needed to get her off the wreck and away before the sinking barge dragged them both down into the depths.

He tried yelling to her, but the wind whipped his voice away, too. His mother stared dumbly at him. He thrust out his hand in a demand that brooked no argument.

She took her savior's hand and slithered off the tortured deck to safety. Safety in which churning water <u>on the inside</u> of David's boat came up to her mid-calf. Dully, she concluded that wasn't a good sign. A worse sign: David without Joe. Where was Joe? That bastard.

Joe reminded her of Mary Ann. She grabbed David, pointing to the girl. David stretched out to grab the girl's foot to drag her down the ruptured metal deck plate and into the dinghy. The girl's pretty mouth formed words that could not be heard in the din.

Together, mother and son pushed the dinghy hand over hand along the wrecked hull to disentangle it from the wreck. David tried to turn onto a course toward the island and safety. He couldn't. The wind took control, whipping the little boat away from the wreck. Away from the beach. Away from the safety of the island. Away from the ice chest that he'd protected through everything.

David fought the oar, trying to steer with it, trying not to cry at the loss of everything he'd worked so hard to preserve, trying to assert any kind of control at all.

Deborah watched her son fight the jerking steering oar. The dinghy pitched and rocked, threatening at each moment to overturn. Yet its motion downwind was soothing compared to the last movements of the dying barge. It was soothing to have David in control, too. She looked over at Mary Ann, who returned a weak, exhausted smile.

The smile enraged Deborah. She cupped her hands and started to bail the water that had now risen to her knees. "Bail!" she yelled at the girl, who did not understand. The girl and David had not even exchanged a glance. They should both be embarrassed, Deborah thought, at what she must have done in front of him. And now to be face to face with the mother of the boy she'd performed in front of—

Distracted by her emotion, Deborah's bailing was startlingly inefficient. Her cupped hands removed cups of lake water while gallons slopped over the gunwales and more poured from the sky. My shirt, Deborah thought. I can use my shirt as a makeshift bucket as she was taught in a Power Squadron lesson. The girl could help too. But Deborah would be damned if she would tell the girl to take her shirt off in front of David. Deborah slipped her own shirt off to use as a makeshift bucket. She pantomimed a command that Mary Ann start bailing with her hands.

At the stern, David hung tight to the steering oar. "Just keep it downwind," he chanted to himself. Over and over: Just keep it downwind.

By the grace of the killer storm, with the ballast of three waterlogged bodies and the water half filling the boat, the dinghy sailed majestically. Away from the barge. Away from the safety of the island. Its motion was almost peaceful as it sailed into the maw of the howling storm.

Hours later, in the afternoon, when the winds had eased and the lake subsided into glassy calm, the crew was shivering, drenched, and exhausted. But the dinghy held on. Mostly submerged, its crew half-drowned, the little boat still floated bravely. And David Doorman still clung with dogged tenacity to his oar and to his duty of saving his two passengers.

Chapter Twenty-Four

By early afternoon, the storm had blown itself out. The dark clouds and rain disappeared. The wind still blew from the north, but now as gentle as a sleeping puppy. The unencumbered sun burned off a thin high overcast, warming all the soaked bodies still out on the lake. The surface of Lake Lanier subsided into a sheet of green glass, almost as flat as the top of a coffee table. Five knickknacks were arranged on the glass.

One, at the south end of the lake, flying north at top speed, a speedboat. The driver intended a course toward the north end of the lake, though in the confusion that is Lake Lanier, it actually had to head east to head north. Spray from its bow wave nearly hid the flashy FLEET logo. At the helm, Special Agent in Charge Brashears Livingston Thomas III stood, bouncing on the balls of his feet as his boat bucked against him.

Another speeding boat, in the far north, well out of sight of the FLEET speedboat, charged south. The Hall County Maritime Patrol boat in the charge of Deputy Martin was searching for the distressed *Admiral Byng*, following a hunch about the barge's path as it was pushed by the storm.

At the southern expanse of the lake, near the dam, two other boats lolled, oblivious to the speed of the others. The two sailboats, swimming together in elegant state on the placid water, looked like nothing so much as beautiful swans, paddling in perfect harmony.

Somewhere near the middle—north of the swans, north of the northbound speedboat, and south of the southbound speedboat, smack in the middle of the lake's widest expanse—a bit of jetsam bobbed. A closer look would have revealed a small dinghy. The little boat wallowed, dead in the water, nearly capsized, almost submerged.

The dinghy's occupants sat huddled and stuporous. They seemed not to notice the sun, or the warmth, or the passing of the storm, or the fact that the water level in the hull had risen above their waists as they sat immobile on its thwarts. In fact, the water in the boat had almost reached the gunwales that topped the hull. But for the flotation built into the hull, the dinghy would have sunk long ago. Joe Doorman, had he known, would have been proud of the success of the flotation he'd built into the little boat.

All night, David Doorman had sat up to his waist in freezing water, steering the boat with the single oar. His efforts had taken all of his strength; the waterlogged boat barely budged at the tiny distraction of the oar. The wind had buffeted the crew all night, freezing their exposed skin and driving the boat ever farther southward. The waves tossed the dinghy in ungraceful lurches, so that each of the passengers had exhausted their strength scrabbling to hang on. David, terrified of losing the oar, juggled constantly to keep a hand on the oar and a hand on the boat. Now, even as the sun cast its welcome warmth on the calming lake, he did not notice that the storm was over.

The sound of a speeding powerboat roused David Doorman from his exhausted stupor.

He looked up and quickly pinpointed the approaching boat. He'd heard the sound before. He'd also seen the boat generating it before. In fact, he'd been run over by this very boat before. He wasn't even surprised that now, just when the sky was clearing and things seemed to be brightening up, it was coming for him again. He struggled painfully to his feet in the stern of the dinghy, holding the oar to keep from toppling over.

Did he stand to warn the approaching boat? Did he stand to warn his passengers? Was he merely preparing to dive overboard? He himself wasn't sure. His movement was the last straw for the dinghy, though. The weight shift dug one gunwale into the lake, allowing the water to rush in and fill the hull. With great, slow dignity, the hull turned right over. David, his mother, and Mary Ann slipped leisurely into the lake.

The overturned hull, mostly submerged, lurked for a few moments at the surface, as if taking a breath before sinking into the deep water. Its crew was too surprised to do anything more than listlessly tread water, trying to wake up and trying to wake up to what had happened. The dinghy still floated, just barely. Even awash, if intact it might still have provided some protection, or at least kept the survivors together.

The patrol boat, however, had other plans. The sharp deep-v of its hull bisected the dinghy with a sharp thump. Then it sped on without a pause up the lake, disappearing in the distance. By some miracle, its churning propeller missed dicing the swimmers into chum.

The cold water of the patrol boat's wake slapped David in the face and then dunked him. That finally brought him back to consciousness. On reflex, he reached first for the oar he'd been protecting all night. He saw his mother and the other woman treading water, spitting and coughing, clutching at pieces of the wooden hull and the shreds of their life jackets. David looked around in amazement. The only evidence that there had ever been a hand-built sailing dinghy was pieces of oddly shaped wood and pebbles of flotation foam.

Boy, is Dad going to be pissed, David thought. At least it wasn't his fault this time.

"Better grab on to something," he croaked out dully. "It's a long swim."

Chapter Twenty-Five

Aboard *Käseria*, Billy Bob Kaufman stood tall at the wheel, feeling proud. *Damn* proud. He'd survived the storm, saved his boat, and beaten the assassins. He'd spent hours at the helm, fighting the storm. *Käseria* had fought the storm only under power, it was true. Kaufman would rather have been sailing under storm canvas, because that's the way Captain Jack Aubrey would have done it. Honestly, though, Kaufman figured that even Aubrey would have used a motor to navigate a storm if he'd had one.

Motor or not, nobody could take this from the Cheese Man: he'd stood his ground, clung to the wheel, motored hour after hour into a blistering hurricane of wind and rain. Well, running away from it, actually. Whatever. He fought it and won. Pride energized him. He fought the urge to tear off his soaked shirt and scream his defiance at the retreating storm. "I'm still here!" (he wanted to yell as he beat his chest). "I'm still here and you're running away!"

He was proud of his boat, too. She'd motored for hours in survival conditions, her engine ticking over like his Rolex watch, never missing a stroke during hours of fighting wind and waves. *Käseria* had performed like the pedigree animal she was. That the motor had started sputtering and coughing this morning as the storm died away didn't particularly bother him. He figured that the motor was as tired as he was after their ordeal. He'd throttled back to idle to give it a well-deserved rest.

He was proud of how he had dealt with the killers, too. He'd always heard that if you were kidnapped, you were supposed to establish a bond with your captors. He'd made a big effort to get them talking, connect with them like a real person. He had succeeded; he and they had a personal bond now. He hadn't earned Top Sales awards as Georgia Cheese Inc.'s "Top Cheese" three fiscal quarters for nothing.

He'd finally managed to get them talking in the wee hours of the morning, when the storm started slacking off and the two killers started shaking off their torpor. "You folks been doing this a long time?"

"This is our first hit," Lynette responded brightly.

Buddy shot her a nasty glance. "Lynette!"

"It's OK," Kaufman assured them. "It's not like I'm going to tell anyone."

"Oh, we know you're not." Lynette's ambiguous reassurance hung between the three of them for a moment. She hurried to change the subject. "We used to be in a different line of work, you know. But our suppliers kind of dried up. So we thought we'd try a new line of work. This is our first gig."

"Thank you, 'War on Drugs,'" Buddy muttered.

"This isn't really our style. We tried some other things to supplement our Social Security—"

"Walmart!" cursed Buddy.

"—but it didn't really work out. *Some of us*"—she glared at Buddy—"don't really go in for customer service."

Buddy leaned toward his captive, his face screwed up in an evil counterfeit of a smile. "'Can I tell you about our specials today?' Like I got nothin' better to do than suck up to a bunch of old farts who got to shop discount." He spat over the side. "Let me tell you something, bud. I used to be able to buy and sell people like that. One time, I could'a bought the whole damn store. Cash. We used to move more product on the East Coast than—"

"Honey," Lynette cut in. "I'm not sure he really cares about your resumé."

"It's not like he's ever gonna get to tell anyone, Lynette."

The implication chilled the conversation once more. They were mostly silent in the ensuing hours. Later, with the dawn, Kaufman sent Lynette below to make coffee. He could smell the weak aroma of instant coffee drifting up through the open companionway, mixing with the persistent fumes. The scent of fresh caffeine filled him with gratitude for being alive. Lynette came up the companionway with a scowl and three cups of coffee.

She put them down out of Kaufman's reach and rubbed her eyes. Then she pointedly turned away from Kaufman's outstretched hand. Daylight and calm weather seemed to have restored the killers' insolence. She put a cup down in front of her partner.

"Here, sweetie," she said. "This will make you feel better."

Kaufman left the wheel and stepped forward to snatch a cup. He drained it in one swallow. The scalding liquid felt as smooth as a single-malt scotch. He put the empty cup down and picked up another. It was probably supposed to be Lynette's cup. Well, tough for her. He was the captain, he was in charge, and she better get used to it. He downed hers too.

Buddy drank and sat up stiffly. Revived, he handed the cup back to Lynette and clawed his way to his feet. Lynette finished the coffee in her partner's cup and stretched, a cat stretch that began at her feet and spread slowly up along her slender body all the way to her fingers.

Kaufman found himself entranced. She was actually not a bad-looking woman. Kind of old, but that wet suit showed off delectable curves. It made Kaufman think. If Buddy was as old as he looked, maybe Lynette might welcome a little manly attention—

An exclamation cut through the fantasy. "Damn! Look!" Lynette and Kaufman turned to follow Buddy's pointing finger. Less than a hundred yards away, another sailboat drifted in the glassy water. Its stern faced *Käseria*, and on the stern was painted the name *Caesaria*.

"That's it," yelled Buddy. "That's it! That's his boat!"

There wasn't any question whose boat he'd seen or what Buddy would do if he got over to it. Billy Bob felt his happiness chopped off right at the root. They'd order him to motor over. They'd jump aboard the target's boat. They'd off the poor guy, right in front of him. And just like that, they'd turn Billy Bob Kaufman, Cheese King of the Southeast, from a life of innocent blamelessness into an accessory to murder. Worse: an eyewitness that these two had done it. And that meant that the killers would have to—

He turned to the killers to remind them that they had a deal. "Remember," he croaked out of a mouth suddenly dry. "Remember you agreed—"

"Get me the binocs," Buddy ordered. He sounded like his old self again. Lynette jumped below, then dashed back up with the binoculars. Buddy started swearing as he adjusted the focus. Not in anger, Kaufman realized with his stomach suddenly churning. No, it was joy. Pure, unadulterated joy.

Buddy lowered the binoculars. "That's the guy, the one at the wheel. Sitting there fat and happy. Looks just like his description. 'Bout time we got some good luck. Let's get to work." Buddy took another look through the lenses. He turned from appraisal of their target to appraisal of Kaufman. The Cheese King's blood ran cold as Buddy stalked over to him, nearly chest to chest. "Give me the gun. Then drive us over there."

Kaufman had been reviewing his options since the moment Buddy pointed to their prey. He could always just refuse to cooperate. He had the gun. He had the boat. They couldn't sail it without him. He was irreplaceable.

His mood lifted. Then it flagged. There were two of them and only one of him. They were vicious killers. He was just a salesman.

Another thought buoyed him up again. He didn't have to refuse to help. He could agree to help but gum up the works. Discover a problem with the steering. Go the wrong direction. Make stupid mistakes in sailing toward the other boat. One mistake after another would frustrate the killers and maybe make them give up their planned murder.

His courage wilted again. The killers wouldn't be fooled forever. Sooner or later they'd figure out what he was doing. His resistance might prevent the murder of this guy—what was his name? Doorman?—but they were likely to take their frustration out on him.

There were lots of good reasons to stop them. What they were going to do was wrong. It was murder. He could stop it and be a hero for the first time in his life. Not just a salesman anymore: a hero. Whatever the cost.

Cost: that was the problem. At the very least, physical injury. Likely severe physical injury. Even more likely, the cost of his life. He might become a hero by saving Doorman, but he'd most likely be a dead hero.

Maybe it was worth it. He was going to be dead anyway, one way or the other. Eventually. He could be a hero right now. He could save an innocent man's life right now. Which sounded pretty inspiring until you put it up against the fact that being a hero probably meant being dead not in some distant future but more like *right now*. And anyway, wasn't he just as innocent a victim as Doorman?

"Right now." That brought a different perspective on the problem facing him. Right now, they needed him. That meant that right now the couldn't dispose of him right now. That gave him time to find a way to avoid taking part in a murder. While they were distracted with trying to get that Doorman, he'd have time to think about a way out. Possibly even something to save the other guy, too.

Kaufman looked into the cold eyes of the killer bellying up to him, hand extended, palm out, demanding the weapon. The Cheese Man couldn't find it in those eyes to believe in his own salvation or Doorman's. But given time something might develop...

Kaufman pulled the gun out of his waistband. Buddy snatched it away without a word and turned to his partner. The two killers huddled together and exchanged urgent whispers at the forward end of the cockpit. Buddy then climbed over the cabin roof and made his way to the base of the mast. He peered intently at the quarry, fondling his handgun.

Lynette stalked over to Kaufman. "Drive right over to them," she ordered. "Buddy wants to be real close, you understand? And you probably want to do what he wants."

"We had a deal."

"We had a deal," Lynette agreed.

Kaufman stared. Was there a slight emphasis on "had?" Or was it on "we"?

Kaufman shriveled under her steely look. He took the wheel again and moved the throttle up a notch. Barely above idle speed, they closed smoothly on *Caesaria*.

Kaufman saw that there were three figures in the cockpit of the other boat, not just the one at the wheel. The other two were sitting, oblivious. None of them looked up. It was odd. As still as the lake was, *Käseria*'s motor had to be audible. But nobody on the other boat seemed to notice until *Käseria* was within fifty yards.

Kaufman glanced at Buddy, still at the mast. He was now sighting along the barrel of his weapon, taking careful aim. Kaufman's knees failed at the thought of the imminent murder. He fell into the helmsman's seat, feeling sick.

There had to be something he could do to stop it. Turn *Käseria* away. Dive over the side and swim for it. Let *Käseria* motor on, out of control. Let the killers yell and scream as they tried to figure out how to steer.

The problem was the gun. A big gun in the hands of a hired killer. They were not going to let him live. He'd seen it in their eyes. The man was cold and heartless as a snake, and the woman wasn't any better. Whoever Doorman was, Kaufman was sorry for him, but he himself deserved to live just as much as this Doorman guy, damn it. He stood back up, grasped the wheel, and did what he was told.

Käseria glided ahead. In the other cockpit, Kaufman saw the man steering look up, finally noticing their approach. As *Käseria* came arrowing right at him, the man stared. He roused himself and began waving his hands and yelling. After a few seconds, he jumped up to the boat's cabin top, signaling ever more frantically.

On *Käseria*, Lynette stood so close to Kaufman that he could feel her body heat. Now, her iron focus shriveled whatever prurient interest he had felt. "Park us right next to that other boat," she ordered.

Just before the boats collided, Kaufman turned his boat away hard. He hoped the sharp turn would throw Buddy off the cabin top and into the lake. It didn't. The assassin stood steady, one arm out in front of him, steadied by the boom, his aim trained on Doorman from not more than a few yards.

Käseria glided up behind *Caesaria*. The abrupt turn had slowed her almost to a stop, just enough headway to pirouette in place. For a second, the boats floated almost transom to transom. The crews of the two boats stared at each other. Frozen. Mere feet away from each other.

Then the gun in Buddy's hands went off. A surprisingly small pop. Kaufman started. He'd never really believed that Buddy would shoot someone. He hit the throttle lever in a panic. *Käseria* dug her stern down into the water and accelerated away.

Kaufman turned to see what had happened behind him. He looked back in time to see Doorman fall to his knees. At first, Kaufman thought that the wake of *Käseria*'s acceleration hitting the other boat had toppled him. Then he saw the blood.

The other two men in *Caesaria*'s cockpit suddenly stood up, looking around wildly. They seemed to see the blood at that moment. Yelling broke out that sounded like panic. The smaller man dashed below.

Scared, thought Kaufman. He turned *Käseria* back to get a better look. Shot, for sure, but not enough blood to be more than winged. Kaufman wouldn't have thought it possible to miss at such a close range. Yet the victim was standing, albeit hanging onto the shrouds to keep from falling. Kaufman peered at him, trying to figure out how badly he was hurt. Then he realized that he was giving Buddy another chance for a killing shot. He pushed the throttle lever forward to speed away.

Käseria's motor coughed. Not just a hiccup this time: a serious cough. Kaufman was about to check the fuel gauges, but events on the other boat distracted him. The big man on *Caesaria* suddenly jumped up on the side deck, brandishing a gun. A big, ugly gun. A gun pointed right at Kaufman.

A voice in his head shouted: Me? Why me? He jammed the throttle forward again, hoping the motor would catch. Then he watched in silent terror as the big man with the gun, not more than a couple of yards away, pulled the trigger. *Käseria*'s motor coughed, died, coughed again, but Kaufman heard only the metallic click of the pistol in the big man's hand. He watched the man's trigger finger clutch wildly at the trigger. More clicks. The gun jumped in the man's hand as he pumped the trigger. Click. Click. Click.

Kaufman didn't feel any of the bullets hit him. He must be in shock, he knew, from the impact of the three bullets. He looked down at his body, then patted himself desperately to confirm. No wounds! How could the shooter have missed from so close?

He looked gratefully up at the shooter. He caught the man's eyes just in time to see the gunman's arm finishing a long follow-through. A follow-through as though he'd just thrown a fastball. Kaufman saw the flash of a hurtling missile leaving the man's hand. Almost at the same second, an impact staggered him. An explosion of light and pain knocked him off his feet. His last conscious thought was that the gun had hit him squarely in the forehead.

Kaufman fell backward, his hands reaching spasmodically for the flying pistol. It bounced off his forehead, clattered to the side deck, then slid overboard. Kaufman saw none of it. He fell as his last conscious thought faded into nothingness. The thought was wordless, the product of his brain trying to process the sound of *Käseria*'s motor coughing and dying.

Kaufman's next thought might have been to check *Käseria's* fuel gauge. But he had already hit the deck, senseless.

Chapter Twenty-Six

Roaring north from his base, Special Agent in Charge Brashears Livingston Thomas III balanced on the balls of his feet to ride his bucking patrol boat as it slammed over the waves at top speed. He'd carefully watched Sergeant Pitts drive the FLEET boat hard and now, blasting over the waves, he felt more like a mariner than ever. His interagency contacts from the Department of Defense and DEA had helped to triangulate the fading distress call from the *Admiral Byng*. Now he was almost airborne as he flew toward the position he'd entered into the GPS. His attention was fixed on his radar, straying occasionally to his GPS. There was no reason to keep the 360-degree watch of the empty water around the boat that the boat geeks insisted on. Clearly the storm had chased everyone else off the lake.

No locals would obstruct the work of justice this time. Not that he hadn't done his duty to invite them to join the Bureau's effort. He'd called the County Sheriff's Department several times and hadn't managed to fight through the dispatcher's obstructionism to Deputy Martin. The man was probably home, tucked safely in bed.

Thomas himself had been up and out early. He'd left his own rack at 5:30 A.M. for a combat-booted run along Peachtree Street. The lowering clouds and threatening sky reminded him of a TDY in Northern Ireland back in his Corps days. He regretted that it wasn't raining as he ran. Thomas never felt as alive as when cold rain sloshed in his boots with every step. It was something you learned to love on Parris Island that never went away, something that every day made his morning constitutional of six-and-a-half-minute miles (five of them, to be exact) worthwhile.

He returned to his apartment, dressed, and then hit the office by 7:15. Being out of DC didn't change his work ethic. He still got to the office early, still took lunch at exactly 11:45, still filled out his daily T&A reports at 4:45 every day, even if, out in the field, there was nobody to approve them.

This morning, he'd barely started working through his stack of intelligence briefings when he heard radio chatter about a distress call from a boat on the lake. He laid the *Atlanta Journal Constitution* on top of the *Chattanooga Times Free Press* and the *Birmingham News* and tuned in to the emergency channel on his VHF. Only static rewarded him.

Thomas felt a jolt of adrenaline at hearing about the emergency. It reminded him of his duty during the Gulf War. Just like back in the old days, he'd immediately grabbed his "scramble bag" as he would have in the Sandbox, and ran out the door. In seconds he was roaring up the highway into action. On the drive, he phoned around to his contacts within the local law enforcement agencies to try to put together a task force. He got no volunteers.

That was only the first of his frustrations. Traffic on I-85 North up toward the lake was at a dead standstill. There was no telling why. It seemed like every time a cloud blew across the sun, some idiot in a rusted pickup collided with a semi hauling chickens. Then the local police would close down ten lanes of interstate north and south while scratching their heads and debating what to do. Meanwhile, a few thousand people sat and waited patiently for the road to clear. Back home, the traffic police handled things better. They pushed the wreck off the road so people could get on with their business. Apparently, that was too complicated for the locals to think through down here.

Sitting in his car in the traffic snarl, Thomas didn't waste time fuming. He worked through contacts gleaned from interagency task force meetings. The name Federal Bureau of Investigation still carried some weight, despite the Deputy Martins of the world. It had taken only forty minutes to get technical assistance from some agents he knew.

Arranging for triangulation of the distress call had been easy enough. When Thomas called the Bureau contacts in the military bases around town, *Admiral Byng* was still broadcasting. Sporadically broadcasting, weakly broadcasting, but broadcasting enough to get a fix. Plotting the location of the victim on the DIA satellite map had been a piece of cake. In fact, the FLEET boat would have been on the scene conducting a rescue within forty-five minutes from the first call, if it hadn't been for the traffic on the interstate. Nevertheless, the Bureau was here. Even on that huge expanse of lake, the Bureau was on it! Or was going to be there, if the gosh darn traffic would just move aside.

He got the FLEET boat powered up minutes after arriving at HQ. The boat's VHF radio remained startlingly quiet. There had been no distress calls since he'd gotten to the lake around noon. Maybe someone else had gotten there first. Maybe it hadn't been an emergency. Or maybe—and this last alternative was the one that made Brashears Livingston Thomas's heart race—maybe only the Bureau was prepared to dive into a rescue mission.

Despite the National Weather Service warnings about bad storms on the lake, it sure seemed calm to Thomas. All there was to deal with was a little light rain. Low, dark clouds, some wind, but just a few drops of rain. The locals were a bunch of fraidy-cats. A little precipitation made them want to crawl under their beds and hide.

Thomas was soon motoring clear of the FBI dock at Port Hideaway Marina and running at full speed. He'd headed northeast toward the incident scene. Now he was speeding along with his eyes glued to his large-scale DIA map of the lake, trying once again to confirm his position with his electronics.

Suddenly the boat lurched. He grabbed for a handhold as his boat stumbled. The hull chattered as it lost stability and then bounced around until it found its groove again.

He wondered what that bump was. He looked around. There was nothing. A couple of sailboats almost invisible in the far south. Some garbage bobbing in his wake. That was all. The lake was empty.

The agent shrugged. It was the second or third time he'd run into flotsam in just a couple of days. The sitrep had warned about it, but nobody had told him the lake was so darn *dirty*. He turned his attention back to planning the rescue.

Thomas blasted up the lake for what seemed like an hour, checking the map's landmarks against the radar and GPS. He guessed he was getting close now. He finally lifted his eyes off the instruments to scan the lake itself, but in an emergency, he didn't want to slow down. The triangulation had been good enough to give him a few thousand square yards of target area. But now that he was close, islands surrounded him. Would the boat have piled up on one of those? No, he decided: you have to be pretty stupid to hit an island, even in the dark. But then where was that gosh darn wreck?

Thomas was leaning down to adjust the gain knob on his radar when he found it.

There was little enough left. The wind and waves had stripped the *Admiral Byng* of nearly every identifying feature. All that remained were two pontoons and the warped steel framework, partially attached to the steel deck, all of them submerged. The rivets had long ago failed, and the pontoon cylinders were filled with water. The deck plates lay just under the surface, held up by the drowned pontoons supported by the reef that had been the cause of *Admiral Byng*'s demise.

The FLEET boat, running on a plane, might have missed it. Thomas, however, had steered to starboard to avoid the island dead ahead, onto a course that ran right over the carcass of the *Admiral Byng*. The topmost edge of the *Admiral Byng*'s deck plate, that jagged edge of serrated steel, filleted a thick slice of the speedboat's deep v-hull like it was cutting through butter.

The damage would have sunk the patrol boat immediately had Thomas not been traveling so fast. Not even the mortal blow could stop the speeding hull, though. The hull continued forward like a stone skipped across a pond. It might have continued skipping even farther than it did if not for the outdrive that Thomas had been planning to research when he got the chance.

The patrol boat boasted a high-performance inboard-outboard motor. Its propeller and transmission hung down below the hull in a structure the locals called an "outdrive." Milliseconds after the performance deep-v hull flayed itself on that submerged steel plate, the outdrive did its work. The lower unit snapped up when it caught the plate and then, when the lower unit reached the limit of its movement, stopped swinging. The hull jackknifed up into the air at the sudden check, then crashed down as the lower unit sheared off. When the hull slammed back down, the bow dug in, causing the stern to fly up and over the arrested bow. The speedboat cartwheeled, end over end, in slow motion, down the lake.

Brashears Livingston Thomas III found himself ascending to heaven to the sound of a fiberglass hull being shredded and then a high-performance inboard-outboard destroying itself. Stupid with surprise, while airborne, he caught a glimpse of his ride cartwheeling transom-over-bow beyond him. The concrete-hard water knocked him senseless before he could finish saying "golly gee." The cold water inflated his Type V Special Issue experimental life jacket but did not rouse him in time to see the apocalyptic finale.

As his boat cartwheeled beyond him, the wild jackknifing of the outdrive shredded the fuel lines and sprayed gasoline everywhere. The red hot motor—running at top speed for too long—ignited the aerosolized fuel, now as explosive as TNT. The cloud of aerosol blew up, and the fire instantaneously followed the fuel lines upstream to the gas tanks. The gas tanks blew spectacularly.

The ruined hull continued cartwheeling forward, now an undifferentiated ball of flame skimming over the lake, accompanied by a meteor shower of burning debris. Flaming pieces of the patrol boat rained down in a cone-shaped field of debris, all of it hitting the water beyond the fortunate but unconscious Thomas.

An island away, bleary-eyed Tramp Martin was searching for a boat in distress when the double explosion brought him fully awake. A fireball mushrooming over the trees of the next island caught his attention.

Well now. That just might not be a good sign.

He jammed the throttle down hard as he reached for the radio to report the fire.

Chapter Twenty-Seven

Aboard *Caesaria*, Doorman lay where he'd fallen at the foot of the shrouds. Blood leaked between his fingers as he held on to his wound. He struggled to get back on his feet, but the weight of the blood flowing down his side pinned him to the deck.

He wasn't quite sure what had happened. He assumed he'd been shot. He knew he was hurt. He knew he was bleeding. He might well be dying. But none of those puzzle pieces fit together.

As for dying: well, Doorman examined the possibility dispassionately. He'd imagined his own death countless times. He'd lived most of his professional life with the knowledge that at some moment he might end up looking down the barrel of a gun. He'd seen it so many times in dreams, in nightmares, in waking fancies, with every telephoned death threat, with each snarling curse by a defendant or by a defendant's family or by a disgruntled victim, that it had become just background noise. Until this moment, he would have said that he had learned to live with it. But he never envisioned dying this way. Not on his own sailboat.

What shocked him now that it had happened was that he'd never given consideration to an obvious consequence of being shot: the pain. The incredible, soul-destroying pain. Which was blossoming right now like a mushroom cloud expanding to fill up every nook and cranny inside his body.

Gritting his teeth was all he could do as the pressure of pain built within him. Maybe he could have managed the pain if his life had flashed before his eyes like it was supposed to. All those decades of experiences might have assuaged the agony that flooded through his entire body, or at the very least distracted him. Instead, the moment that the gun discharged now expanded like a supernova, one single moment of burning bleeding pain becoming his entire universe, eclipsing every other moment of his life that had come before the moment he felt the bullet's punch. The hot blow of being shot; the numbing trickle of blood leaking through his fingers; his freezing, burning side; the competing waves of fiery and icy pain that swept through him: together, they wiped away anything that might have happened before the shot. He wondered if the same unbearable flood of agony might wipe out any chance of there being a "later."

Doorman lay on his side and watched over *Caesaria*'s side as *Käseria* took his assailant away. Gasping, he struggled to get up, fighting the force of gravity that had become overwhelming. Finally, he gave up on getting to his feet. No, he wasn't giving up, just gathering the energy needed to stand. He inspected the hand that had been holding to the wound. He wiped his bloody hand on his pants and then pressed it again to his sticky side. The flesh below his shirt felt shredded.

"Get the first-aid kit," Doorman heard himself order. It amazed him that his voice sounded calm and controlled. He wanted to laugh out loud about how well he was hiding the hysteria coursing through his body and the agony that was arriving like a big freight train. Slow, relentless, unstoppable.

He wanted to laugh again at the pirates. Billy shrieking, "Is he dead?" Blackbeard demanding, "What did he say? What did he say?" Billy's wild-eyed cry for the first aid kit as he dived down the companionway.

Blackbeard grabbed Doorman under the arms to haul him off the narrow side deck onto the cockpit sole. As the big man dropped him to wipe the blood off his hands, Doorman thought he might burst out into sobs. The pain he'd concluded just moments ago was "incredible" or "soul-destroying," was bad, but this was...this was...

A wave of indescribable sensations lifted Doorman and then slammed him down. His eyesight narrowed to a tiny core of clarity surrounded by curtains of flashing lights and shifting patterns of static. He saw Billy appear with the first aid kit, only vaguely visible through strobing stars and curtains of searing heat. The agony seemed to push him far, far away, to where Doorman could only barely hear them talking about him. From miles away, he felt them tearing open his shirt, then turning away to retch over the side. At least not on my clean decks, Doorman noted with gratitude. The two pirates grimly slapped a series of gauze pads over his wound. Doorman reached to hold them in place and felt liquid immediately begin trickling through the pads and then through his fingers.

Wound. Doorman turned the word over in his mind. Wound. Not a wound, actually. More like a leak. He was leaking like a boat. Except that a boat leaked fluid in, and he was leaking fluid out. Slap a patch over my leak. Fother me. These motherfothers. He stifled a laugh at his own wit. He didn't want to laugh at a time that was so serious to his two crew members. Instead, he closed his eyes to save them the embarrassment of seeing the blood.

In the panicked moments after the gunshot, Blackbeard had rooted around wildly for his gun and finally found it. He hadn't thought about the first-aid kit or about patching a gunshot wound. He'd focused on one thing. Payback. Returning fire. Not letting the shooter get away. Getting revenge.

Blackbeard found the gun just in time to draw a bead on the shooter. The movement of the boats put masts and rigging in his way almost immediately. The big pirate ran toward the bow for a cleaner shot, fixing the shooter in his sights. Then their hunter turned—Blackbeard saw the name of the other boat in big bold letters and wondered why it looked familiar—and the guy at the wheel of *Käseria* blocked his shot at the shooter. Blackbeard pulled the trigger anyway, incensed at everyone on the attacking boat. The pistol produced a dry click. More feverish pulling, more impotent clicks.

Enraged—his own boat attacked, his own captain shot, his own weapon useless, a perfect shot wasted—Blackbeard cocked his arm back and pitched the useless gun with all of his might at the closest target. A lucky throw, or a skilled one: the useless gun flew straight and true at the target.

It conked the man steering the other sailboat in the forehead. He fell comically, just as if his bones had melted away. The other boat slipped away, its crew members staring with their mouths open in matching sets of *o*'s at Blackbeard or at their fallen comrade.

Blackbeard climbed back to the cockpit. Doorman lay where he'd been dropped. His eyes were open, but he wasn't moving. Blackbeard stood over him, helpless.

"Is he dead?" he asked his partner.

"I dunno," Billy choked out, sounding near tears. "Why'd they have to shoot him?"

The pirates looked over the stern. They were practically face to face with *Käseria*'s two crew members, yet there were no answers there.

The four crew members faced each other, unmoving, as the boats drifted apart.

"I don't like the look of this," Blackbeard whispered.

Billy nodded. "This sure looks like a hit to me."

It stunned his partner. "Hit?"

"A hit. You know, a hit." Billy pantomimed firing a gun. "Like on TV."

It made sense. The pair on *Käseria* were both dressed in black, just like on the crime shows, and they had a gun. They'd shot the Captain in cold blood, just like you'd expect from hired killers. "But why are they trying to kill this guy? He must be important. Or he really pissed someone off. Maybe we better get outta here before we end up as collateral damage."

"How?" Billy cried. "The motor don't work. You know how to sail a sailboat?"

Blackbeard shook his head. He looked over at the crew on the other boat. The guy, the one who'd killed Doorman, started to toss the murder weapon overboard. The woman stopped him. They looked over at the place where their fallen crew member lay, out of sight, then turned and disappeared down the hatch together.

Blackbeard's mind worked slowly. If Captain Bligh was important enough to kill, wouldn't the killer come back to finish the job? Not only to make sure they'd killed Doorman, but to get Billy and Blackbeard too. Blackbeard knew from TV that hired killers didn't leave any witnesses.

It wouldn't be just two against one, either. Two of them and a gun. And all Blackbeard had to fight them was a dying man and a partner afraid of lake beavers.

"He got any guns on this boat?" Blackbeard demanded.

"I don't know. Why'd you throw yours away?"

The big man grabbed his partner and shook him. "You're the one who searched the boat, damn it! Did you find any guns?"

"No, no, no. I didn't find nothin'. I don't know why there ain't no guns. Ask Captain Bligh."

"I think he's dead."

Doorman groaned. "Not dead," he grunted. Pain had pulled him back to consciousness. "No weapons."

"No guns? You don't have a single gun?"

"Flare gun," Doorman grunted through gritted teeth. "That's it. Flares. Behind the starboard cushions in the salon." Billy jumped quickly down into the cabin and sounds of wreckage following him as he rooted around. "But you'd better get this boat moving the hell away from them."

"Just how do we do that?"

"Raise the sails," Doorman gasped out. He pointed weakly at the boom. "Get the cover off."

Hearing a rattling behind him, Blackbeard turned and looked back at the other sailboat, slowing drifting away from *Caesaria*. The woman on *Käseria* was standing on the roof, stripping the mainsail cover off the boom. Blackbeard reached up to the cover over his head, discovered the clips, and began twisting them to unhook the cover.

Billy came out of the cabin with a red canister marked Flares. "Flare gun's in here. We gonna shoot off a few flares to call for help?"

"Help me," Blackbeard demanded. Together they wrestled the cover off the boom. Then they stared at each other, befuddled, trying to puzzle out what to do next.

A running clatter from *Käseria* made them look over. The man was hauling on a rope. The big sail inched up the mast as he pulled.

Blackbeard leaped into the cockpit. "Which rope?" he demanded Doorman. The man seemed to barely recognize him. Blackbeard prodded him roughly. "Which rope?"

Doorman pointed vaguely to the ropes piled up on the right side of the main hatch. Blackbeard started pulling them one by one until he found one that pulled on the sail. He grimly hauled at it, called Billy to help, tore his flesh and fingernails as he raised the sail. It snapped and popped lazily right over his head. *Caesaria* didn't move.

Billy slid down into the cockpit. Pawing through the first-aid kit, he found pain pills. He fed two pills to Doorman. Then he spared a glance for the other boat. "Hey," he warned Blackbeard, pointing.

Now there were three figures in the other cockpit.

"Isn't that—" asked Billy, pointing. Both men finally noticed the silent figure just now sitting behind the wheel, rubbing his forehead.

"That fat pig," spat Blackbeard. "We should'a shot him when we had the chance."

"No, no, no, no," cried Billy. "Then we'd really be in trouble."

The statement struck Blackbeard dumb. He looked at his partner with disbelief.

Finally, the big pirate turned his attention to the tangles of ropes. It was hard to concentrate under the threat of imminent death and harder to distinguish one rope from another. He eventually figured out that one of the ropes pulled on the aluminum stick thing that held out the bottom of the sail. The others...well, maybe Doorman would wake up again.

Blackbeard watched as over on *Käseria*, as the killers followed the directions of the pig who'd been beating up on Mary Ann. With the big main sail up, *Käseria* started drawing even with *Caesaria* and then started away toward the northeast, up the lake. Blackbeard watched as the front sail billowed out to the side, flapping. The boat turned slightly, causing the sail to wrap around the front wire. From the way everybody on *Käseria* started yelling at each other, that apparently wasn't good.

Blackbeard hopped back into the cockpit and started searching for the rope that worked the front sail of *Caesaria*. Billy somehow understood. He pushed his partner out of the way and grabbed onto the rope running forward to the front sail. He loosed it from its cleat and let the wind take it.

The sail opened up, ballooned out, and flew out in front of *Caesaria*. Blackbeard looked over to get a clue about what to do next. Over on the other boat, they were pulling in on some side ropes. He looked around, found ropes on the side decks and started pulling them at random. Eventually he pulled on the right one. The jib popped into a neat, sensuous curve.

Above the pirates' heads, the main filled with an audible snap. The boom trundled over the pirates' heads. Blackbeard stepped on the rope that was running wild through the cockpit as the mainsail filled, acting out of instinct to keep things from just happening on their own. *Caesaria* lunged forward, turned in a half circle, and took off toward the north, angling away from the attackers.

Billy yanked the rope out from under Blackbeard's feet. He didn't know he could cleat it off by snapping it between the jaws of the quick-release cam cleat. He held the mainsheet in his hand, fighting to hold on as the sail tried to pull the mainsheet through his burning fist. He noticed that now that he was holding the rope, the sailboat became like a living thing. It scared the hell out of him.

The combined errors of the pirates put *Caesaria* on a close reach. The boat sailed into the wind, a few points away from *Käseria*'s course.

"Get the wheel," Doorman croaked, waking again.

Billy stumbled over the prosecutor and started turning the wheel. His experience steering the boat yesterday didn't guide him in what to do now.

Blackbeard wanted weapons. "Where's the flare gun, Billy?"

Billy pointed to the flare canister, still laying where he'd dropped it. Blackbeard promptly forgot it as the boat picked up speed and started to dance. Blackbeard had to grab frantically for handholds to stay on his feet.

The boat didn't seem to respond to Billy's frantic turning of the wheel. "How do I steer this thing?" cried Billy.

"I'll do it," Doorman said, trying to sit up. "Get me over there."

The two pirates exchanged looks. "Can you handle it?" Blackbeard looked dubiously at the man whose blood stained the cockpit all around him.

Doorman hacked out a sound that sounded like a death rattle. It just might have been a laugh. "Dying I'm a better sailor than either one of you living."

Blackbeard wasn't sure the "dying" part was all that funny. He pulled Doorman over to the steering pedestal. He had to lift the man's hands up to put them on the wheel. He hoped Doorman could keep his eyes open. "All you've gotta do is just get us the hell out of here," he assured the dying man.

Doorman nodded, looking like he was going to collapse onto the deck. "Trim the jib," he ordered weakly. The two pirates looked at each other. "Trim the jib," Doorman insisted. Then he said something under his breath and tried again. "What you did before. Pull that rope in. That one over there."

Billy pulled it. The boat immediately tilted over under their feet and accelerated. Blackbeard let out a curse as he grabbed for a handhold.

"S'normal," Doorman slurred. "Where're our friends?"

Billy understood. He pointed back behind them. "Back there. Going the other way."

"Won' be for long," Doorman said. "They got to come back to kill me."

"What did you do to them to them that makes them want to kill you?" Blackbeard demanded.

Doorman shook his head. "Never seen 'em before. Pull in that rope over there a lil' more."

Caesaria ran northeast, close-hauled into a gentle north wind. *Käseria* had turned in a broad circle and then headed south on a dead run directly away from her quarry, rapidly diminishing toward the horizon. Billy watched the killer's boat as it turned back, this time coming after them. "They're coming back," he cried out, starting to bounce.

"Gotta come," Doorman agreed, his head nodding sleepily. He turned bloodshot eyes on Billy and mumbled. "Gotta get away. Get that rope over there." His hands were shaking and he was barely able to lift his arms from the wheel to point, so Billy had to guess which rope. Head lolling, gasping between syllables, Doorman explained what they had to do. Blackbeard and Billy jumped to do it, guessing more often than not. Whatever they did worked. *Caesaria* accelerated once more.

As *Caesaria* sped up, both pirates turned to watch the other boat. Its sails filled. The ship spun, sails flapping like a windblown clothesline. Angry yelling erupted from the cockpit. Then, after a few seconds, *Käseria* turned around again, the sails filled again, and then it did the same doughnut turn all over again. It looked to Blackbeard like their attacker was out of control. Angry voices came dimly over the water, confirming his guess.

Soon, however, *Käseria* seemed to get itself together. It charged back toward *Caesaria*. There wasn't any doubt now: it was attacking them. Within a quarter of an hour, the boat had pulled behind them, only a hundred yards back, right in their tracks, its bow splitting *Caesaria*'s wake. Billy kept staring at it, trying to decide whether it was staying even with them or catching up.

"We gotta do something," Billy pleaded.

Blackbeard shrugged. He didn't have a clue what to do. But wait a minute. "What about the radio? Why don't we call for help?"

"Antenna's gone," Doorman gasped out. "Storm got it. Couldn't raise anybody this morning."

This morning? The pirate frowned. The son of a bitch. He'd tried to call the cops while they were sleeping.

Son of a bitch or not, Captain Bligh was the only one who could drive this damn boat. He wasn't looking good. His skin had turned distinctly gray. What would they do if Doorman died on them?

"Get up front," Doorman told Billy. "Can't see over the cabin. You gotta look. Check for boats. Reefs. Rocks. Stuff. In the water." Doorman waved him away bloodily and wearily.

Billy scrambled up over the cabin to the foredeck. He didn't like being up there. The bow wave streaming by on either side of the hull scared him. With the water from the bow wake rushing just below him and the vibrating sail next to him, he feared falling off. Or getting slapped off by the sail pulsing beside him. If he fell in the water, they'd never get back for him before he drowned.

He eased himself forward until he was kneeling just behind the bow pulpit, his hands clutching the metal rails. He could see nothing in the water ahead of them. It looked like clear sailing.

Billy smiled at the thought: clear sailing. That was a good one. He'd have to tell Blackbeard—

Billy the Kid glanced up and almost fell overboard. He saw, dead ahead, three rocks. He yelled out "Rocks! Rocks! Look out! Mayday! Dead ahead!" as he stood to point to them. He lost his balance, grabbed at the smoothly flowing jib for an elusive handhold, and kept yelling and pointing even as he searched for any handhold to keep from going overboard.

At the wheel, Doorman vaguely heard a raised voice from the foredeck. He couldn't make out what they were saying through the roaring in his head. He could see only the top part of the little guy's body over the hump of the cabin top, his hands scrabbling at the jib, then hanging on the forestay. He's going to rip the damn sail, Doorman thought. The damn fool, jumping up and down and pointing toward something in the water ahead. Whether he was pointing to port or to starboard was unclear. What he was exercised about was unclear. Which way to turn was unclear.

Doorman did the only thing he could. He turned the wheel hard over and let the main go, trying to turn back away from whatever Billy was yelling about. *Caesaria* spun on her keel. The sails flapped and protested. The bow turned quickly through 90 degrees, then crept around to complete a perfect circle and head into the wind, sails luffing and the boat slowing.

Billy came stumbling back from the bow at a run, still pointing and calling out warnings. He ran back and jumped down into the blood-splattered cockpit, gesturing and shouting about rocks, now right next to *Caesaria* as her momentum died. Then he stopped, his mouth open. "Oh, my lord."

Blackbeard studied the adversary, futilely trying to come up with a plan. Now that *Caesaria* had stopped, *Käseria* came at them like an angry freight train. Blackbeard expected Captain Bligh to take some action, but he huddled unmoving behind the wheel. His hands never strayed from the wheel, but his pale face was pinched and his eyes closed. Blackbeard looked up, gazing past the injured man at the wheel, toward whatever Billy was yelling about.

In the water, not ten yards away, three faces poked up out of the lake, streaming water. Expressionless. Lifeless. Staring with the dull, disinterested eyes of lake beavers.

Chapter Twenty-Eight

The swimmers looked pale, listless, nearly lifeless. The pirates saw that the swimmers weren't going to be able to help themselves climb onto the sailboat. Both men reached down to haul the first of the swimmers aboard with brute strength.

"Mary Ann," Billy cried out when he hauled the limp girl aboard. They fell into each other's arms, both crying.

That left Blackbeard alone to help the next one up. He leaned down over the transom and stuck out his hand. He almost fell overboard trying to haul a woman up the ladder. She was dead weight, clearly incapable of helping herself. She came aboard as a shivering mass, collapsing in the cockpit, unaware of anyone or anything around her.

Blackbeard leaned down to offer a hand up the ladder to the next person. He'd thought it was another woman. It turned out to be a boy. A boy who slapped aside his offer of a helping hand and returned it with a punch in the nose. Blackbeard cursed, grasping his nose with both hands and letting the boy fall back into the lake. "What the fuck did you do that for?" the big pirate yelled.

David hauled himself numbly up the stern ladder and mumbled through lips stiff with cold. "For hitting my father."

"I don't even know your damn father!"

"You hit him yesterday. You didn't see me, but I saw you. You hit him with a gun. For no reason."

"Yesterday?" Before the storm. Whatever portion of Blackbeard's life that had been lived back then was only a dim memory. And the only people he remembered hitting recently were Captain Bligh and the porky middle-aged guy he'd beaned on the other boat. He had no regrets that he'd thumped the captain of the other boat. He wished he'd hit him a whole hell of a lot harder and a whole lot sooner. Bligh, though: Blackbeard felt kind of guilty about that. He'd turned out to be a pretty decent guy.

"Wait a minute." Blackbeard pointed at Joe Doorman, now just an inanimate lump of bloody clothing discarded under the wheel. "That's your father?" All of a sudden the extra clothes and the extra food and some of Doorman's strange behavior and even the noises around the boat that first night... "Oh, no. Your father. I'm sorry I clobbered him, man. And I'm sorry he got shot."

"Shot?" Deborah Doorman thrust herself between David and Blackbeard. She was still little more than a heap of wet rags shaking with cold and exhaustion and relief. But at the word, she cried: "Shot? Oh my God!" She looked around, seemed to see the body for the first time, and scrabbled over to Doorman's side.

"You shot my father?" David looked around the cockpit sole at the blood and the body of his father. His gorge rose. He had to gulp breaths of air to keep from throwing up. He doubled up his hands and glared at Blackbeard, ready to attack him again.

Billy piped up. "*They* shot your father." He pointed a finger at the other boat. "And now they're comin' back." He pushed Mary Ann away and stepped up onto one of the cockpit settees for a better view. "Oh, God, they're comin'. They're comin'." He began bouncing on the soles of his feet, and Blackbeard and Mary Ann feared that he would begin his dervish dance.

"Help me get him down below," Deborah cut in. Mary Ann pulled Billy over to the unconscious form of Joe Doorman, as much to stop the demonstration as to help Doorman. They gently lifted him off the floor of the cockpit and maneuvered him down the companionway ladder, feet first. Deborah hovered, trying to stand aside and trying to help at the same time. She ended up just cradling his head to keep it from smashing into something. And found herself looking deep into his eyes. Half closed. Lifeless.

Bleeding out. Dying. Dear God. Joe. That bas—

No. That would have to wait.

David was uncertain about what to do. He stood, fists clenched, ready to attack the pirates again. When they pistol-whipped his father he feared they would kill him. They hadn't, though—if they were telling the truth about who shot him—and now seemed almost...not friendly exactly, but concerned. And they were certainly afraid of the people on the other boat.

Were they telling the truth, though, about the other guys shooting his father? Could he trust them? Could there be two groups of people on the same lake wanting to hurt his father? It was hard to believe, but he didn't know. David wished somebody could explain it to him.

Doorman, body maneuvered halfway down the companionway, came to with a start when they twisted his body to slip it by the nav station. His eyes sprang open. He looked wildly around. "Let me go, let me go," he insisted, struggling weakly to fight his handlers. Deborah tried to comfort him, but he talked over her. "That boat," Doorman gasped out, fighting for breath. "Kill us all. Have to get away."

Deborah shushed him. Mary Ann said soothing words. Blackbeard yelled from the cockpit to shut the fuck up if he wasn't going to help. David glared at the big pirate, incensed once more. But when he looked back and forth between the pirates and the crew of the other boat, it became clear to him that those guys and these guys weren't working together. Suddenly his father's words fit all of the pieces together.

"You have to let me up!" Doorman howled piteously as his strength failed. "I have to con the boat!" His head fell back into Deborah's hands. She thought he had lapsed into unconsciousness. Or worse.

He rallied, clearly summoning his last reserves of energy. He twisted his neck around to look back up toward the cockpit. "Is that David out there?" His eyes sought out Deborah's. His voice turned to pleading. "David. David can sail the boat. David can get us away from them."

Then he passed out.

Chapter Twenty-Nine

Blackbeard stood, peering at *Käseria*. The other sailboat was heading for them at a good clip. Doorman called it right: *Käseria* was on the attack.

Blackbeard wanted nothing to do with what was about to happen. Whatever he and Billy had done, they didn't deserve to be killed by hit men. Particularly when they'd just be incidental victims. It was hard to believe that Captain Bligh had done anything to deserve to be killed either, but he must have done something to piss those people off. Whatever it was that he'd done—or whatever the killers thought he'd done—it had nothing to do with Blackbeard or Billy. They just needed to get the hell out of the crossfire. Now.

The big pirate looked around desperately, trying to figure out how to get the sailboat moving. *Caesaria*'s bow pointed north, directly into the wind. The sails flapped ineffectually. The boat drifted, almost unmoving. The big pirate was pretty sure that meant they weren't going to be able to sail that way. What a ridiculous thing about a boat powered by wind, that you couldn't sail upwind when you needed to. And right now, they needed to.

But how were they going to get the damn boat moving to escape? Neither he nor Billy knew how to work a sailboat. With Doorman out of commission, they were pretty well screwed.

Unless...unless the kid really could sail the boat. He looked again at the sodden, disheveled boy, shivering with cold. Nothing about him would lead anyone to suspect that he could tie his own shoes, much less sail a sailboat. "Can you really drive this thing?"

"Give me one reason why I should," David snapped, still trying to figure out for himself good guys and bad guys.

"Your father. That's the reason. There are two killers on that boat. They're coming back to kill your father. And if that's not good enough for you, there are those two women down there who need your help. Everybody here needs you. Including you, hotshot."

"Why do they want to do that?"

"Why? You'll have to ask your father. All I know is, they shot him point blank a few minutes ago. It was no accident. They gunned him down. In cold blood. You understand what I'm sayin'?"

"When you bashed my father in the head, that wasn't an accident either." David wasn't sure anymore who were the good guys and who were the bad guys. The blood all over the cockpit certainly made it clear that his father had been shot. He didn't *know* that the other guys did it. It might have been these pirates. These guys were vicious criminals. Pirates. Liars. He had no reason to believe anything they said.

Except that these pirates were afraid of those other guys. And so was his father. The pirates' explanation made sense. Except that didn't mean it was true. "Why should I believe you?"

"You don't have to believe me. I prob'ly wouldn't if I was you." Blackbeard's smile was so lacking in guile that neither his last arresting officer, nor his probation officer, nor Billy, would have recognized it.

"But the thing is, if we don't work together now, there won't ever be a later. And fortunately or unfortunately, you're all we got to drive this boat. Assuming you actually know how." He glanced toward *Käseria*, got a shock at how quickly the attackers were bearing down on them, and then back at the boy. "It's now or never, kid."

Assuming that it was all true, the question was: could David get them out of this? He assessed the situation around him. Wind. Water. Waves. The other boat coming on, right on a collision course with *Caesaria*.

It certainly looked like it was now or never. And it was what his father wanted him to do. David stepped up to the wheel pedestal.

Could he do it? He put his hands on the wheel, not committed to taking the responsibility. One of his hands reached down for the ignition. The instruments lit up. The fuel gauge read empty. The engine cranked but did not turn over. The diesel tank was empty, then.

David looked up at the sails and then the wind indicator and then the lake. He took in the other boat approaching steadily from upwind. From the north, David knew. The sails of the other boat were set wrong for this wind and for their heading. The fabric luffed and popped loudly as it approached. But it still came on.

The sails of the attacker were so clearly wrong that they must not know how to sail. But something niggled at his memory. It reminded him of a trick he'd read about. One he'd seen in one of Patrick O'Brian's novels his father kept pushing on him. Captain Aubrey tricked a more powerful French warship. He'd set the sails intentionally wrong, wanting it to appear to the French that the English boat was trying to get away, when Aubrey was actually maneuvering to attack.

Could that be it? Did the killers on the bigger boat want *Caesaria* to think they were coming at full speed so they could force *Caesaria* to commit to a course? Meanwhile, they would creep up slowly, waiting for *Caesaria* to declare its intentions, and then move to counter whatever *Caesaria* did. Or maybe the other crew was just incompetent. Either way, the two boats' courses would intersect in just minutes. And lives might be at stake.

If David could get the boat moving quickly enough, maybe they could catch the attackers by surprise. Get enough of a lead to get to safety before the bad guys caught them.

The quickest route to safety for *Caesaria* was to go south, toward Lanier Bay Marina at the south end of the lake. It was close to the city of Buford, which must have doctors and hospitals. But that would mean running downwind in front of their pursuer. If David was the only one on the boat who could sail the boat, he wasn't sure that by himself he would be able to cleanly tack the boat, never mind jibe it. That's what he'd have to do to turn the boat onto a southern heading without broaching.

Nor would he be able to handle the sails on the tricky downwind tack while also steering. Better to head upwind, north toward Gainesville. Surely there was a hospital up there. And it was a direction that would require less technically demanding sailing. That would put the attacker behind them, chasing, having to respond to *Caesaria's* moves, rather than in front of them, able to block them.

David frowned. It would be a lot longer trip to safety. That was bad if his father was seriously hurt. To pick up any headway from a standing stop was going to take some time and some space. He glanced over the side. There wasn't much leeway to the west. They'd have to fall off to the east to pick up speed. That meant crossing the attacker's path, possibly even crossing its bow. Dangerous. But the only way to get to Gainesville.

Without deciding that he was going to accept the challenge, David turned the wheel to starboard, staring up at the wind indicator at the top of the mast. The wind played with the sail before filling it. In a few seconds—never taking his eyes off the wind indicator—David unconsciously reached forward to adjust the jib sheet and, next, the main.

Blackbeard watched him, amazed. This wet, bedraggled kid seemed to know all the ropes cold. He looked like his father, his entire attention on the sails and the wind. If a few minutes before he'd looked like a little lost boy, now he looked like a sailor. He looked bigger and more mature than the drowned puppy Blackbeard had pulled out of the water. Occasionally, the kid leaned forward to pull on this rope or loosen that. Each time, the sailboat picked up speed, almost like the kid was part of the boat, or the boat was part of him. The big man could not suppress a pang of jealously that this kid's father must have taken the time to teach him.

For a moment, the big man's eyes misted. He wished he'd been lucky enough to have a father who taught him stuff. He'd never learned anything from his old man other than getting high and getting in the first punch. That and disappearing when the going got tough.

Blackbeard shook off the thought. He bent to pick up a rope lying tangled on the cockpit sole. "What do I do with this here?"

"Just wrap it around that winch." David pointed without looking down. "Don't pull it." Then he called down into the cabin. "Mom!"

Blackbeard started. *Mom*?

The older woman they'd plucked out of the water appeared, framed in the hatch. She'd rallied. Her cheeks had color now. She looked intense. Worried. "David, I'm kind of busy right now."

Blackbeard stared. That woman was this kid's mom? A "mom" who was trying to save a dying man? A "mom" who was saving a life but only "kind of busy"? What the hell? And the way she said it. *Kind of busy*. Like: *I'm kind of busy cooking dinner.* Or, like: *I'm kind of busy knitting a comforter.* Who were these people?

David's next question broke into the big pirate's thoughts. "How's Dad?"

The big pirate watched Mrs. Doorman weigh her words. She finally admitted, "He was shot. It's an abdominal wound, David. I don't know how bad it is. He's lost a lot of blood. We need to get him to a hospital." She added cautiously, "Your father seems to think that there are people on another boat who are trying to hurt him."

"I know." David's eyes flicked over to Blackbeard. People on this boat, too. He smoldered with hatred for the big pirate. Maybe he was not the one who'd shot Dad, just like he claimed. But until the two pirates appeared, it had been a perfectly normal cruise. Everything bad happened after they invaded the boat.

David's thoughts dissipated. Mom still stood in the companionway. The look of concern on her face made his eyes tear up. "You take care of Dad. I'll get us to a hospital. I can handle it."

"I never had any doubt." She flashed him a tired smile and disappeared back into the cabin.

Blackbeard watched the kid with awe. A simple *I can handle it* when all their lives were on the line. His own father would be bellowing and throwing things and looking for somebody to blame. His own mother would be doing her usual: screaming about calling the police. Nothing like this dialogue would never have happened in the house he grew up in. It was more like a '50s sitcom: "Would you please save our lives, son?" "As you wish, Mother."

David had been talking without ever taking his mind off the boat. *Caesaria* rewarded him by picking up speed. Now he focused on tactics. They'd be better off, he decided, to rely on strategy to evade

Käseria rather than trying to outsail her. If he could attack the other boat, make her turn away, get some breathing space...

That was it. He decided instantly. He commanded, "Hold on!" and hauled the sails in. *Caesaria* heeled and accelerated yet again. The movement launched Blackbeard toward the low side of the cockpit. He managed to grab a handhold before the heeling boat could launch him into the water.

David loosed the sails' sheets from their clam cleats with two quick whipping movements, spinning the wheel to turn to port. Heading west, where land loomed not very far away. But he needed speed and needed it now. He didn't have much room to build speed, but if he work up a little, then he could turn back east and cross in front of *Käseria*, maybe even make the attacker sheer off to avoid collision.

Caesaria turned onto her temporary new course. David quickly reset the sails for the quick tack toward the west and, with a few efficient motions, trimmed them. The big pirate staggered again as the boat leaped forward eagerly. He watched David handle the boat, not losing his balance—not even appearing to notice—the new tilt of the deck. The sailboat moved as though excited now. She raced toward the shore, water singing along her waterline, singing as if she was excited to be part of a deadly race.

Chapter Thirty

Billy Bob Kaufman, Cheese King of Atlanta, was weighing various tactical plans as he stood at the wheel of his sailboat, watching the boat they were chasing. In the last few minutes, he'd watched the profile of *Caesaria* change. Her sails filled neatly, then she tacked away. As he watched, she fell off the wind to a close reach and then on to a run. They would try to get away toward the east, he guessed. That's where they'd have the most space to maneuver.

Which was great for Billy Bob. It meant the chase would be longer. More distance; more time for something unexpected to happen; more opportunities to find reasons to slow down; more chances to create space; more possibilities of finding a way to tip the assassins overboard.

Billy Bob looked ahead and gulped. He'd mistaken what he'd seen. *Caesaria* was heading west, toward the looming land and a broad arc of islands that would block their escape. Why would they sail into a dead end? Now *Käseria* could corral them in minutes. It didn't make sense.

Worse, it made Billy Bob's graduation from innocent bystander to accessory to murder imminent . There was no question in his mind that if he managed to corral Doorman's boat, the killers would finish Doorman off if he was still lucky enough to still be alive. And then everyone else. Including Billy Bob Kaufman.

After a couple of confounding minutes of continuing toward a dead end, *Caesaria* pirouetted and tacked back. Back east, toward more open water. Also, directly at *Käseria*. A chill ran down his spine. Now they were hunting him!

It didn't make any sense. *Käseria's* crew had guns. The crew were professional killers who'd already exhibited their willingness to kill. Doorman's boat should be running, not attacking.

An unpleasant possibility nagged at him. Maybe he'd underestimated the quarry. Maybe the guy—what was his name? Doorman, that's right—wasn't just a guy off the street. Clearly he had balls. Being hunted didn't seem to faze him. Neither did being shot. It was obvious when Billy Bob thought about it. The target had to be important enough to justify hiring contractors. It was just their bad luck—and Billy Bob's—that the victim had the balls to stand and fight them toe to toe.

Which begged the question that now seemed of paramount importance. Kaufman called out: "Buddy, who is this guy?"

Buddy snarled. "Hey. Pay attention to your driving. Your only concern ought'a be doing your job and doing it right. You're going to snuggle this big hulk right up next to that big hulk. Then you're done."

Done. *Done* like *not likely to be alive tomorrow*. "I want some assurances," Kaufman croaked out through a mouth suddenly dry. "I want some assurances you're not going to do to me what you're going to do to that Doorman guy."

Buddy enunciated carefully. "What are you worried about? Obviously we need you to get us back to dry land when we're done here. Lynette and me can't drive this thing. After that, you'll never see us again. I can assure you of that."

Kaufman heard the confirmation of his fears. *Never see them again* because his eyes would be permanently closed. Permanently open, actually. Still, if they needed him alive until he got them close to land, that meant he still had time to figure out how to save himself.

But there was not much time left for planning his own salvation. Not right now, with *Käseria* was on a dead run, heading south. *Caesaria* was south of them, heading northeast. Toward them. Fast. Their courses would intersect in minutes.

Intersect, hell. If *Käseria* didn't jibe, or if *Caesaria* didn't turn away, the two sailboats would collide. Either that, or *Caesaria* would pass them by, sailing east, and seize the initiative. And as O'Brian's captains knew, if *Caesaria* passed *Käseria*, *Caesaria* would seize the advantage. Aubrey called it the "weather gauge:" the ship that stayed upwind had the advantage of always being in a position to make the first move, in a position to decide to attack or to escape. If *Caesaria* got past them, *Käseria* would only be able to react.

It gave him an idea. If Billy Bob let *Caesaria* get upwind, that meant that *Käseria* would never catch up. Doorman wouldn't end up dead. Billy Bob wouldn't end up an accessory to murder. Lynette and Buddy would have to give up the hunt—

—and take out their frustration on the nearest handy target. Which was Billy Bob Kaufman. He might end up dead because he'd saved Doorman's life. Crap.

"Hey," he called to Buddy. "We got a problem."

Buddy jumped down into the cockpit from his perch on the cabin top. "What? You need help driving?"

"It's like this. They're trying to cross us." Billy Bob Kaufman tried to draw a diagram in the air with his hands. "If they cross us, they can make a run for Lazy Holiday Marina or Lakeland Marina or even Hall County Marina near Gainesville. By the time we turn around to go after them, we might have lost too much ground to catch them. Not without some first-rate sailing, and I don't have a racing crew I can rely on. All I've got to rely on is just you fu—" He swallowed his next word in time to save himself. "Uh, guys. Rely on you guys. Once we end up downwind of them, we're sunk."

Buddy stared, squinting.

The Cheese King watched Buddy's face. He could read faces like Helen Keller could read signs. He understood that the squint meant Buddy thought he was being played. And that Kaufman's explanation didn't sound even faintly likely. Buddy tried again. "See, they'll have the weather gauge—"

"What kind of crap you feeding me?" Buddy spat. "You got all the gauges you need right there in front of you."

It was too difficult to explain. In fact, Kaufman himself didn't entirely understand it. But maybe it was an opportunity. If he made it sound really difficult to chase *Caesaria* down, then when he failed it wouldn't seem like he did it on purpose.

Buddy slipped into his most unctuous tone. "See, we can't go directly into the wind. We can't just point the boat there and get it there. It's not like a powerboat. The boat that's upwind controls the battle. See? We gotta be between them and the wind to control things. They control the whole shooting match if they get past us. We can trap them against the land as long as we have the weather...that is, as long as we're upwind. Right now we're upwind, and we can block them in any direction they try to go. But if they get by us and they're upwind and we're downwind, we'll have to catch them by tacking over and over—" Billy Bob stopped, seeing the look on Buddy's face.

"They're coming right at us. We don't have to chase anybody."

"Yeah. OK. Right now, I can get us right alongside that boat as they try to pass us, and you can do whatever you need to do," Kaufman assured him. "But if you miss, and if they slip past us, we're going to have to chase them upwind. We may never catch them."

"I guess you better make sure they don't get past." Buddy turned away. Conversation over as far as he was concerned.

Kaufman began to feel desperate. "You gotta choose. I can block them and make them turn away and stay south. Or I can try to put us alongside and you can shoot at them or board them. But if I try to get us alongside and something happens and you don't stop them, it may be the only shot you get. It's only a few hours 'til dark. We might could lose them in the dark, or they just might outrun us or whatever. If they get upwind of us, we damn sure ain't gonna be able to trap them against an island or the shore."

Lynette had been listening intently and, despite herself, found the strategy interesting. "What happens if we get in their way? You know, block them?"

"See, I think the thing is that if we go up that away"—Kaufman pointed northwest—"we might could pin 'em against an island. That'd give you your best chance. It would take longer, but it would let you take your time and do it right." And Kaufman might be able to slip close enough to shore to dive overboard and swim for it.

Buddy pulled out his pistol and checked the load, keeping his eyes locked on Kaufman to make a point. "It's simple. We don't need any fancy maneuvering. All you gotta do is put us right next to them."

Kaufman started. Almost exactly the instructions of Admiral Lord Nelson to his captains: "Never mind maneuvers, just go straight at 'em!"

Kaufman wondered if Lord Nelson looked as bloodthirsty as Buddy did at this moment.

Chapter Thirty-One

David steered *Caesaria* on a close reach to the northeast. He pushed her as close to the wind as he could, using every input from each of his senses to edge so close to the wind that he was in danger of stalling the boat. He sensed slight irregularities in the wind as it played in his hair. He felt slight variations of pressure on the rudder through his fingertips on the wheel. He sensed the boat's balance through his feet on the cockpit sole and the minute variations in the sound of the bow cutting through the water. He saw and played every puff of wind, every crease of the sails, driving the boat as if it were a living being, totally unconscious that he was sailing the boat better than he ever had.

For a little while, David hoped that he might sneak past their attacker: pass it cleanly, leave it behind while beating upwind. Doorman had taught David how to judge whether another boat was on a converging course. He tried various combinations of adjustments to the sails, played with different headings. But no matter what he did, *Käseria* stayed stubbornly in place, on a course that would intersect *Caesaria*. David looked at his sails and the wind indicator and shook his head. Nothing he did coaxed any more speed out of *Caesaria*.

He had to avoid the opposing boat getting too close at all costs. If Blackbeard could be believed—if his father was right—they had to get away or die. Yet *Käseria* in position to block their escape northward. She seemed cemented in a controlling position.

What were his choices? He could jibe the boat and run away, but then he'd be giving *Käseria* the power to chase them down and herd them into a corner. He could slow down just a little and pass behind the big boat, but he would have to steer close to fool them into thinking the courses were still converging. "Close" wasn't healthy when they had a gun and a willingness to use it.

There was only one other possibility. A long shot. He couldn't do it by himself, and he wasn't sure he could do it with the help he had available. But with no time to second-guess himself, David snapped the orders out. "We're gonna have to tack. Get your friend up here to help."

Blackbeard hesitated to follow the orders of a kid. But this was not the same sodden urchin he'd pulled out of the water. A different kid from any of the kids he'd known in school or, for that matter, in Juvie. David stood behind the wheel, fully invested in running the boat. When he gave orders, it wasn't like he was a kid playing captain. He was the captain.

Blackbeard did as he was told, not quite believing he was letting a tyke tell him what to do. He called his partner.

Billy came up. David pointed at the jib sheet. "When I say so, you unwind the line—that rope right there—off the winch. Stop! Don't do it until I tell you." To Blackbeard: "You. Pull really hard on that rope over there until I tell you to stop."

David looked them each in the eyes to make sure they were paying attention. "Look sharp and keep your heads down. We're going to be real, real close. If they want to shoot at us, they're going to get a great chance." David looked at their pursuer. In the few seconds of instructions, *Käseria* had gotten close. Maybe he'd hesitated too long.

David saw the captain of the other boat staring anxiously at *Caesaria* and then at his own boat, as though measuring them against each other. The guy clearly feared that *Caesaria* was going to ram his boat. And in a second, *Caesaria* would in fact hit them.

Käseria's captain flinched, turning his boat west to avoid the collision.

"Get ready," David warned, not looking at his crew. "*Now!*" David swung the wheel hard over. Billy let the port-side jib sheet go. The sail flogged as the boat turned into the wind and then through it onto a port tack. "Now you," David called to Blackbeard. "Do it." The big man pulled in the starboard-side jib sheet. When the jib popped into shape, *Caesaria* set off like a racehorse, bounding over the other boat's wake. David told him to stop hauling on the rope, looking around for their rival.

For the moment, it was dead astern of them. Going the other direction. Seemingly retreating in disgrace. The two pirates stood up and gave each other high fives. Then they turned and shot obscene gestures and insults at their attacker.

"Get back to your places," David snapped. They looked at him with surprise. There was no time for David to explain that their advantage was momentary and that now they were going to undo what they'd just done. "Wrap those lines around the winches like I told you. We'll have to tack again."

He didn't want to take his eyes off the sails. It boiled down to a game of inches. *Caesaria* wouldn't be able to make up any ground they lost it this next maneuver didn't work. To pull it off, David would have to get the sails drawing perfectly.

"Oh darn," Billy clucked. David didn't have to look to know what the little pirate had seen. No doubt *Käseria* had headed up into the wind and chased after them. If that guy set the sails right, David knew, the other boat would catch them in a minute. That would be the end. The killers' boat would pull alongside and shoot everyone on *Caesaria* full of holes.

The solution was to tack back. A snap tack, like he'd seen in the America's Cup races. One night when he was sitting with his father watching the America's Cup on TV, he'd seen the Australians pull a surprise tack on their American challengers. The Aussies had left the Americans in their wake, struggling to catch up. A snap tack might work if David did it fast and timed it right and caught the other captain by surprise.

He pointed at the jib sheet to direct Billy. "Loosen up that rope again when I tell you." He peered at their enemy, judging speed and angle without realizing he was doing geometry. When it was time, he called "Now!" He whirled the wheel. *Caesaria* heeled with the sharp turn. Billy had gotten the starboard jib sheet caught and struggled to loosen it. The snagged line held the sail in place, causing the boat's head to swing through the wind more quickly than David intended. Now they were not going to be able to accelerate out of the tack because they'd lost the jib's power. Blackbeard, meanwhile, following directions, started hauling in the port sheet, robbing *Caesaria* of additional speed.

It was a disaster in the making. The boat would turn in a full circle while they untangled the snag. That would cause them to lose their lead over their attackers, let the bigger boat pass them and get upwind, or let the killers pull alongside at their leisure to take potshots.

Suddenly the starboard sheet popped free of its entanglement. The jib snapped into place. *Caesaria* leaped forward, passing *Käseria* on the opposite tack. The killer's boat had started to accelerate out of its tack, but, surprised by *Caesaria*'s tack, headed stubbornly in the wrong direction. *Käseria*'s helmsman stared at them, open-mouthed, as *Caesaria* passed upwind, pulling away.

Käseria's sails luffed for a moment. David wondered if the other boat had been getting ready to tack when *Caesaria*'s snap-tack caught him by surprise. Now, *Käseria* tacked to get back in the game, bringing the two boats running side by side. A pure race on parallel courses. *Caesaria* pulled away momentarily as *Käseria*'s crew struggled to get the sails set after the tack. The only good news about the other boat running parallel was that it kept the killers' hands busy trimming sails rather than using whatever ammunition they had left.

"Great job." David grinned. "Now, let's do it again." The pirates jumped to set the sails as if they were experienced crew.

We're in control, David thought. For the moment, and if we can manage to stay ahead of them, and if they don't start shooting, we're in control.

***

Shooting was precisely what Buddy and Lynette were discussing. They were discussing it loudly. They were discussing it angrily. And they were discussing it within the hearing of their intended target.

Kaufman did his best to ignore them as he concentrated on *Caesaria*. The other boat had outsmarted him again. The boats diverged on opposite tacks. Kaufman ran from one winch to the other, letting the sails flog on one winch as he left it to manage another. With every tack he lost ground, then had to fight to make up the lost ground.

Now Kaufman turned hard to port, tacking the boat alone as the killers stood discussing how they would manage the boat if they dispatched him. Once again *Käseria* pulled close to *Caesaria*, but still behind. Much to the frustration of the assassins.

Right now, the boats were neck and neck, not more than ten yards apart. The kid at the helm surprised him with each tack. There was no reason that *Käseria* couldn't beat *Caesaria* flat out, tack in front, and take back the weather position. The larger boat had a longer waterline and carried more sail. Even Kaufman knew that meant that *Käseria* was faster. No reason they were losing the race except for lack of hands.

Sailing the boat himself, trimming the sails too, there was no way Kaufman would win the race. Not even against even a damn rowboat. Well, screw this, Kaufman muttered. He wasn't going to do all the work.

"Hey!" he bellowed. The killers' conversation stopped dead, their faces frozen in mid-discussion. "You wanna catch that boat, you gotta goddam help! Now quit bitchin' and trim those damn sails!"

Lynette paused in her expostulation. The woman looked over at the Cheese King, then back at Buddy and then back once more. "OK. Tell me what I need to do."

Buddy eyed Kaufman with a stony glare, flamboyantly caressing the gun in his hand, contemplating a different course of action.

***

The boats flew, side by side, eastward. A puff of wind here or there favored one boat or the other momentarily. *Caesaria* pointed closer to the wind, so was able to edge slightly north-northeast to separate from *Käseria*. But the bigger boat carried more sail and had more power at its disposal. It gradually inched ahead, even with Kaufman doing most of the work of sailing and trimming the sails.

David kept an eye on the opponent, knowing he would have to find the right moment to tack away again.

Kaufman peered at the Doorman's boat as he inched closer. *Käseria* would soon be racing side by side with *Caesaria*, then pull in front. The Cheese King watched closely, moment by moment, judging when he'd be able to tack in front of the smaller boat and cut it off or, even better, force it to tack back downwind to avoid a collision. Either way, in a few moments *Caesaria* would have to concede the weather gage to *Käseria*.

Slowly, slowly, *Käseria* pulled even. In a few seconds, *Käseria* would pass. Then a quick turn and Kaufman's boat would be blocking the other boat, forcing them to tack away.

Then *Caesaria* tacked suddenly, taking Buddy by surprise. The Doorman boat sped away from their attacker. Racing westward.

It took a moment for the uncoordinated crew on *Käseria* to respond, but they tacked to follow. For a few minutes, *Caesaria* pulled away as the other boat's crew struggled to get the sails set properly. Slowly, though, *Käseria* clawed its way inexorably back, even pulling slightly ahead. David tacked *Caesaria* yet again. *Käseria* stayed right with her, tacking again, pulling even, starting to inch ahead. Their wakes cut parallel *z*'s in the deep green surface of the lake as they raced.

David muttered something under his breath when he saw the new teamwork on the opposing boat. The curse rang out clearly in the fraught silence of the cockpit. His mother would not have approved. The word David uttered made Blackbeard look back at him with a censorious look. A look at the ragged boy at the helm softened him. He asked, "How long can we do this?"

"We can do this until we run out of lake or they cut us off. The trouble is, sooner or later he's going to get in front of us and then between us and the marina. And I have to get my father to a hospital."

Blackbeard thought he heard an unusual strain in the young captain's voice. He put a hand on his shoulder. "You OK?"

David shrugged the hand away. "What do you care?"

All of a sudden he was that kid once more. Sullen. Hostile. Which was understandable, given the way they'd met. But now he needed to get over it. He was their only hope.

Blackbeard softened his tone. "Listen, dude. Just because I hijacked your boat and knocked your father around doesn't mean I don't care about getting away." David shot him a poisonous glance, and Blackbeard grinned at him. "Seeing as how I prize my hide."

The boy snorted.

"Is there anything I can do?"

It seemed to focus David. "Weapons. Find some weapons. We got those flares and a flare gun. If we don't have anything else, we'll have to use them."

Blackbeard called Billy over. Together they crawled all over the boat, above decks and below, collecting everything that could be used as a weapon. It wasn't much. Just the three measly flares they'd found before and the flare gun. A couple of carving knives. A few unopened bottles of wine that might serve as clubs.

Meanwhile, the boats raced together for the western shore. *Käseria's* crew had gotten their act together. Their boat was pulling ahead in fits and starts. David muttered another curse.

Looking ahead, he could tell that they'd be OK on this tack for a while: there was an island ahead that they'd manage to squeeze by. When they did, *Käseria* might have to tack away and would lose ground. The next tack after that would be tricky, though. It would be a long tack, toward the east, where there was plenty of open water. That meant plenty of opportunity for the faster *Käseria* to pull ahead. Then *Caesaria* would be finished.

Unless he did something now. But nothing occurred to him. He'd tried everything he could think of. Sooner or later *Caesaria* and everyone aboard her would be lost.

When you don't have any options, redefine the problem. Right. Sure, Dad. Let's redefine ourselves to already be safe and sound in the ER in Gainesville. That would solve this problem pretty quick.

David looked at the other boat, the wind, *Caesaria's* position on the lake. "It's got to be the next tack," the boy muttered to himself. His voice quavered as the enormity of the next decision hit him. His knees shook. His breath came short and shallow. Imagining the likely results of their long tack to the east made him sick to his stomach.

Wait, though. He shouldn't be scared. This was just like a race. He'd crewed for his father a few times when they raced *Caesaria* in the informal sailing club races. After everything else that had happened to him today—never mind yesterday!—this race was nothing. There. How's that for redefining the problem?

Still, David found himself trembling. He was afraid of losing his father if he didn't get to a hospital soon. Afraid of putting his mother in danger. Afraid most of all of failing to live up to his father's confidence. *David can do it.* David wasn't so sure.

The question was, was there anything he could do to win the race? *Käseria* could grab the upwind position—it *would* grab the upwind position any moment now—and *Caesaria* could do nothing but run away. In the end, though, the result of the race was already clear. And it wasn't giong to be pretty for anyone on the Doorman family sailboat.

Think it through, David's father said in his ear. As though his father was there next to him, not down below, wounded, or worse—

David shook his head to clear the inconceivable. Dad's voice insisted he pay attention to the problem he faced. *Decide what the problem is, not what you wish it were. Then make your best choice.*

Thanks, Dad. Great help there. Maybe you could tell me what's my "best choice?"

Your "best choice" is your best choice given what you know. Nobody can expect anything more from you. You shouldn't expect any more from yourself. Make your best choice and execute it. That's all.

When had Dad told him that? He couldn't remember. In any case, right now there was really only one choice. If *Caesaria* couldn't get away—and she couldn't—there was nothing to do but fight. He'd have to put *Caesaria* right alongside *Käseria* to give the pirates their best chance to attack the killers and their guns. His scratch crew would have to use whatever weapons they could put their hands on.

David let the pirates distract him for a moment. They stood around the cockpit, staring around without any apparent understanding of what they were seeing. The pirates and the girl didn't look like fighters. He himself and Mom certainly weren't. But pirates were pirates, weren't they? There was no reason they couldn't be called to step up and act like pirates.

Would they follow his orders, though? David's hands tightened on the wheel. He'd find out soon enough.

"Listen up. We are going to have to fight them. No, don't argue! Just listen!" Oh, God, now his father's imperious tone of voice was coming out of his own mouth! "I'm going to tack again in just a minute. That boat over there is going to want to tack after us, just like he's done all day. When he starts to tack, I'm going to put us right alongside him. After that, it's up to you. Hit him with everything you've got."

Billy gaped at him, then Blackbeard. "Us? Why us?"

Blackbeard slapped Billy. "Get your girlfriend up here. I've seen her fight. She ain't no wimp." *Unlike you* remained unspoken.

Billy jumped below. Mary Ann came up, Billy following reluctantly. David breathed deeply for the first time in minutes. The potential mutiny was over. His scratch crew seemed ready, even enthusiastic. Mary Ann most of all.

They divvied up the weapons. Mary Ann got a bottle and a handheld flare. Billy got a knife, a bottle, and a flare. Blackbeard took the flare gun and a knife. He tried to hand the remaining handheld flare to David, who refused it with a shake of the head.

"I'll sail. You fight. First, we tack. Got it? You two are going to do what you've been doing. I'm going to put us alongside. They aren't going to expect us to stop and fight. We'll surprise them. You're only going to have the advantage for a few seconds."

Billy asked, "What if they have guns?"

It shocked Blackbeard. The killers in fact *had* guns, they'd already *used* guns, Doorman was below bleeding *as the result* of a gun. But right now, Blackbeard figured Billy needed to be calm more than Blackbeard needed to needle him. So for once, Blackbeard kept his snark to himself.

Mary Ann stepped in. "Look at it this way." Mary Ann patted Billy's shoulder. "If they've got guns, we have to face them sooner or later. Personally, I'd rather do it when I've got something in my hands." She hefted the bottle. "I already took one screwing today. I don't feel like taking another one. Now without a fight." Blackbeard noticed Mrs. Doorman's face, framed in the companionway, flashing disapproval at the girl's language.

Suddenly Mary Ann let out a squeal and pointed at *Käseria*. "That's him! That's him!" Even Deborah Doorman came a few steps up the ladder from the companionway to see what the noise was about. "He's the one," yelled Mary Ann, catching Deborah's eye. "He's the one who..."

Her voice trailed off. She didn't know quite how to explain exactly what Billy Bob Kaufman had done. Not in polite company. She glared at the men around her. "That pig is *mine.* Got that? Him and me—we got business to finish."

Deborah looked from the girl to the man piloting the other boat. If she'd been doing "business" with that guy, it must have been a transaction performed on another boat. Maybe even the boat that was chasing them. That put another complexion on the girl's stories: she was on "a date" on "another sailboat;" she was kidnapped and dumped, hog-tied, on *Caesaria*; she'd never seen Joe before; never saw a boy. Maybe her ridiculous story was the truth. At any rate, was it any more ridiculous than Deborah's riding out a storm in a rusty barge or David's saving her with a sinking dinghy?

With a softening expression, Deborah went back to tending to Joe, that b—

Deborah swallowed the thought and amended: Back to tending her husband.

David had ignored them all, shifting his gaze back and forth from the water to the wind riffles on the lake surface to the position of the two boats. Then: "Let's tack." David started to turn the wheel. Then he stopped. "Wait a minute. Light those flares. I'm going to tack; then I'm going to give them time to tack behind us, and then I'll jibe around and come up alongside." Three faces looked at him blankly.

He tried again. "We're going to turn around. That'll take them by surprise. When I tack to starboard—that way, over there to the right—they're going to follow. I'll cut right in front of them and spin us around. That'll put us right up next to them, side by side. That's your cue to attack. You two land some of those flares on that boat someplace where it will start a fire. Into their cabin or up in their sails. If you can start a fire, they'll be so distracted they won't be able to chase us. But we have to take advantage of that second or two, because after that—“ He turned his attention to Billy. “You stand by those winches. You’re gonna have to do the jib sheets by yourself.”

Blackbeard hurriedly lit his own flare, then Mary Ann’s. The flames were blinding even in the daylight. The thick, acrid tails of smoke were a dead giveaway of what they had planned. So much for surprise, David thought.

If surprise was gone, then he could not wait another instant. “Now,” David called out, his voice betraying his nervousness. He swung the wheel hard over.

Chapter Thirty-Two

Billy Bob Kaufman knew *Caesaria* would have to tack away as soon as *Käseria* sailboat threatened to pass them. They'd been doing it all day because they couldn't afford to give *Käseria* the edge. Kaufman had an answer this time, though. If he got this right, the strategic advantage would be all *Käseria*'s.

He was up on his toes, eyes flicking from his sails to the other boat, ready to counter the maneuver. A doubt flashed through his mind. What the hell was he doing? Losing was the plan. He had to lose the race to foil the assassination of Doorman. But he hated to lose, even when he should.

Kaufman pushed his resistance out of his mind. There was still time. Right now, he just wanted to prove a point to the killers that he wasn't just a salesman. And there was a reason to win the race: he had to make buying in to their plan look real. He didn't need to make it all the way to the finish line ahead of Doorman's boat; he just had to prove to everyone that he could do it, before he threw the race.

So he watched *Caesaria* carefully, waiting for the right moment. He saw the other boat's sails shudder. Tacking. He didn't even take the time to warn his crew. He spun the wheel.

Caesaria didn't tack, though. She jibed, spinning on her keel. Jibing meant turning around 180°. The maneuver produced a thunder of flapping sails. Both boats accelerated onto their new courses, now toward each other, on an even closer collision course.

In a panic, Kaufman clawed at the wheel to avoid the collision. *Käseria* turned and kept turning. In seconds she was pointed downwind. The sudden move threw both killers to the deck. Buddy landed on his butt on the cabin top where he was standing waiting for a shot, then started to slide with the suddenly tilting deck. He dropped the pistol at his feet, grabbing wildly with both hands for something to hold on to. The pistol slid away from him, bounced off the cabin top, then heavily to the side deck. Before Buddy could retrieve it, the gun plonked into the lake.

Buddy nearly followed as he slipped toward the water. He caught himself, an arm and a leg hooked around the lifelines, his body half overboard. Kaufman was in no position to enjoy the sight, much less save him. He hung on to the wheel and looked wildly around to see where *Caesaria* was.

Following them! *Caesaria* was now behind *Käseria*. Billy Bob jumped to trim his sails appropriately. *Caesaria* charged right at them.

It perplexed Billy Bob. Why would they jibe? If the other boat was trying to get away, why turn back toward *Käseria*? Billy Bob pondered the problem as he jumped back and forth between adjusting the headsail and mainsail. It looked like they were trying to come alongside. In fact, now *Caesaria* was alongside, bucking in the bow wave of Billy Bob's boat.

Just as he was trying to figure it all out, he saw something fly up in the air. A missile! A burning flare! Billy Bob ducked instinctively even though the sizzling flare whizzed over his head and landed on *Käseria*'s foredeck.

The bitter whiff of burning fiberglass resin reached the Cheese King. He called frantically to his crew, pointing. "Get that thing!

It's gonna ruin my fiberglass!" Lynette scrambled to the foredeck and kicked the flare over the side.

Another flare flew over. Kaufman was gratified that this one missed his boat completely. Except...it didn't miss. It hit the mainsail and stuck there for long seconds before succumbing to gravity. Sliding down the sail, it left a scorch mark on the sailcloth and fell onto the cabin top. On her way back from the bow, Lynette grabbed it and tossed it over the side, too.

Buddy suddenly appeared at Kaufman's side. "Why are we standing here?" He pointed at *Caesaria*, which seemed to be accelerating past them. "Get us moving. Get them!"

Kaufman had been, until that moment, nothing more than a sailor caught up in a race he was going to lose to try to save his own life. But now he was pissed. Burn my boat? Kaufman ground his teeth. He turned the wheel to put *Käseria* right into other boat's wake.

Buddy turned to Kaufman. "Burning their sails down. How come you never suggested it, eh?" The killer grabbed Kaufman's arm with an iron grip. "You got a flare gun on this boat?"

Billy Bob told him where to find it. The assassin turned to Lynette to send her below. "Go get the flare gun. I'm gonna beat those bastards at their own game. See how they like it. Soon as the Admiral here gets us close enough."

***

On *Caesaria*, David watched the flares hit *Käseria*, but his mind was on the problem of breaking away from the enemy boat. The flares hadn't worked; his maneuvering had been muddled; now the big boat kept pace just behind him. Once the killers got their sails set properly, they could pull even with *Caesaria* once again. If he turned back north, *Käseria* was in perfect position to move in front of him to block him.

He cursed his stupid mistake. He hadn't thought it through properly. He'd blown what might be their only chance to get past *Käseria*. So now they were speeding away from the nearest town and further from the closest hospital. Stupid, stupid, stupid. For the first time in twenty-four hours his eyes well up with shame. He'd screwed up yet again.

Yet *Caesaria*'s quiet grace under pressure didn't flag. The boat responded to his every movement of wheel, sheet, and rudder with calm, confident assurance. She held her own against the bigger boat. With *Caesaria* on his side, there was still a chance.

It was true that his plan so far hadn't won the fight. But it was also true that the tacking duel had kept the enemy at bay. It had placed *Caesaria* in position to attack. And David's quick tacking had placed them alongside *Käseria* for a moment, at least, exactly where he wanted them. The execution was off, he conceded, but not the strategy. It would have worked. And they might still get another chance.

If they did, this time he'd nail them. He would just have to find a way to set up another chance. David concentrated on trying to pinch every possible advantage out of every waver of the needle at the top of the mast.

On and on went the race, ponderously cutting wakes into the emerald green water. The long afternoon waned as, inevitably, working her greater sail area and longer waterline to advantage, *Käseria* again began to inch up even with *Caesaria*. And *Caesaria* maneuvered to keep away.

***

Billy and Blackbeard stood by in silence and watched David. He struck the pirates as master of his boat in every way. But helpless in the face of the stubborn attack.

They watched their adversary approaching inexorably. There was nothing for them to do. Nothing David could do to speed up *Caesaria.* Nothing to beat back their attacker. Nothing but wait for the inevitable collision.

Soon the frothing bow wave of *Käseria* crawled into the wake of *Caesaria*. The crew of *Caesaria* watched helplessly as the big sailboat inched closer. In the enemy's cockpit, they saw Kaufman concentrating on keeping the sails filled and his course true. They saw the two other people in the cockpit watching *Caesaria* intently, like hyenas eager for the kill.

David glanced at his crew of pirates, saw their expressions, and looked quickly over his shoulder to see what they were staring at. The killers' boat was right on their tail. The race was over. There would be no more running.

There was room—barely room—for only one more maneuver. Right now. Only if David did it now. If he moved right now, he could cut in front of them. Head north, right into them. Turn and confront them. Ram them if he had to.

There was no time to weigh the odds. No time to think about alternatives. If he didn't act now, then *Käseria* would be all over them. They'd all be at the mercy of the killers. And if he acted and failed...well, they'd still be at the mercy of the killers.

There was simply no choice. If he didn't try, there was no chance he'd be able to save his father. Unless he managed that, Joe Doorman would die even if the killers didn't shoot him again. If they really were killers like Blackbeard said, then they'd kill not only his dad. They'd get his mom. The girl. The pirates. And David himself.

The laborious weighing of alternatives had taken less time than a heartbeat. David straightened up at the wheel. "One last trick, guys. I'm going to loosen the mainsheet a little." To the small pirate: "Let that jib sheet—that one, right there—loose a few inches. Give it some slack. That's right. That will slow us down real fast. They won't know we've slowed down, and they'll come up almost next to us. Then I'll jibe again. That'll put them right abeam of us. Right there." David clarified, by pointing to a spot at *Caesaria*'s side so that the other three would understand what "abeam" meant. "It'll be the last chance we're going to have."

David got Blackbeard's attention. "Load that flare gun. Put a couple of flare shots into their sails. Don't waste them. And you," he instructed Mary Ann, "try to get that last flare into the cockpit. If you can get them jumping around the cockpit, or even start a fire, maybe you'll get them distracted enough that we can get away."

They started to argue with him, mostly because they didn't understand what "abeam" meant or how stopping would save them. David ignored them. "Mom," he called out. Deborah Doorman popped up in the open companionway. "I'm going to attack them. Get Dad down below the waterline. Get down yourself. There's going to be some shooting."

Deborah blanched. She started up the companionway hatch. "David—"

David held up a hand to stop her. "Get down! Your job is to help Dad. Go!" He was dimly conscious that his mother stood open-mouthed at the companionway for a few moments. "Go!" he repeated. She drew herself up to object to his tone, then thought the better of it and returned to doctoring her husband, below.

David turned his attention back to his crew. "Ready?"

Billy leaned over Mary Ann's flare, lighting it. "OK. We're ready."

Blackbeard checked his flare gun. "Ready." The three exchanged a quick grin, grim but determined.

David uncleated the main sheet and let the rope run between his fingers. The boat slowed, but not enough. He caught the little pirate's eye and pointed to the jib sheet. "Let that jib fly." Billy uncoiled the line from around the winch and let it run. The jib luffed out, too far, snapping and popping. *Caesaria* settled in the water as if someone had slammed the brakes on. In a moment her stern lifted as her stern wave caught up with her.

Käseria kept on, charging toward them on top of a thick bow wake like a battleship under full steam. David used the last of his sailboat's momentum to spin 180 degrees, turning *Caesaria* into the wind. There it stalled, as he'd hoped. *Käseria* ended up right next to them, on the port beam, just where David wanted them.

Billy grabbed his partner. "Wow. You see that? He done just like he said."

"Fire!" David called.

Time slowed to a crawl.

Blackbeard stood at the rail, the flare gun extended as he aimed, looking like duelist in an old daguerreotype. The flare gun had two barrels, which he assumed must mean two flares. He'd choreographed his moves in his head. One shot at the big sail, another at the smaller front sail. And then a jump over onto the other boat to kick some ass.

David glanced over at their adversaries, where the crew's mouths were open in comic *o*'s of surprise again.

Fire, fire, fire, David pleaded silently.

Finally, Blackbeard fired.

The flare popped into *Käseria*'s mainsail. It stuck there, smoldering and smoking. From the cockpit of the big boat, the Cheese King screamed at his crew to put it out.

The killers—shocked to be the recipients of incoming fire again—stood immobile, looking back and forth between the burning flare in the sail and the flares they held in their own hands. The three alternatives froze them, unable to decide. Use the flares to return fire? Put out the fire on *Käseria*? Or jump in the lake and swim away?

On *Caesaria*, while Blackbeard fumbled to load another flare cartridge, Mary Ann stood up on the cockpit seat. The burning stick flare fizzled in her hand like an oversize sparkler. She balanced for a second, carefully judged her throw, and then lofted it gently, underhand, toward the target.

The flare arced up in the freshly washed air.

It reached its zenith and paused. Then it began a slow descent, followed by six pairs of eyes.

Five people thought the flare was going to miss. David, standing useless at the slack wheel, was certain Mary Ann had overshot the mark. Blackbeard figured her throw would land short and one of the killers would just kick the flare overboard. Buddy and Lynette came to the same conclusion: the flare would miss them entirely and fizzle into the water.

Only Kaufman watched with trepidation. His eyes stayed glued to the flare as it described a fiery arc up into the air and then lazily down toward *Käseria*. As it began to fall, he breathed a sigh of relief. She'd mistimed her throw. Now he would have time to luff up into the wind to check out the damage to his mainsail.

Mary Ann, though: Mary Ann wasn't paying attention to the path of the flare. She'd done exactly as she intended. She'd lettered in volleyball in high school, where her best skill—on the court, at any rate—was not blocking or setting or hitting a killer spike. It was her magical ability to dink the ball precisely at the spot an opposing player was just leaving.

Behind her back as she turned to find her next weapon, her flare drifted nonchalantly down from the sky. *Käseria* ran eagerly forward to meet it. The flare tumbled end over end through the pale blue sky, burning bright against the faded blue sky of afternoon and the too-white sails. It dropped toward the big sailboat, floating neatly down toward the big, open companionway that led into the sailboat's cabin, down toward a target that rushed forward as if *Käseria* were rushing to embrace the bright spark of light falling out of the sky.

The flare passed cleanly through the spiderweb of rigging, bypassed *Käseria*'s sails and fell with a ballet dancer's grace right down through the open companionway of Billy Bob Kaufman's prize sailboat. It disappeared out of sight. Buddy, Lynette, and Billy Bob stared, stupefied, into the cabin now lit by blinding light. On *Caesaria*, Blackbeard lifted one long leg over the rail, holding a shroud for balance as his boat came close enough for him to easily vault over to wreak revenge on the other boat. Mary Ann snatched the bottle Billy held and turned back to find a target on the other boat.

A deep bass *whomp* made Mary Ann pause and Blackbeard freeze. The sound caught the crews of both boats off guard. They looked around, trying to figure out what the muffled sound was. A fiery explosion blew them all off their feet.

The gasoline vapor that had been leaking out of *Käseria*'s fuel system had been causing eyes to water for hours, days, weeks. It had been gathering unvented because Billy Bob Kaufman didn't know to run the engine-compartment blowers to clear out gasoline fumes. That gasoline vapor now embraced the burning flare with spirits as ardent as the arms of a waiting lover.

All anyone remembered later was the tongue of flame vomiting out of *Käseria's* companionway. A heartbeat later, the hatches blew out of *Käseria's* hull with champagne-cork pops. Fire snaked hungrily out of every opening in the hull. Then the fire, fueled by the mixture of gasoline vapor and air, ate its way along the fuel line to *Käseria's* gas tank, and the whole boat exploded with a roar.

The explosion knocked Kaufman out of his cockpit into the lake. It blasted Buddy and Lynette overboard. It ignited *Käseria*'s sails. The explosion blew out the portholes and hatches and a handful of through-hull fittings. As if that wasn't enough, it also found a weak spot in the fiberglass of *Käseria's* expensive but thinly constructed hull and peeled it open. The lake poured into the gap. *Käseria* settled heavily in the water, and still ablaze, began to sink.

On *Caesaria*, a shocked Mary Ann turned to Billy, her face white. "Did I do that?" Billy hugged her, himself horrified at the flames. Blackbeard, dumbstruck, caught between preparing to board the enemy jumping into an inferno, paused with one leg over the guardrail, one hand on the shroud. His whole body vibrated, ready to jump, held back by his brain slowly processing that his intended landing place was now a raging fire.

The explosion brought Deborah Doorman charging up the companionway ladder. She wanted to know what the heck all the noise was about. She couldn't process the scene just outside *Caesaria's* lifelines.

Käseria settled into the emerald green water. The water rose in the cockpit and cabin, forcing the fire to climb away from it. It ignited the cushions and devoured the ropes, the canvas, the sails: everything that would burn. Then sought more flammables to consume.

The crew of *Caesaria*—captives, pirates, warriors—suddenly found themselves at a loss. In an instant, the threat to their lives simply disappeared. Now they all stood still, staring stupidly at the ugly charred thing that the sleek sailboat was rapidly becoming as they coughed up the acrid smoke the light wind blew at them. They looked at each other for confirmation that what they were seeing was real, their faces highlighted by the fire that burned with increasing intensity as the water rose to choke it off.

"Well, damn," Blackbeard muttered.

David discovered the wheel under his hands as if someone else had placed it there. His boat was out of control, having turned upwind like a wind vane. The wheel twitched ever so slightly, telling him that the boat was about to broach. What he really wanted to do was stay and watch *Käseria* burn. *Caesaria* reminded him of his duty: to get his boat away from the fire. And to get his father to a hospital.

The boy glanced up at his boat's sails, looked quickly around to make sure he had room to maneuver, and turned the wheel. He continued to turn the boat back onto the starboard tack. He groused at Billy to let go of the port-side jib sheet clutched in his hand. *Caesaria* started forward again. Gradually she picked up speed. Soon she had enough speed to tack.

"Tacking," David announced. Billy understood the drill by now. He turned away from the spectacle to do his job. He quickly figured out which rope to pull and set the jib.

Caesaria's head came around. The boat picked up speed, then accelerated with the jib set. It ran on a fast broad reach for a hundred yards. David swung the wheel to tack, the pirates trimmed the sails in without being asked, and *Caesaria* headed back toward the bubbling water where *Käseria* was almost awash. They would pass the three swimming figures by a few yards.

Deborah Doorman climbed further up the ladder. She looked ahead and saw the swimmers. She pointed them out to David. "Are you going to pick them up?"

He avoided her eyes.

"David? David!"

"I'm going to run their sorry asses over."

Deborah stepped up into the cockpit and pushed past the boy. She pulled a life jacket and two flotation cushions out of the stern locker. "You can't just let them drown." David looked away, checked the surrounding area, and turned the boat slightly. When *Caesaria* was close enough, Deborah tossed the lifesaving gear toward the swimmers.

Blackbeard and Billy watched their enemies swim for the life jackets as *Caesaria* moved away from the flaming rubble. The killers dwindled into mere specks on the water behind them. Both pirates breathed a sigh of relief that they had survived the battle. Blackbeard reflected that the day had turned out OK in the end. All's well that ends—

Then Billy grabbed him. He pointed up the lake and moaned. "No, no, no, no, no."

Blackbeard's blood ran cold. The attackers couldn't possibly be back! He turned to look, dreading what he would see. Coming straight at them with lights blazing and siren blaring: a police boat.

Shit, Blackbeard thought. Perfect. This would be a great ending for almost everybody.

The killers would get arrested. Doorman would get to the hospital. Mom and the kid would get to dry land. Mary Ann would get a ride home. The terrifying day could end with all the loose ends tied up. He slumped down on one of the cockpit lazarettes, his head in his hands.

It couldn't end up better for almost anyone. Except him and Billy.

Chapter Thirty-Three

Earlier that afternoon, while two sailboats were still dancing their *pas de deux* at the other end of the lake, Tramp Martin had come around the island blocking whatever was producing the smoke he'd seen over the trees. His throttle was bulled back to barely above an idle. Where there were two fiery explosions, there might be a third.

He came upon pieces of steaming debris, scattered over the water. A boat had obviously exploded. He didn't see any survivors.

Finally, he saw a life jacket. He pushed the patrol boat's head around and motored slowly over. A human form came into sight. Suspended by the life jacket. Not moving.

Martin was hauling the unconscious man aboard before he realized it was Thomas. He dragged the man into the boat and onto the floor of the cockpit. Tramp checked his vital signs. For a man floating unconscious among smoking debris, the vitals weren't too bad. Still, he better get this guy to a hospital.

He'd made a few circles through the flotsam to make sure there wasn't anybody else floating in the wreckage. He scanned the nearby islands with his binoculars but found no other survivors. He wondered what had happened.

It must have been the FLEET boat that exploded. For the briefest of moments, he regretted missing the conflagration. He decided that it made him almost as happy to never have to see the FLEET boat again.

He nudged the throttle into forward. Thomas suddenly sat up, holding his head. He pointed vaguely. "Watch out for the wreck! Watch out for *Admiral Byng*!"

Martin throttled quickly back down, scanning the water for the missing barge. There was no other boat. The federal agent was talking gibberish. No surprise there. But even if he might have a head injury to add to his other deficits, it would be foolish to ignore a warning, even if it came from a loopy FeeBee.

Memory told him that somewhere out here was a reef, just under the surface. He peered at the water, trying to penetrate the flotsam and the late afternoon glare. Then Martin caught sight of the surface water swirling. Deep lake water didn't swirl.

There it was. A submerged steel deck plate. A second later he made out one of the sunken pontoons. Nothing more. They must be all that remained of the *Admiral Byng*.

It painted an eloquent picture of what must have happened to the FLEET patrol boat. Thomas wouldn't have known about the reef. He probably didn't actually know where *Admiral Byng* was, or that the barge had sunk and posed a danger to navigation. And he drove like a crazy man.

Tramp Martin would have loved to rub it in a little. Except that Thomas was looking around at the debris field, shaking his head and murmuring to himself. It was hard not to feel sorry for him.

In the end, Tramp couldn't help himself. "Well, hey. Look at the bright side. You found the *Admiral Byng* before me." He nudged his patrol boat onto a slow plane. He steered out into the main body of the lake, then north for the city hospital.

The FeeBee had struggled upright in one of the cockpit chairs, insisting that he was all right. Still, Tramp Martin knew trauma well enough to know that he couldn't trust the victim's self-appraisal. Buford's clinic in the south and the medical facilities to the north in Gainesville were equally far. Six of one and half a dozen of the other. But the fact that his home dock—the sheriff's dock—was in Gainesville, made up his mind for him.

Tramp pushed the throttle gently forward to put his boat up on a faster plane. He called his dispatcher. "Do me a favor. Call General. I've got one on board who survived an explosion. Condition unknown. Have them meet me at the docks in fifteen minutes with an ambulance."

Thomas spent ten minutes bitching in a voice growing steadily louder and more obnoxious. He was OK. He'd been in fights before. He wasn't hurt. He didn't need a hospital.

The deputy thanked the heavens that the motors drowned out his passenger's whining.

They were only a few minutes away from the docks when the radio burst to life. This time it was the chief himself. "Hey, Trampster!"

Martin grinned. The chief would ride anyone else using improper radio procedure, but his radio discipline was pure trucker. Tramp keyed the mike. "Go ahead, Chief."

"Got a report of fireworks down near Marker 6. Or maybe across from 6. Ol' coot who lives down near Shady Grove was sitting out on his balcony with a pair of binoculars—probably watching the drakes do the ganders, if you know what I mean—anyways, he saw some flares around a couple of sailboats, then heard a couple of explosions..."

"Nah. I just came from that scene. That fire was a lot further north, Chief. I just picked a floater out of a powerboat explosion and fire–"

"No, Trampster, liss'n 'ere. Marker 6. Flares, fire, explosion. Could'a been out on the water between 6 and 5. Get over and check it out."

Tramp looked over at Thomas. The FeeBee was holding his head with one hand, but with the other he waved Martin on. "Roger, Chief." Martin hung up the microphone, then turned a tight circle to head south again. He maxxed up both motors to put the boat up on a fast plane toward the reported location. The vibrations on a high-speed plane rattled everything and everyone on the boat. Particularly the poor, potentially concussed FeeBee.

It took more than a quarter of an hour to get down to where the flares were reported. The bumpiness of the ride as the patrol boat flew down the lake had the salutary effect of silencing his passenger's whining.

The first thing Tramp Martin saw was the smoke hanging low over the lake. Next he saw two sets of sails right in the middle of slowly dissipating smoke. One hull was visible. The other was invisible, apparently obscured by the smoke. As he got closer, he saw that one sailboat was already leaving the scene under sail. That seemed a little odd.

The other boat, though...

Tramp stared, squinting, but couldn't quite make it out. The hull and sails seemed to shimmer. He kept staring, trying to get a fix on an image that wouldn't hold still. The black-and-orange sails wouldn't come into focus. Must be one of those expensive new metallic fabrics, Tramp speculated. Kevlar or something.

Then it all came together and his blood froze. They were sails—sails on fire! As they got closer, he saw that the hull of the burning boat was awash. Tramp circled around the burning hull, keeping his distance. It had exploded once; it might again. It was a new record for him: two exploding boats in one day.

There were no survivors visible. The boat was sinking fast. If there was anyone below, they were either being toasted or already drowned.

Meanwhile, the first boat sailed calmly away. The detective grabbed his binoculars. He saw what looked like a young boy at the wheel. A woman stood next to him, holding on to the shrouds and to all appearances, dressing down the boy. Two other guys sat in the cockpit, paying no attention.

Tramp flicked on his siren to get their attention. At the same time, he called it in to Dispatch. He gunned his boat up to the fleeing sailboat and hit the siren again. Got on the loudhailer. Ordered the helmsman to stop.

As Tramp pulled alongside, the boy helmsman luffed skillfully up into the wind and held the sailboat there. The kid's touch on the wheel was confident and steady. Tramp wondered where he'd learned to handle the boat with such confidence.

The woman aboard the boat rushed to the rail and started gesturing and calling to Tramp: a great flood of words, too urgent and too fast to comprehend with the patrol boat's engine noise still echoing in his ears. As Tramp glided up next to the sailboat, the woman's words became audible in disparate phrases as his ears adjusted to the near silence.

"Husband shot."

"Lost a lot of blood."

"Need to get him to a hospital."

"People drowning."

"Trying to kill us."

She looked crazy. Her words were crazy. And she continued talking crazier still.

"Blew up."

"Can't leave those people to drown."

"Husband...medical care...right now."

Tramp looked over at Thomas. "You know any first aid?"

The federal agent nodded, squinting as though the light hurt his eyes.

The deputy handed the FeeBee a handheld VHF unit. "I think she's talking about a gunshot wound. That radio's tuned to Channel 16. Climb aboard, see what you can do for the man. Get one of the passengers to start calling a mayday and see if there's any medical help around." He helped Thomas climb up the high freeboard of the sailboat, calling out, "I'm gonna go check out the wreck."

Rid of his patient, Tramp peeled off to go back to check out the sunken boat. Most of the smoke had blown away. The mast—the top few feet of it, anyway—still stood proudly upright as the hull continued to settle into the deep emerald-green water. Bubbles and chemical slicks effervesced around Tramp's boat. The smell of burning plastic and smoke and gasoline loomed around him. A few pieces of wreckage still smoldered in the water.

The biggest things identifiable in the water, however, were the heads of three swimmers. One was trying to wave with one hand and swim with the other, all the while shouting like a walrus in heat. The other two splashed the water with inefficient movements, apparently trying to get away.

The deputy put his boat alongside the swimmer. "Come on up." Killers, the woman had called them. Seemed unlikely, but no reason to take chances. Tramp loosened his weapon in its holster.

He guided the man toward the stern ladder, reaching behind his back for his handcuffs. As the man pulled himself up the swim ladder, Tramp snapped his handcuffs open and waited.

The man had one foot on the ladder when he saw the handcuffs. He froze. The blood drained out of his face. "No, no, no. You got it all wrong. It's not me! It's them!"

"Keep your hands on the ladder, sir. I'm going to cuff you, then you can come on up." The man started to protest more, but the deputy cut it off with an eloquent gesture toward his service revolver. In a minute he'd handcuffed the man with one practiced hand, never letting go of his service weapon.

Tramp helped him into a seat in the bow cockpit. The man stared at the cuffed hands in his lap. Soon enough, however, the guy's shocked silence gave way to outraged protestations of innocence. Pirates had robbed him, a storm had tried to kill him, assassins had almost murdered him, maniacs had destroyed his boat, and now, as if that weren't enough, he was being falsely arrested and would sue everybody.

Tramp shook his head and let the guy rant. He nudged the boat over toward another of the swimmers. The next one was an older woman in a form-fitting wetsuit. Tramp motored up next to her. "Climb aboard."

Lynette uttered two impolite words and swam away. The deputy picked up his boathook and deftly caught the woman's life jacket. She turned, trying to fight the restraint. Tramp put all of his weight into pushing the pole down to dunk her. When he hauled her back up spluttering and coughing, she was still fighting, so he did it a few more times. Finally, the lake washed the fight out of her.

Soon she was cuffed and puffing in the bow next to the first guy. You would have thought that with another of his confederates aboard, the first guy would have shut. But no. He kept yammering as though she were the author of every one of his troubles. At least Tramp didn't have to listen to the FBI man. The big guy yammered at the woman. "You thought you were going to kill me." "You thought I was finished." "Who's finished now, Babycakes?"

The deputy listened idly while maneuvering the boat toward the last swimmer. The man in the boat kept on yammering. On and on and on and on, until Martin considered opening the woman's handcuffs and letting her shut the guy up.

The last swimmer proved easier to corral. He swam obdurately, trying to dog–paddle away from the police boat even as it loomed over him. His heart wasn't in it, though. When Tramp snagged his life jacket with the boat hook, the man simply gave up. He allowed himself to be towed to the swim ladder without a word. He climbed up on his own, submitted to the handcuffs with a whispered "Thank you," and meekly let himself be led forward to where the other two captives sat.

Martin made sure all the passengers were secure. He turned the patrol boat back toward the sailboats and called in a report to the chief. He barely paid attention to the movement in his front cockpit.

Lynette had wiggled her way over to Buddy. "I'm so sorry. So, so sorry."

Buddy's voice was quiet, but not meek. "It's your son who's going to be sorry. I'm going to find his ass and kill him."

"Now Buddy." Lynette managed a weak attempt at a smile, at the same time pointing to the policeman with her eyes. "You know you're not going to kill anyone. And hey! Look at the bright side. We aren't going to have to go back to Walmart any time soon."

***

Within minutes, the county patrol boat was back at the waiting sailboat. The boy captain quickly set out bumpers and rafted the boats.

Tramp pocketed the key to the ignition of his patrol boat and clambered up the high side of the sailboat.

He looked around curiously. A dark brown pattern splattered the white fiberglass of the cockpit and side decks. The boy appeared not to have moved from where Tramp had left him. He looked wet and exhausted, hanging onto the wheel as much to support himself as to steer.

Behind him, standing near the companionway hatch was a fetching young woman, and beside her, a young man. Tramp knew the young man immediately. He looked around for the guy's buddy.

"Well. If it isn't my two old friends." Billy and Blackbeard looked at each other sourly. "Say, you guys wouldn't have any information about a whole slew of stolen Sea-Doos, would you?" The two pirates remained silent. Mary Ann looked curiously at Billy, then to the other partner. Her pretty lips froze into disapproving silence as Billy blushed.

Martin shrugged. "Oh well, I guess we can talk about it back at the station." He nonchalantly cuffed them both. "You two are under arrest for...let's see now...how about 'Unsafe Boating.' You got to remember to wear your life jackets, boys. We can talk more about it downtown. And maybe you can tell me about those missing PWCs, too."

The sound of boats roaring toward them interrupted the conversation. There were two. One was a bass boat. Its driver, it turned out, was an emergency room physician taking a day off to fish. He quickly tied off and jumped aboard the sailboat with his black bag. (They take their doctor bags fishing? Tramp wondered.) The doctor quickly ducked down into the cabin to take command of the wounded patient.

Another was the AmeriBoat towboat. Since Thomas insisted that he himself didn't need medical care, Martin put him to work. He passed along custody of the prisoners to the towboat and sent the FBI guy along as custodian. The towboat set off up the lake toward the sheriff's dock at Hall County Marina.

Tramp Martin sighed as he watched it go. He knew the Feds well enough to know that he'd just given the FeeBees an excuse to assert jurisdiction over all of the incidents involved. At least he'd given the possible concussion victim the pleasure of a couple of long, pounding rides up and down the lake. If the Bureau was going to steal the case, the least their local representative could do was suffer for it.

The doctor took charge of Doorman, quickly making arrangements to rush him to the hospital in Buford. Meanwhile, Tramp heard him order the older woman around like she was a servant. Mrs. Doorman, it turned out, was a nurse. She was clearly used to taking peremptory orders from doctors, even doctors who spent their days out fishing. Tramp would have seriously considered kicking the guy's teeth in if the doctor had talked to him that way.

Tramp helped them lift the unconscious Doorman up into the cockpit and then gingerly down into Tramp's boat. Tramp left them to get situated as best they could for the fast run to the hospital and turned to the kid. He hadn't budged from the sailboat's wheel. He told the boy to get on board the patrol and sit down.

"What about my boat?" the kid demanded.

Well, hell. Should'a thought this through.

The sailboat was too big to tow behind the patrol boat. The water was too deep to anchor. Tramp could hardly leave it adrift. He obviously wasn't going to leave the kid to sail it alone.

Tramp asked the doctor if he could handle the patrol boat. He could; doctors could do anything. The detective worked it out with the doctor. The fishing doctor would take the patrol boat up to Gainesville and leave it at one of the courtesy docks at Hall County Marina. On the way up, the doctor would call EMS to meet him there. Tramp would tow the doctor's bass boat up to the sheriff's dock for the doctor to pick up later.

He assured Mrs. Doorman that David would be right behind them and assured the doctor that he'd take care of the bass boat. He tied the doctor's boat to the stern cleat of the sailboat to tow it behind them as they sailed north.

The doctor sped off, the doctor pushing the patrol boat as fast as possible without starting to plane. The doctor clearly knew his boats. And his patients.

Tramp stood next to the boy. "Let's get the motor cranked up and get going."

"Engine," the boy corrected. "Not 'motor.' It's diesel." Saying it like anybody with a brain would know the difference between a diesel engine and a gasoline motor. "And it's dead. We have to sail."

Tramp absorbed the information and the boy's grasp of mechanics. "Can you sail this thing?"

David chortled, a sound not entirely encouraging from the person at the wheel. "Yeah."

Tramp settled himself in the cockpit. "OK, son. Get us to Gainesville, OK?"

David moved about the cockpit, trimming sails and then taking the wheel. Once they'd gotten underway, he pointed out the lines that needed to be trimmed. Once he'd followed orders, and with nothing to do for a moment, Tramp sat down and leaned back against the cockpit coaming.

"Looks like you know what you're doing. Lucky you weren't out here in that storm we had last night." Tramp took in the boy's disheveled clothing and his evident exhaustion. “But I’ll bet you have a hell of a story.”

David didn’t look at him. Tramp watched his eyes cycling between wind vane and sails and the riffles on the water and the minute movements of wind in the sails. When David spoke, Tramp could barely hear him.

“Story? You’d never believe it.”

Chapter Thirty-Four

On the long ride to jail in the towboat, Blackbeard leaned over toward his friend. "I'm sorry, man. I thought this time I'd figured it out. I thought this Sea-Doo thing was gonna make us rich."

Billy shook his head. "Wadn't your fault. We got bad luck, that's all." They rode in silence for a while.

Blackbeard hung his head. "I keep getting you in trouble." Billy protested, but Blackbeard talked over him. "I've been getting you in trouble for ten years. Ever since that fight with Randy Parker in seventh grade, I been getting you in trouble."

Billy sat up, incredulous. "How'd you have anything to do with that?"

"Hell, Billy. If he hadn't called you a little faggot, I wouldn't've beat him up and we wouldn't *both*'ve ended up in the Detention Center."

"Called *me* a faggot? He didn't call me a faggot."

"Sure he did. Don't you remember?"

"You! He was calling *you* a faggot!"

Blackbeard waved his manacled hands in dismissal. "If he called me a faggot, then why did he jump all over you?"

Billy swung his handcuffed body around to stare. "He didn't jump all over me. I jumped all over him. He called you a faggot, so I punched him in the face, and then I started hitting him and it felt so good I just couldn't stop. I was havin' a good time giving him back some'a the shit he'd been giving me since third grade. Until you got in my way."

"You were protecting me?"

The surprise on the big pirate's face almost made Billy break out laughing. "I di'n't want him goin' around sayin' it to everybody."

They sat silently as the boat sped them to jail. Finally, Blackbeard spoke, looking out at the passing lake. "Look, Billy, there's something I should'a told you a long time ago."

Billy shook his head violently and pushed his friend away. "I don' need to know nothin' OK? I already know and I been knowing since you and me was in grade school. And no, I ain't one myself, and double no, I don't care you are. OK? We clear on this? I'm your friend and that's it. So now let's just leave it."

Blackbeard stared, his mouth open.

On the opposite side of the cockpit of the towboat, the killers glowered in seething silence at the pirates, the whole reason they were in custody now. They knew what their immediate future held. In an hour, they'd be getting printed and mugshotted. Within a few hours after that, they'd be sitting in separate interrogation rooms, trying to trade information for jail time. Now they were plumbing their memories for anything that might make the investigators happy without incriminating each other. They weren't having an easy time coming up with anything.

Between killers and the pirates sat the Cheese King, a look of smug triumph on his face. He couldn't wait to tell the police about the two who threatened to kill him and the other two who'd sunk his boat. And get an apology for being arrested and cuffed when he was nothing but an innocent victim of criminals. Justice would be sweet.

Now if he could just get these damn handcuffs off.

***

Hours later, in the hospital in Gainesville, the surgeon came out of the swinging doors of the emergency room, snapping off his gloves. He knocked on the wall next to one of the curtained enclosures of the critical care unit.

A voice from behind the curtain groused. "Oh, come in, for God's sake. Heck, invite the whole floor why don't you so we can get it over with and I can rest."

The doctor slipped through the curtain. He saw the patient struggle into a sitting position.

Deborah Doorman recognized the surgeon who had come in to get permission to operate on Joe. "How is he?"

"Mr. Doorman will be fine." After describing the medical genius he'd deployed to save Doorman's life, he congratulated himself on the positive prognosis. Deborah Doorman heard only a few phrases: "no major organs," "prognosis is great," "recovering nicely."

"Fine, fine, fine. What about my son?"

The surgeon wasn't used to having his works of art dismissed. He blathered about things like "exhaustion," "exposure," "full recovery," and the best news: "not to worry."

Deborah wriggled more upright. "Great. Now, how about release me so I can go home and get some rest? It's like a Little Five Points on Halloween in here."

"I want to keep you overnight for observation. Not many people spend the night on the lake in a storm."

"*In* the lake. Not 'on the lake.' Up to my neck *in* the lake. If you're not going to write release orders, can you at least get me moved somewhere quieter? Like the maternity ward or the psych ward or something?"

The doctor laughed nervously, looking around for help. The unit clerk intervened before things got ugly. "Mrs. Doorman, I just spoke with a Detective Martin. He said your son's doing well, and he made sure to tell me the boat's fine, if that makes any sense. The doctor wants us to keep your son for observation, too." She nodded at him to let him take over.

"I can't believe you both spent the night out on the lake," the doctor interrupted. "Not with that storm. You'd have to be some kind of idiot to go out in weather like that. I've lived here my whole life, and I never went out when a norther was coming in. You're lucky to be—"

"Oh, shut up." Deborah closed her eyes and lay back.

The unit clerk blanched. "We talked to your insurance company," she assured Deborah, "and they're going to let us move you and your son both up to the same room." She frowned. "They did say that, um, your daughter isn't covered by your insurance. Is that right?"

Deborah sat up in surprise. "My daughter? We don't have—" Deborah could feel her brain slowly grinding into gear. "Oh. Yes. My daughter. No, she's not covered on my policy." She closed her eyes and lay back, silent for so long that the doctor and clerk thought they should creep off. Then Deborah opened her eyes, having thought the whole thing through. "It'll be private pay. Get me a bill and we'll settle up. How is she?"

"She's fine. Just a little exposure. The nurses are all amazed about how good she's looking."

Deborah snorted, then turned to the doctor once again, her eyes blazing. The unit clerk scurried away, determined not to get caught in the crossfire again. "Did my husband say anything?"

"What he said didn't make a lot of sense, and he kept talking until we put him under to fish the bullet out. He said to tell you he was really proud of your finding him. And he wanted to tell me what a really fine job his—your?—son did." He let out a disparaging laugh. "He also wanted me to promise he'd be OK for a trial next week. Next week! Can you imagine?"

He excused himself and disappeared through the curtain like the Great Oz. In the cubicle, they could still hear him muttering: "Lawyers!"

Deborah Doorman fell slowly back onto her pillows and within seconds dropped into what seemed like her first deep sleep in years.

Chapter Thirty-Five

The man formerly known to the Milan Family as Number Two hunkered down on his rattling seat. It was only a smelly, tattered Greyhound bus, but it gave him the sense of being safe and secure and—most importantly—invisible. He'd chosen a seat in the dark middle of the bus, trying to sink into the deepest anonymity he could manage.

A few hours ago, he'd slipped out of the milk truck and walked casually away, feeling the milk-soaked trousers clinging to his skin. When he turned a corner that hid him from the truck, he started running, zigzagging randomly through block after block so that nobody could follow him.

He had no destination in mind other than to get as far as possible from the guys in the truck. The bus station was a surprise, but he didn't hesitate. Whatever the Universe gave, you took without hesitation. So he didn't pause to consider what he was doing. He stumbled into the bus station and purchased a ticket on the first bus going anywhere.

In the first long hours after leaving Atlanta, as the bus shuddered and shook through a terrific storm, Two had huddled down in his seat, more fearful of everyone knowing who he was and what he was running from and the way he smelled of soured milk than he was of the hurricane buffeting the bus. His fear of the FBI or the Mafia, or whatever they were, eclipsed his fear of the storm battering the old bus.

The bus's destination was a mystery to him. His destination, though, was quite simple. He was headed anywhere, on the first bus headed wherever that was, as long as the bus was leaving *right now.*

Only after the storm subsided did Number Two begin to relax. As the sky cleared, so did his mood. He sat up and started to notice the scenery as the bus headed through the countryside. The view seemed to stretch out endlessly, the land broadening into one huge plain from horizon to horizon.

There was a lot of land out there. All empty. Plenty of places to get lost. Maybe this would work. Maybe he would actually find some little town where no one ask questions and where he could start to get on with his life. He'd never have to worry about his neighbors wondering who he was or where he was from. And maybe the FBI or the Chicago family would not find him. Or they'd just let him go.

Endless hours on the bus dissolved his unease. Bored, he took stock of his assets. He still had a hundred and something dollars in his wallet. He only had the clothes on his back, but he hadn't had a lot more getting out of the pen. All he had to do was get to wherever he was going, find a YMCA or something, and get a job. Start over. Only this time he'd be smart: he'd steer clear of people like...well, like the idiot he was when he stumbled up the stairs onto the bus.

Where was this bus going, anyway? He pulled the crumpled ticket out of his pocket. It was hard to read in the dark, rattling cabin. He twisted and turned the crumpled piece of paper to catch what little illumination the courtesy lights provided. A one-way trip, he thought it said. Which was fine. He wasn't going near Number One or his crew ever again.

He kept peering at the faded print on the ticket, trying to decipher the smudged print. Suddenly it snapped into focus. The sight gave him a sudden, spasmodic pain, a lightning bolt right in the middle of his chest. Almost like having a heart attack. Or getting shot.

It was a one-way ticket, alright. Atlanta to Chicago.

A Pirates' Glossary

beam: The side of the boat running from bow to stern; hence a "beam reach" is a course with the wind coming over the side.

below: Anywhere below the deck, generally referring to the cabin, salon and berths. Hence "down below" means in the cabin.

bilge: The lowest portion of the hull inside a boat, where the water inevitably collects and from which it can easily be pumped overboard; hence "bilgewater."

Bimini: The folding canvas canopy covering the cockpit of a boat.

boom: The horizontal spar extending from near the bottom of the mast toward the stern, which, as the foundation for the mainsail, holds the mainsail open and controls the angle of the sail.

captain: In modern recreational sailing, the person directing operations on the boat and usually the one steering. The person steering is technically called the helmsman, since they control the "helm."

chart: A navigation map, characterized by showing features of the water (land, obstructions in the water, and useful navigation landmarks) but devoid of most terrestrial features.

cleat: A piece of wood or metal—usually t-shaped—to which ropes are attached. Hence "cleat hitch," a knot tied around a cleat for mooring.

close-hauled: Sailing into the wind, which is to say with the wind anywhere in the arc from 45 degrees to the right of the bow, around the bow, to 45 degrees to the left. Note, however, that in those 90 degrees of range, the middle portion—a dozen degrees to either side of the bow—is a no-go zone in which the sails will not fill and the boat will stall. Also generally referred to as sailing "upwind."

cockpit: The rear portion of the deck of a sailboat from which the boat is steered and the crew works or rests.

companionway: A stairway that leads from the cockpit down into the cabin via steep stairs sailors call a "ladder."

con: As a verb, the informal word for the act of steering the boat.

cross: To intersect the course of another boat and pass in front of it.

dinghy: A small open boat, often propelled by oars. Sailing dinghies have movable masts and booms.

dodger: A smaller version of the Bimini, which usually covers only the front portion of the cockpit.

downwind: Sailing with the wind coming from any relative direction behind the boat. Gentlemen only sail downwind.

engine: A propulsion unit powered by diesel. (Compare: motor, powered by gasoline.)

flemish: To coil a rope artistically in a pattern of concentric circles.

gunwale: The top edge of the side of the hull. In the days of wooden boats, it was the name of the wooden member that ran bow to stern on each side and topped off the planks making up the side of the boat.

fother: To wrap a sail around the outside of a hull; as a verb, a technique to stop or slow a leak by wrapping a sail around the hull, where the specific hull defect cannot be identified or immediately addressed.

gauge (or **gage), weather ~**: Weather gauge (or gage) refers to the position of one boat positioned upwind of another boat. In this position the boat with the weather gauge (i.e. that is upwind of the other boat) controls whether the two boats' courses will intersect or diverge. The downwind boat is generally in a defending position, and in a race or warfare can only react to the movement of the boat possessing "the weather gauge."

halyard: A rope or wire that, through a pulley at the top of the mast, raises or lowers a sail.

hatch boards: Material (often wood) that close off the companionway to shut out water or visitors.

helm: The device (wheel or tiller) that controls the boat's rudder and therefore its course. Hence "helmsman." (Distinguish "Captain .")

jib: The triangular sail that is the front sail on a single-masted sailboat, flown between mast and bow. (Compare "jibe.")

jibe or gybe: To turn the boat by turning away from the wind. In a gybe, the wind driving the boat passes from one side of the boat, over the stern. A gybe always results in the boom swinging in a large arc over the cockpit where helmsman and crew work, making the motion of the boom dangerous. It is the mirror image of a "tack," but gybing is often an unintentional error and always more dangerous than a tack.

ladder: Any stairs on a boat.

knock down: When the wind pushes boat so hard from the side that the beam and sometimes the mast come in contact with the water. While not catastrophic, it is indicative of dangerous conditions, including hard winds and big waves. A knock down is not necessarily a capsize, but it is closer than any sailor wants to come to that emergency.

lazarette: A storage area in the cockpit, the top of which provides seating.

locker: Any closet or storage space.

luff: (1) To luff is to turn the sailboat dead into the wind, so that the sails lose their ability to drive the boat forward. In this position the sails "luff," which is to say, flap impotently rather than capturing and directing the wind like a wing. (2) The "luff" is the portion of a mainsail running parallel to the mast. Since this is the first part of the sail to show turbulence as a sail begins to lose it driving force (by forming a kind of blister on the upwind side of the sail), this region is referred to as "the luff."

mainsail or "main": The aftermost large sail of a sloop, set on the main mast and running laterally from the mast to the rear end of the boom. It provides the greatest part of the motive force of a sailboat.

mast: The largest spar on a sailboat, often longer than the boat itself, supported by various types of rigging.

mooring: As noun, a mooring is a place where a boat can be tied up as a substitute for anchoring. As a verb, mooring is the act of tying a boat to an object to secure it in place.

mooring knot: The knot used in connecting the boat to any other stationary object. Usually based on a series of loops in the rope and almost always capable of being tied quickly and untied even more quickly. Almost always affixed to a metal fitting on a dock or on a boat called a cleat.

motor: Auxiliary power on sailboats (since the main power is the sails) which may either be a diesel-powered engine or a gas motor.

nav station: A flat-topped cabinet in the cabin, usually located where someone can quickly swing down from the cockpit to consult it. This is where the paperwork of navigation is performed. It provides a dedicated space to read and mark navigation charts, and in many sailboats the top lifts to provide a space to store charts.

port (see starboard): To the left of the centerline of the boat while the observer is facing forward.

reach: A point of sail in which the driving wind comes over the side of the boat. It can be a "close reach" if the wind is coming from an angle close to the bow, a "beam reach" if the wind is coming from the side, or a "broad reach" if the wind is coming from a the rear quarter of the boat.

reef: 1. A rocky obstruction in the water, sometimes but not necessarily created by coral polyps; 2. As a verb: To reduce the area of a sail to counter the effects of strong wind.

rigging: The collective name of all of the ropes and wires that support sails and masts.

rode: The anchor line.

rope: Any non-working piece of cordage. It becomes rigging, a sheet or a rode when used for a specific purpose.

sail cover: Canvas that wraps around the sail to protect it from the weather when the sail is furled.

sheet: Cordage that controls a sail. In a small sloop, the "main sheet" is rope tied to the trailing corner of a sail to control the sail's angle with respect to the wind. In a smaller boat, sheets are always led back to the cockpit and can be controlled without leaving the cockpit.

sole: The floor of the cabin, covering the bilge.

spinnaker: A large sail similar to a jib and also hoisted forward of the mainsail, used specifically for sailing downwind.

starboard (see port): To the right of the centerline of the boat while facing forward.

stern: The rear of a boat.

stern ladder: A ladder attached to transom at the rear of a sailboat to allow someone in the water to climb from the water into the cockpit.

swim platform: A platform on the stern which accomplishes the same function as a stern ladder but provides easier access than a vertical ladder.

tack: To turn by moving the bow of a sailboat through the direction of the wind. The opposite of a jibe, a tack is the usual method of changing the direction of a sailboat. In a tack, the wind generally does not wildly sweep the boom over the cockpit, so tacking is much safer than gybing.

transom: The vertical panel at the rear of a sailboat hull, where a stern ladder or swim platform might be situated. In a "walk through" transom, the structure opens like a door to allow someone boarding to get into the boat without climbing up and over the transom.

upwind: Sailing into any wind coming from forward of the beam (i.e. over the bow). "Gentlemen," sailors say, "do not sail upwind," or risk spilling their martinis.

v-berth: The triangular area directly under the foredeck of a sailboat where the two sides of the hull join to form a v-shaped space. This space is sometimes used for sail storage because it is accessible to the foredeck through a foredeck hatch. In pleasure boats, the space can also be used as a berth and is furnished with a mattress to provide sleeping space.

winch: A mechanical device that controls the sail's sheets lines, flattening the sail or allowing it to belly out. A winch applies the mechanical advantage of gears to multiply the force a sailor can apply. The pressure on the sails by even a moderate wind is enormous, much greater than one person can counteract by pulling on the line unaided. Manual winches use lever arms called "handles" that allow the mechanical advantage of a long lever arm to augment human strength. Winch handles are almost always separable from the body of the winch to get them out of the way when the winch is not in use.

Acknowledgements

This novel owes its existence in no small part to Saul Elbein, who co-wrote the initial story when he was not much older than David Doorman. We both owe heartfelt thanks to Rivka Elbein, who—without writing a word—bore the entire burden of the creation of this book on her superhero shoulders.

The genesis of this book has been so long that there are generations of readers in numbers too numerous to count who have commented on various drafts. Among them are: Junab Ali (r.i.p.), Asher Elbein, Saul Elbein, Dr. Deborah Blaine, Tobi Cooper, Rabbi Danny Horowitz, Jeanette Burney Sullivan...and so many more that by this point, even they have forgotten yeoman's work in giving their time and attention and patience to help pave the way for its publication.

Finally, I owe an inestimable debt to my editor, Sarah Walker. She always brought to the work studious copy-editing, excellent insight, fearless critique, and an unflagging sense of humor. It is she who wrestled a mere typescript out of the cold, grasping claws of the Drawer Where Novels Go to Die and she who birthed it as a novel.

About the authors

T. Seamus Farley has worked at many things: busboy, prep cook, waiter, short-order cook, trial lawyer, prosecutor, adjunct professor. But any time he could steal a few minutes from "real life," he could always be found doing his real work: writing. He's published widely: short stories, scholarly articles, essays, and poetry. *Pirates* is his first published novel.

Seamus and his wife live in the southeastern United States. They are the parents of two fine young men, both successful writers. The Farley household includes a Golden Doodle, a Standard Poodle, and the spirit of The Best Dog Ever. When not writing or reading, Seamus can be found building stringed instruments, fly fishing, cycling or sailing.

Seamus can be contacted at the email address specially reserved for readers: **seamusfarley.readers@gmail.com.**

Coming soon are other novels in the Doorman saga, including *Just Cause, Down the Road,* and *Dead Letters*. In the meantime, you can find Seamus' short stories, essays, excerpts and prequels on his website, **seamusfarley.com**.

***

Saul Elbein Saul Elbein works at the nexus of science, business, and politics. He focuses on the critical intersection of business strategies, environmental challenges and political decisions. He pioneered a widely read Sustainability Newsletter for a national online political magazine. His work has highlighted the rise of new forms of energy, the insurance crisis, and the remaking of the state GOP. His expertise in science and policy reporting, coupled with an understanding of analytics and email marketing, helps him turn complex issues into compelling narratives. He and Asher Elbein are co-founders of the newsletter "Heat Death" https://heat-death.ghost.io/He lives with his wife and their two boys in the Southwestern United States. The entire household is subject to the rule of two Bengal cats. This is his first published work of fiction.

Also by T. Seamus Farley

Just Cause (a Doorman novel): forthcoming, March 2026

Down the Road (a Doorman novel): forthcoming, June 2026

The Letters (a Doorman novel): forthcoming, August 2026

Their Story: forthcoming, October 2026

See Seamus' website for additional free materials. Sea musfarley.com

Made in the USA
Columbia, SC
23 January 2026

77954849R00212